Us, in Pieces

ALSO BY TASHA COTTER

Astonishments (2020)
The Aqua Notebook (2019)
Some Churches (2015)

Us,
in Pieces

a novel

~~Tasha Cotter~~ and
Christopher Green

Shadelandhouse Modern Press
Lexington, Kentucky

A Shadelandhouse Modern Press book

Us, in Pieces
a novel

Published in the United States of America by:
Shadelandhouse Modern Press, LLC, Lexington, Kentucky, smpbooks.com.
First edition 2019
Shadelandhouse, Shadelandhouse Modern Press, and the colophon are trademarks of Shadelandhouse Modern Press, LLC.

Library of Congress Control Number: 2019937297
ISBN 978-1-945049-11-8

Book design and page layout: Benjamin Jenkins
Cover design: Jennifer Carrow
Production Editor: Stephanie P. Underwood

to my teachers, Tasha

for Mom, who was right all along and for Granny
Most of what I do is probably because you read me Cars and Trucks
and Things That Go. Christopher

If there is something to desire,
there will be something to regret.
If there is something to regret,
there will be something to recall.
If there is something to recall,
there was nothing to regret.
If there was nothing to regret,
there was nothing to desire.
—*Vera Pavlova*, "If There Is Something to Desire"

The course of true love never did run smooth.
—*William Shakespeare, A Midsummer Night's Dream* (I.i.134)

Us,
in Pieces

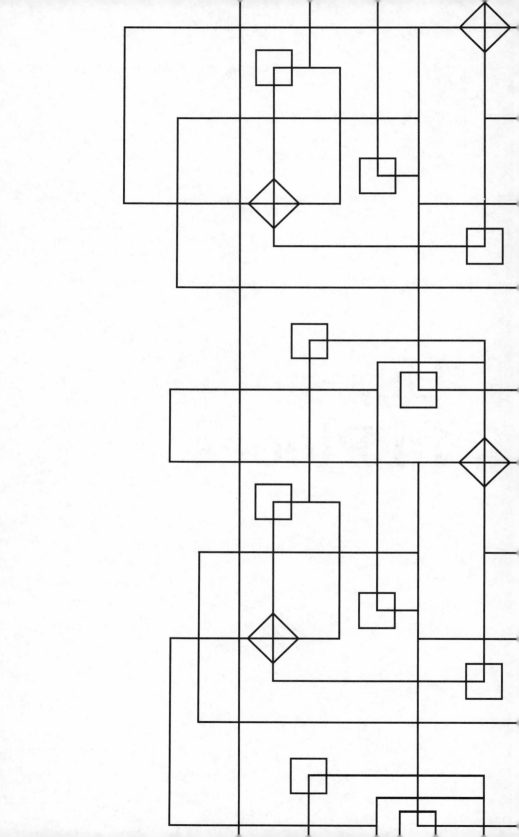

Part 1

October 4, 2013

Adin

Here's what I thought a tractor pull was: A functional event turned into a community project, sort of like an Amish barn-raising. There's a tractor, obviously, pulled around for...some reason. Who knows? Farm stuff. It was an ineffable mystery to diehard urban types like me. What I imagined, essentially, was that everybody got together and did generic manual labor, something rural and wholesome, and then went back to the house for apple pie and hard-boiled eggs.

Here's what a tractor pull really is: You take a bunch of tractors, stack V-8 engines on them, paint them like stock cars, and then use them to pull giant sledge weights down a 100-meter track, in a race to see who can pull the biggest weight the farthest and fastest. Some of them even do it with radio-controlled tractors now. Meanwhile, people sit in stands eating nachos and drinking Mountain Dew, cheering them on. It's like if NASCAR cars entered a Strongman competition, and all the competitors were using performance-enhancing drugs. Yes, swear to God, this is a thing.

So, as you might imagine, I was a little disoriented at my first tractor pull. Especially when Lilly's mom suggested that I ride *in the damned tractor* with her husband.

Lilly hadn't even gotten there yet. I was only there to see her, honestly, but her mom was just *so* excited, and her dad was shouting, "C'mon, Boy! There's girls watching!" He assumed that I was the sort of insecure twit who would immediately cave to that sort of inelegant pressure—and I was. I hadn't even been there two hours before I was on the back of this something-thousand horsepower metal-fanged demon horse, and her dad was laughing his head off at the look on my face. "Sure beats the metro!" he cackled.

And that, of course, is the precise moment Lilly got there. Right about the time I was attempting to remove myself from the material world, like disaster victims do, trying to find this happy place somewhere inside myself filled with spiced chai lattes and community theater and those little ribbed plates you put your finger foods on at Christmas parties. All I wanted in the world was not to empty my bladder all over the seat. I could entertain nothing beyond that one dire necessity; there was no room. And yet, there she was at the edge of the crowd. Grown-up Lilly. Just like I'd hoped for.

She seemed a little taken aback when I made my way over to her afterward, my whole body still humming like your hands after mowing the lawn. She was holding lemonade in a little plastic cup. She was dressed more fashionably than I remembered her being in college, standing straight-backed and stern-faced, surveying the whole of the scene around her. Her hair was in this gorgeous long ponytail, much longer than it had been the last time I saw her.

When I told her it was good to see her again—over the roar of all those terrifying machines, lions of the South Carolina Serengeti—the first thing she said to me was, *"What?"*

Later, when I suggested we keep in touch, she said, "Yeah, that would be great. I'd love that." This was a terrible lie, and we both knew it. We exchanged email addresses, in that way that friends do when the flame of their friendship has been standing in the rain for the better part of a decade.

I went home defeated, dejected, disillusioned. Any number of alliterative feelings collided inside of me until I thought the chemical reaction might shatter me like a glass beaker. It was the best day I'd had in years.

When Lilly and I stumbled back into each other's lives, I was still in the death grip of family photography, which is only about 10 percent snapping pictures and 90 percent telling that bratty kid in the Ohio State cap to tilt his head to 18.4 degrees. Small consolation, in other words, for a man who spent most of college in a darkroom, with big glossy prints of bluebells and courthouses and the shadowed profiles of all his laughing, indulgent friends. I was unspeakably miserable and alone. I entertained fantasies of scribbling on the camera lens so it looked like all the families were on fire. I was in the market for a change so enormous it would shift the tectonic plates of the ground I walked on, and Lilly was it, although if you'd told me so at the time I would have laughed. Or punched you in the face. Or both.

And then, one morning in September, I rolled out of bed and there it was, waiting for me on my bedside table, so simple, so small: a text from Tristan Rawlings, best friend and onetime college go-between for me and Lilly. *Don't know if you heard,* it read, *but Mrs. Jameson just went back to* Miss *Jameson.*

A chill shimmied up my spine—how did he even know this? I'd heard some years back of her marriage (no small amount of despair there, I may as well admit), but not from him. We never talked about her, in fact, me and Tristan. I hadn't known up to this point that he was in a position to hear of her goings-on. But Tristan was like that. He kept his fingers dipped in the lives of everybody he met.

Later I'd find out the whole provenance of this wild scoop, how it went from Lilly to a friend to a friend and on down to Tristan and, at last, to me. But, in that moment, where it came from wasn't half so consuming as the news itself. Lilly, unbound, a free agent. The woman I had lost and never hoped to see again, back again after a long absence. I was shocked, bewildered, and secretly elated. That same afternoon, I tried calling her old home number to see if I could get in touch with her, to check up on her.

Why did I do this? you may ask. Was I genuinely concerned? Or was I scheming even then to have my shot with her, before the ink was dry on the paperwork? I don't know. Column A, Column B. I'm almost sure it was a little bit of both.

I knew the odds that she would pick up were against me, because she was twenty-eight now, a big girl, well past living with her parents. She'd long since disappeared into parts unknown, and I might have had a better idea where if we had spoken at all in the last 9 years. But we hadn't. I hadn't seen her since the summer after our sophomore year. But then, what alternative was there? God knew I wasn't going to hit up Tristan for her cell number.

Lilly did not pick up, of course. But her mom did.

She was tremendously excited to hear from me. Polite, enthusiastic exchanges ensued, and inquiries were made as to my job and my family. She gave me a rundown of the Jameson's B&B, and told me how they'd converted Lilly's room into a guest room. In a moment of touchingly accurate recollection she asked how my dad was doing; she had remembered our great family tragedy in January of that second year. She even invited me to her husband's tractor pull—which, looking back, was more than a little strange. I'm not sure what impression, at nineteen, I'd given her that I was into tractor pulls. But it was a chance to get out of Ohio and away from my awful job, to see some of that old Southern scenery I so missed. And maybe—my guilty, giddy heart insisted—it would also be a chance to have my first glimpse of Lilly in almost ten years. Grown-up Lilly. Her mom didn't mention the divorce, and I didn't ask, but it was there, in between every word.

And then, the pull itself—a bust. One last painful memory of a squandered opportunity to lay on my pile, years after all the others. After I got home from South Carolina I agonized over whether to even write to her at all, given how awkward we had been with each other.

The opening dispatch in our correspondence took a week for me to finalize, and even then I was woefully dissatisfied with the results.

> **from:** Adin Driscoll
> **to:** Lilly Jameson
> **sent:** October 7, 3:13 p.m. EDT
> **subject:** Long time no see
>
> Hey!
> It was good to see you again. I had a lot of fun (although I'm fairly certain I'm never going near a tractor again). I'd like to talk to you some more sometime, maybe catch up a little. Also tell your mom thanks for the little cake things that I forgot the name of.
>
> Adin

How hard was it to do this? The world may never know. I must have rewritten the third sentence about eighteen times. In my head it started as something like, "I've missed you so much, missed having you in my life, please for the love of God don't leave it again." On paper it started as, "We should really get together again and talk," but even that sounded too...eager. I went through various iterations, each one increasingly distant and cagey, until I got to this one. She probably knew.

[◦] [◦] [◦]

October 11th

Lilly

I KNEW.

from: Lilly Jameson
to: Adin Driscoll
sent: October 11, 5:53 p.m. MDT
subject: Re: Long time no see

Adin,

It was nice seeing you again, too. My dad still talks about your face at the tractor pull. Were you wearing a helmet? Someone told me they saw you wearing a helmet? Not saying it's a bad idea, necessarily. (I never in a million years thought I would see you on a tractor.) Anyway, Dad won't stop talking about you.

Seeing you there was, well, just really unexpected. Mom didn't tell me she invited you. But it was good to see you—you haven't changed much.

Catching up would be good.

Lilly
p.s. The cookies are called *madeleines*...

The irony of Adin inquiring about madeleines was not lost on me. I'd read my Proust. The whole time he was in Beaufort I felt like I was reliving some alternate version of my past that I couldn't get a handle on. I saw him and a thousand memories rushed back, making me feel laid bare—and, well, a little embarrassed. I recalled all the meals we'd shared in the dining hall, the CDs we made each other, studying in the library, walking to class together, a slow dance that I'd never forgotten, shopping together, smoking the occasional cigarette in the courtyard, and even sharing the same bed at times, though nothing ever happened. It struck me how intimate our past life had been. There was a period of time when my life was very much braided with his. Did he remember those things? Did he recall any of that stuff? Was he just another guy coming out of the woodwork since I was now single? He showed up in my hometown, so it kind of looked like it.

I wasn't exactly thrilled to see him. His timing couldn't have been worse.

Lilly: hey, you there?

Jane: hey. I am. Just put harlow to bed. I saw your fb status finally changed…Big step.

Lilly: Yeah… Now I'm getting all these sad messages from ppl. I meant to call you. There's been so much going on here. Meetings w/ lawyers, moving stuff. …ALSO, btw, you'll never guess who was at my dad's tractor pull IN BEAUFORT.

Jane: a thousand men drinking Pepsi, chewing tobacco and spitting on the ground?

Lilly: YES. All of the above. And Adin Driscoll.

Jane: ? Adin? From college?

Lilly: Adin. Driscoll. Can you believe that?

Jane: whaaaaat? No! Why was he there?

Lilly: Yes! How crazy is that? Mom invited him w/o telling me. It was weird. …He wants to "catch up" and everything. What's your take?

Jane: well…I'm betting he still likes you. Is he still cute?

Lilly: Im not really thinking about that right now. But yes. He is still very cute.

Jane: he still likes you—does he know about the shit going down w/ tim?

Lilly: he clearly knows about the divorce, he doesn't know the geography of it, per se

Jane: how'd he look?

Lilly: Good. He was really out of his element, though. It was fun to watch. I'd had a shitty day and seeing him ride on a tractor made things much better.

Jane: he was at a tractor pull…is he still into photography? He used to win all those awards…

Lilly: yeah. He said something about that. I don't know the details. I think that's his job. A photographer. In Ohio, I think.

Jane: I always liked Adin.

Lilly: yeah, he was just always kind of up in the air about everything. He was so shy. He never had…a plan. I remember how you all used to bug me about him.

Jane: you remember those looks he used to give you? We'd pick on him about it once you were out of the room.

Lilly: Yeah, I do.

Jane: he was kind of lovesick there for a while.

Lilly: to this day I have no idea what was going on in his head. Anyway, what I really want to know is, what's it like being a mom?

Jane: I'm trying to get used to this stay-at-home thing…i don't love it.

Lilly: Really? So do you guys have a joint division of parenting?

Jane: a myth as far as I'm concerned. But it's amazing. I mean, I love being a mom, but is it weird for me to miss being young and careless and…looked at? Dancing at parties til 3 am?

Lilly: Trust me. You're golden right now. Husband, child, a home. Now, the being seen part…

Jane: you know, everything just felt different, it was all so exciting.

Lilly: We were teenagers! First experiences—parties, lights, music.

Jane: FRAT PARTIES! And occasionally the rare person who could see right through you.

Lilly: …yeah. That too.

Jane: God. What was Adin Driscoll doing in beaufort?!

Lilly: Attending my Dad's tractor pull?

Jane: Come on. why was he really there? We both know.

Lilly: He wants to be friends, again, I guess.

Jane: He wants something more than your friendship, Lilly. He did then. He does now.

⊠ ⊠ ⊠

December 2nd
Columbus, Ohio

Adin

IT HAD BEEN ALMOST TWO MONTHS SINCE I'D heard from her. I assumed the promise we made to each other was a casual one, easily forgotten, that we'd probably ask a few basic, impersonal questions and then drift apart again. But this was worse than I expected. She said yeah, let's do that, and then I didn't hear from her.

Time passed. Weeks collapsed into one another, messy and indiscernible. I remember nothing of what happened in them. It's as though someone has gone back and redacted them, black streaks across all the long hours that I did, at one point, actually occupy.

One day at work this skinny suburban matriarch in a sweat shirt and yoga pants came storming in with a copy of her son's senior pictures. Something had happened, in development or in transit, and the largest of the photos were smeared in several vital areas. Every copy looked as though someone had spilled bleach on it. This, of course, had nothing to do with me, but mine was the only face she had to connect with the job. It took twenty minutes to hand her off to Bill, the owner. I had to call him at home because, as the owner, he took no actual part in the business, preferring instead to play golf and watch *NCIS* on his 80-inch television with his young blond wife—who, it's worth mentioning, was much prettier than the mother in the sweat shirt.

I came home weary, bitter, despairing of my lot. I dived deep into my personal reserve of Grey Goose, a bottle I normally saved for special occasions. No big loss, I told myself. To what special occasion was I looking forward? An engagement? A promotion?

My dead mother's birthday? I poured another shot and toasted my empty apartment. "To life!" I said. *"L'Chaim!* May your old crushes send you wedding invitations and your dreams desiccate like pinned butterflies—beautiful but forever grounded."

Several hours later I emailed her.

from: Adin Driscoll
to: Lilly Jameson
sent: December 2, 3:01 a.m. EST
subject: Breaking radio silence...

Lilly,

How are things going? I haven't heard from you really since we hung out in October. I'm wondering if i did something wrong. I hope everything's okay. Things were really shitty when you stopped talking to me last time, so I'm just not wanting that to happen again. I hope that's not what's happening. I was thinking about you earlier, especially your room at school, and I ws thinking about how happy we were back then. I hope you're still that happy.

I liked seeing your house again, you know. It's not like I remember it at all, but it still felt so familiar. Like all the really important stuff was still there you know? I read that poem again that your mom framed by the stairs, the one about the orange tree and I think some guy you were in love with in highs chool. Are you in love with anobody now? Do you still write? I tried it for a while after I graduated, but it was a disaster I use too many adverbs, and I can't seem to think of a plot that doesn't have a love story in it. But that was always my thing, I guess. Love stories I mean not adverbs. Maybe that didn't need clarification, but just in case, right.

Hope to hear back from you soon. i have a lot of other questions.

Adin

I woke up the next morning, found my email account still open. I clicked on my "Sent" folder. I wailed.

❖ ❖ ❖

December 4th
Fort Collins, Colorado

Lilly

from: Lilly Jameson
to: Adin Driscoll
sent: December 4, 12:12 p.m. MST
subject: Re: Breaking radio silence....

Oh, Adin:
Sorry I am just now getting back to you.

Man, shit is happening....

I *do* still write. It's kinda my life. Are you still doing nature photography? I write children's books. My first book won an award last year (still don't know how that happened). But there it is, that's what I do.

I'm in the process of separating from Tim, that's why I haven't written you. We've been separated for a while now, but it's all kind of wrapping up, legally, at this point. I'm getting through it, though. I've just launched myself into the work as a way of trying to blot out reality, which I'm sure must sound like real healthy behavior. How am I feeling? I've had "The Past and Pending" by The Shins on repeat for days now. I've been boxing up stuff, labeling things. ...

The truth is somewhere along the way things got kind of toxic between us. He spent all his time at the law firm (he's a lawyer) and I busied myself with writing. I don't think we missed each other.

I think I got married because I wanted to be like everyone else and to want the same stuff everyone else wants. I didn't know how to just be myself. I'm not sure Tim really knew what he was getting into. We were really young when we got married. We were naïve, but we cared about each other. Slowly all the small fractures became deep cracks.

We got to a point where things couldn't be repaired. Things were said that couldn't be unsaid. It felt like we weren't on the same page about anything. I felt myself disappearing inside myself, not wanting to come out. I'm sorry if I'm talking too much—I don't think I've told that to anyone.

I'm thinking of moving out this next month and am trying to figure out where the hell I should go. Denver is #1 on my list so far. I've traveled through there a lot and absolutely love it—the mountains, the air, even, but I don't know many people there. I feel like I could go anywhere I want at this point in my life, and for the first time ever, I can. I just don't know where. Where would you go if you could go anywhere? Honestly, I'm scared shitless. I would have called, but I'd probably be crying in minutes because I'm actually freaking out and I don't want you to have to deal with that. A long time ago you and I could talk about anything. Maybe that's still the case. Maybe not. Time will tell, right?

Lilly
p.s. You *were* drunk in that last email, right?

⌗ ⌗ ⌗

December 5th
Columbus, Ohio

Adin

I TRIED VERY HARD TO BE POISED AND dignified and aloof this time around, as if that would somehow undo the incredible lapse in judgment presented by the previous message. And somehow I managed to do reasonably well, even if just beneath the surface of my words I was screaming that I couldn't contain myself, that the thought of knowing Lilly again made me pace my apartment just to get the energy out of me, that all I wanted in the world was to go back to what I had been able to say to her when I was drowning in vodka.

How did I manage this? Very carefully, that's how.

from: Adin Driscoll
to: Lilly Jameson
sent: December 5, 10:25 a.m. EST
subject: All's well that ends well

I really thought I was going to get away with it until your PS. I'm not even sure how that email happened, honestly. I have zero memory of that whole experience. I don't remember reading that orange tree poem, either, although apparently drunk me remembers it really well. Is there actually a poem like that in your mom's house? I guess I just wanted to know why you hadn't written, but was too nervous to ask about it while in my right mind. Oh well. I guess my wrong mind says hello.

I never met Tim, so I can't say I know what's being lost there, but if you both want jet-setting careers more than you want each other, that does sound like kind of an irreconcilable difference. It still sucks, though. Believe me, I've never been married, but I know what it's like to lose something you worked so hard to build. I've lost a couple of them since college.

Honestly, if I could go anywhere it would probably be back down south. Not to Savannah or Georgia specifically, but somewhere down there. When I have bad days at work, which is often, I come home and make tea and Google pictures of some beautiful Old South town like Charleston or St. Augustine, have fantasies about getting some great little apartment in a complex where they all party until four in the morning. I've only ever known it as a vacation spot, but the more I think about it, the more I realize I never felt more at home than when I was there. I need to be in a place that's both as old and as young as I feel. If money weren't an issue, I'd probably go to one of those towns, or someplace similar, somewhere with antebellum architecture and strangers who tell you hello as they pass you on the street.

But where you should go? I'll have to think about it. My first instinct is to say Columbus, because, well, that's where I am. But Columbus isn't the best place for a writer, and the weather sucks. Although it does have some really good music, and I remember you liked music as much as I did. There is some cool stuff here, if you're out of ideas and just need to get out now.

Wow, that got heavy real fast. I don't know what to say. If you want to call, I'm okay with crying. Believe me, it wouldn't be the first time I've had a phone call like that. I'm just glad that we're talking again.

Adin

I navigated the part about suggesting Columbus like a bed of hot coals.

Tristan: sup

Adin: hey

Tristan: what's goin on

Adin: guess who i started talking to again

Tristan: telling me is easier

Adin: fine. Lilly

Tristan: what? jameson?

Adin: the same

Tristan: no way lol

Tristan: because of the divorce? you still trying to bone her?

Adin: i wasn't even trying to bone her the first time, asshole

Tristan: because i will take zero responsibility for telling you she was single

Tristan: oh right yeah. in love or whatever

Tristan: so how's princess handling the single life?

Adin: she's moving back from wherever. I suggested she go to columbus, for some reason

Tristan: columbus lol

Tristan: you are TOTALLY trying to bone this girl

Adin: no, I'm not

Tristan: again! you're trying again!

Adin: will you shut up. she was a really good friend of mine, and i missed her

Adin: i don't want to bone her. i just want to talk to her

Tristan: whatever, you never said one word about her after she left Ohio U

Adin: yeah, well

Adin: i wanted to

Oh, Tristan. Always yanking me out of the dim bunker of my own delusions. I was going to make him the best man at my wedding, if I ever had one.

⟐ ⟐ ⟐

December 10th-13th
Denver, Colorado

Lilly

from: Lilly Jameson
to: Jane Thomas-Barczak
sent: December 10, 1:13 a.m. MST
subject: Good evening!

Jane:

my agent just sold my NEXT book. I opened a bottle of wine to celebrate (have almost finished bottle) Wish you were here listening to p.j. harvey w/me. remember when we used to hang up twinkle lights in the dorm and have dance parties? miss those times.

Yes, Adin and I are still emailing. Actually, need to talk to you about him—he is being nice and suggested I move to where he lives. not sure what he is getting at.

You and Philip have something special. I need to follow my dreams for once and well, maybe someone sees me as being worth the trouble, but if not, then I won't worry (will try not to worry—would be a lie to say will not worry at all). I just want someone who would like, pick me up and spin me around and eat cotton candy with me at a fair and then the next day get hyper-caffeinated with me and watch *CBS Sunday Morning* and eat croissants in our PJs. And have loads of animals. My life is all in my head. You know that. I just want someone I can break free from all that with. Lightness. I need lightness.

I feel very raw right now. I feel like such a cynic and raw in the sense I second-guess everything now. Where did my confidence go! Well, I told you about this a little already. wish you were here. PJ harvey is playing your favorite song. May buy a self-help book—do you have recommendations? dont tell Adin i am asking, etc.

Another thing in potential companion: Must like the Me They Get.

Dad always hated the guys i dated. They were all losers in his book. I remember when I was like 18 and some guy, I think it was Jason, showed up and I had to go get something upstairs, I return and dad had him in the basement showing him his gun collection. Creeped me out. Dad continues to bring up Adin since that tractor pull. The other day when mom called, it was Adin this and Adin that. She said dad wants me to invite him out anytime. I mean, they are NOTHING alike. Adin wore a helmet during the tractor pull. I think Dad wants to make Adin his protegee, like the son he never had. Dad wears cowboy boots with manure on them to church and Adin wears these fancy Alden loafers and cardigans to his job as a family photographer. did i tell you he is in columbus, ohio? He actually asked me to move there, suggested it, I mean.

Lots of questions
Lilly

∎ ∎

from: Lilly Jameson
to: Brenda Jameson
sent: December 10, 7:49 a.m. MST
subject: Hey Mom

Mom:
I was writing mostly because I think it would be a good idea to have Adin in for the holidays. A week sound okay with you? I think you know his situation and yes, he stays in the guest bedroom. Don't get any ideas and no matchmaker stuff.
Love you,

Lilly

. . .

from: Adin Driscoll
to: Lilly Jameson
sent: December 12, 5:05 a.m. EST
subject: So what's going on here

Hey,

So your mom called. She wants me to come stay a few more days at Christmas. Was this your idea or hers? I can probably get the days off work, and I'm not going to see Dad until close to New Year's. And honestly, I don't have much going on here for Christmas; I was going to bust out my three-foot plastic fir and depress myself watching *It's a Wonderful Life*. I'm available, is what I'm saying. I can drop down for a day or two, have lunch, see a play, leave before it starts looking like I'm moving in.

She said you were going to Denver. I'm jealous, you know. West of the Mississippi is like the dark side of the moon to me. I don't even know if the grass is the same color there, or what language they speak. I'd love to get out of Ohio, after all these years, see the Rockies or the West Coast. Maybe I'll come visit, get the lay of the land. Everybody else is gone—Micky, Jane, Giselle, Julianna, Tristan. I do still talk to Tristan, though. He says hi.

Maybe I've said this already, but I'm really glad to be hearing from you again. It was a lot more boring without you all those years. I'm going to the library tomorrow to get one of your books. I know I'm not your ideal audience, but I like the idea of seeing first-hand what you've been up to. It helps me close the gap a little bit.

Adin

...

from: Lilly Jameson
to: Adin Driscoll
sent: December 13, 8:10 p.m. MST
subject: Christmas Plans

Adin:

You coming to Beaufort for Christmas was my idea. I just think my mom got super excited and beat me to the actual invitation part, which is very much like her.

I moved into my new place in Denver last week. I wonder what you'd think of it. Not much in the way of grass. That's something I miss about Beaufort (and the South in general)—the green grass, the trees. Though Colorado is something to see—there's wild sage growing all over the place—and pine trees, and the mountains. Breathtaking mountains. If you ever make it out here, I'm sure you'd love it. It's a photographer's paradise.

Why don't we coordinate our flights around the holidays so we each arrive in Charleston together, rent a car and drive to mom and dad's in Beaufort from there. Meeting a handsome man in the hustle and bustle of a busy airport is on my 100 Things to Do Before You Die List. *Very Sleepless in Seattle / When Harry Met Sally,* I know, but a girl can have romantic fantasies, right?

Lilly

⟨·⟩ ⟨·⟩ ⟨·⟩

December 14th
Columbus, Ohio

Adin

So she moved to Denver. Land of...wow, I really didn't even know what was in Denver. Rocks, I guess? All places have rocks. Honestly all I knew of Colorado was *South Park*. That's how remote she'd become. Just when I thought I'd have her back in my life again, off she charged into the unfathomable West. But that was what she did best: intangibility.

I would, however, see her in two weeks, which was intimidating. I found myself marveling at her now, at how she'd changed, matured, gotten more beautiful than I remembered. I hated her for that. For keeping up with me. It would have been easier for her to marry some asshole and get fat with babies and chocolate and chronic unhappiness. But she had to grow from the girl I always wanted to the woman I always wanted. I wasn't sure I could take that in the flesh.

Everything had come tragically full circle. Here it was again: the old misery, the consuming desire. I must have been secretly craving it, all this time. That must have been why I threw myself into ridiculous and untenable situations, why I was even now falling twice for the same girl, in the same situation, for the same reasons, and with almost definitely the same results.

I spent far too much time now wondering what this divorce and the other foggy details of her life had led her to believe about love, and what I might have done to change it if I could. I don't know why. I was scared of seeing her, of what would happen. Or, more precisely, what would *not* happen. I was scared of going there, saying hi to her mother, eating some sort of fried bird, taking a walk along some windy beach, and going home.

And that being it.

God help me, I prayed. God help all of us.

from: Lilly Jameson
to: Adin Driscoll
sent: December 14, 7:30 a.m. MST
subject: Re: Christmas Plans *attachment*

Adin:

Hey, well, I got us both flights that arrive in Charleston on December 20th.

You should have received everything via email. I'm looking forward to getting back to Beaufort. It's freezing here, but there's nothing like looking out your window and seeing snow-capped mountains—not the sissy mountains either. I don't know much about Ohio, but I think I've got you beat when it comes to jaw-dropping earthly splendor.

Speaking of which, there's a story I've been meaning to send you called "Splendor." I wrote it a few years ago. I know we've talked about how unexpected it is for us to be talking again. I see it as a sort of microcosm of us.

Sometimes I feel like our whole relationship was based on half-truths. Do you ever feel that way? We think we grow wiser and more mature, only to be knocked back by life and suddenly I'm no wiser than I was at eighteen, sitting on our bench on the college quad, watching the leaves fall, wishing I were older. And you wished for that, too. What were we after, exactly? I think we've always been like that—old souls drawn to old things.

Sometimes I think the tragedy with Tim lay in the simple fact I expected wrongness to announce itself boldly, right up front. Back then I didn't understand the concept of nuance. I suspected that something tragically bad would look *really bad*, but Tim was great in a lot of ways, which I interpreted as meaning he was perfect for *me*. I find myself wondering if what's right for us wears a mask, too. Like, there is no parade when the *right one* appears is there? And maybe you don't even like the way the *right one* kisses you at first, but still…life can surprise you. At my core, I want every kiss to be one of the better ones mankind has ever known. Is that unreasonable? I don't know. I'm just talking to myself here.

Lilly

As I READ HER PLANS, I PICTURED OUR meeting at the airport. In my version it was a slow-motion collision, with Tchaikovsky's *Romeo and Juliet* playing. I wanted the sappiest, soggiest reunion imaginable. Any less would be crushing. But this was impossible. Lilly's casual discussion of our relationship, the words she used for it—"unexpected," especially—cut deep. She wasn't imagining anything like the elaborate film sequences running in my head. She'd devoted more words to her ex-husband than to our meeting. Probably she imagined shaking hands, a discussion about what brand of car to rent. She wasn't the hot mess I was. Our fated reconnection was little more than a curiosity to her. She hadn't spent the last several years wishing for it.

And then I read this:

Splendor

They met freshmen year. She was holding her denim bag tightly in the college parking lot, waiting for her boyfriend to get his SUV working. She walked over to a grassy spot and sat down. The guy walked over to where she sat. He was saying something to her, but between the occasional roar of the engine and other people she couldn't really hear what this guy (and who was this guy?) was saying to her. Do you know Splender? She thought he asked her. She smiled. She asked him to repeat the question and when he did she realized he meant the band Splender. Yes, she knew the band. The guy liked that she knew this. They talked until her boyfriend came over, asking her if she was ready to leave. She got up and followed her boyfriend, waving goodbye to the guy.

This guy did not take her to the formal. He was not her date to anything. He rarely went to the library with her where she made large stacks of French flash cards or took notes on Pride and Prejudice. But the guy found his way to her dorm room where they listened to music and watched indie films together. He found his way to the table she ate at each day. He knew when she would arrive at the cafeteria. He watched her go to frat parties with other people. Sometimes they raised a glass to each other and when she danced, he'd disappear.

The girl remembers some moments with him perfectly. Like the night he followed her back home after they escorted her drunk boyfriend back to his dorm. They were alone for once, in the dark. It was late and there was a song playing. They slow-danced to the song. The girl remembers feeling steadied. The girl never asked the guy if he remembered that night, though she never forgot. As an adult, this memory became a sad thing. She assumed he had forgotten it, or worse, had shared similar dances with many girls since.

The girl transferred schools and the guy stayed behind. The guy didn't visit her or email or phone. Nothing. The girl was quietly devastated and distracted herself with schoolwork. Inside her, their clearest moments and their deep bond ebbed and flowed. Months passed and she grew uncertain. Questions disappeared. Answers were given. She tried to forget the guy who introduced her to music, slept head to toe beside her in a bunk bed, and, for a reason she couldn't identify, seemed to want her. But there was no proof of that. Her new mind was years in the making and a great deal was put away. Over time, thick walls were built. He became ghostlike and walled off from her.

Years later the guy would finally get up the nerve to call her, but it was too late.

He sounded like his old self. Her husband was at the dining room table drinking coffee, working on a laptop while she talked to the guy. When she hung up she turned to look at their backyard, her eyes landed on someone else's property. Her mind was racing. She sensed her wall had just taken a huge hit.

Again the guy dropped away and again she tried to rebuild that wall brick by brick and it mostly worked. Sometimes she would miss a spot, sometimes she would leave and come back to find pieces of the wall had vanished in the night. She worked and worked until one day the guy emails to ask how she's doing. What could the girl say? How could he even ask the question? Years pass and variations of this occur until one day she does not answer him.

from: Adin Driscoll
to: Lilly Jameson
sent: December 14, 7:48 p.m. EST
subject: That story

Okay, we need to talk about this.

How much of this is true? I mean, how much of it do you think is true? Because I can promise you that most of it is fiction. Here's the picture you're painting: we're good friends, and then I abandon you. Sorry, Lilly, but that's not what happened. From where I stood, it was the other way around—you switched schools, you got married and moved away. I mean you had my number. You didn't call, either. And the only reason I didn't call was because I thought you were washing your hands of me, of all of us. I had to find out from *other people* that you were gone. I figured if I wasn't worth a phone call, there was no point in trying to get back in your good graces. I spent a lot of that year beating myself up about it, actually, thinking that I had done something to deserve your contempt.

No, I didn't know you were building a wall. I didn't know you needed to. But good for you. I didn't get a wall. I got this blasted-out no man's land. There was no cover available for me. Even when I dated other girls, I worried that whatever misstep I had made with you would get repeated with them. And we were never even together! How fucked up is that?

Make no mistake: I've been just as haunted by you, Lilly, as you seem to have been by me. Almost certainly more so. You think I don't remember those French flashcards, or the mornings we got coffee at the cafe by your dorm? I remember them so vividly it's like you're still here, walking around my damn living room, tilting your head at me when I make a dumb joke. You're the best connection I have to the person I was that year, right before everything changed, before Mom and Dad moved back to Savannah, before Mom got sick. How could I forget you, or the perfumed smell of your room, or the strands of hair hanging loose from your ponytail, or the careful loops of your handwriting, or you playing the flute in bed at two in the morning? How could you think that I could be the bad guy here?

If this story is our future, it will be because you do the leaving again. It even says so—"until one day she does not answer him." I never went anywhere the first time, and I'm not going anywhere now. I hold the things I care about close to me, and you are chief among the things I care about. I hope that this is just fiction to you, that this tirade has been all for nothing, because if not, then I'm at a loss. I don't know what else to say.

Adin

Call it courage, call it rage. Call it unjustified or overdramatic or batshit crazy. I'll be the first to admit it was all of these things. But what it was most of all was the truth. I was so caught off guard that I didn't have time to sit and think of how to word this diplomatically. All I had to work with was raw feelings, which I splashed all over the screen like mismatched paints. I was pained and angry and weirdly, *weirdly* relieved. I had been living with these words for so many years, and I wanted, just once, for all of them to be made clear to her. I could not possibly care less what the effect of this message was. I cared only about the sending. I cared only that she know how wrong she was.

☒ ☒ ☒

A few hours later
Denver, Colorado

Lilly

I WAS TOTALLY UNPREPARED FOR HIS RESPONSE. I *haunted* him? I reread the email. He would *never leave me*? We never even dated in college. He had never asked me out. We'd never even kissed. Yet somehow, he became the one person I could not shake. Despite the difficulty of leaving Jane and the heartbreak of losing Jason, Adin had been my best friend, the one I truly mourned, the source of my sleepless nights. I walked the halls of the University of South Carolina a zombie, emptied out, a shell of who I was. I could not bring myself to smile. I could not wake myself up. And the more I thought about it, the more I started to think that maybe he was my other half. And maybe that's why I was feeling only half-alive. Adin knew my secrets. Adin and I knew the words to the same songs. We came to the same conclusions. We were drawn to the same ideas and stories. When he didn't try to reach out after I moved, I fell into one of the darkest periods of my life. Each day, my body contained a hurricane of our shared memories—a life I could not get back. All at once, I'd remember a look he'd given me on a bench or the feel of his hand on my back and it would collide with the hundred-mile-per-hour winds of a dream I had of us. There was never any stopping it. The force of that weather took years to contain and manage. Did he think leaving everyone had been easy for me? The truth was, leaving other people *had* been painful. But leaving him had brought a level of pain and sadness into my life I hadn't believed possible. He'd been silent. Remember all that white space? I wanted to ask him. Remember all those years apart?

> **Lilly**: So, Adin, you said we needed to talk. ...
>
> **Adin**: okay, well i mean i did my talking already

Lilly: I wrote it a long time ago. It's ok if you hate it.

Adin: i didn't hate it, it was good, that's not the problem. is that really how you see the way things went down?

Lilly: well, yeah, mostly

Adin: well, the guy in your story is this douche who abandons you, her, whatever and that's not how that happened i thought you were the one who wasn't interested in talking anymore

Lilly: I was just surprised by your reaction. I should have told you I was going to USC. It was my parent's decision. The out-of-state tuition.

Adin: Really?

Lilly: That. And you.

Adin: me? what?

Lilly: And Jason—because of all the drama. Do you remember how nonstop it was? Between you, me, and jason? All the frat parties I was expected to go to—I'd get there and he'd have frat duties. All the time.

Adin: i remember, yeah.

Lilly: I felt like i was so far from...myself. I went to OU for the creative writing classes and i felt like i was becoming someone i didn't recognize. I hated always being dragged to one fraternity event after the other...I knew things were bad with Jason, he was always handling frat stuff. it just consumed him, but i kept hoping things would calm down and we'd go back to how we used to be, but then they started talking about him taking on a leadership role...and i knew it wouldnt stop.

Adin: oh, trust me, i knew. that shit is hard to not notice

Lilly: and i felt like i was always caught between you and Jason, and the idea of choosing between you two...i just felt like it would ruin our little circle. And yet you were always there for me, always around and jason hated that. He and i fought all the time, and i tried to shield you from it.

Adin: Look, Lilly

Lilly: you and I were great friends, but I felt like you never respected my choice—you'd make these fairly obvious comments about me (us) and it would put me in an impossible situation with Jason. At the time I really liked him and felt like things would improve if I just gave him more space. I know you and I had a great friendship, but i wasnt sure about anything more, so i didnt want to risk it.

Adin: so you left? just like that? eighteen-year-old me was not so great at navigating that sort of thing. and i guess if i'm being honest there's probably still more of him in me than i'd like. so you decided to just remove yourself from the picture?

Lilly: yes. I thought it was the best way. I was always at the center of all this drama at OU. I hated it. And i felt like no matter what i did i couldnt escape it. at some point over the summer i made the decision not to return. i felt like you would all be so much happier without me there. I really believed that.

Adin: so you didn't call because you didn't think we needed you to. you thought we'd be glad to see you go.

Lilly: that first semester at USC i was too scared to call. I kept imagining how happy you all were—later that semester i knew things had changed with the group. I was miserable. I guess i just didnt think you'd miss me that much

Adin: yeah, well…i did i can't even tell you

Lilly: and i got to USC and didnt realize how much i needed you in my life

Adin: wait, what? you needed me in your life? how?

Lilly: Adin we were great friends at OU i guess i thought i could find that anywhere i never did

Adin: oh…okay

Lilly: thing is i meant everything in my last email. the fact that we've known each other so long and know so much about each other is what i find so hard to lose when i think about us trying to be anything more…that scares me i dont want to hurt you or build a wall but i felt lost without you

Adin: i did, too it would be funny if it weren't so tragic or maybe it's funny because it's tragic but you said that story was a microcosm for our relationship. i mean do you see the future being me leaving you again? or you someday not returning my calls?

Lilly: i think i do all this as a way to protect myself from you dropping off the face of the earth...

Adin: well, to be fair i only dropped off the earth because the earth moved away from me i don't plan on doing it a second time

Lilly: I can't believe we're meeting at the charleston airport in December

Adin: ...and then what?

Lilly: I don't know what do you want to happen?

Adin: honestly, it doesn't matter. i'll be happy with anything i just want to see you again

Lilly: Yeah, talking to you like this...exchanging all these emails. I want to see you, too

Adin: well, i'll be there

Lilly: Okay. I'm glad you're not mad. ...I was scared to be this honest w/ you. Looking back, I know it wasn't your fault. It really wasn't. I think I just convinced myself it was.

Adin: i was never really mad i was just hurt and worried that you thought i was something i wasn't

Lilly: well, you're showing me who you are and i like what i see i hope you still like who i am

Adin: you have no idea

Lilly: Hey—Mom is calling. I'm sure she'd love to know we've been talking.

Adin: yeah, probably, haha

Lilly: Okay. I'll talk to you later.

Adin: okay. Later

MOM WAS NOT CALLING. I COULD FEEL SOMETHING happening between us that I wasn't ready for. Something I couldn't articulate. I wasn't ready for this new Adin. This Adin who spoke his mind and wasn't afraid to go after what he wanted. In college, he could see right through my BS and my sometimes cowardly behavior. He could tell when I was being fake. He could pick out my white lies and detect my insecurities. I could misdirect others, but Adin was smarter than the rest. His insight had always impressed me and confounded me. Being around him made me feel like I'd been taken apart and rebuilt, the weak parts stripped away and made steadier. I always felt like he could see everything about me, as if I was a walking, breathing spectrum of color that only he could see in its entirety. To learn that he may still care about me was almost too much. What would he see when he saw me in Charleston? I was afraid there'd be nowhere to hide. I was afraid *to* hide. How to explain it? I was afraid I was falling in love.

❖ ❖ ❖

December 20th
Charleston International Airport, South Carolina

Adin

I MET LILLY AT THE AIRPORT IN CHARLESTON as planned. She sent me a text before I was even off the plane, telling me to meet her on the top floor of the terminal. I'd figured we'd just meet at the car rental place, somewhere practical and efficient. The sort of place friends meet. But she seemed insistent, so I agreed. But then the plane was forever late—I didn't hit the tarmac until 12:30. When I got up to the little Starbucks where she'd been waiting, she looked tired, stressed.

She was sitting by the railing overlooking the terminal, staring down, I guess searching for me so intently that she missed my actual approach. And I have to admit that I watched her there, just for a minute or two. Is that creepy? I don't know. But how many chances would I get to see her like this, in her genuine state? Before she knew that I was back in her life, before she was changing herself accordingly? This was my only chance to see what had become of Lilly, this girl who had become almost like a character from a book that I had once loved as a child.

She was beautiful. Of course she was beautiful. That was impossible to miss. Her hair was still long and dark, and I wanted, as I always had, to feel it slipping through my fingers. She sat with her legs neatly crossed, a habit she'd never had in college. An expensive wool coat and trendy boots had replaced her ripped jeans and Chucks. I appreciated these differences. They reminded me of some of the ways I myself had grown up. I liked the idea of us being new people together.

The craziest thing of all, in a way, was that she seemed comfortable and poised sitting there by herself. Watching it all. The way she had at the tractor pull. In college she was always surrounded by people, a habit I suspect was at least partly rooted in four lonely years of high school. She had a boyfriend, and me, and our circle. The closest I ever saw her to being alone was when it was just the two of us. But now here she was, back straight, head tilted gracefully toward the railing, hands steady on the table, or her lap, or her coffee cup. She might have sat there all day if I hadn't shown up.

I smiled at her—this big, helpless, blood-rushing smile that I knew I'd have to ditch when her eyes finally found me. The dopey smile, the betrayer. The one that gives it all away.

Then she took out her cell phone, slid her finger around, hit a few buttons. I couldn't read the screen from where I stood, but I knew what it was: she was waiting for me to text her, saying where I was. She pocketed it again and sighed deeply, this forlorn sound. Not a sigh of impatience or frustration. Something else altogether. Nervousness, maybe. Or a lot of other things I wanted to hear but couldn't be certain of.

I set my suitcase down. She turned. And there was this ever-so-slight rupture in time, like a record skipping. We stayed where we were for a long second before her face registered me, and then she rose, left her coffee cup and her purse and her great big rolling luggage, and crossed the cafe floor to me. I started toward her, she lifted her arms, and then we were actually touching each other. No more emails, no more phone calls. Just two bodies brought together from two sides of the void. It was everything I had wanted out of our reunion in October, everything I had fantasized about in those last lonely nights before I boarded the plane. I gripped the wool of her coat, and she lay her head against my shoulder.

"It's good to see you again," she said, her voice quiet, subdued.

"It's better than that," I told her.

We were a freeze-frame of one of those airport reunion scenes that people whisper about among themselves and cry over in movies. We didn't care. This was all there was to care about. We stayed in each other's arms for so long that it started getting difficult to pretend like we were only doing what close friends do. She finally let go of me.

On the escalator we began the long giddy process of catching up—both of us glancing away every time one of us gazed at the other too long.

⟨•⟩   ⟨•⟩   ⟨•⟩

December 21st
Beaufort, South Carolina

Lilly

from: Lilly Jameson
to: Jane Thomas-Barczak
sent: December 22, 7:30 a.m. EST
subject: Tell me what's happening…

Hey Jane,
I saw baby Harlow's pictures! He's got Philip's bright red hair! I really hope I can get over and see you all while I'm in town. Maybe Harlow will be a fan of mine.

Oh, Jane. Will someone ever want the kind of life I want?

What am I doing back in Beaufort, waking up alone in this stupid king size bed they put in my room when they transformed it into a guest room?

I guess I'm not *totally* alone. Adin is here for the holidays. We'd been talking on the phone and emailing about every day... and it just feels like things are progressing. Which is crazy right? Toward what, I don't know. He is actually upstairs, still asleep. I invited him to have Christmas with us and he has been, well, in a word, amazing. I'm kind of in shock about the whole thing.

We've had a few guests here at the B&B and Adin helped mom prep breakfast for the guests. I should admit that his interests are not wholly innocent—they seem to lie in ensuring she makes triple-berry pancakes rather than buttermilk. Mom seems to like having him around and he and Dad have been getting along well, which is surprising since I thought my dad hated everyone. Sometimes it feels like Dad likes Adin more than me. I walked downstairs to find he and Adin sitting in front of the plasma TV, eyes glued to some Area 51 marathon on the Discovery Channel.

There seems to be something more between us than I remember there being in college. You know what our crowd was like. Adin and I were always close, but nothing serious ever developed there. And I'm trying to pinpoint why. I was always dating Jason, wasn't I? There was this chemistry between us, or maybe *magnetic pull*? Never a romantic relationship.

There's definitely something more here. I need a second opinion on all this. ...

Right now I'm sitting at the dining room table waiting for him to wake up and have coffee with me on the screened-in porch. I keep thinking about going upstairs to his room and just, I don't know, asking him if he'd like for me to make us breakfast. If I made him breakfast would it look like I wanted to impress him? Seduce him? Or that I wanted to make him think I'm a domestic goddess—which I'm not...? See, there I go second-guessing things. I guess I'm just sorting out what "we" are.

Funny how now we're adults, having our college relationship recalibrated to these new roles. So why do I just want to walk up to his room, lock the door, crawl into his arms and never look back?

Lilly

[✤] [✤] [✤]

December 23rd
Beaufort, South Carolina

Adin

ON OUR THIRD DAY, WE WENT TO SEE Lilly's best friend Jane. This had been our sort of holding pattern since I arrived—accompanying Lilly through her old house, hanging out with her parents, being a temporary part of the B&B staff, going on outings like this one. I felt uncomfortably like a surrogate husband, performing a whole suite of husbandly duties. And no one seemed to be saying anything about it. On paper and on the lips of polite guests and relatives, I was just an old college friend. Good Old Standby Adin. But that very morning Lilly had snuck into my room and claimed she was freezing, that her dad kept the house too cold, that she needed a good snuggle like we'd had in college.

A word about the snuggling, by the way: I was *never* okay with that arrangement to begin with. (Well, no. I was okay with it in ways that I suspected were different from Lilly's, and so I often dreaded it and the things that it might reveal about where we stood with one another.) In a way, it was a good emblem for our whole relationship, both then and now. We were way too close, physically or otherwise, to call ourselves friends. But Lilly was unwilling to call it anything else. In fact, it was worse than that. It didn't seem to occur to her to call it anything else.

We spent the day bouncing Jane's kid Harlow on our knees and catching up. I had known Jane in college but had never *known* her, exactly. Her existence was a combination of photos and anecdotes and my own imagination, with some connective tissue made up of the times she and I actually occupied the same room. But she was nice, polite, well-recovered from the birth. She juggled breastfeeding and preparing lunch for three like a pro. The Jane that I remembered— the one who drank double shots and rode on the backs of motorcycles and mounted a ceaseless campaign to corrupt Lilly—seemed to have retreated, replaced by this docile doppelganger.

"I can't wait to have a good martini again," she confessed, and then I recognized her.

Whatever was going on between me and Lilly, we hadn't brought it up yet. And I was having trouble enjoying myself, because at any moment—back in the car, at her dinner table, in my bed again—we might blink and there it would be again, that Feeling, right there in between us as it had been when Lilly and I met at the airport. What would we do when it came? Because every hour I was more sure that it would. Already I had nearly said something to her a few times. My lips had hovered over her neck when I played big spoon. She could probably feel the hitch in my breathing.

There was one moment, especially, while Jane was discussing the merits of various baby formulas she was researching for the long-awaited respite from sore nipples, when we looked at each other and something aligned itself, like the lenses in a kaleidoscope. We both saw through to each other, and there, with a baby gurgling between us, I felt sure that our suspicions about each other were correct. The mood seemed to transition quietly from tension to inevitability.

Lilly decided to take Harlow for a few laps around the house, like she was training for some infant-toting 5K. I figured I'd get some air; the mild Southern winter was a fleeting privilege I hadn't taken the proper time to relish. So I grabbed my beer and stepped out to the yard, going for a few laps of my own around Jane's enormous woodsy property. Tall, conical cypresses, long-needle pines, and oaks that shivered in the wind. A vast swath of neatly kept grass. Real, honest-to-God pine straw. I listened to the crunch of my steps and felt a rare brand of peace.

After a minute or two, Jane came out to meet me, falling in step with my route. She held some sort of orange juice/tonic water concoction; even with an empty tank again it seemed she was still keeping booze at arm's length.

"So," I said, glancing back through the glass at Lilly's shadowed form, the small form of the baby in her arms, "Jane Thomas. It is still Thomas, right?"

She smirked. "Thomas-Barczak, actually."

"Woof. The hyphenate. Jane *Thomas* would be slightly mortified by this news."

"Yeah, well, that bitch is buried beneath the dance floor of some cheap, scuzzy club now, where she belongs. So I'll name myself what I please." She let out a weary grunt, the distinctive battle cry of the new mother, reaching behind her to rub out the kinks in the small of her back. Then, seemingly out of nowhere, she let out a chuckle. "How about you?" she asked. "Adin Driscoll. Living the dream, huh? After all these years."

I turned to find her giving me a particular sly smile. I recalled that smile from numerous occasions. I was unused to seeing it aimed in my direction rather than Lilly's, and I confess I was a little bit thrown off. "I'm afraid I don't know what you mean."

"Oh no?" She pulled the tie from her hair, started combing her fingers through it. "Well. I'm sure you'll figure it out soon enough."

"If I were to...let's say if I were to interpret that question *very* liberally."

"Yes?"

I looked away from her again, with a dumb kid's bashful grin—the same one I'd been wearing at the airport. "I'd say that it's nice. Puzzling, but nice."

"Puzzling how?"

"Just...," I shrugged. "Look, Jane, you know the backstory to this week better than most people would. But there's still no way I can tell you how it feels. To not know what's going on here—"

"You know." She was nodding, fixing me with this steely, scolding stare. "You're just doing what you've always done and pretending like you don't. You want this to get any farther, you want to make up for all those years of you sitting on your ass, you're gonna have to take the initiative. You're going to have to *make* it happen."

"Are you trying to tell me that I *should* do that? Are you giving me the green light?"

"You know I couldn't do that. I would never betray my best friend's trust that way."

"Are you implying," I asked her with much deliberation, "that there is something there *to* betray?"

After a moment Jane replied, wide-eyed and innocent, "If I told you that, that would be a betrayal, too."

"Hey!" Lilly called to us. She was standing in the open doorway to the house, bouncing Harlow against her chest. Harlow's eyes bugged like he was riding the Tilt-A-Whirl at the state fair. "You guys forget about me or something?"

"That's what you get for stealing my baby!" Jane yelled back, and then said, lower, "Come on."

She had gotten a few yards away from me when I called out, "Wait." She turned, eyebrows raised. The December wind flattened the loose bundle of her hair against her cheek. "Let's say something happened," I told her. "Let's say that what I wanted to happen happened. What do you think Lilly would say about my moving to Denver?"

Jane glanced back over her shoulder, making sure we weren't still being observed, but Lilly had disappeared inside again. Her face was, for the first time, genuinely taken aback. "Adin—"

"Forgetting, for a second, how crazy that would be. What would she think?"

"I...," she opened her mouth, but for a moment couldn't manage to eke anything out. She just shook her head a few times, and the *O* of surprise collapsed into a bewildered laugh. "Well," she said, finally, "I can't tell you what she'd say. But I know what I'd say."

"Which is?"

"If my husband is carrying half the torch for me that you are for Lilly," she said, "then I'm proud as hell to have the hyphenate."

⌖ ⌖ ⌖

December 26th
Beaufort, South Carolina

Lilly

THE NEXT MORNING, I TIPTOED THROUGH THE HOUSE making coffee and filling our thermoses as Adin gathered his camera bag. He'd wanted to get up at dawn to go to the beach and watch the sunrise. Mom and Dad's place was less than a quarter mile from the beach. A five-bedroom Victorian they'd converted into a B&B right after I'd graduated high school. It was the house I grew up in. Barefoot, we walked to the beach. I spread a blanket on the sand, and we lay back and listened to the seagulls. We had the whole place to ourselves. You could almost hear morning spreading over the coast.

He took my hand and we watched the sky shift from darkness into a whisper of light. At one point I sat up and looked at him over my thermos. His eyes seemed to be focused on the shifting clouds. As if sensing an imminent change in the weather, he got up and took a few shots of a far-off tugboat, bobbing in the choppy water. He got closer to the water, adjusted his lens, and then turned the camera on me. I figured he would. For once, I didn't care.

"You smiled!" he called out, peeking at me from behind the lens. "I was not expecting that."

I nodded, raising my thermos to him. "I know. I probably scowled at you enough in college."

He laughed. "To be fair, I was probably kind of annoying about it."

I nodded in agreement and watched him head back my way, the white sand kicking up around his ankles. After all this time, Adin Driscoll was back in Beaufort, South Carolina.

I couldn't get over it.

"I think it was your way of taking everything in. I would love to have those kind of memories."

"You had your journals," he said.

I'd been wondering if he'd miss this once he returned to Ohio—the lazy days together, the long conversations, the tingly feeling that this was something to hang on to. I knew I would. He sat down beside me. I took a sip of coffee and he reached for my hand, setting his camera aside. Looking out over the water, it felt like we were trying to hang on to a tiny, beautiful thing between us. I couldn't even name it, but it was there: this feeling from long ago. Something I recognized the contours of.

He brushed the sand off his ankles. "You know how I take pictures. How do you write those books?" he asked. "You never told me."

I draped my arms over my legs and gave his hand a squeeze, turning a little toward him. "It all starts with an idea. I guess. A very good idea. A promising idea. That's the first thing. Then I start building the story around the idea."

He nodded, his eyes focused on one of the far-off boats. "So is it a linear thing? Do you write it straight through, or is it not like that?"

"Sometimes it's linear, but I go back all the time and change things around. It's not all straight, forward motion. Something will click in the middle that didn't in the beginning. That's exciting," I said.

"What? When things make sense?"

I nodded. "Yeah, and just...being in control of that world. The idea is the easy part. It starts to feel like you're putting together a puzzle. You begin to feel all the pieces come together and finally make sense. But it takes time. A lot of time."

He lay back on the blanket and stared up at me. "You make it sound simple."

I shrugged. "A lot of it's intuition, I guess. You ask yourself if something makes sense. In your gut, you know. And you follow that feeling."

There wasn't another soul on the beach. The wind was starting to kick up. I ran my fingers along his arm and sat the thermos back on the sand. I lay down beside him, and turned toward him, a cool morning rising around us. The waves crashed on the shore, and that sound, that soft backdrop was the sound of my childhood. I sat up and pulled my knees to my chest so that I could watch him watching the pale clouds shift above us. It felt like he was making an effort not to look at me.

There were things I wanted to say that I knew I couldn't. Things that would confuse him. I wanted to tell him that by far the worst thing about leaving Ohio had been leaving him. He would never know the pain; how much I hated myself once I realized the mistake. Back then I hadn't realized that his love, friendship, and understanding were everything to me. It was Adin that I'd missed more than anyone. It was Adin that I dreamed of, that I wanted to call, that I wanted to go on long walks with, that I wanted to listen to music with. And now? I loved this electric joy that ran through my veins when he was near; this shimmering wave of happiness that pulsed through my body. Had I for once figured out what it meant to be certain of something? It was all I could do to maintain the responsible veneer that I presented to the world.

But why was I suddenly ready to give him anything and everything he wanted? I realized that if I had children I would want them to grow up and be just like this man who would follow me to the ends of the earth, who never ran from his feelings, but stared them down. I loved that he saw the world in a way that I wished I could.

We left the beach at 9 a.m. and headed back to the house to get ready for the day. I told him about a used bookstore on the square in downtown Beaufort and he wanted to check it out, so we went.

It was one of those tiny hole-in-the-wall places, stocked floor to ceiling with books and towers of books and overflowing bookshelves. We were the only ones there, except for the owner, Roy, who was watching a Christmas parade that was being broadcast live from New York. His cat, Hazelnut, was there, too.

"Want me to show you the Art and Photography section?" I asked, taking Adin's hand.

"You know me well," he said, following my lead.

I pulled a cord that lit a bare bulb dangling from the ceiling. Art and photography had always been his thing in college, and he'd been talking about getting back into nature photography a lot lately. I picked up a Robert Doisneau book and handed it to him, but he took the book, sat it down, and pulled me to him. There was a split second where we looked at each other, letting a thousand questions and answers pass between us. I took a step closer, allowing his hands to travel down my hips, his lips grazing the tiny wisps of stray hair behind my ear. I circled my hands around him, moving him into a corner, out of view. He swept my hair back and when I looked up at him, he kissed me. I wrapped my arms around his neck and I felt his hands lock around my waist. We stood like that, surrounded by language—new and old—for a long time. The bare bulb overhead crackled like a firework about to fizzle out, but it never did.

❖ ❖ ❖

January 1, 2014
Columbus, Ohio

Adin

WHEN I PUT MY ARMS AROUND LILLY AT the Charleston airport, something snapped, something started pouring out of me. Having her there, within arm's reach, having her close enough to smell her perfume and her shampoo, to feel her brush against me when she turned, it was all too much. By the day after Christmas, I was insane with wanting her. So, against all my reason and fear, I kissed her. It was barely even a choice. My body basically did it for me. And she kissed me back.

Hold on, I have to write that again.

She kissed me back.

Everything that has happened since is all because of her doing that.

She freaked out after it was over. She couldn't stand the thought of us finally being together and then immediately coming back apart. She would rather not let us start anything at all. This of course made *me* freak out, because I felt like I had jumped the gun, like our ship was going to sail that week and I'd never get another chance. I was still crazy for her, still ready to throw aside everything resembling sanity to keep her. So I proposed something utterly ridiculous, something that, for all its childishness, would have seemed impossible to us when we were in college.

"Let's just be a couple for forty-eight hours," I said. "After that, we know I have to go. We won't leave it open-ended, we won't disappoint ourselves with trying to make long distance work. We'll just say that we're a couple for these two days, and then we'll go back to how we were. It's better than going the rest of our lives never knowing what this would have felt like."

She said no, and no again, and still no. We debated it for hours, until finally I gave up and just kissed her, hard, with total abandon, with a love that was ragged at its edges with melancholy. I kissed her in a way that said, if this was going to be my only chance, I was going to take it, in a way that might begin to make up for all the ones I hadn't taken before.

Then she said yes.

It was the best forty-eight hours of my life. We sat leaning against each other on the beach, watching the sun drift across the water, while I played with her hair and she squeezed my hand. We went to Waterfront Park downtown, sat in the swings in the playground there. We lay with our arms around each other in the bedroom she grew up in (our heads now, all these years later, occupying the same end of the bed). I was dizzy with happiness. I caught myself breathing quickly, had to chill myself out again. I got no sleep in those two days, because I spent the nights watching her while she slept and thinking, *This can't be real, this can't be real.* Every minute of that time I spent celebrating, keeping her close to me, fighting off any notion of the time when I would have to leave. But that was a hopeless battle, because no matter how much I didn't want it to come, it came.

I had planned to go see Dad in Savannah for a couple days before I came home, so she drove me to the car rental place the morning of December 28. From the moment I woke up that day, all the giddiness was gone. The whole drive was quiet. We were still happy, I think, still relieved, but something had slipped in and made it murky, like ink in water. I reached over and put my hand on the back of her neck. She sighed. I could tell she was already in the first stages of regret.

Then we were standing in the parking lot. My car was loaded. It was sunny and bright and cold. She was trying not to cry. And I did exactly what I had known I would do the whole time, the second the idea came to me: I started trying to argue for keeping it going. We can talk every day, I said. And I can fly out there to visit. I have all this time and money and no one to spend it on. We can do this. We can make this work.

She stood there in silence, looking down at her shoes, letting me let it all out, knowing how important it was to me to make this speech. And then, for the last time in those two days, she told me no. And this time I knew there was no changing her mind. We were too far away from each other, she said. And there was no way to know when we'd actually be together. Who was going to leave their job and home and everything else behind to be with the other? How long were we going to keep trying to be a couple when we were more than twenty hours apart?

As she asked me these questions something welled up in me. It rumbled in my gut, squirmed up my throat, lay in wait at the back of my mouth. I wanted to tell her that this was a non-issue, that if she asked me to I would walk out the door of my apartment, leave everything to my name behind, and be at her door the hour she got back from South Carolina. But I fought it down, so hard it gave me a stomachache when it was over. I let her end it, there in that parking lot, because I was afraid that if I told her I was ready to drop everything I had after just two days she would wonder what the hell was wrong with me. She would get in her mother's car and roll away into my unreachable past, and I'd be left crying into my complimentary coffee all the way to Georgia.

It shames me to think about this, that I gave up on it at the last second. But here we were, having come together after the better part of a decade with no correspondence, having only spent six days in each other's presence, only two of them *together* in the way I had always dreamed about, and I was ready to suggest something just shy of marriage. There was no way she would react to this positively. There was no way anybody would. So I bit my tongue. We held each other one last time, and she wept a little into my coat when we said our goodbyes. Then she composed herself, turned back into the woman I met at the airport, and we both left.

By the time I got to Dad's place, I had exhausted myself with grief. I told him hi, gave him a hug, and asked if he wouldn't mind if I went to the guest bedroom. I slept for fifteen hours. When I woke up, it was gray and rainy. I looked out the window, shivered, and went back to sleep again.

How do you start moving again from a screeching halt? I wondered. How do you come back to that life—the frozen North, your bare apartment, the canned food, the framed photos under cold glass—and find it as bearable as you left it? How do you go back to talking to letters on a screen when you've felt the warmth of the one they belong to?

Maybe I wasn't going to find a way to keep going after this. Maybe tomorrow morning I'd call work and tell them I was quitting and going on disability. Maybe I'd sell all my things and just lie in the middle of the empty living room, imagining it was still the day after Christmas and I was still the kind of man who could risk everything and put my lips to hers in the middle of all those dusty, sun-bleached books. Or maybe I'd plod on in a world of gray, take photos of people happier than I, drink myself to sleep on the weekends, and try not to think about the day I'd get that call or email that told me she'd met her next boyfriend, the one she'd be with for longer than forty-eight hours. Either/or. I supposed it didn't matter.

to: Lilly Jameson
from: Adin Driscoll
sent: January 4, 10:54 p.m. EST
subject: Back in the real world

Hey,
Man, it's been a weird day. Going back to work was unreal after that trip. There was all this snow everywhere, and nobody offered me any more hot cider. I hope the transition back to reality goes better for you tomorrow! I had a really great time with you and your family. Even if it got kind of crazy there at the end. I'm glad we did what we did, and I hope you are, too. Thanks for the awesome Christmas.

Adin

There's no love in this message. Just fear. I was afraid of belaboring the memory, nagging her with the possibility of reliving it. And in that respect it was sort of like a New Year's resolution, because fear was what drove my words to her for a long, long time after this.

[◈] [◈] [◈]

January 6th
Denver, Colorado

Lilly

to: Adin Driscoll
from: Lilly Jameson
sent: January 6, 8:31 a.m. MST
subject: Hey

Hi Adin:

I keep thinking of our 48 hours. For so long there was all this distance between us. And now we have the chance to change that. We have the chance to find a way to be together. I feel like we fell apart just as I was starting to see what *we* could be. Maybe it's for the best. I mean, I know we have very different lives. We have our own careers. You can't just be away from someone for almost a decade and not build a life for yourself in all that time. I don't mean for this to sound so heavy. Please don't think I'm saying, "Hey! Let's do that long distance thing! I'm in Denver. You're in Columbus! We can do this!" Cause I'm not. I wanted you to know that when I feel myself trying to turn my back on you and move on, I can't. Ever, apparently.

I feel so stupid rehashing Christmas again—I get the sense it's kind of behind you and here I go bringing it back up. But here's what I'm thinking: I leave tomorrow for a four-week book tour. There are ten cities, nine of those places are decided on by the publisher, but the tenth city is a place I can choose. I just chose Columbus. I made the call yesterday. I thought it would be an easy way for us to see each other again (read into that what you want).

The truth is I'm nervous about what we're doing. What *are* we doing? Who says, okay, I'll pretend this is something more than it is for the next forty-eight hours, then step away, no strings attached? There were already a lot of strings there in the first place, Adin. I never in a million years imagined myself being OK with something like that, but I think I *would* do that again. I would do it all again with you.

I just wanted you to know that I don't regret anything, if that's what you're worried about. Your email sounded a little... careful...and you're not as careful as *College* Adin. You've changed. You're not the same person you were.

Maybe I'm just blowing this all way out of proportion. Maybe you've done this with other women. I don't know, but that doesn't seem like you. You're too much like me for that. Taking this kind of emotional risk is new to me. I'm a planner. A long-term sort of girl. I don't date around, really. I suppose I'm a pretty traditional girl at heart. Maybe that's why I feel like I'm exploring new territory here. What I mean to say is: I wouldn't be telling you all this if I thought there was any way I could ignore it.

It meant something to me and I hope I don't sound ridiculous for telling you all this. I know I don't typically pour my "feelings" out like this (try to avoid that at all costs, mostly), but I'm trying to be different, too.

I'm sorry about how we left things. Hope to see you in Columbus on February 1st.

Lilly

❖ ❖ ❖

A few hours later
Columbus, Ohio

Adin

Adin: hey

Tristan: whats up

Adin: so you know that girl i didn't want to bone?

Tristan: u bone her?

Adin: well, no. although i will concede i want to now.

Tristan: great. our long national nightmare is over.

Adin: right. but here's the problem

Tristan: no hold on, i can do this part for you

Tristan: "i'm like so Goddam in love with her, and i want to bone her, but you know, in a nice loving way, forever and ever"

Adin: truly, sir, you are a poet

Tristan: yeah it's a gift

Adin: but she's some crazy number of hours away now, and she was very serious about not doing long distance

Tristan: oh noes!

Adin: so i'm not sure what to do

Tristan: not holiday sex! heaven forbid!

Adin: can we skip to the part where you stop being stupid and care about this?

Tristan: ugh, fine

Tristan: look, if you saw her for the first time in nine years and had her tongue in your mouth inside a week, there's still something there. just man the hell up and go to her. that's what people do when they're in love.

Adin: i think that was actually good advice

Tristan: i have my moments

Adin: so i see. there's still the manning up part though

Tristan: that has always been your weak point, it's true

It was true.

⟨•⟩ ⟨•⟩ ⟨•⟩

January 7th–13th
Denver, Colorado

Lilly

from: Lilly Jameson
to: Brenda Jameson
sent: January 7, 7:34 p.m. MST
subject: Re: How things going? *attachment*

Mom:

Tim just told me he will be at one of my tour dates. Did you give him my tour schedule??

Next week is our last meeting with the attorney. Tim's practice is doing really well, and so he seems upbeat despite everything. Things have really taken off since he moved everything to Fort Collins. I was up there for a couple of days when I got back to Colorado. I wish you could see his office—he bought this red brick building downtown and hired a decorator and the place looks incredible. (I attached three pictures, but the pictures don't really do it justice).

Adin is doing well. He's in Columbus (a photographer). He told me he had a great time when he was down for the holidays. I think Adin and his dad usually just hang out in Savannah, so he liked the festivities at the B&B in Beaufort.

One of these days you should visit me out here.
Talk to you soon.

Lilly

I kept thinking about Adin and going over everything that happened over Christmas. What was it about him that kept asking to be *thought through*? I'd forgotten how much sense we made in each other's presence, and the fact that this feeling could exist between two people wouldn't leave me alone. I'd forgotten what it felt like to be so fully understood by another human being. To have that in my life again was a revelation, so I was hesitant to forget about us. I'd learned a little bit about what you could and couldn't expect to find again in life.

Adin's presence, his affection, his attention, and his desire were disorienting to me.

Then I got this email.

from: Adin Driscoll
to: Lilly Jameson
sent: January 9, 6:01 p.m. EST
subject: (no subject)

Hey,
I don't really know what to say. I didn't want to talk about Christmas so much in my last email because I wasn't sure how you would take it. But now you're talking about it, kind of intensely, in fact, and about coming to Columbus and seeing me, and I don't know how to react to all that. That couple of days meant a lot to me, too, but I'm afraid of seeing you and having to say that horrible goodbye again. And I'm afraid that I'm going to campaign for long distance again and you're going to get angry with me. God, this would be easier if I could just move to Denver, or you could move here.

I don't know. Maybe you shouldn't come. Is it bad that I'm saying that? I want you to, obviously, I would love for you to come. I would redo Christmas, in a heartbeat, absolutely. It's just that for all these years I have wanted you, and the fact that it was so incredible to finally have you just made it worse to lose you again. I don't know if I can handle that twice, at least not that close together. Those couple of days I spent with Dad were pretty rough. I'm scared of going through that more than once.

If any of your other cities are near here, I'll totally come and see you. Seriously, though, please don't think I didn't want you to come. I did, I do. I just can't hear another *no* this soon.

Adin

He was *scared* to go through this more than once? Did he not think I was uncertain, too, but willing to take a risk? I was floored by his cowardice. *Be a man!* I wanted to write back. Fuming, I canceled my reading in Columbus. There was no way I could face Adin. Not after that email. I felt humiliated for going out on a limb and for being as honest as I'd been with him. I felt politely rejected, and it stung. When a girl named Maggie from Public Relations suggested I read in Toledo instead, I said, "Sure, why not?"

from: Lilly Jameson
to: Adin Driscoll
sent: January 13, 6:40 a.m. MST
subject: Sorry I made things weird

Adin:
Sorry about my last email. I could feel myself going out on a limb when I wrote it. I should have kept it all to myself. I probably shouldn't have said half of that. Let's put it behind us. Deal?

I canceled my reading in Columbus. I'll be in Toledo, instead. One of my books is being used in their school district this year, so it should be a good crowd. I wonder what you'd think if you attended one of my readings. Talking to the kids and parents after the reading is the best part, I think, though half the time I just feel jealous of them for having what I don't—you know, the whole American dream thing. I try to be content with my career and the path I've chosen, but sometimes when I watch a mom and dad lead their daughter out of the bookstore I feel myself staring at them a little too long. I gather my messenger bag and my wool coat, shake the store manager's hand one last time, and leave.

I wonder if you ever feel like that—satisfied in some ways, but strangely empty in other ways. I just realized I have no idea what your goals are, or what you want out of life. I hope it's not weird for me to ask this, but I'd simply be curious to know—what is it you really want? Where do you want to be in five years?

I recall you once told me during college that you wanted to do something with photography. I guess I'm almost exactly who I was at eighteen. I always wanted to write—I never would have guessed I'd be writing children's books, but hey, it counts, right?

Lilly

⟡ ⟡ ⟡

March 28, 2003
Ohio University, Athens, Ohio

Lilly

"I FEEL LIKE IT SHOWS TOO MUCH SKIN. Like I'll need a sweater to go over it," I said, reaching for a turquoise cardigan I kept in my closet.

Jane shook her head gravely, from the bunk bed to my left. "No, no, *no*. We talked about this! There will be no cardigans. That ruins the look."

"It's just March. It's kind of cold out," I said, rubbing the white, slinky fabric between my fingers.

"But it's a halter dress!" She stood up and marched over to where I stood in front of the mirror, snatching the sweater away from me. "Nope. Sorry. This is the spring formal. You look hot in that. Really, *really* hot," she said, her eyes landing on the bouquet of red roses Jason had sent me for my birthday just days earlier.

I looked at myself in the mirror one more time. "Do I even have the cleavage to, like, justify this dress?" I turned, critiquing my silhouette in the mirror.

She crossed her arms. "Hell yes. And now people will know. *Jason* will know," she said with a wink.

I rolled my eyes. "Okay, okay. I'll wear the dress. I paid good money for it, after all." Which was a lie. She and I had bought it at a consignment shop in Athens last week. I'd paid $5 for it.

Satisfied, she gathered up her things. I knew she wanted to start getting ready herself. She had a whole ritual planned: shower, shaving, hair-curling, spray tan, pedicure, teeth whitening. It was a little more work than I was willing to put in to achieve a good look, but Jane went for polish and I admired that. I was too lazy to invest all that time and energy into a formal. I wasn't sure that Jason would notice if I did. He never really commented much on my appearance. I just tried to shoot for a messy yet pretty sort of look. Anyway, I didn't like all the fuss.

"I'm heading out. Lilly, your phone is buzzing. Want me to get it?"

"Yep," I said, wrangling a bobby pin between my fingers.

"Oh, let's see if I can predict who it is."

"It'll be Adin. He mentioned he may come over."

"Yep. It's a text. Adin."

I sprayed a bit of perfume on my neck and clipped in a bobby pin. The clock read 4:30 p.m. Jason was supposed to get here at 5 p.m. I knew it wasn't the smartest idea to let Adin be around when Jason got there, but Adin was practically my best friend and I was pretty sure Jason was starting to understand that Adin and I hung out. A lot. Besides, Jason and I were going to an Italian restaurant in downtown Athens with some of his Sigma Chi friends and we would be together all night. If he wanted to sulk and get jealous, he could, but Adin wasn't going anywhere. I'd made that clear. It had, in fact, been the source of two of our more epic fights.

I went to my computer and clicked on a playlist Adin had made me several months ago. He always sent me good music. It was something I loved about him.

"Is Adin coming over?" I asked.

She nodded and tossed my phone on my bed. "He is. And he may go into shock, seeing you in that dress," she said, hands on her hips, assessing things.

I looked at her in the mirror. "Is it weird that I actually had a dream about him the other night? Did I tell you that?" I asked, lowering my voice.

"You had a *dream* about Adin?"

I looked right at her and slowly nodded, mouthing the word *yes*.

She threw her makeup bag onto the bed with such force the mattress shook. "Oh my God. What happened? Tell me all the details."

I knew this side of her—she would want to know everything. She was a voracious consumer of rumors and campus gossip. And she could be relentless.

I fiddled with something on my dresser. "Um, I can't really remember..." I felt my face getting hot. Why did I even tell her anything in the first place?

"Bullshit, Lilly!"

I shot her a look and cleared my throat. "All I know is I woke up and felt...like I'd cheated on Jason or something. I felt weird about it all day. I could barely look at Adin in the cafeteria. I was sitting between him and Jason and—"

"Oh my God. You didn't tell Adin?"

"Hell no! And you better not tell a soul, either. The last thing I need is for Jason to hear that I'm dreaming of other men. He would lose his mind."

"*Okay*. But how did you feel when you woke up? Like, was it a *sexy* dream? Do you think?"

I ignored the question, mentally picking apart what I would and would not tell her.

"Lilly, you have to tell me. I tell you *all* my embarrassing shit!" she said, hitting the mattress.

"Then, *yeah*," I ventured. "It was...kind of sexy." I turned to slowly face her, propping myself against my closet door. "It was actually... *great*. The sort of thing you don't want to wake up from." She burst out laughing, cackling almost, and I had to laugh, too. "Which is why I feel so shitty about it, Jane! Because it was extremely vivid and realistic..."

"And *great*, apparently!" she laughed.

"I've been thinking about it all week," I said, lowering my voice. I took a deep breath. It felt good to tell someone.

After a lot of going back and forth and dabbing our eyes from tears of laughter, she shook her head in disbelief and walked over, taking both my bare shoulders in her hands. "But seriously, are you telling me I can't tell Adin you had a sexy dream about him?"

"No. You really, *really* can't, Jane," I said, stretching out each word, so that I was being crystal clear.

"Lilly!"

"I am being dead serious!"

"Why not? He would *love* to know that."

I looked down, trying to think of how to explain it all to her, feeling a rush of adrenaline course through me. "Because, Jane...if he knew something like that, then we probably couldn't be friends anymore. He would see me differently, and I couldn't take it back. And, next to you, he is my *best friend*. The minute that information enters the picture, things change. *He and I* change. So you *have* to promise me—"

She groaned, cutting me off. "Oh my *God*, Lilly. You've spent far too much time working all this out."

I nodded once and looked away. I couldn't argue with that.

"Wait—was this the first time? Have you had *other* dreams about Adin?"

"What? Have I had other dreams about him? Adin, you mean?"

But she just stared me down. She wasn't buying it. I felt a knot tighten in my stomach.

"Lilly *Jameson*!"

I slowly nodded, fighting back a smile. "Promise me you won't say anything to anyone."

She doubled over as if I'd just punched her in the stomach. "*Fuuuuuck*."

"Jane! Promise me—"

"Okay. *Shit*, Lilly. I promise." But her voice had changed, had taken on a tone of seriousness. "But did you ever think it might *mean* something?" she asked, her voice steady and inquiring.

I slumped against the bedpost. "Yeah, I have. I mean...I don't know."

She nodded solemnly and looked at my alarm clock. "Wow. Okay. I've really got to get ready." She folded her arms and gave me one last long look. "Marvelous. I'm so glad you took my advice on that dress. I love how it ties around your neck. It's so sexy."

I still felt self-conscious and a little unsure about the whole thing. "Yeah...," I said, feeling for where the dress tied at the nape of my neck, making sure it was tied tight. "I feel like—"

"A million bucks!" she said, plucking one of my roses out of the vase to take with her and then heading for the door. "Like Marilyn Monroe."

I called out after her to give the rose back and, when she didn't, I went after her. I had just rounded the doorway when Adin appeared in the hall, camera in hand. Jane came to an abrupt halt and I grabbed the rose away from her, tripping a bit in my heels when Adin's eyes met mine. Seeing my surprise, she buckled with laughter. I knew what she was thinking. I looked away from him, bracing myself for what might be coming.

"Okay, Lilly! Learn to walk in those," she turned to Adin. "Adin! Make sure she can walk. There will be no flip-flops or sneakers or Doc Martens. Those heels are hot."

"Yes, they are," Adin said.

I blushed, glancing at the rose dangling in my right hand. I gave her a quick hug and promised I'd text her later. She shot me a knowing glance, looking from me to Adin, and for a second I thought she was going to confess everything I had just told her. But, after an excruciating few seconds of suspense, Jane spun around and disappeared down the hall.

Once she was gone, I pointed the rose right at Adin. "No photographs!" But as I said it, he snapped one anyway.

He smiled helplessly. "You looked very *Mask of Zorro* there for a second."

Seeing the camera, I sighed. "Been working on Humanities today, I guess?"

"Yep."

"I've been meaning to ask how your portfolio is going," I said, leading him to my room.

"It's going."

"I need to work on mine."

I went to open the door, aware of Adin right behind me, his breath on my neck, where my dress was tied in a small bow on my bare skin. He felt really close, but maybe I was still just getting used to the dress and how I looked and felt in it. Maybe I was imagining him that close.

We walked in and Adin collapsed in my desk chair as he always did, glancing at the screens, tabs, and websites displayed on my laptop.

"I see you've been listening to the mix I made you," he said, swiveling to look at me in the mirror. I could hear the note of approval in his voice.

I met his gaze and continued getting ready, as he said, "A *perfect* mix, I might add." I watched him for a moment, as he read and scrolled through the playlist. I put in my sparkly chandelier earrings. I reached for a hair tie, turning to see Adin studying me.

"I think maybe I should confiscate the camera," I muttered.

"I promise, *no more* photographs," he said.

I smiled and stared him down in the mirror. I wished he was going to the formal, but I knew he wasn't. This was for guys rushing Sigma Chi. Every guy was supposed to bring a date, and Jane and I had been asked.

"I feel too exposed in the dress. I didn't want any pictures to exist of me in *this* dress."

"Are you mad at me for taking your picture?"

"I just wish you hadn't taken a picture of me like this."

He didn't say anything for a minute. "Well, I didn't mean to make you mad."

"Oh, I'm not mad," I said, flipping my head over and putting my hair high up in a ponytail, realizing as I raised up that I probably should have been more careful to cover myself when I bent over. I was not used to being mindful of my cleavage, and this was a dress that required it. I prayed Adin hadn't been looking too closely. I turned my back to him and busied myself getting my hair in place, turning to him a minute later, once I was sure that my cheeks were no longer burning.

"What do you think of the dress? What do you think of the *effect* of the dress?" I asked, twirling a little so the soft white ends fluttered up, just like I'd seen in the movie. When I looked up, he was headed for the window.

"What are you doing?" I asked.

"It's kind of warm in here. I was going to crack the window."

"You're *warm*?"

He nodded, opening the window a bit. "*And* I don't think I'll need any pictures," he said, so softly I could barely hear him.

I blushed, wondering what he was referring to. Likely, he'd seen something, but I was not about to bring it up. "I wish I took more pictures. I never think to do that," I said, turning the volume up on an acoustic song I knew we both liked.

"Yeah, but you write things down."

I nodded. "But you have the images. You have all these photographs of everything exactly as it is. You can piece them all together and have everything right there in front of you, so you never forget it."

He stood there facing me for a moment, considering this. "Some things you just remember," he said, turning from me to face the cool air streaming in from the window that overlooked campus. "Some things you never forget."

❖ ❖ ❖

January 13, 2014
Denver, Colorado

Lilly

Lilly: jane!

Jane: hey! Still liking denver?

Lilly: yeah, pretty well. Just sent an email to Adin. Wasn't a happy one.

Jane: thought you really liked him?? I know he liked you...

Lilly: I did. I do. I mean... I don't think he's ready for a relationship. Seems very much on the fence about me. I get the feeling some girl broke his heart or something or he's seeing someone in Columbus, maybe.

Jane: Huh. I didn't pick up on that, but you always knew him better. He seemed...in love...big time.

Lilly: I don't know. he sent this email after I told him I'd be in Columbus and totally freaked out. He was *scared* to see me again. I read it a few times to just make sure I wasn't misinterpreting things—I had tried to be more honest w/ him about how i felt and he didn't take it well. Basically, he told me not to come. He doesn't want to see me.

Jane: I don't know. when you two were here I talked to him about you—he asked my opinion on what you'd say to his moving to denver. he was thinking about moving out there for you. he seemed serious…

Lilly: he asked you what I'd think if he moved to Denver?? Like, got a place in Denver?

Jane: he wanted my opinion on how you'd react if he moved to Denver. It was a serious question. I think he's struggling with what he should do. This is Adin, Lilly. I don't think he ever stopped loving you.

Lilly: But why wouldn't he want to see me in Columbus? I was trying to meet him halfway.

Jane: He wants to protect whatever you two have, I guess. Probably just scared of making a move—scared the wrong step may mean another decade without you. I don't know. But you know how timid he always was in college.

Lilly: you think he loved me in college?

Jane: Well, yeah… Jason, Tristan…all of us just kind of knew. You remember those parties we went to and how he'd go, but only to kind of hang out…Tristan used to joke that Adin only went to parties he knew you'd be at. Jason couldn't stand him. Adin was in our dorm all the time…the cds he made you, the way he always sat by you in the cafeteria…

Lilly: I just keep feeling like I messed up somewhere, like I said too much too soon, broke a rule somewhere, I was actually trying not to be so guarded. You've always told me to be more expressive, and to say what I'm thinking. I was trying to do that.

Jane: Adin just needs to get his shit together a little bit. Is Tim doing ok?

Lilly: yeah, he's good. He may be seeing someone new,

actually. I think he's going to be at a reading of mine in the next month. he sent me an email out of the blue saying he'd "try to catch one." apparently mom just told him where all I'd be. I swear, someone could call and ask her for my cell phone number and home address and she'd say "hang on, lemme get that for you."

Jane: Tim's going to a reading of yours? That is *nice* of him.

Lilly: tell me the truth, though, is it crazy that I already feel so much for adin? The email he sent just... crushed me, and I'm kind of embarrassed about it. I mean, it really, really stung. Am I in the crazy-in-love phase that inevitably disappears?

Jane: oh my God. are you in love with ADIN DRISCOLL?

Lilly: I will neither confirm nor deny. ...

Jane: But i mean, it doesn't have to go away. You're just being cynical. There comes a point where you have to take a risk— which it sounds like adin isn't doing. You're just being overly cynical because of everything that happened w/ tim. I'll be honest. I never in all those years saw tim look at you the way adin looks at you.

Lilly: i know...I feel that when you're young you're always waiting for something bigger, better, more awe-inspiring (stupidly assuming there's something better) and over time 1 person can come to be the standard everyone else is measured against.

Jane: What? Has Adin been the guy you measure other people against the whole time?

Lilly: Yes. It occurred to me when I was writing that email to him.

Jane: Shit. I never knew that. I think he's scared to face he could actually get what he wants.

Lilly: yeah...Im losing sympathy there

Jane: but I think you're scared of maybe getting what you want too.

⟦❖⟧ ⟦❖⟧ ⟦❖⟧

January 15th
Columbus, Ohio

Adin

from: Adin Driscoll
to: Lilly Jameson
sent: January 15, 9:47 p.m. EST
subject: On being alone

Believe me, I know how you feel. Think about what I do. I take pictures of happy people for a living. Mothers and their tiny daughters with big shiny braces, smirking high school football players, little bundles of gorgeous sorority girls in shiny dresses and sky-high heels. They all walk out of the studio with these big shit-eating grins on their faces, and I just sigh and get another bottle of evian and look over their shots, perfect little permanent reminders of just how appallingly content they all were together.

What do I want? Actually, I can tell you in more detail than is appropriate in an email, but I'll try to keep it brief. First and foremost, what I want is to be a nature photographer. I want to stop spending fifteen or twenty minutes getting babies to smile, children to keep still, and senior boys to stop snapping the bras of senior girls. I want to shoot something enormous and tranquil and bursting with subtlety. I want to be one of those guys who camps out in the African grasslands for forty-three hours so he can get that perfect golden-hour angle of sunlight, that perfect windswept wave across the sea of blades. I want to publish photos that will make people erupt in little tiny gasps and say, "God, I never knew it was *that* pretty there."

Here's the problem, though—I lied, just now. That's not the first thing I want. If *Aperture* wanted to do a piece on me and they asked me what my greatest passion was, of course I'd tell them the same lie. But the truth is there is something else in the world I want even more than that. If I sit down and work very hard to clear away the careful traps of self-deception I set for myself every morning when I wake up, what I *really* want the most is this:

To wake up at 7:30 on a Sunday morning and find the woman I love lying in our cozy full-sized bed with a big white down comforter and big fluffy white pillows. To hear, from somewhere down the hall, our two daughters already playing together in their room. To trace the peaceful lines of my wife's face and rest my fingers on her messy bed-hair. To have her wake up as I'm getting out of the bed and insist that I stay for ten more minutes. To jump back in, maybe put one of my icy feet on her, so she slugs me one in the shoulder, and then scoop her into my arms and tell her that, after three minutes, this is already the greatest day of my life.

I'm sorry about your canceling Columbus, even if you insist that I shouldn't be. I did desperately want to see you again. Maybe you think I'm a spineless twit for letting my fear of separation keep us apart, but I can't help thinking you might feel differently if you had ever spent ten years hauling around the burden of secret feelings for somebody. I mean, for more than a third of my total life you were squarely confined to my wildest dreams. And then, suddenly, for two days, you stepped out of my dreams into my life, only to leap back out again. I can't tell you what that's like, and believe me, I tried. I've been writing this paragraph over and over again for an hour. I can tell you that it causes massive upheavals in the way I think about things. This isn't an excuse, just an explanation. I would never take back that kiss in the bookstore. But I need time to ready myself for having you snatched away from me again. I'm sorry for whatever that's done to you, if anything. It's just how I'm built these days.

Adin

꘏　꘏　꘏

February 10th
Toledo, Ohio

Lilly

from: Lilly Jameson
to: Adin Driscoll
sent: February 10, 7:32 a.m. EST
subject: Re: On being alone

Adin:

I know you getting to the Toledo reading last night must have taken some planning and I'm sorry we didn't get to speak much. I'm even sorrier for the way I acted. Was it weird for me to introduce you to Tim afterwards? I didn't know he'd be at that reading, actually. I feel like I should apologize to you—I wasn't very nice. I was a little rattled. Tim told me he would be at one of my readings, but I didn't know which. I hope I at least remembered to introduce you to my agent Nate. He was the one sitting in the front row when I was being introduced and the one kind of managing the whole thing. The guy in a bow tie.

I guess what I wanted to ask you was why did you decide to come? I mean, I'd wanted to go to Columbus, *where you live*. I changed my schedule to Toledo because I thought that was what you wanted. And then Nate and I get there and I see you in the corner with Tim.

My feelings got a little hurt after reading your last email, honestly. When I read it, I felt like Julia Roberts in *Notting Hill*, when she goes back to Hugh Grant's bookstore and he's being a wimp about being with her and she gives her speech about just being a girl in front of a guy pleading for his love, but it's not enough and so she walks away from him, stunned, because Hugh Grant feared his rookie heart wouldn't heal if she were to reject him.

Of course, I didn't get to say any of this to you in person—wrong time, wrong place. Nate had booked us reservations downtown—a celebration dinner. Anyway, I acted like a broken-hearted teenager hell-bent on making you pay for simply watching out for yourself. You said I was "confined to your wildest dreams" and if that's what you want—a fantasy, then I'll accept that. I know you have a life in Columbus. I have a life in Denver. Maybe you could visit someday? It just seems like we shouldn't be putting distance between us. Maybe I've not told you this enough, but I really missed having you in my life, too. So was it was dumb of me to think that the bond we had in college could be something more? There will always be a part of me scrutinizing every word and look that passes between us (I think you know this about me).

Lilly

It had been weeks since we'd spoken. He tells me he can't deal with seeing me again, but he *shows up* to see me. The fact of the matter was this: I was spending far too much time thinking about him—about what his emails meant, about what he was keeping from me, about what he was afraid of. I went to get a cup of tea and sat back down to reread my email one more time before sending it. Even I was surprised by how candid and frank I was being with him. I knew the terrain of my heart was uneven. I knew he was trying to protect himself. I knew I was letting all my messy feelings out of the bag. That's when it hit me: I had fallen in love with Adin Driscoll.

⊡ ⊡ ⊡

Several hours later
Columbus, Ohio

Adin

I KNEW THAT THIS WAS LILLY'S WAY OF giving me one final chance. I knew it as sure as I knew that my last email, the one about waking up in the white bed, had been my rather clumsy attempt to say I was willing to give up everything for her. All the *Notting Hill* stuff, on down to that last question ("Was it dumb of me to think" etc. etc.), she was dripping with anger and resentment and, loud and clear above everything else, longing. I knew it from the first of the many times I read it, and I knew that something had to be done, or I'd lose her.

But, when you spend so much of your life loving someone who doesn't love you back (not to mention any number of minor someones who don't even seem to try), when you spend all those long nights spoon-feeding yourself reasons why she isn't worth your agony, why it would never work, why she'll never want you, and why you should find something else to pour all your desire into (photography, for instance), it becomes difficult to take that same little voice seriously when it's trying to tell you that, somehow, after all those years, she *does* love you, she *does* want you, and, in fact, she wants no one *but* you.

This was the uncertainty I was dealing with. I wanted to write back to her with feverish ecstasy bursting from my every word. I wanted her vision to swim with kittens and daffodils when she read my sweet, swooning reply, my weeping acquiescence. But then what? Could I really quit my job and move out there to the snow-smothered West to play house with my old college flame? Wouldn't there come a day when she woke up and realized she'd only been caught up in a whirlwind fiction? Platonic innocence had been our natural state;

wasn't it inevitable that we return to it? And where would I be left then? Stranded in the Rockies with the love of my life, whom I couldn't touch with anything more than a handshake.

I couldn't do this on my own. I decided to take a poll.

Adin: hey

Tristan: hey player

Tristan: how's the love life treating you?

Adin: that's exactly what i need to talk to you about

Tristan: shocking! film at eleven!

Adin: yeah, hold on, i'm sending you something

Adin: okay, i sent it

Tristan: lol

Tristan: christ, i would never have thought that you two had it equally bad if you hadn't sent me that

Tristan: that is hilarious. you two are perfect

Adin: really? that's what you get from that?

Tristan: come on, man. how many reasons you think a woman has to ask you to fly across six states to visit her?

Tristan: people talk about how chicks are all intense with their feelings, but that's total bullshit. chicks are just like everybody else. they're not going to show all the cards. they don't want you seeing the dirty laundry on their bedroom floor unless they're inviting you to sleep in their bed

Adin: you're getting awfully wise about this

Tristan: we've been talking about this same crap for weeks. we've already pretty much had this exact conversation. i should be getting credit hours for this.

Tristan: i want to see you be happy, because you're my friend, but i also want you to get this all over with so i can go back to calling you funny names without feeling bad about it

Adin: fair enough

Adin: so then what's your verdict?

Tristan: you know what? she's testing you.

Tristan: she literally asked you… hold on

Tristan: "so was it dumb of me to think that the bond we had in college could be something more?"

Adin: yeah, yeah, I know

Tristan: well, then i don't know why you're even talking to me. i know you, i know how long you've been hardcore pining for her, and how stupidly stupid you are about anything with the word love attached to it. you already know what you're supposed to do, you're just trying to get me to tell you something that will make you less scared of it

Adin: ouch

Tristan: yeah, well, i tell it like it is, man

So. One vote for "Do it."

from: Adin Driscoll
to: Arthur Driscoll
sent: February 10, 10:38 p.m. EST
subject: Advice about Lilly

Hey Dad,

I need your advice on something. I don't think I can decide what to do without your help. Lilly sent me this email, and it's kind of been freaking me out. She seems pissed that I said I couldn't see her in Columbus, and now she's talking like we're never going to work out *ever* and she was stupid to think we would and on and on. I was thinking that maybe we'd figure out how to do this somewhere down the road, but I don't think we have that kind of time now. She seems pretty serious.

But then again, I don't know if she is that serious. That's the rub. I'm afraid that being in love has a shelf life. That I'll get there and she'll realize that it wasn't as big a deal as she thought. Or maybe she won't trust me now that I've put her through so much. There's at least two hundred different ways this could go wrong, and only one way it could go right. And I've never been very brave with odds like that.

I know you are not well-versed on Lilly and me, but I have to ask this anyway, because you're the person I trust the most: what should I do?

Adin

One thing about my dad: he is not a long-winded guy. Not because he's emotionally pent up, like we imagine most people's dads. He doesn't shy away from talking about feelings. In fact, he's probably better at it than most dads, precisely because he hates beating around the bush. He just likes to get it *done*. He says what he means, what he thinks you need to hear, regardless of how hard you might take it, and then moves on to his next task.

He called me that night, about half an hour after I sent that email. Our whole conversation took about five minutes.

"Adin, what is your worst-case scenario here?" he asked me. "What is the thing you're most afraid will happen? What is the most horrible way you can imagine this going?"

"Well," I said, swiveling in my desk chair, "I guess the *worst* thing would be that I get there, I'm there for a week, everything is great, and then she wakes up and tells me it's not going to work."

"Let me see if I've got you right," Dad said, without a second's hesitation. "You're afraid of one week of this great love with the woman you've always wanted most?"

"Well, not the week itself, just everything after it."

He was quiet for a long time. I heard a few ambient noises as he performed some domestic task in the kitchen and then a groan as he settled into his chair. I could picture Dad, with his salt-and-pepper beard, in one of those hard-backed maple numbers at the kitchen table, with that one dim light over his checkered tile floor. "Son," he said, a form of address reserved only for his most earnest speeches, "If Jesus Christ himself came down and told me I could spend one more week with your mother, what do you think I would say?"

My reply was so sheepish that he probably didn't even hear me, but he still must have known what I said. "You'd tell him yes."

"All right," he rumbled, with the same stern finality he had used with me when I was a little kid drawing tigers on the wall with yellow crayon, "then you've already got my advice."

Two votes.

AFTER I HUNG UP, I SAT IN MY cold bedroom, thinking, and I went on thinking for the rest of the night, right through half the morning. I knew I was going to call in sick at work the next day. But I didn't care. This deserved my time.

⊠ ⊠ ⊠

February 11th
Toledo, Ohio

Adin

I HAD GONE TO THE TOLEDO READING BECAUSE I couldn't stay away. I intensely regretted causing Lilly to cancel her Columbus reading, and that scared the hell out of me—knowing not only that I had kept this woman away from me but also that I had lied to both of us to do it. I would have been perfectly willing to endure another goodbye if it meant another day or two with her. But if that was the only day or two ever again? Because of something I said?

I got to the bookstore early, hoping to have a chance to talk to Lilly beforehand. But all I found was a room full of children and their weary parents. In the back row, I spotted the only other child-free adult, a nicely suited guy fiddling with his BlackBerry. I sat next to him—not for conversation but for something like security, safety in numbers. I was entirely too nervous to talk to anybody.

He glanced up at me and then did a double take. "Oh my God," he said, with a disbelieving chuckle. "You're Adin."

If you've never had a complete stranger come to a similar realization right in front of you, then I'm at a loss to describe it to you.

He gave me his hand and, somewhere through the murk, I shot an impulse to take it. "I'm Tim," he said. When I showed no signs of recognition, he added, "Tim Beals. Ex-husband Tim."

I got hot-cold. I suddenly recalled seeing him hovering in the background of pictures that I'd seen of Lilly on Facebook. I had seen him, registered him on some level, but it never occurred to me that he was *the* guy. "Wow, God, I'm sorry," I fumbled. "Yeah, Tim. Nice to meet you finally."

He replied with a kind of smirk, not unfriendly. "Not quite as nice on my end, to be honest. But yeah, it's a pleasure. Lilly's told me an awful lot about you in the last couple weeks."

And so began the most awkward conversation of my life, which, shockingly, was also one of the most enjoyable. Against all my expectations (and my hopes), Tim was a good guy. He was polite, affable, gracious. He seemed to concede defeat in a manner devoid of all embarrassment, as if it couldn't so much as chip at his sense of himself as a man to be envied and admired. And I liked that about him, that he wasn't jealous, or insecure, or hostile. There was no reason to be anything but warm and chatty. He gave me his business card, and I laughed at him when he asked for mine.

It was Tim, later that night, who had to tell me how worked up Lilly had seemed. I didn't see it, and I didn't buy it. I thought he was trying to be encouraging; I assumed he had been notified of my ambivalence and was trying to give me a gentle shove for her benefit. But then Lilly herself confessed to being thrown off by my presence and to feeling guilty for her cold shoulder, which did hurt me.

I think it wasn't until that confession, and especially until I talked to Dad, that I realized the stakes. I had assumed that Lilly, with her gorgeous smile and her blossoming success and her total lack of discomfort with the rest of the world, would move right along from my cowardly ass. But as I thought back on Lilly at the Toledo reading—the way she took long pauses for swigs from her water bottle, the way she had to take a few breaths before she answered questions, the way she was just a little bit halting with all the children, the way she had been a little *too* eager to give my book a hasty couple of ink loops and then send me on my way with a "Thanks for coming" and nothing else—it suddenly came to me. More than a month had passed, and Lilly was still rattled by whatever it was that persisted between us. And I hadn't even been there at all during this whole time.

⊠ ⊠ ⊠

That evening and the next morning
Toledo, Ohio

Lilly

LATER THAT EVENING, I WENT OUT WITH NATE to a café bistro near the University of Toledo campus. I'd made only one request: the place we go must serve alcohol.

We were seated right away, and Nate got out his iPhone. I ordered us two glasses of wine and took a deep breath, thinking about how the reading had gone.

Nate looked up at me. "So, that was *extremely* interesting. You okay?"

I crossed my legs and reached for my glass of water. "I already know what you're going to say."

"Well, then I'll skip the predictable part." Nate smiled and put his phone on the table. "The *un*predictable part starts with me saying I've never seen someone drink so much water. In the span of two hours I think you consumed about two liters, possibly *three*." He picked his phone back up. "I bet it'll be on YouTube tomorrow. I'm betting your face will be hidden completely."

I buried my head in my hands. "Oh, this is bad."

"You had a glass hovering around this general area the whole time," he said waving his hands around his face, smiling. "It was like you were embarrassed to be seen or something."

"I wasn't *embarrassed*."

"Okay. Maybe you were nervous. But why would you be nervous? You do readings all the time."

I looked away, shaking my head. I knew I had been a little awkward, but I was starting to realize how poorly the night had gone.

"I was a little off. I know that."

"You still sound nervous, or rattled, or *something*?" he said leaning in.

I nodded, not even sure where to begin. "I am, yeah. A little bit."

He paused, likely trying to connect the dots of what I wasn't saying to what I was thinking. "It must have been Tim *and* Adin. Who would have suspected they'd show up to the same one? It was a book reading for children. Not *Love Connection*."

I sat my glass of water down.

He continued, "Why would they come to a reading aimed at children? In *Toledo*? In *February*? Wait, wait, I know, they are *both* in love with you. You wouldn't tell me who initiated the divorce, but it must have been you."

I shook my head, wishing the alcohol would hurry up and arrive. "We are *definitely* not talking about that—"

"Fair enough. But I saw Adin getting you to sign a book, and the look you gave him...was not one of love," he said, relaxing in his seat.

I fidgeted with my napkin, sensing I'd made a bad impression—and wondering just how bad—when the waiter came and sat the two long-stemmed glasses of Malbec on the table.

I smoothed the napkin. "Tim has moved on. I'm pretty sure of that. He probably came to be supportive, I guess. And, as for Adin, well...that's one I've not totally figured out."

"What do you mean?"

"I don't know how to explain it..."

"Well, you're a storyteller, so *try*," he said, straightening his bow tie and scooting into the table.

I wadded the napkin up and ran my finger along the base of the wine glass. "Okay. For example, I have this memory of me and Adin from college. We're leaving a party and it's maybe 2 a.m. and I'm rummaging in my bag for a hair tie to put my hair up. I'm getting mad because I *just had one*, and Adin says to me, 'It's in your pocket.' I look up at him and reach into my pocket and *there it is*. My hair tie. And he says, 'I think you put it in your pocket when you let your hair down.'"

Nate nodded and looked away, a smile spreading across his face.

I took a drink and set the glass down. "That's when I knew Adin was different from everybody else. And that's just one example."

"He paid attention to you. *Close* attention."

"It was the way he said it, too, so quietly and matter-of-factly, *'Your hair tie is in your pocket.'* I was completely taken by surprise. It was like this momentous thing. And we were great friends. The way he'd watch me sometimes, it was like he was memorizing something. I think he was memorizing—"

"But you two never..."

"No, no. We weren't anything like that. But we may have been more than that, if that makes sense. Anyway, I'm still trying to work it all out. Because most people don't care nearly as much as he does, do they? Most people don't stick with you. He's the one person who has always stuck with me. Even when we were apart. And we were apart for years. It's like we found each other at the wrong time, and we've been trying to get it right."

Nate leaned in. "Adin looks *different* from what I pictured," he said, taking a drink.

I smiled, settling into my seat. "What'd you picture?"

"He looks so young! He looks like a skateboarder!"

"Nate, he does *not*. Why do you have to say things like that. He's as old as I am! Let me guess, you think he plays *Dungeons & Dragons*, too? You think he's into comic books?"

"Well, I mean, it's fine." Nate took a sip of wine and glanced toward the bar area, the black rim of his glasses catching the light. "You know, he never spoke to me all night, which I thought was odd. I don't know him. He seemed a little shy, insecure maybe." Nate sat the glass back on the table.

I shrugged. "What if he is?"

"Okay, let's just say, I thought he was the *opposite* of Tim."

I nodded. "Business-minded, politically correct, and overly confident Tim? That makes more sense."

"Bingo! That is all."

from: Adin Driscoll
to: Lilly Jameson
sent: February 11, 3:46 a.m. EST
subject: Well, here goes...

I'm going to keep this very short, because if I give myself too long I'll think too much about it and call the whole thing off.

I came to the reading because I love you, and I told you I would not be at the Columbus reading because I love you, I've loved you since our time together at OU, and I've loved you enough to crumble under the weight of it. Maybe that makes sense to you, maybe not. But it's true, and I have to say it to say this. I was stupid to think I could have your love without risking mine. I don't want to be stupid anymore. If you tell me to come to Denver tomorrow, I will.

Adin

• • •

from: Lilly Jameson
to: Brenda Jameson
sent: February 12, 7:02 a.m. MST
subject: Need Advice

Mom,
You know how I told you about Adin being at the reading and how uncomfortable everything was? Well, he sent me this email saying he'd be willing to move to Denver to be with me. That's crazy. Right?

We haven't spent much time together since college and I don't know if Beaufort counts since it was more like a holiday thing. I don't know that we could live together and not kill each other in the process. I don't know his habits. I mean, who just up and says, *tell me to come to Denver and I will*? Not that I don't want him to move in, per se, but you know that old saying, fools rush in? Wouldn't it be foolish of me to say yes?

I've got to go to a book signing in Tampa and I don't know what to say to him. Maybe you and Jane are right—maybe we do just click and we'd be happy and make it work, somehow, but what if it's a total disaster—then I'd feel guilty that he up and moved across the country for me. I couldn't live with myself. He could get to Colorado and hate it and then I would feel responsible for ruining what he had going in Columbus.

Lilly

Mom called ten minutes later. I was throwing my iPod and a bikini in my carry-on while trying to awkwardly position my phone between my cheek and my shoulder, listening to her. She thought I should let him move in and just see how things go. But this was Adin, after all, the Adin who helped me find the books I needed in the college bookstore, the Adin who would bring me hot cocoa in my favorite study carrel, the Adin who held my hand and helped me cross the road when the freak snowstorm blanketed everything in ice and I was too scared to walk outside because I knew I'd fall.

But more than that, this *new* Adin was willing to meet me on my terms. Hadn't I essentially dared him to do exactly this? To man up and give this a shot? Weren't we both curious about what could have been and what still might be? I couldn't say *move in*, because I wouldn't be home for another week. That afternoon I was leaving for Tampa and I would be there through Valentine's Day.

I leaned over my suitcase and mashed it down until it zipped all the way. I blew some stray hairs out of my face and stood up and looked around at the little piles of clothes on my floor. I walked over to my bookcase and glanced at the very top shelf where all my old journals were lined up. The red journal was from freshman year—the year when Adin and I first met in a Humanities course where we each had to produce a photography portfolio. I'd known immediately I'd do badly in the class. I was a lousy photographer. Adin had been the standout student.

I took down the journal, flipped it open, and started looking at all the images I'd collected and taped in. Some of them Adin had taken on the college grounds. He liked to photograph nature and, as a joke, he photographed flowers, developed them, and then gave them to me. He thought that since my name was Lilly I would love pictures of flowers. I ran my fingers over the black-and-white images and laid the journal on the bookshelf beside all the others.

I glanced around the room and imagined Adin walking through it.

I imagined him in my bed, and I let my thoughts wander. I was late. I needed to go. But his words were still ringing in my ear. I got to my doorway and imagined him sitting by his computer in Columbus, hair unkempt, dark circles under his eyes, drinking tea in his pajamas, and waiting for a response.

I couldn't let that kind of information—that kind of *question*— linger. I took a deep breath, glanced at the clock, and wrote him back.

from: Lilly Jameson
to: Adin Driscoll
sent: February 12, 8:10 a.m. MST
subject: A Proposition

Adin,
My plane leaves for Tampa in two hours. I'll be there until February 18. I'm staying at the Grand Hyatt Tampa Bay. Here's what I propose: spend Valentine's Day with me. I'm still trying to wrap my brain around what you said.

Lilly

[◦] [◦] [◦]

A few minutes later
Columbus, Ohio

Adin

Adin: hey

Tristan: hey killer!

Tristan: what did she say?

Adin: honestly?

Adin: i wish i knew

⊠ ⊠ ⊠

February 14th
Tampa, Florida

Lilly

from: Lilly Jameson
to: Jane Thomas-Barczak
sent: February 14, 6:32 p.m. EST
Subject: Valentine's Day

Hey Jane,

I'm sure you are out with Philip, having an amazing meal and drinking wine as I write this, but I am having wine too. nate said I didn't have anything until late afternoon. afterwards I am going out with some local authors for dinner then maybe coming back for drinks I don't know. It will be fun though. Tomorrow night will be my fun night. I'm betting you are having a great night, but you know what, valentine's day never meant much to me like most people. Seriously. Who cares? (i do not)

Did I tell you Adin wanted to move in with me and I told him to meet me in tampa so we could talk about it like normal people? I am no fool. I am NO fool. So he's not here and I guess he is still acting like a child. Why did I think things would be different? This is his one great flaw isn't it? Inactivity. he has these crisis (crises?) of indecision. I am naïve. No wonder tim liked him so much. Adin is incapable of action. I need to forget and move on. He's not even called me, jane. I say all that to him and nothing.

Things are going okay on the tour. Toledo was just so weird. I still feel shaken by the whole thing. Some kid's mom posted this video on YouTube (from the Toledo reading) where

I basically ignored her child who had a final question (I was trying to wrap up the Q&A) and I look like a jerk. I was telling Nate and he said who cares? I do!

I keep trying to forget adin, but he's a jack-in-the-box that keeps popping up to say I love you—and I believe him. Screw all this indecisive crap. I'm done. I've even stopped taking my b. control pills. I figure I don't really need the constant reminder that I'm with no one, will not *be* with anyone, etc. i hope you are having a good night. feel like Im sort of done w. life for the moment, so, wine.

Still. I thought he would be here. I thought we were going to really do this. What was I thinking?

There is *nothing* on TV!

Think I am just going to go walk on the beach and pretend it's a day like any other.

Lilly

☒   ☒   ☒

That same day (Valentine's Day)
Columbus, Ohio

Adin

FOR ABOUT FOUR HOURS AFTER I SENT THAT email, I was suffocating in what I'd done. It's over, I thought. I've gone from one extreme to the other, and even someone who loves me isn't going to be able to take that transition gracefully. I've messed it all up. I waited too long and then played catch-up a little too fast. There is no way that any good can come of this.

For just a few seconds, when I got Lilly's reply and saw how short it was, shorter even than mine, I was certain that I had been right. My heart dropped like an anchor. And then, just as quickly, it was buoyed up by the words. Not *yes*, per se. In fact, I wasn't sure exactly what she was saying. But it was enough for me. If all I had to do was buy a plane ticket to Tampa, well, it was a small price to pay.

I called work to tell them I was taking the last few of my vacation days. Only two, but that was okay, because Lilly's time in Tampa stretched until Tuesday. It would work out perfectly.

Work had other ideas. "Your PTO expired at the end of the year," Carrol in Human Resources told me flatly. "You'll have two days sometime in March."

"For Christ's sake," I pleaded. "Could I just have the two days now?" I had earned them, after all.

"No," she insisted. "You had your chance, and now you have to earn them again. By the way, aren't you scheduled to work *today*?"

My mind was racing along at such velocity it threatened to jump the tracks. I would take a day off next week to spend the weekend with Lilly in Tampa and fly back on Monday. But just one day to avoid arousing suspicion. It would have to be a sick day, too, since that was all I had left. But I was already taking a sick day today. Wasn't I?

"Yeah, sorry," I said. "I had to take my dog in to the vet this morning. He was having trouble breathing. His surgery is Monday. That's why I needed the time off. I'll be there in an hour. I can work late."

"Adin, you don't have a dog."

"No, I do. I just found him last night, on my way home from work. I think he's sick. That's why I had to take him in."

There was a pause. A long, suspicious, my-hands-are-tied pause.

"Oh," she said. "Well. Congratulations, I guess."

I had turned the time-off thing around, but I couldn't make it to Tampa until late tonight. How could I tell Lilly? I made a decision that any man might have believed was the right one in the moment: I didn't tell her. Anything. I thought I would just show up. You know? Like a surprise! I didn't want her to think I was just making excuses, to assume that I wouldn't show up at all. I knew that she would struggle to have faith in me until I was in Tampa, in the flesh. So I figured why not wait until then to contact her?

Yes, I do know how nonsensical that is. Yes. Sure. But I was groping for a plan, only a few shades away from a panic attack. I did what I had to do. I maintained radio silence for three days after getting her *proposition*. Then I got on a plane.

⌗ ⌗ ⌗

February 14th–18th
Grand Hyatt Tampa Bay, Florida

Lilly

IN TAMPA I SPENT A LOT OF TIME in conference rooms, answering questions and smiling for the camera with fans, my heart jumping a little each time a door opened. I checked my email every five minutes. It was Valentine's Day, after all. I expected Adin to show up any minute. The hotel had these outrageous Valentine's Day parties, and everywhere I looked couples were getting dinner or having drinks. Men were proposing, women were dressed in low-cut gowns, teary-eyed with sentiment, and everywhere I looked lives were changing for the better.

My head and heart were all over the place.

Things went sharply downhill when I was trying to talk to aspiring children's book authors later that afternoon. I was in a room of about thirty people—MFA students, from what I'd been told. Ten minutes into my talk, the door opened and a young man who looked remarkably like Adin had looked in college ducked in. Embarrassed, he apologized for arriving so late. And that reminded me of Adin, too. Adin was usually late to class in college. He never *missed* class, but he would always arrive four to five minutes after it had started. I was always the early bird, saving him a seat in the back.

I was thinking about all this as the guy awkwardly made his way to an empty seat between two young women in the last row. I swallowed hard and turned away. Of course, I was really just trying to suppress a need to…what? Vent? Shout? Cry? Bargain with God? I turned to face the board where I had written little clusters of websites and books I thought the students would find helpful. I tried to pick up with where I had left off, but a photographer came in, a large Nikon draped around his neck, just like Adin in college. He smiled politely and went to the back of the room.

I kept taking off the marker cap and putting it back on again. *Stop it*, I told myself. *He's not here. Get over it. He's not coming.* I looked down at the red felt tip of the marker. I'd been talking about archetypes of fairytales. I could feel the lump in my throat. I could feel the anger bubbling to the surface. I had to get out of there.

"You all will have to excuse me for a second. I'm not used to this Southern humidity! *Allergies.* Be right back."

I quickly moved to open the door on my right and tried to discreetly make my way down the hall, which wasn't easy since I was a headlining author at a children's book festival. I just wanted to cry. I just wanted to give a sound to the confusion and hurt. I had to find a release. From him. From me. From whatever we had that was wrecking my life without it.

I got to the bathroom, locked myself in a stall, and took my phone out of my pocket. I scrolled through my contacts until I reached Adin's name and grabbed some toilet paper to dry my eyes. I checked my voice mail. I checked my texts. Nothing. I wanted to call him and tell him how confused I was, but I couldn't do that. How I didn't just *want* this to work—I *needed* it to work. I wasn't going to call him, though. I knew this was him saying goodbye. And I worried he'd respond with another one of his thanks-but-no-thanks statements, and I would feel only more disappointment and humiliation.

Standing there, dabbing my face in a bathroom stall, I realized this is what had kept us apart in college: I had feared this very experience.

How many times had I wondered about the two of us? It felt as if we'd come close to this same edge. But he'd never said anything. He never asked me. He didn't show up. He never followed through. And so I'd have these dreams of us. I had so many dreams about him. It seemed my body and subconscious were trying to satisfy that need in my life, subconsciously trying to fight my way through the fucking mystery of it all and just see *what that would be like.* The body wants what it wants.

Something great was passing me by, and I was starting to feel the sting of its departure. Logic was begging me to move on, but this was Adin. He was, by definition, not someone I could just blot out of my life. He meant too much. He mattered too much. He *was* too much.

And then the crushing reality hit me: I didn't matter enough. Despite all his protests and adoring looks and the immensity of what I felt between us. *I* didn't matter enough. That's why he never showed up.

I didn't matter.

I dried my eyes and unlocked the stall door, my hands shaky as I pushed it open. I looked at myself in the mirror. My eyes were bloodshot. My skin was splotchy. My nose was red. I wiped the last tear away with the back of my hand and reached for a paper towel. I felt slightly neurotic and questioned whether I should even go back into that classroom. I'd had one other emotional break like this that I could remember—the last time I saw Jason at OU. I had completely lost it. What would I do? How could I go back in that classroom? Why did I let Adin do this to me? My hair was stringy in the front from the mix of tears and hairspray. I tucked my long bangs behind my ears and touched at my loose bun which was still in place but just barely. I sniffled and turned, facing the stainless steel stall door again, my body shaking. I stared into it, trying to make my mind go blank, trying not to see Adin's face when I closed my eyes. I felt the room go completely still—the only sound was my jagged breathing. Without a thought in my head, I slammed my fist against the steel door and immediately reeled from the impact. I felt a satisfying pain shoot through my hand. My hair fell down, and I didn't bother fixing it.

Walking down that hall, my sadness gave way to a shimmering, radiant anger. It was February 14.

⊡ ⊡ ⊡

Adin

I GOT THERE JUST BEFORE NINE O'CLOCK, jittery and damp around the armpits and back. I rented a car and searched GPS for directions to the hotel. My heart was pinballing around inside me the whole way there. What if Lilly was too pissed to be happy that I had come? I was terrified that I had flown down for nothing, that I would be back on a plane in three hours crying into my cocktail napkin. What if three days without me was enough to make up her mind? Suddenly the whole radio-silence gambit seemed idiotic rather than playful. But I was here now. There was nothing left to do but follow through.

The Grand Hyatt was enormous, sleek and glowing in the night. It loomed over me almost threateningly, like it was trying to protect her. The lobby was tall and filled with white stone and marble, like I imagined the Forum in Rome. I stood out awkwardly in my hooded jacket and kneeless jeans. But I didn't care. I was here for Lilly, not for the guests or the staff.

I spotted Lilly at the bar in the hotel lounge. She was dozens of yards away, but I could pick out her coat and her long hair in any crowd. I stopped behind one of those obscenely large columns, shielding my eyes from the harsh chandeliers, and texted her.

Adin: hey, lilly, how's Tampa?

Lilly: Fine. It's great. Adin, where are you?

Adin: why? were you worried I wouldn't come?

Lilly: ??

I had come up with a plan during the flight—one that I thought at the time would be cute and romantic and possibly run some damage control. Should I draw this process out, toy with her just a little longer? Then I saw her shoulders heave with an angry sigh. I cut to the chase and texted her one final bit of cleverness:

Adin: Turn around

And she did. Grinning like a lovesick idiot, I started walking toward her.

She jumped off her stool, power-walked up to me, and slapped me hard across the face with what I am guessing was all her might.

❖ ❖ ❖

Lilly

MY JAW DROPPED WHEN I TURNED FROM NATE and saw Adin standing there grinning like he had somehow swooped in and saved the day. Who did he think he was, showing up whenever it suited him, leading me on and being an indecisive jerk who couldn't be bothered to pick up his phone?

I didn't mean to make a scene in the lobby.

Or say the word *fuck* that many times.

Or so loudly.

Fortunately, Nate ran over and intervened before I could truly hurt Adin, but what was originally a *heated quarrel* between myself and Adin spun out of control. The confusion started around the time Nate called me *Darling* (he sometimes called me that). This led Adin to think the two of us were together (*a couple*, is what Adin later told me), but Nate was only trying to get me to stop insulting Adin and to lower my voice. Adin and Nate exchanged words (okay, provocations, *derogatory remarks*). Basically their exchange, if I remember correctly, went something like:

"Oh, come on, you're the one who's been stringing her along."

"Who do you think *you* are, asshole?"

"Excuse me, I'll call the cops if you don't leave here immediately! You do know you're at a children's book festival?"

"I'm not fucking going anywhere!"

"Oh yes you *will* go somewhere or I'll have security—"

And at that point, Adin punched him, sending Nate's glasses skittering across the marble floor. Then Nate ran at him.

THAT WENT ON UNTIL THE HOTEL SECURITY CAME over, which stunned us all into temporary adult-like behavior. I had never, ever been in trouble with the law. "I'm a children's book author!" I yelled as security hauled me to this dark room with the others. Adin was sweating, and Nate's bow tie was crooked. They sat us down at a large circular table and made us watch the footage of the brawl, which was extremely humiliating. Nate sat there with a black eye, smirking as though he wanted to get the final punch in. After we had been talked to (it was awful—the most embarrassing experience of my adult life), we were free to go. The three of us walked back into the lobby. Nate quietly found his glasses near a giant palm, glared at Adin, and announced he was going to put ice on his eye. Adin was silent. I looked at my watch and then at Adin. It was almost eleven. He looked alert, like he was ready to fight anyone or anything else that may come between us.

"Adin, what the hell are you doing here?"

The chandeliers overhead dimmed a bit, and Adin glanced up toward them as if he was looking for an answer in the distant heavens. A lonely saxophonist began playing "Someday My Prince Will Come" in the bar area. Adin was looking at everything but me. Like he was rehearsing something in his head or trying to remember lines. I grabbed his hand to bring him back to reality.

"Adin."

This time he looked directly at me and, after stammering for a few seconds, told me exactly what I had been needing to hear for a long time.

⟨◊⟩ ⟨◊⟩ ⟨◊⟩

Adin

"I'M HERE BECAUSE YOU ASKED ME TO BE," I said.

The lobby just felt darker after that. Not as scary, maybe, but not as glamorous, either. We walked around aimlessly until we found this little restaurant overlooking the water, with paper-shaded sconces on the walls and napkins folded into attractive shapes on every empty plate. Nobody wanted to eat at the hotel on Valentine's Day. It was just us and one lonely-looking businessman. But the water looked gorgeous at night.

Lilly ordered a lobster bisque, so quietly the waiter had to ask her to repeat herself. I guess she was trying to make up for all her screaming profanity. A friend of hers had posted a video on Lilly's Facebook page of the Toledo reading, with Lilly, in her distraction, missing some poor kid's earnest question. Lilly had been mortified. I imagined now a Facebook video of the scene in the Hyatt lobby, already an internet meme—do something shitty and then scream, "I'm a children's book author!"

"When do we get to the part where you tell me why you showed up days late and didn't call or write or anything?" she asked. She was still looking haggard and bewildered. She had sobered up with impressive rapidity, but there was something about her that was still a little shaken, a little inside out. I had expected that my dramatic entrance might cause trouble, but I confess I hadn't quite been able to forecast this reaction.

"I had to work today and I wanted to surprise you," I said, guiltily, like I was telling her I ate the last of the peanut butter. "I'm calling in sick on Monday." Then, and this is proof enough of just how exhausted we both were, I added, "I told them I had a dog," as if this might be the last puzzle piece she needed.

She was quiet for a long time. Even in the South, it was chilly in February, so all the big storm windows were closed. I couldn't hear the sound of the waves outside. I wished that I could; I felt like that might make all of this better. "I love you," I told her. "I don't mean that as something that will make you less angry at me. You can be angry, that's fine. It's just that I flew a thousand miles to say it to you, so I thought I would just get it out of the way while we have a quiet moment." There was something conflicted about the way that I said it—genuine, yeah, but also a little heartbroken, a little bitter.

Her phone buzzed loudly, like it was trying very hard to cut me off. Lilly sighed and picked it up to check it. "It's Nate," she groaned. "He wants to know where we are."

"Who the hell is he, anyway?" I asked, hoping that this time I could get away with posing the question without punches being thrown.

"He's my agent. And a really good friend of mine. He thinks you're just messing with me, treating me badly. He's trying to keep me from getting hurt."

"So you can write better books." I thought about staring her down on that one but decided that if it wasn't the worst possible time, it was close.

She pinched her lips anyway. "Because he cares about me," she said. "Agents are just like this with their authors, okay? It's a—it's a unique relationship, you know, it's hard for someone outside the industry to get. We're in constant communication, and he's really invested in my well-being, and I mean it's almost like a—like a marriage, really."

I took the napkin from my plate and unfolded it. I felt like destroying something carefully made. "So are you registered at Target? I have a rewards card there and I want to get ahead of the gift-buying herd. Otherwise you end up buying towels and...," I almost spilled my glass of water trying to end my jab on a casual sip, "and silverware."

She might have gotten up and left then if the waiter hadn't shown up with her bisque. "Holy God, that was fast," I couldn't help but tell him.

"You're the only ones here," he replied, with this look that was like a scowl wrapped in a smile—not even a half-assed attempt at politeness. I suspected he knew who we were. I also suspected it might be in Lilly's best interests not to eat anything here. She didn't lift her utensils once the whole meal.

"So you thought the best thing to do would be to just not call for seventy-two hours?" she asked finally. "And then you blindside me while I'm crying on Nate's shoulder, you *blacken* his *eye*, and I mean put-a-steak-on-it kind of blacken, and your only explanation is *I love you*?"

I shrugged helplessly. The only other person who could ever put me on the spot like this was my dad. Except my dad was always stone-faced when he did it. Lilly's eyes were like the headlights of a locomotive. "I love you a whole lot?"

She shook her head and started typing away furiously on her phone. "I have to be honest, Adin. I'm glad you actually came, I really am. I had convinced myself you wouldn't. It's a relief that you meant what you said. But this whole thing..." She trailed off so she could finish typing and then practically threw the damn thing down and let out a big, bursting sigh. "But this whole thing has just been so crazy, and I don't want to make any huge decisions while we're all still so rattled. I need more time to think about all of this."

"Did you just text something to Nate?"

She stared off toward the water, as if noticing it for the first time. "I am glad you came, though."

"Did you tell Nate where we are?"

She snapped toward me then. "Adin. Stop. He's my agent, okay? And when he gets here, you are *both* apologizing, and then he and I are going to go find out how to put the kibosh on this disaster before anybody's parents read the paper tomorrow. I'm sorry, but I have to fix this before I worry about anything else."

"Well, what should I do? I can't afford to stay here." I unsuccessfully tried to fold the napkin back the way it had been. I laid it on the plate, tortured, ruined.

"I'm sure there are plenty of hotels around here that aren't the Hyatt. You can stay wherever you want."

"What about tomorrow?"

She shrugged.

"I mean, am I going to get to see you at all?"

"I don't know. The whole thing tonight is making it more complicated. Just let me know tomorrow if you're staying. I should have my schedule mostly hammered out by then."

IT WAS ONLY FORTY-EIGHT DEGREES WHEN I left the hotel, but I was so hot I took my hoodie off. The streets were filled with cars, half of them classic, like some kind of club was in town. I searched around on my phone and got a poor-people motel eleven blocks away. I walked the whole way there not thinking about anything—except maybe to wonder why so much of Florida was pink.

from: Adin Driscoll
to: Lilly Jameson
sent: February 15, 6:38 a.m. EST
subject: About last night

Lilly,

I woke up this morning with one very important realization, which is that I never told you I was sorry. So here it is now: I'm sorry. I'm sorry for screwing up my big surprise, I'm sorry for letting you spend all that time worrying, I'm sorry for hitting your agent. And mostly I'm sorry for not telling you what I needed to tell you in a timely and elegant manner, for waiting until it was very possibly too late and then flying down like a chump to hear you tell me so.

I don't know if you'll be busy today. I guess with everything that's happened it would make sense if you are. But if not, I've been up since 5:30, and I found a highly reviewed Cuban place called Holy Havana. We could get lunch. Or something. I could tell you I'm sorry in person. And that I love you. It didn't come out right last night. I still need to do it right before I go.

Adin

. . .

from: Lilly Jameson
to: Adin Driscoll
sent: February 15, 6:45 a.m. EST
subject: Re: About last night

Adin:
I'm really sorry, too. For a lot of things. I should have been more understanding about your job. Last night after you left I felt awful about how I treated you. I was mad. I was a mess. I was relieved you actually showed up....Would you want to meet me for breakfast? It's Tuesday and my schedule is wide open. I can be downstairs in forty-five minutes if you're up for it.

Lilly
p.s. Bring your luggage.

WE NEVER MADE IT TO THE RESTAURANT DOWNSTAIRS. He got to my hotel around 7:15 that morning, still looking as haggard as he had the day before. I wondered if he'd even slept. He sat his luggage down in the corner of the room, hardly taking his eyes off me. I thought he might yell. I thought he might say he'd had it with me, that I was too much trouble. I felt like I deserved that. I knew he'd made the trip to Tampa in order to see me and I knew the whole thing had been a disaster so far, and I was mad at myself for that. But he *had* finally come through. It dawned on me that he was risking a lot to be in Tampa with me.

I told him he could share my room. I gave a flimsy excuse about not wanting him to waste his money on a place down the road since he came here *because* of me. *I had room to spare*, I'd said, motioning toward the two living rooms, the unmade king-sized bed, and the kitchen. He nodded. Like an idiot I walked over to the windows that faced Tampa Bay and proceeded to tell him about the view and how gorgeous the coast looked at night. I was nervous to have him there. I'd spent weeks, if not months, thinking about being alone with him. Not to mention all those far-off daydreams and fantasies that followed me from the past. I didn't want him to leave, so I was playing the role of kind, informative hostess, which Adin must have picked up on right away.

I was pointing out a yacht with what looked like two huge dogs running around the deck when I realized the drapes were closing around the window as I was talking. I spun around and Adin was untying the knots that held the silky long blue fabric back.

"Oh? Not interested in the dogs?"

Adin smiled. "Not interested in dogs, the bay, boats, any of that," he said, fiddling with the long, mustard-colored tassel.

I walked over to him. "I really am sorry about yesterday. I just didn't think you were—"

"I know, I know."

Adin wrapped his arms around me from behind and we stood there holding each other in the soft morning light. I was glad he had shut me up. *Closeness* was in fact all I'd wanted. I folded my arms around his. The drapes gave a soft blue glow to the room that made it seem as though we were underwater. I felt his lips on my neck and let my head slip toward his chest. He brushed my hair aside and continued, his lips leaving hushed echoes at every point they touched. I opened my eyes and turned to face him. His face was soft and inquiring. I reached for him and he leaned into me, kissing me harder than before.

Half-dressed, we shuffled over to the bed, smiling past each kiss as if we were both trying to keep a secret from the other that we had every intention to tell. We fell onto the messy bed, reaching for each other's remaining clothes until we were both undressed, kissing each other with such ferocity it was as if we were determined to erase the lost time and make up for every lost second. Every kiss seemed to matter. Every touch seemed like a bolt of color filling in a lost, colorless picture.

We were unrestrained. We were indelicate. I pulled him against my body. I didn't want him to have any uncertainty about what I wanted. There would be no side-stepping this time. No impasses. No half-hearted hints. My lips grazed his chest and neck and my head bent into the crook of his neck. I felt like someone who had been lost at sea and had finally (miraculously) reached a shore. I trembled with relief. I held on to the land. He tightened his arms around me, encircling me as he moved against me in waves. I closed my eyes tightly and felt my cheek brush against his temple as the blue silk drapes slowly lit with the light of the bright, breaking day.

◙ ◙ ◙

February 13, 2003
Ohio University, Athens, Ohio

Adin

It wasn't immediately clear which was going to be the bigger warning sign—that Tristan had brought two bottles of Mad Dog 20/20 (fruit punch flavor, because that was a *thing* somehow) or that one of the bottles was half-empty when he showed up. "Why's one of them half-empty?" I asked him, and he told me not to be a pessimist.

I myself was drinking Pinot Noir, splitting a bottle with Lilly. We'd bought it two hours earlier, out of a room at the Phi Tau house everybody referred to as The Commissary for some reason. It was an illicit thrill we both tried to play off as no big deal. Truthfully, at nineteen, maybe I would have preferred the Mad Dog, but I didn't want Lilly to know that. We were all together, us and Tristan and Jane, as well as a couple others, minor players in the cast of that year, having a drinking party in the first-floor room that Lilly and Jane shared. Jason was out, gone upstate with friends for a Foo Fighters concert, which I thought was a little odd, this being both a Thursday and the eve of Valentine's Day, and that being one of Lilly's favorite bands.

Lilly sat at her desk, nursing her glass with a far-off look. I knew that expression well, and the wish that I could be the one to chase it away was like cold metal in the back of my throat.

"Aight, aight," Tristan announced, leaning forward on the bottom bunk, making the distinctive crunch of cheap box springs. He spoke in that MC voice he always adopted when he was drunk among friends. "Let's do something risqué. We're young and dumb, and I count at least six bottles of various types. There is no excuse for not making this a night to regret."

"How about you do something to regret," I suggested, "and the rest of us just come away with a good story to tell our friends tomorrow."

"Okay, well, A: all our friends are already here, unless you've got some other secret coterie I don't know about. And B: stop drinking crushed grapes like a tittering socialite, and live your life a little."

I cocked my head at him. "You know Mad Dog is mostly wine, right?"

Tristan peered at me skeptically and then at the bottle. "Bullshit," he said, but he sounded unsure.

"It's literally wine. They literally call it bum wine. You didn't know that?"

"Okay, well, it's wine with less girly stuff in it."

"What, like mixed fruit?"

Tristan glared at me, red-faced, and then gave a petulant shrug as he scanned the laughing faces around the room. "Shut up," he said, otherwise speechless, and retreated toward the wall. This was a rare feat, getting Tristan flustered over something. I should have been prouder to have managed it—and with an audience, no less. But I just chalked it up to him getting an early start on the booze.

A few feet away, Lilly sat in her ancient wooden chair (she and Jane had tied cushions to the seats, but honestly, there was no saving it) and rolled the wine around in her glass. She was smiling, a little. Only a little.

"Hey, Lilly," I said. "Think fast." And I raised up the camera and flashed her with it before she had a chance to think at all.

"Adin!" she protested, her smile dissolved, replaced by an angry scowl. "Don't take a picture of me right now!"

"You weren't smiling. I figured you'd smile if you had a camera aimed at you."

She scoffed, held the glass up for me to get a good look at it. "We're *drinking* right now. Seriously. I don't want pictures of me drinking when I'm underage. My parents would have a litter of kittens. And then train them all to murder me."

"Somebody top that girl's glass off," Jane grunted. She was on the floor, leaning against the frame of her bunk, holding a bottle of Jim Beam between her crossed legs. (Tristan sat above her, scheming, no doubt, for excuses to give her affectionate pats on the head and shoulders.) "I can still hear all the wheels turning in her head." She took a long pull from the bottle, as though to further the point.

Lilly gave a big sigh, either showy or genuinely exasperated, I couldn't tell which. "Fine," she said, lifting the bottle up from the floor beside her, pouring herself a generous refill. "Adin? Need any more?" She offered the bottle to me. I was on the floor, too, and she had to lean over the head of Julianna to get it close enough for me to reach up and take it. I had a moment of hesitation, until I pictured spending the rest of the night watching her miss her boyfriend, and then I downed the rest of my glass and took the bottle by the neck.

"*Any*way," Tristan said, "I vote for *Truth or Dare*."

"What is this, eighth grade?" Jane demanded. "Because I left my copy of *Mall Madness* at home."

"Jane. Honey." Tristan reached down and gripped her near the base of her neck, with mock gravity. It was one of those moments— everybody knew he just wanted to touch her. Jane knew. Even I knew, and flirting was like a foreign language to me. But we all let it go. We were kids. We never stopped wanting to touch each other. "If you've got a better way to loosen up this roomful of nerds, I would be eternally grateful to hear it."

Jane rolled her eyes. She didn't shrug his hand away, though. "Whatever. Let me just finish off this bottle so we can spin it afterwards."

"Awesome. Forward, then. Let's start with Adin."

Shock rippled up my spine. Tristan was looking at me with what I could only think of as an icily jovial expression, whatever that meant. I'd had this recurring dream, in the last few years, of driving my car onto a bridge and realizing too late, that it was raised up in the middle. I'd go flying off toward the water, frantic, paralyzed. That was the feeling I had now. "Uh huh?" I replied.

"Truth or dare?"

I hated this game. It was always a trap. Truths and dares, at our age, were basically the same thing. They both amounted to clandestine attempts to out all your biggest secrets. Luckily I had a simple but brilliant strategy, a ploy I suspect no player of the game has ever thought to attempt—just pick truth and lie. "Truth."

"Cool." Tristan rubbed his fingers across the thing on his chin that he seemed to believe qualified as a *beard*. It was clear that he had known before he suggested the game what the question would be. This was his particular brand of revenge. "Adin, tell us: Do you have a thing for anybody in the group?"

"Um. The whole group, or just the people in the room?"

Tristan smiled, gave a slight shrug, as though this were a trifling distinction. "I don't know. In the room, I guess."

"Dude," Jane interrupted, glaring up at him. "That's not cool."

"Well, I could ask him what his favorite foods are, but that wouldn't really uphold the spirit of the game, would it?" He turned back to me. "So?"

I mulled it over, with the same deliberative expression he'd worn. "Uhhhh," I thought aloud. "No. Not really."

In the corner of my eye, Lilly raised her glass and took a sip. Don't, I thought to myself. Don't read into that. It's a drinking party. People drink. Don't—no, goddamn it, *don't*.

"Ah, well." Tristan sighed, long and loud, like a damsel in distress. "Worth a shot."

We went around the circle. One of the guys dared Jane to take a shot off of Julianna's stomach, but Jane was a table dancer at all the parties; she didn't flinch at such basic indiscretions. She did it but kept it so quick and perfunctory that none of the guys assembled had a chance to relish it. Someone asked Tristan if he'd ever had sex while I was in the room, and his answer was a surprise to nobody, least of all to me, who, you know, lived there.

Lilly, of course, chose truth. Neither of us was the dare type. "If," Jane asked her, "I go up to Madame Noir's after class tomorrow, for my own Valentine's Day celebration, will you buy a vibrator with me?"

This had the effect of making Lilly sort of half-disappear from the room. She reddened, hid her mouth behind the glass. "Sure," she said. "I'd help you pick one out."

"No, kid, I mean one for *you*."

She achieved some deeper shade of red not found in nature, the kind that can only be mixed in industrial facilities. "Uh—" she stammered. "Well, I don't really need one."

At this, Jane gave her *the face*—raised eyebrow, pinched lips. "Like hell you don't."

"No, I mean," Lilly took a deep breath, closed her eyes tight, "I mean I don't...*need* one."

The message clicked, and the room caught fire with uproarious laughter. Lilly doubled over and covered her face with her free hand, did something that might have been laughing or sobbing. Meanwhile, I sat there, dumbfounded and (it must be admitted) shamefully excited by this revelation. Lilly Jameson. Holy shit. She was so shy about this sort of talk it was easy to forget she might have a sexual nature. I had hoped, in the darker parts of my adolescent heart, that it was there, and to see it laid bare now brought on a nasty shiver. I had to take a large swig of the wine to hide it as it went through me.

"All right," Tristan said, wiping tears of mirth from the corners of his eyes, "fair enough. That brings us back around to Adin. Okay, Adin. Truth or dare."

Something went wrong in me—wires crossed at some junction, my whole nervous system still reeling from the wild gunfire of my synapses. "Uh, dare. I guess." Wait—*what*? What did I just do?

Even Tristan blinked in surprise. "Well, Jesus, Sailor, all right. Ima have to think this over a second. This is a unique opportunity." This time, when he set aside a moment to ponder, you could tell it was real. I waited there on the floor, like a prisoner waits for his sentence. "Okay, I got it," he said. "Kiss a girl. You can pick which one."

There was an immediate consensus of understanding. Every face in the room, Lilly's included, went to me. I glared at Tristan, who was so red-eyed and unsteady it wasn't even clear he understood entirely what he was doing, although probably he did. I stood, grabbing the nearest desk corner for support, and after a moment's thought turned to Julianna, right next to me. "Okay, Julianna. Sorry to do this to you."

A titter of giddy laughter went around the group, and Julianna gave a bashful grin as she started to stand. This won't be so bad, I thought. Julianna's pretty. It won't be a chore to kiss her. In fact, she really—

"Oh *come on*," Tristan moaned. "We all know that's not who you wanna kiss."

Every body in the room froze. Mine froze so bad it could have shattered, except for my face, which was on fire. On the floor, Jane stared up at me in horror, but also, I could see, in curiosity. What would I do? she was wondering. They were all wondering it.

What I wanted more than anything, *anything*, was to look at Lilly. To see how she was taking this. It was like when you think you see something in the corner of your eye and you just turn, you just have to, without thinking. But I couldn't. I could never. I had to keep my neck in a vise grip, let the heat in my face start to pass.

Somewhere below me, Julianna was still poised to stand, one palm pressed to the ragged rug underneath her. I sat back down, leaned over and kissed her, not an actual kiss but just this hard press of puckered lips against her unsuspecting *O* of shock. "There," I said. "All done."

Behind her, Lilly moved slightly, some gesture I didn't dare to watch. I couldn't be sure—it was almost certainly wishful thinking on my part—but it seemed like she had taken another drink.

⌑ ⌑ ⌑

February 15–18, 2014
Tampa, Florida

Adin

HOW CAN I DESCRIBE WHAT IT'S LIKE TO be with a woman who was once a girl I couldn't have? For years she was neatly filed away under "Never" (or even "Who, Her?"). And now here she was, smiling up at me in that gray Southern half-light, skin tinted blue from the drawn curtains. It was Zen, almost—I could feel every point where our skin touched, separately, its own private intimacy. Every whispered word between us seemed to hover and mingle in the space between our lips. I started to lose track of who was saying what.

In my mind I was retracing our steps, all the way back to that phone call to Beaufort. It wasn't even six months earlier that I could make it through a day from start to finish without a single thought devoted to Lilly Jameson. Not even four since we had actually seen each other for the first time, again. And now I was in Tampa wrapped in her arms, making little sounds of relief.

So I didn't call in sick at work on Monday. Or Tuesday. We stayed in that hotel room for four nights and three days, ordered room service, loudly performed her books to each other, consumed each other, and generally didn't speak or write to anyone. By this time tomorrow I'd be back at—

"Oh shit," I said aloud, snapping cleanly out of it.

"What?" she whispered.

"I forgot to call in sick at work."

She grabbed my jaw in her free hand, the one not making shallow claw marks in my back, and told me to shut up. And I did.

Mid-morning on Tuesday work called. My cell was sitting on a chair by the window, where it was plugged into the wall, and I nearly didn't answer it in time because I was trying to see if I could reach it without extricating every part of my body from the sheets. It was the same woman, Carrol (or Miss Benedict, apparently), and she sounded much less defeated this time. She sounded *joyous*.

"Mr. Driscoll," she squawked, "I have to tell you, unless you have a very good and very provable explanation for this week's absence—"

"Hold on, actually, I have the proof right here," I said, and handed the phone to Lilly, who had a mouthful of Pop-Tart and was in the middle of cracking up at Conan's monologue from the previous night. She gave me a puzzled look, and I just shrugged and grinned like a mischievous schoolboy.

She took the phone and mumbled, "Hewwo?"

Even though the words on the other end were tinny and distant, I could still hear that total bewilderment. There was a lot of rising intonation. Then there was stern, subtle voice-raising. Lilly just gave a lot of one-word answers like, *Yeah, Okay, No, Maybe, Probably.*

Then she suddenly switched to the voice I imagined her using during business calls and said, "Okay, well, have a good day. Mm-hm. You, too. Okay, bye." And she hung up.

"Well?" I asked. "How did it go?"

She tossed the phone in my lap. "You are so fired," she said, and face-crammed the rest of the Pop-Tart.

from: Human Resources – Family PhotoWorks, LLC
to: Adin Driscoll
sent: February 18, 11:31 a.m. EST
subject: Notice of Termination

Mr. Driscoll:
Following your misconduct in attendance, as well as the unprofessional attitude and dishonesty shown to Miss Benedict in Human Resources, Family PhotoWorks will be terminating your employment as a Grade 3 Photographer effective Friday, February 28th. You may finish out your work until then as scheduled or seek new employment as you see fit. If any equipment owned or leased by Family PhotoWorks is currently in your possession, please see that it is returned in full before the official date of termination.

Your four years of service to our company are appreciated, and it is with much regret that we notify you of this decision. We at Family PhotoWorks wish you much luck in your future employment and endeavors.

Regards,
Gary Roethlisberger
Vice President of Human Resources
Family PhotoWorks, LLC

This email transmission is intended only for the use of the individual or entity to which it is addressed and may contain information that is privileged, confidential, and exempt from disclosure under applicable law. If the recipient of this email is not the intended recipient, you are hereby notified that any dissemination, distribution, or copying of this communication is strictly prohibited. If you have received this communication in error, please return it to the sender immediately and then delete the email and destroy any copies of it.

OUR LITTLE HOLIDAY DIDN'T LEAVE HER MUCH TIME to get ready for her next gig, a book festival in Atlanta. She gave me her spare key and the apartment's address and said that I was free to move in whenever I wanted but that she wouldn't be back until early March. After the festival, there were a few other cities that Nate had lined up at the last minute, as a way of trying to counterbalance all the bad press Lilly had been avoiding.

I bristled at the guy's name, and I think Lilly must have noticed, because she kept the discussion of her work to a minimum. "I'll call you from Atlanta," she said, "and then from Grand Rapids. Last stop is Seattle, in a couple weeks."

"How will I survive that long?" I asked, thrusting on the other leg of my jeans. I was trying to watch her and a daytime talk show at the same time.

She smirked. "We've done the last five months with email, text, and voice mail. What's another few weeks?"

We checked out together, waited at the airport together. Her flight came first; mine wasn't until later that afternoon. We kissed like two clumsy, overeager kids at her gate, like we should have kissed all those years ago, and then I went to Starbucks and gushed about it to Tristan, whose chuckling semi-disinterest I could hear even in silent black lettering.

I walked around the concourse in a daze, as if I still couldn't figure out quite how I got there. Lilly texted an hour and a half later that she'd gotten in and that she missed me and would think of me that night when she was alone in her hotel room. It was the one bright spot in that whole day, because after that I had to get on a nonstop flight to snowbound Ohio, where my empty, unheated apartment was waiting for me.

And that email from work.

THERE WAS SOMETHING BITTER IN ITS UNRELENTING POLITENESS, something that carried me toward despair. Losing my job had seemed like little more than a punchline in Tampa; now it was something real, something shaming. I truly had given up everything, and for at least a couple of weeks I'd have nothing to show for it except another empty apartment in another chilly city. I got loaded on the rest of my Grey Goose and waited for Lilly to call. She never did.

■ ■ ■

from: Adin Driscoll
to: Lilly Jameson
sent: February 21, 7:28 p.m. MST
subject: Landed in Denver

Hey,

Well, I'm finally here. It took longer than I thought it would to get my stuff in storage back home, to break my lease (ouch), to drive all that way. Well, the last part took about as long as I expected. Everything else was pretty rough. But it's over, and here I am. And I miss you. I hope Atlanta went okay. I know we haven't gotten to talk much the last couple days, but hey, I signed on to love a writer. I get it. Hopefully there'll be a lull in there somewhere so we can talk more than ten minutes.

I start job hunting tomorrow. I had nothing to spend my money on back in Columbus, so I've managed to save up quite a bit of it. I could last probably eight or ten months. But I need something to occupy my hands and my brain. I don't want to spend these next several days just reading your books and flushing your toilet. I'm hoping I can find a job that involves putting something other than suburbanites in front of the camera. Denver's unlike anywhere I've ever lived before. It's a little intimidating, but there are a ton of jobs, so I'm holding out hope.

It's so weird, though, being here. I got in finally at about 12:30 in the morning. I was so tired I left most of my stuff in the car, where it's still sitting, waiting to be shown its new home. It was cold as hell, colder than Ohio. I just kind of stumbled in the front door, spent three minutes staring open-mouthed at everything, then collapsed atop that big four-poster bed that feels like a hill of kittens. When I woke up I took the longest, hottest shower of my life and went out for groceries. I don't think I realized until I was out on your front step that I had absolutely no idea where anything was.

That's how my whole life feels right now, actually— untethered. Which would be great if you were here. I never would have guessed it, but I think I might like that feeling, untethered. But only with things. Not with people. I hope the next couple days go by quickly. This bed is too big for me, and besides, I don't know when to put out the garbage or how to open the mailbox.

I need you. Come home soon.

Adin

✦ ✦ ✦

Atlanta, Georgia

Lilly

AFTER I READ ADIN'S EMAIL I SPUN AROUND on my swivel chair, stood up, and then collapsed on my hotel bed. The Atlanta reading didn't go as planned. My parents had taken the liberty of showing up unannounced. They wanted to show their support. (*We only ever went to one reading of yours!* Mom had pointed out while sliding into the Red Lobster booth later that evening.) I knew it had been Mom's idea—Dad would never have thought to come to a reading of mine. He hates books. I'd never actually seen him read a book, other than the Bible. He disliked that I pursued a *hobby* as a career (his words), and children made him nervous (something he'd never admit to but was obvious to me). He simply had nothing to say to them. Clearly, my scene was not a father-friendly environment. What I had not counted on was his stance on my love life.

I was in a Barnes & Noble on Peachtree with three other authors, and it was standing room only. I didn't realize my parents had been there the whole time until the signing, when I noticed them standing in line with everyone else. When it was their turn to get a book signed, Mom shouted, "Look who it is! My big author girl!" And practically flung herself over the edge of the table to get at me, knocking over someone's half-filled water bottle. Water splashed onto the crotch area of my jeans.

"Mom!" I said, frantically looking from her to the line of kids behind her.

Mom was a whir of energy, donning a pair of gaudy hand-painted reading glasses, picking up my books and then setting them back down. I used to hide those same glasses from her because I thought they looked tacky. Dad was shifting nervously from me to a little girl in pigtails standing beside him and watching me with her big, brown eyes.

"Lil, look at these *people*. They've all got your little books!" Mom cooed, as I leaned in to hug her.

I decided I would do Dad a favor and talk to the little girl who was quietly swinging her book back and forth, brushing his leg. I knew she had to be making him a nervous wreck, trying to figure out if he should talk to her and all.

"Hi sweetheart, is that a book you got there?" I said, settling back in my seat, reaching across the table for her copy.

She looked up at Dad then back at me. Her face had gone sour. Something was wrong. I wondered if Dad had shot her a look.

"You got a wet spot," she said. Her voice was raised in a way to get the most attention possible. People began craning their necks, looking past her. A slow, chaotic uproar of shouts, laughter, and pointing began. Kids darted in and out of the line. Pee was big news for the ten and under crowd.

I glanced at my mom. She was trying to stifle a laugh. "It's water!" she shouted to no one in particular. Dad wasn't amused. For a moment I wondered if he'd missed mom knocking the bottle into my lap. *Did he think I really pissed myself?* I thought, shifting in my seat.

I leaned in to talk to the little girl. "No, sweetheart!" I reached for the empty plastic bottle that had landed on the floor and sat it on the table, explaining to her how the water bottle had fallen and splashed me.

She had a quizzical look on her face. She was grinning, eyeing the others. *Not buying it!* She might as well be saying. There was no contest between my story versus the one in her head.

She raised her index finger to her lips then, as if she'd had an epiphany. "But it could be pee, too!" she said, enunciating every syllable.

"No, no, it *couldn't* be. Because it never was!"

The little girl shook her head in an exaggerated way, allowing her pigtails to sweep past other kids. Then someone came and picked her up, a teenager whom I assumed was her older sister.

I leaned over to Mom, who'd been standing to my left the entire time, not doing anything, but gleefully watching as the whole scene unfolded. It bugged me that she was watching this exchange as though my life was nothing more than an ice show at Disney World.

"Mom, I need you to go get me some new pants."

"New pants?" she said, glancing from me to Dad.

"Yes! I have to be here for another hour. I can't be walking around in wet pants. I think they want to do pictures. Can you go grab me some new pants?"

"Well, sweetie, where? We don't *know* this place."

"Mom, we're in a mall. I don't care. I know you know *malls*."

"Well," she said turning to Dad. "Okay, we'll take a look. I'll try to get a couple of things," she said shuffling past a manager.

"Okay, that's fine. Just try to be fast. The first person who wants a photo…"

Mom seemed to catch on then.

"Ew! That's right, isn't it? Okay! Okay!" Mom said something to Dad and then directed him toward the exit as if the place was on fire and he was incapable of moving himself out fast enough. I watched in horror as she began shouting "Coming through! *Pants emergency*!" into the crowd, waving her hands in the air.

The real trouble began after they got back.

Mom returned twenty minutes later, Dad and shopping bag in tow. She now wore a look of determination. It was like she'd realized she had a *daughter in need*. These were the moments Mom lived for, only she was out of practice since I had been on my own for many years. When she reached me she tossed a Lilly Pulitzer bag on the table. She loved all things Lilly Pulitzer, but I could never get into the Easter egg colors, the tropical prints. She cut in front of twins, each wearing identical eye glasses with soft, baby blue frames. Amazingly, ten-year-old twins wore glasses that weren't as loud as my mother's.

"Sweetie, put these on," she said pointing to the bag.

I smiled sweetly at the kids and then took the bag, excusing myself for just a minute.

The two of us walked to the bathroom in the back of the store, me trying to covertly cover the wet spot with the huge shopping bag. I dug around in the shopping bag and found two options: Option 1: Turquoise blue velour lounge pants (in medium, therefore not my size); and Option 2: Poplin print Bermuda shorts in a color that most closely resembled limeade (one size fits all). I grimaced.

"*Mom...*" I pushed open the bathroom door. "Really? Why the bright...*everything*?" and here I realized I would have to choose my words very carefully. She had bought things *she* would wear. "Pretty, pastel? I'm wearing a black cashmere sweater. Either one of these will make me look as wide as a sailboat."

Sailboat? I had to stop reading so many children's books.

Mom's face fell, and she reached for the lounge pants. "You ought to be wearing these anyway. They're comfy. You can tie them so they're tight. Look..." she said, demonstrating. "You can't sit like that in those fancy tight denim pants, Lil. You're liable to cut off circulation in those."

I held the pants up, studying them. I had to get a picture taken out there in just a few minutes. It was going to be hung up in the bookstore—me with the staff. An author photo—in these?

"*You* knocked the water over, and you bought me the sort of pants you'd wear to the Red Hat Society in Beaufort!"

Just then the back stall opened and a mother and daughter crept out. I noticed they skipped the handwashing part and went right for the door. If that wasn't a sure sign that I was basically in a nightmare, I wasn't sure what was.

I closed my eyes and hung my head, listening as the door softly closed.

Mom was silent. She held both pants at her side, as if they were (ugly) flags. I had to get back to the table. The day was wrapping up. I grabbed the lounge pants.

"I'm sorry," I whispered. "I shouldn't talk to you like that. I'm sorry." I ran a hand through my hair. "I'm just a little tense is all." I took a deep breath. "I appreciate you getting them."

She lowered her voice a notch. "They're fun, Sweetie."

I rolled my eyes, went in the back stall the lady and her daughter had come out of, and changed pants. I tied the pants (yes, they tied) into a very big knot that seemed to ultimately only draw attention to the fact I couldn't dress myself properly because the pants were clearly too big. The pants pooled at my feet, which was saying something since I'd worn three inch heels.

I walked out and looked in the mirror. I glanced from my reflection to Mom's. She stood firm, her arms crossed against her chest. I knew her this way. My whole teenage existence she had spent pretty much wearing that exact look, locked in that same pose, unshakable.

"Okay. I think these will work," I said, touching at the fabric.

I look like I am going to the fucking beach, I thought. Or a pajama party.

Mom studied me in the mirror. "They look just fine to me. I always liked bright colors on you."

I looked at her, biting my tongue.

"It looks good with the black. I like the pop of color. You always wore too much—"

"I know. I know. Thanks for getting them," I said, opening the door for her.

"We can go to Red Lobster afterward if you want," she said.

It was her favorite restaurant.

"Sounds perfect," I said.

FAST FORWARD TWO HOURS LATER, AND WE'RE ALL settled into a corner booth at Red Lobster in the same mall. Dad is asking me all the questions that inevitably lead to what I like to refer to as *Potential Landmine Moments*. It's also worth noting that these questions haven't changed much since I was oh, seventeen. Here's a few of the biggies:

Still writing?

What's_____ doing these days? (blank = ex, formerly equaled ex-boyfriend, now ex-husband)

You thought about writing adult books? (Note: He doesn't mean X-rated erotica or anything. He means literary fiction. Something that would indicate I'd reached a level of maturity.)

When are you coming home? (Translates as: When are you going to stop living out West and move back to the South like a normal, responsible person?)

My dad never liked the path I followed. He wanted me to bring yet more tradition to our already very traditional family. He was especially troubled by my divorce, though he never brought it up directly; it was as if there was something undignified about addressing it. He needed me to fit in to his view of *how things should be.* He needed me to be married. He thought writing books for kids was childish of me. There was something not legitimate about it. And he thought Beaufort was the center of the universe.

Which brings me to Adin.

Thing is, Dad liked Adin when we were friends in college at OU. He'd met him during one of the Parents Weekends Mom had dragged him to. He shook hands, he took note of names, and I suppose he noticed a bit more, too. Like, who his daughter seemed to gravitate toward and who gravitated toward his daughter. Dad had liked Adin back then, or at least he liked him tolerably well. I assumed he still liked him.

"So, what's new with Tim?" he asked. (He liked to talk about Tim as if we were still married. It was his way of tricking me into thinking I was still married to Tim or could still be married to Tim.)

I took a long sip of my unsweetened tea. "He's really liking Fort Collins." I dipped a steak fry waist deep in ketchup. "He was at a reading not too long ago."

Mom leaned over Dad to get a napkin. "Oh! That was nice of him, Lil."

I took a bite of the fry and glanced from Mom to Dad. I had by then already formulated my own hypothesis as to why Tim had shown up in Toledo—it was his covert way of learning more about Adin. He'd been curious about him ever since our split, and all he knew at the time was that Adin lived in Ohio. And that I was giving a reading in Ohio. He thought showing up may present an opportunity to see Adin for the first time. Tim was smart. He'd been right.

"Yeah. It was nice." I continued. "Adin was there, actually. It was the Toledo reading. The two of them met, and it went well."

"*Lilly*! What happened to your hand?" Mom asked, reaching for my right hand. It was the hand I'd punched the door with in Tampa.

She turned my hand over in hers. I swallowed hard and let her run her fingers over my red knuckles.

"Oh, I hurt it in a kickboxing class."

"Kickboxing? Are you doing *that* now?" she said, looking from me to Dad.

"One class. In Tampa."

I took my hand away. She looked worried.

Dad looked up at me. "Adin? You still seeing him?"

"*Yes*, I'm still seeing him," I said calmly. "Mom didn't tell you?"

He looked at Mom. She set her napkin down and didn't say anything.

"I just thought he was in town, visiting last year. I didn't know you two were seeing each other. I thought you and Tim were trying to get back together."

I slowly shook my head. I hated how clueless he could be. I pushed my plate away. "Dad, I moved out. We're *legally separated*. The paperwork is going to be processed in the next week. What is this about? I'm happy with my life. No, I am *thrilled* with my life at the moment." I relaxed in the booth and crossed my arms. "Do you not get that? I wasn't happy. Now I am, and believe it or not, so is Tim!"

"Tim was a good guy," he said, reaching for a knife.

"He was a nice person." I agreed. "But I think we're beyond that."

"Lilly, your father's just concerned…" Mom said, raising her eyebrows at the word *concerned*.

"I mean, Dad, I'm sorry if I'm not creating the all-American family or whatever it is you're after."

As he looked down at this plate, I detected a smirk. Silence was deadly in my family.

"I always really liked Adin," Mom ventured, folding a greasy napkin and laying it on her plate. "What is it he's doing now? He was at a newspaper, right?"

I shook my head. He was never at a paper. Where'd she get that idea?

"No, he's a photographer. A really good photographer. He's moved in to my place, actually."

Mom leaned forward. "So he's there now? He's in Denver?"

"Yeah, he's in Denver now. We've known each other forever. We both want to make this work. He quit his job in Ohio and just recently moved in."

Dad was still silent, not making eye contact as he worked at his steak.

"Well!" Mom glanced at him and then cleared her throat. "So he's not here with you then?"

"No, he's in Denver."

"What does he *do* in Denver?" Dad asked scooting an empty Coke glass to the edge of the table, leaving a wet smear across the table.

"Nothing, right now. He just got there, Dad."

"Nothing? He moved out there with nothing lined up?"

"Well, yeah, he quit his job and he's living at my place. He's a photographer. He wants to do something. I got an email—"

"So he's out there. Doing nothing. While you're out working?"

"Dad, he's looking for a job. He's a great photographer. You saw the stuff he brought to Beaufort? The nature album? You liked it. You said it was good. Remember? The landscapes?"

Dad was silent. He glanced around and lowered his voice. "Your choices are *not making sense*."

I sat up in the booth, ready to fire back at him, but all I could do was sit there, watching the storm roll in. I was not going to defend myself or explain myself to him anymore. I was a grown woman. I waited for Mom to take up for me or to reason with him, but she never did.

⟨·⟩ ⟨·⟩ ⟨·⟩

February 22nd
Atlanta, Georgia

Lilly

from: Lilly Jameson
to: Adin Driscoll
sent: February 22, 1:10 a.m. EST
subject: Missing you (again)

Adin:

God I miss you. How many days has it been? Atlanta was OK. I'm headed to Grand Rapids soon. I can't wait to hear about how you are liking Denver. I know it's still cold, but look out the dining room window! I chose the place because of that view of the Front Range. What do you think of the mountains?

So you feel untethered, huh? Well, you're not the only one. My parents showed up in Atlanta and it was sort of like one bad thing after another. Mom spilled a bottled water on my crotch and now a lot of Atlanta kids think I pissed myself.

Also, there's a new picture of me on the internet wearing turquoise baggy velour pants! When the picture was being taken I imagined you were the guy behind that camera. Somehow, I think I know what the photographer was thinking. Probably some variation of *God, I hate my job* or maybe *Christ, what's she wearing? Stupid dork.*

But maybe the biggest thing I'm dealing with (and losing

sleep over) is whether or not you are happy. My dad made a comment at dinner that really bothered me. I'm trying not to think about it, because I've never been able to make him happy. I know I'm not crazy and you're not crazy. I'm convinced that as soon as I get there things will smooth themselves out.

One last thing—I could have sworn I saw a man who looked a *lot* like your dad. Of course, it's been years since I last saw him, so maybe I'm misremembering, but I know Arthur lives in Savannah and everything—and I hope to *God* that wasn't him—I was standing up frantically dabbing my crotch with a small pile of Kleenexes at the time. He was walking out. I thought I saw him trying to conceal a smile. I almost said something, but I figured what were the chances of it being him.

I miss you.

Lilly

☒ ☒ ☒

Denver, Colorado

Adin

from: Adin Driscoll

to: Arthur Driscoll

sent: February 22, 9:15 p.m. MST

subject: A possibly weird question

Hey Dad,
So I hate to be the whistle-blower here, but did you by any chance go to Lilly's reading in Atlanta yesterday? She says she

thought she saw you leaving right in the middle of the crotch-wetting incident (Well I hope you were there now, or that will sound very, very strange). At first I thought she was crazy, but then I realized it's a feasible day trip from Savannah. I know you do the food column writing thing now, so it's not hard to imagine you trying to line up a visit to some undiscovered barbecue joint next to a sneaky drop-in. So if you were there, this begs the question(s): *Why* were you there? And why did you not *tell me* you were there?

Denver is a bit of a mixed bag right now. I'm trying to stay positive with Lilly, but the truth is I'm really starting to wonder what I'm doing here. It's going to be almost another week before she gets here, and meanwhile I just eat corn flakes and watch TV and try to think of things that are worth going outside for. I make a real hard go at reading, but I can't latch my brain on to something for longer than fifteen minutes (except for TV, which is less of a latching and more of a distant orbit). I've applied to a few jobs, but I can't shake the feeling that Denver's going to be really unimpressed with several years of Family PhotoWorks experience. I want to go out and take pictures, even if it's only for myself, because hey, I'm in this totally new place, and it's so different and exciting etc. etc. But honestly, it's just cold and wet and dispiriting. I didn't realize it would be this hard to adjust by myself. Every day it's like this weight on my chest gets heavier. Just walking from one end of the apartment to the other feels like a marathon.

I told Lilly that I feel *untethered*, but it's worse than that. Untethered can be fun, under the right circumstances. It invites an analysis of risk-reward. But that's not what's going on here. What I really feel is lost.

I've never been fired before, and I've never uprooted myself for a woman, and I've never been by myself in a place that was so unforgivingly big and strange. I still have a lot of faith in your advice—your analogy of you and

Mom was probably a good one. But would Mom make you wait all this time outside the Pearly Gates while she was cavorting around with her agent?

It feels bad, being that harsh about Lilly. But it's true, isn't it? That is what she's doing. And she writes that she misses me and she can't wait for us to be sharing our lives here and all I can think is well, if you want it that badly why are you tacking yet another week on to your schedule? Why am I still waking up in this enormous empty bed every morning without you?

I feel ashamed now of the graceless way I left Columbus: shrugging off a job that's been good to me, tossing all my things in this crappy storage unit where pieces of the ceiling are now covering it like a layer of ash. When did I become that sort of man? I've always been careful, premeditating, thorough. What has possessed me? Is it love? Is this romantic—having thrown away so much of who I was before Lilly stumbled back into my life? You're the crazy one, Dad. You're the one who wooed Mom out of her van on the way to Woodstock, in the middle of gridlock on some Ulster County back road. I'm a straightlaced family photographer with a spreadsheet budget and three pairs of leather shoes. I am not *this*, whatever this is.

I guess I'm just anxious and rambling. Maybe I'm hoping I'll stumble on some wisdom alone so that you're not obligated to find it for me.

Adin

[◊] [◊] [◊]

February 23rd
Grand Rapids, Michigan

Lilly

from: Lilly Jameson
to: Nate Samuels
sent: February 23, 7:15 a.m. EST
subject: Book Idea

Hi Nate:

Just arrived in Grand Rapids. I need to ask you about the tour and some other things. I've wanted to get into adult fiction for a while now and I think I'd like to take some time off after this tour to focus on my life and to flesh out that idea a little more.

Also, Nate, I need to be at home right now. I feel terrible being on the road while Adin is in Denver. He has basically uprooted his entire life to move in with me and I'm not even there for him. I feel like the biggest asshole. If I knew you wouldn't be completely opposed to the idea of canceling the Grand Rapids events, I'd fly right back home. Is that in any way possible? Could I cancel? I know this is kind of last minute, but I need to be with him. I think he's having a hard time. I know you two didn't quite hit it off. I wouldn't ask about canceling if it weren't really important. If I could get out of the Grand Rapids events, I'd be happy to attend the Seattle events. I could go to Grand Rapids next year.

Anyway, about the book. I don't know what it'll be yet, but I want to figure it out.

I want to write a love story—maybe one of those love stories across time.

Please let me know ASAP if there's *any way* I can cancel the Grand Rapids events.

Lilly

. . .

from: Nate Samuels
to: Lilly Jameson
sent: February 23, 7:25 a.m. EST
subject: Re: Book Idea

Lilly,

There is *no way* you can cancel the events we've got planned. We've had ads on the radio and in the local newspapers. If you canceled, the *entire town* of Grand Rapids would think you're an asshole. I'm sorry, but we can't afford that. You *cannot* bail.

Adin will be OK.

I like the book idea. Keep me posted.

Nate

⊠ ⊠ ⊠

February 25th
Denver, Colorado

Adin

I HAD EXPECTED DENVER TO BE BITTERLY COLD and buried in snow. It was in the mountains, right? That's how mountainous areas are in movies and stuff. White as rice, cold enough to require long johns.

Here's what I didn't know about Denver: the mountains aren't under it. They're next to it. Which creates a strange sort of meteorological phenomenon called *orographic lift*. Essentially, orographic lift is when air is forced to gain altitude rapidly because of the terrain, which makes it get cold very fast, which raises humidity to 100 percent and then causes precipitation. The effect of which is that it might be snowing like hell right *near* Denver but not *in* Denver. And the highs in Denver are usually in the 40s in February.

For some reason, the labyrinthine streets of this city were not the thing that got to me. Neither was the altitude, which was wreaking havoc on me even if it wasn't drawing blizzards. It wasn't even the sheer magnitude of the place, the urban reach and the dizzying openness around it. It was when I read about orographic lift on Wikipedia that I broke down, because I realized as I read that I knew less than nothing about this place. Even my best guesses had been off base. I was a total stranger, and the only person who could let me in, really give me my formal invitation, make me a Coloradoan, was still gone, still out with this guy Nate. I needed her there to remind me of who I was now. Everything else had been lost or discarded; the only thing left was my love for her. Without her there I was eroded, nebulous, a ghost.

I didn't use the word *depression* when I wrote to Dad. Maybe I didn't even use it in the long, tortuous dialogues I maintained with myself. But that's what it was. That was what it had been in Columbus, too, only now focused, now intensified, given a tangible source and tangible implications. There was no way for me to know, living inside those days, what the real scope of what I felt was. That would take a long time.

I had with me the only two cameras in my possession now that I was no longer a member of the Family PhotoWorks cabal—a small Kodak point-and-shoot, bought on a whim at a Walmart in Kansas City, and my phone. I left them both on the glass-top coffee table in the living room, where they looked at me pleadingly through those long afternoons as I sat drinking coffee in my pajamas, staring out the window into the cloud-flecked sky. I thought about going out, maybe taking a trip up one of those mountains. The pictures would be low-res, and I wouldn't be able to zoom for shit without a lens, but it would be something to do. And I wanted to. My hands itched for it.

And yet, somehow, the days passed in increments of commercial break, one by one, without me ever moving. The phone I used to play solitaire and text with Tristan; the camera collected dust. I daydreamed a lot about getting a good shot of the city from above, some long view to the horizon that laid out the sprawl like a quilt beneath me. But there was something in the beginning of that process—getting on shoes, putting gas in the car, bracing myself for the stiff winds—that I couldn't stomach.

I satisfied myself that the venture would be useless without a *real* camera. It was ridiculous and juvenile of me to just drop $150 on a piece of hardware intended for birthday parties and pets and think that would be enough. If I still had the Nikon, the one I'd used in college, then I'd have reason enough to go to the trouble. If I only had the right equipment, I could spread my fingers out over the whole city and cradle it in my palms. I could make it mine, the way that Athens had once been mine. But the Nikon was at the bottom of a box somewhere in Savannah, laid up since my last year of college. Without it, anything I might manage would feel grasping and small, the idea of a photograph more than the reality of one.

I made only one attempt, in all that time, to take an actual picture. I brought the Kodak into the bedroom, where I'd arranged a small collage of items on the bed: my car keys, a wallet-size photo of Lilly and me from college, and, from a display in her dining room, a single long-stemmed rose with polyester petals. These I tried to get a shot of against the cream color of her comforter, hoping that the spread of natural light from the window would be enough. But Denver was stubbornly gray, threatening rain, and the room was both too dark and too bright, like someone had turned the contrast up all the way. The cheap point-and-shoot couldn't manage. The only light source was a bedside lamp, and no matter where I tried to place it, its too-focused incandescence ruined the composition. I probably snapped that same picture twenty or thirty times, only to finally look back on them all and wonder why in the hell I'd wanted to try it in the first place. I didn't do this arty, contrived shit. I did landscapes, candid portraits, found scenes. An all-natural palette. What had I thought I could do with random junk and a 60-watt bulb? The whole thing reeked unmistakably of *trying*.

I grabbed my hoodie and left. It was in the upper 30s, cold enough that I probably should have worn more. But I didn't care. My mind was on other things. I shuffled down her front steps and along the sidewalk, bracing myself against that breathless, heart-stopping wind. LoDo rose up around me, big hulking monuments of red brick and glass. They were like a pack of bullies on a prep-school playground, elegantly dressed but aggressive and mean. I felt small beneath them, provincial. I felt like a Midwesterner.

There was a sandwich shop three blocks away, the first place that looked like it might not take offense to my stopping there. I went inside, unzipped the hoodie. The shop was warm and small and smelled powerfully of bread. It was the first time since I'd gotten here that I felt the slightest bit comfortable. I ordered a turkey panini and a coffee, and ate in a corner booth with daffodil-yellow benches. When I was done, I sat there and drank my coffee, looked out the glass storefront, and tried to see if I could glimpse the mountains from where I was. But I saw only more buildings.

I was just skirting the edges of contentment when I noticed a couple sitting on the other side of the restaurant. They were finely dressed, like the neighborhood. And they were looking *not at me* in that way that was very much *looking at* me. The woman glanced over, caught my return stare, and took a sip of her drink. She leaned in toward the man and whispered. The man nodded.

I only had to wonder what I had done wrong for a fraction of a second. Then I remembered I was wearing my worn cornflower-blue pajama pants and my big black slippers. I wasn't dressed for the city streets. I was dressed for afternoon talk shows. I pulled myself further into the booth, but the damage was done, and the gesture served only to acknowledge my shame. The woman was wearing a thick, tan scarf that made her look throaty, like a domesticated bird. Her hair was long and satiny. She could have been a model in a shampoo commercial. She looked at me again, and then they stood and she allowed the man to pull her coat over her shoulders. They left, and I left, too, but not before I had given them a head start.

from: Adin Driscoll
to: Lilly Jameson
sent: February 25, 8:38 p.m. MST
subject: (no subject)

Lilly,

I have to be honest with you. Denver is kind of hard for me right now. I mean it's a beautiful city, and the mountains are just as majestic as they were in the pictures I saw as a kid. But it's just another bunch of city blocks without you here. I've been really down, actually, sitting here waiting for you in this place I know nothing about. I'd probably have gotten drunk by now if I knew where to buy alcohol.

I'm not blaming you. Please don't think that. I know that if you were here I would be sure that I had made the right decision. But it's a little murkier when I face it alone. I got fired and then drove twenty hours into the mountains, and now I just watch daytime TV and get weird looks from your trendy neighbors. I feel like I'm rapidly losing sight of who I am, and more importantly, who I had planned to be by moving here. I don't know if it's just that I need you, or if needing you is in fact the whole problem. Should I just be able to crawl through this existential briar patch solo? It's so hard to tell which end is up; these last couple of weeks have moved so fast my head is still spinning. I at least need you to hold the world in place for a little while.

I'm coming to see you in Seattle. I thought about surprising you again, but I've done that twice now, and both times it's not quite turned out like I hoped it would. I'll be there when you do the reading at the Elliott Bay Book Company. I'm hoping you can get your business stuff out of the way so I don't have to take a number when I get there. Maybe this is asking too much, but considering the sort of gestures I've been making in the last week, I hope you won't mind. I'm not sure what it is that I need from you right now, but it's something. Something important.

I can't wait to see you. I hope everything is going well in the aftermath of the crotch-wetting. Let me know if you can't do that day for any reason. I love you. I miss you.

Adin

⌖ ⌖ ⌖

Grand Rapids, Michigan

Lilly

from: Lilly Jameson
to: Tim Beals
sent: February 25, 11:13 p.m. EST
subject: A favor

Hi Tim:
I hope things are going well in Fort Collins. I'm wrapping up the tour. I know we haven't really talked much since Toledo—and that's mostly my fault. You know I'm the world's worst when it comes to getting back to people. I'm writing because I have a tiny favor to ask of you…

I know you and Adin talked in Toledo, and from what Adin has told me, you two got along well. Recently Adin moved into my place in Denver. Only, *I'm* not there. He actually quit his job in Ohio and moved across country. I'll be back in Denver in about a week, but he's having a hard time adjusting. He doesn't know anyone and may be spiraling toward depression judging from his emails (he's "trying to try to get a job"). I feel terrible about him being there alone and right now I *have to be* in Grand Rapids. I have a young adult series at auction this week and I'm a nervous wreck as it is. I just don't know what to say to him, and I *can't* be there. He needs to go out and explore Denver, but all he wants to do is sit in my apartment in his PJs watching *Tyra* while drinking coffee.

Okay. He *is* depressed.

Would it be possible for you to meet up with him sometime soon, you know, just hang out a little? I'm not asking you to be his friend. Maybe meet him at Starbucks. I wouldn't be writing to you if I didn't think this was important.

I hate to be the sort of person who only writes when they need something, but I promise you I'll give you a call when I get back to Colorado. We'll get dinner together. Did you ever close on that Amelia Island place? I did see the link you sent. I'd love to find a place like that myself. I'm ready to move back south. I think the Florida/Georgia area would be ideal. As soon as my life slows down some I'm going to start looking.

I just texted you Adin's #.

Lilly

• • •

from: Lilly Jameson
to: Adin Driscoll
sent: February 26, 1:10 a.m. EST
subject: Re: (no subject)

Adin:
I want to be there, too. The traveling ends soon. Try to keep that in mind. Can you please, please just hang in there a little bit longer? Soon I'll be back and we can explore the area together.

I just wrote Tim to ask him about meeting up with you. Before you flip out about that, hear me out: He knows the area like the back of his hand. He can show you around a bit. I feel like you're not getting out at all. I think it would do you good to try to find work. Don't you think? You've always loved photographing nature. Why not take a day trip into the mountains? There are guidebooks, you know. I don't know the countryside as well as I wish I did. I think there's a bus that runs from Denver to Colorado Springs and Boulder if you wanted to get out. It would help pass the time at least.

I don't know why you keep making comments about my neighbors dressed so fancy and giving you weird looks. I don't know what's giving you that impression. I don't *think* I live in an ultra-hip area. I think you should try to get on a schedule, go to bed at a certain time, wake up at a certain time, change clothes, you know, it might make you feel better.

I'm really glad you'll be in Seattle. I'm looking at my calendar and that evening I have a dinner with some agents and editors—would you be okay attending that with me? I think it's at a sushi place. Hopefully we will be celebrating a YA series sell, too. Should be fun. The dinner is after the reading. But you and I would still have lots of time together. Nate will be there (I know he's not exactly your favorite person).

I want to make this work. I want to make *us* work. But right now I need to be doing what I'm doing. It's my job and it allows me to have the life I have. I'll be home soon. At the end of the day I'm just happy to have you back in my life, no, *overjoyed* is more like it. I know things are not ideal at the moment. I hate knowing that you're there alone.

Did I mention I gave Tim your number? Please, please meet up with him. It'll do you good. Please trust me on this.

Lilly

⊠ ⊠ ⊠

February 27th
Denver, Colorado

Adin

TIM CALLED ME THE NEXT DAY.

"Lilly said you're having a hard time of it out here," he said, brightly, almost jovially. "She thought you might need someone to point you in the direction of a good time."

"Lilly told you that?" I was mortified. I felt like he could see me in that moment, literally, me in my pajama pants with my coffee and my cigarette. I had started smoking cigarettes again.

"Yeah. And you seemed like a good guy, and I know how crazy that city can seem when you first get here. You wanna get coffee somewhere?"

"What, like a date?"

He laughed. "Yeah, stud. Like a date."

I switched the phone to the other shoulder so I could smoke more comfortably. I could already see myself drenching the apartment in Febreze before Lilly got home. "Is that going to be okay with you? I mean, it seems kind of weird. Lilly asking her ex-husband to be her new boyfriend's playmate."

"Lilly and I have zero illusions about our relationship. We make great friends, but horrendous spouses. She knows it, I know it. I've got a former client now who likes to get bent over upholstered furniture. Especially suede. It's fine."

"Boy, you're pretty uh..."

"Candid?"

"Yes. Candid. That's good. That's probably better than the word I was thinking of. You're very candid."

"Lawyers are a candid breed. I spend most of my days saying everything except what I mean. I don't like to take my work home with me. How's eleven?"

I glanced at my watch. It was 10:08. "Where is this place?"

"Look out your front bay window."

"Roger. Eleven it is."

He was dressed like a lawyer. His cashmere coat was buttoned up, but if he had opened it I wouldn't have been surprised to see that it was lined with Benjamins. He had tailored slacks and Italian leather shoes. Even his steaming breath looked more expensive than mine. I had done my best to dress for the occasion, in the sort of outfit I had once worn to work, the sort I had, in fact, once worn all the time, before the age of spandex waistbands and band logo tees. But I still fell far short of him, and we both knew it.

"Good to see you again, Old Sport," he said, as I sat down with my coffee. I had ordered it black. I was kind of afraid of ordering a cinnamon spice latte in his presence. He had taken his scarf off and folded it neatly on the seat beside him, but his coat was still on. It was like it was part of his exoskeleton.

"Sport. The last time I came across that word it was from Jay Gatsby."

"The allusion is very deliberate, I promise."

"That's good. You came across so much more hip last time. I'd hate to think my initial estimate was so off." In college I had negotiated this sort of banter like a tennis match, and I never missed a serve. I wore wit like a snug pair of gloves. It was probably part of what first drew me and Lilly together. But it felt clumsy to me now. I had lost my edge in the years of isolation and creeping despair. I felt like I was taking out an old rusty bike and riding it down a steep hill.

"So let's be candid," Tim said after a long gulp of the same black-as-night roast I was choking on. "What's been eating you? Lilly seemed pretty upset about you when she wrote to me. She said your last email was a little pathetic."

"Really? She used that word? *Pathetic*?"

"Not exactly, but that was more or less the gist of it. Should I not have told you?"

"No, I suppose that's fair. I've told my father about it, but I've avoided dwelling on it much because I imagine his diagnosis would sound pretty similar. Something like 'No man pushing thirty should talk like you do.'"

"You're right. That does seem fair."

"Yeah."

He leaned forward. "So what *is* the problem? You seemed held together pretty well at the reading. I'd hate to think my initial estimate was so off."

Fifteen-Love, I thought.

"Yeah, well, the problem is, in Toledo I was on the offensive. That's always been my game, offense. Proving myself. Proving that when I say I'm all in, I mean it. I live in an age where most people don't believe me, because most *other* people are lying when they promise the things I promise. And I do well with that challenge, I thrive on it. But without it, I mean…I went to Toledo to atone for a really big mistake I made, and in a way I think I went to Tampa, and now here, for the same reason. I was driving down court. Now here I am, I feel like I've accomplished something of a slam dunk, and I'm waiting for the drive back to my own basket. Or my own end zone. Or something. And it's not happening."

"You're saying you don't feel like your efforts are being requited?"

I turned my cup around in my hands. It was sleeveless and hot as red coals, but I liked the feeling of it. "Is this conversation off the record?"

"I'm a lawyer. Unless there's a court reporter present, I think all my conversations are off the record."

"Except the one where Lilly called me pathetic." Fifteen-All.

He smiled, and it was a real smile, like he appreciated the precision of the jab. I admit I felt a slight satisfaction at it myself. "Yes, you're right. Except that one. But I promise, this one definitely is."

"All right. Then maybe. Maybe that is what I mean. Or maybe it's just that I'm no good at defense. Maybe I'm so used to the process of trying to win over that I can't see when the game is done."

"What gave you this impression?"

"Well, when I sent her that email, I told her I'd be in Seattle on one of her last nights. I wanted to see her alone. I needed some kind of confirmation that what we were embarking on was worth what I'd given up for it. And her response was to say, well, I'm having a meeting that night, you can have dinner with me and Nate and a bunch of publishing people."

Tim shifted in his seat a little. He took another big gulp but said nothing.

I leaned back, a little amazed (and, I'll admit, a little comforted) to see a flash of irritation. "Oh my God," I said, grinning in spite of myself. "You don't like him, either."

He took a long, slow breath. "Lilly and I got along really well at first," he began, "because we shared this deep devotion to our careers. I was just out of law school, and she was just on the hunt for an agent. We had enough space to live our separate lives but enough in common that we could come home at the end of the day and ask how it went and really give a shit about the answer. But once Nate was in the picture, it was different. It seemed like she couldn't talk about what was up without dropping his name. And I'm the jealous type, I have no problem owning up to that. I like knowing that someone I love belongs to me. So I started taking issue with this arrangement pretty quickly. It seemed like he was always finding ways to keep her close to him, to be the bigger male figure in her life."

"Yeah, I think I know what you mean. I feel like every time she's away from me it's because of him."

"Yes. I thought so, too."

"Is that why you guys got divorced?"

He laughed. "Oh no. No, no, no. We got divorced because being workaholics turned out to be the *only* thing we shared. Fighting about Nate was just one of our pet methods for dealing with it." He finally unbuttoned that regal coat of his and put his elbows on the table. "No, that's not what drove us apart. But I will tell you now: watch out for that guy. He's got a pretty good hold on her. I never felt like they were going behind my back or anything. Lilly's not that kind of woman. But I also never felt like the same could be said for him."

"I see." I glanced out the window. It was even darker out now, a heavy low-hanging sky pregnant with snowfall. It would be the first I had seen since I got there. I looked down at my coffee, still steaming like a hot spring. I wanted to be in Grand Rapids then. I wanted to be on her hotel room balcony, taking pictures of the downtown skyline. Taking pictures of anything.

"So is that all this is? You're just mopey because you feel like Lilly doesn't love you enough?"

I shook my head. "No, it's not that. I think she might be struggling with how to express herself, maybe. But that's just part of it. The part I've kind of latched on to. It's bigger than that. I'm just not used to change, you know? I mean, I'm from Ohio. I've barely even vacationed, much less pulled up roots and relocated my entire life. This is the first time I've been west of the Mississippi. This is the first time I've been anywhere that forces me to drive more than ten minutes for a Walmart."

"Homesick?"

"A little. Yeah. But also under the burden of a whole lot of new life experience, all at once. I'm sure I'll crawl my way out eventually, if I can just stop to see the bigger picture."

Tim shrugged. "What's the bigger picture?"

I thought about it for a second and then shook my head. "That I should have done this a long time ago."

"Done what? Moved in with Lilly?"

"No, moved in with *anybody*. Moved period. For any reason. Just...put myself in a situation that needed dealing with. I mean the last time I did that was..." I almost said *college*, but thought better of it at the last second. That was an entirely different conversation I didn't feel like having.

"Mm," he grunted. I glanced at him, and he was frowning down at his cup, fidgeting with the paper sleeve. Some of what had animated him a few moments earlier had drained. He now looked a little harried, a little lost for words.

"You do, too," I said, half-accidentally. I think I hadn't known until it came out that I was planning on actually saying it aloud.

He glanced up, startled. "Do what?"

"Think I'm pathetic."

This made him laugh, which surprised me at first, until I realized that that, too, was the sort of candor he appreciated.

"You do, don't you?"

"Um." He pursed his lips, crossed his legs. It was clear that he was waging a very small battle between politeness and pragmatic honesty. After a moment, though, he started to nod, turning up his palms. "You know, I...I guess I do, Adin. Now that you ask. It's not as though we're best buds here, so—sure. You're right. Maybe I owe it to you to be honest about that, given the circumstances."

"Well, thanks," I said—meaning it, somehow. "But you're wrong."

"Am I?" His eyebrows rose. Here, then, a challenge of the sort he had not predicted. I wondered what the score might be now and decided that it didn't matter. Because something had occurred to me as he talked. Something about being criticized so directly, so guilelessly, had changed the picture for me, turned it so I could see from a different angle. I wasn't sure how it happened, but I found that I now knew some of what to say in my own defense.

"Yeah," I told him. "You are."

For a few seconds we just looked at each other. His gaze was hard and appraising. I wasn't sure what mine looked like. Then, as though suddenly brought back to life, he leaned forward, started shrugging his way out of his coat. "All right, then. Do tell."

"You and me, Tim, we're two different categories. We are like apples and—I dunno, kiwi fruit. Pomegranates. We're good at different things. You're good at controlling your feelings, and I'm good at *feeling* my feelings. You've got a good job, you dress well. You know how to make people need you. You're like this other guy I used to know, Jason. He knew how to be needed, too. But I'm not like that."

"You're telling me," he said, smirking, "you're good at—if I may—*talking* about the things you want to do, as opposed to *doing* them. You promised Lilly the moon, coming here, but all you seem to have done so far is make her worry about you, make her feel guilty for not being here."

"Yeah," I replied. "Yeah. But here's what you're not seeing: most people wouldn't come at all. *You* wouldn't, I'm willing to bet."

"Goddamn right I wouldn't."

"I know. But I would. And let's be real here, Tim: I've only been here for six days. I've never made a move remotely like this before. And the woman I did this for can barely spare me a phone call. We have both screwed the pooch on this one. We moved fast, with no idea of how it would turn out. We're both doing our best and finding that our best isn't good enough, not yet. But that's fine. I'm *here*. It's not just talk I'm good at. If I fumble, if I come across as inept or impractical, it's only because I'm throwing myself into something very few men would ever consider. I don't care about the risk. I don't care about the possibility that all this will turn out disastrously. I know what I want, and I've come here to work for it. That's what I'm good at. Offense."

There was a long silence, punctuated by the clink of spoons, the hiss of the espresso machine, and the din of conversation both more pleasant and less consequential than ours. It was surreal, this moment, this stalemate. Tim looked at me, and I could see in his eyes that something had changed. Only slightly, almost imperceptibly, but there it was all the same. After a while, he nodded, a slow gesture that might have meant approval or pity, I wasn't sure which. Then he smiled, just a little bit of a lift at the corner of his mouth, and fell back against his seat.

"You know what you are?" he said, pointing at my chest. "You're a late bloomer."

I laughed this time, a bigger laugh, probably, than was appropriate. But hearing those words was an instant relief to me. It felt like he had shined a light on a tiny object casting a big, nasty shadow. Of all people, this guy, potentially my biggest detractor, had given me exactly the words I needed to describe myself. And this was always the best thing you could hope to come away from a friend with—a big, bold name tag. So maybe, I thought, that made us friends. "Yeah, I guess I am," I said. "I'm the chrysanthemum of men."

from: Adin Driscoll
to: Arthur Driscoll
sent: February 27, 1:20 p.m. MST
subject: Just checking in

Hey Dad,
I haven't heard from you in a couple days. I'm still wondering about you or your double at that reading. Write me back just so I know you're okay. I'm leaving for Seattle the day after tomorrow, but you can call me whenever. Just let me know how you're doing.

Adin

■ ■ ■

Tristan: hey stranger, how's colorado?
Adin: hey, it's okay. kind of lonely
Tristan: when's your breadwinner getting home?

Adin: couple days. i'm going to see her on the first though

Tristan: just can't wait? too in love?

Adin: something like that

Tristan: cool cool

Tristan: so I have news

Adin: oh yeah?

Tristan: oh yeah. remember viv? my uh…roommate for the last couple of months?

Adin: i remember you mentioning her a few times, yeah

Tristan: well…we're getting married!

Tristan: PLOT TWIIIIIIIIST

Adin: …wtf

Adin: i mean, congratulations, i guess. but really though, wtf

Tristan: i know, it's nuts. i'll cop to its nutsness

Tristan: but I don't know, it's weird, neither of us has really felt like this about somebody before. we thought it was just awesome sex, but she comes over sometimes and we watch movies and talk about our feelings and forget to even HAVE sex

Adin: you don't forget to have sex. that's not a thing.

Tristan: I know, I know

Adin: you don't talk about feelings either

Tristan: that's kind of a dick thing to say, considering how much i've had to talk about yours lately

Adin: well. okay, touché

Tristan: but anyway, we're doing it in vegas, baby. may 17th. tell your woman

Adin: that soon? In vegas?

Tristan: oh yes, on both counts

Adin: well that does sound more like you, i guess

[⦿] [⦿] [⦿]

March 1st

Seattle, Washington

Adin

I LOOK BACK ON THIS DAY WITH FONDNESS and sorrow, in measures so close as to be safely called equal.

I arrived at Sea-Tac in the late afternoon feeling more than a little proud of myself. I had made a full cross-country trip, from Florida to Ohio to Colorado to Washington, in a little over two weeks. Tampa had been disorienting; Denver had been agonizing. But Seattle—hell. Seattle was like a drug. I had spent so much time pawing my way through the fog of war that I was starting to feel at home in it. I took a taxi to the Grand Hyatt Seattle (*Did she have a discount with these people?* I wondered) feeling like an old salt, like this was just another port on my Magellan-like route. I sprawled across the back seat and gazed out the window at the buildings, several times as tall as LoDo's, keeping track of which would make the best photos. I think just knowing that I'd be seeing Lilly again so soon was a comfort to me. I was only a few hours out of the apartment and already feeling less suffocated.

She was out when I got there, so I had two scotch and sodas at the bar ($19.50—and somehow this, too, made me feel deliciously itinerant) and then called Tristan. He and Viv were planning a full-on wedding to be held in two and a half months, a nightmare that only they could have found enjoyable. "No Elvis Chapel whiskey weddings here," Tristan said. "We're romantics. We want to play dress-up."

Viv said she was trying to decide which bridesmaid dresses would make her friends and her sister look the most hideous. I had never spoken to her directly, but it was plain that she and Tristan were a match.

It got to be evening. I knew dinner had to be soon, but Lilly was still nowhere to be seen. So I politely inquired where the hotel pool was. The clerk gave me admirable directions, and I followed them to their indoor, heated, Olympic-sized, marble-edged behemoth, where I snuck in and used the neighboring showers and then changed into my suit.

I was back in my element. I was on the move, searching out this woman I loved so much. I was making things happen, not waiting for her to come to me. This was what I had been missing in Denver—purpose, a vector to follow.

I was feeling great until I got Lilly's text: *1401 Third Avenue. 8:30. Can't wait to see you!* My first thought was, *Am I her boyfriend or her BFF?* Who sends a text like that, knowing what I'm doing here and what I'm looking for from her? My second thought was: *Chill out. Don't be a baby.* My third thought was: *Fuck you, Conventional Wisdom. This is not what love looks like.*

And that was the condition I was in when I got to the restaurant.

I will say this: the food was really, really good. I had thought I'd be too nervous to eat, but as soon as I smelled the place, I knew I was dropping a hefty sum. Most of the other people were already there. It was a round table, and yet the place where Lilly and Nate were sitting side by side still seemed like the head. Lilly smiled up at me as I approached and pulled out the chair on her other side. "Hey, Honey," she sang sweetly. "I'm glad you came."

"Yeah," I said, smiling back. Just *yeah*.

When it came time to order, I gave the customary, "I'll be paying for her." But Lilly insisted that Nate had already offered, as a gift to celebrate the end of a successful tour and a *very* successful aversion of disaster following what they both referred to (quite confidentially) as *The Tampa Incident*. I tried to fight her on it but backed down quickly when I realized I would only come off as petty. I should say, though, it helped that Nate still had a little bit of discoloration around his eye.

The party assembled rather quickly, and for two and a half hours the conversation rarely diverged from shop talk. I heard the word *market* thirty-eight times—I know this because I counted, because that was the sort of conversation it was. I had nothing else to do. There was an older guy next to me who was fairly quiet the whole time, and I attempted to strike up a separate, less excruciating dialogue with him, thinking that perhaps he was as uninterested as I was. But I gave up when I realized he was using his phone under the table.

Lilly herself was affectionate enough. She kept her hand on my leg for much of the meal, leaned over and gave me a handful of little kisses on the cheek once in a while. But there was something reserved about her, something nervous. She was deeply engrossed in the jargon battle royale, so my time with her was limited. She asked me how I was feeling, and I told her better, and she said she was glad to hear it. That, along with my brief mention of the wedding and my casual invitation for her to join me "if you aren't busy," was probably the longest private exchange of the meal. Every ten minutes or so Nate leaned in to whisper things to Lilly that I couldn't catch. I tried to hear without moving my head. It was tough. I didn't pick up anything.

There was one amusing quirk at the end of the meal once checks were paid—the group broke like a football huddle. People made for their cars and their taxis so fast that the displaced air ruffled my nicely pressed shirt. It took about four minutes for the three of us to be left alone in the lobby.

Nate offered to put Lilly's coat on for her, but she politely refused, to my relief. "Well," he offered, buttoning his own jacket, "where to now?"

I glanced at Lilly and then back at him. "Well, actually, I was hoping we could get some time alone. I haven't seen her in a while."

Nate laughed, like he thought it was a joke. I think, in fact, that he really did think it was a joke. "But it's our last night of the tour!" he replied, with boyish enthusiasm. "It's our celebration party!"

I had expected this, which may be why I didn't immediately start losing my patience. "Nate, please," I said, as evenly as could be. "I have some very important things to talk about with Lilly. I would really appreciate some privacy. You guys have already had so much time together."

"Well, yes, I know, but—" He looked at Lilly, who was watching for a cab. "Is that okay with you, Darling? You want me to go?" I almost punched him again. I hated when he called her that.

Lilly frowned. "Yeah, maybe so," she said, after a pause I held my breath for. "I'll see you in the morning, anyway. We'll have most of tomorrow to have fun before we go."

Nate nodded. "Okay, that's fine. I'll head on down to Dragonfish, I suppose. I've been meaning to find some time to see it again while I'm here, anyway, and it's right by the hotel, so." He offered me his hand, soft in its black leather glove, and we shook. "Nice to see you again," he said. "Sans altercation."

"You, too," I told him, eager to be gracious now that he was finally backing off. He gave Lilly another big hug, tightened his gloves, and started off down Third. If his departure had been any more cheerful, he would have been whistling.

Lilly turned to me and smiled again, but it was a very, very tired smile. "So," she asked, "what would you like to talk about?"

AND AN HOUR LATER WAS THE WORST FIGHT we'd ever had.

It started out so well-meaning, too. She said that she was feeling a little exhausted from her long and hectic schedule, so we went back to the hotel room, where she washed her face and I absently read the TV channel laminate. When she came back into the room, she had her makeup off. I grinned, feeling like I was seeing her for the first time since the last hotel room, and went to kiss her. She kissed me back. It was just what I had wanted out of this trip.

Then I said, "So I decided to stop being pathetic."

It didn't take long to see that this was the worst possible way to start. At first Lilly was angry at Tim for betraying their conversation, which she insisted he had misrepresented. Then she was angry at me for using it against her—*like a weapon*, she said. I had meant it to be a positive opening line, a kind of adorably self-deprecating way of telling her that I was feeling better. But that's how these things go sometimes. The best intentions make the most colossal mistakes.

The whole thing spiraled fairly quickly. She accused me of giving in too readily to my emotional turmoil, and I accused her of not giving a shit, which (pro tip, boys) is never a good thing to tell a woman. It took five minutes just to convince her not to throw me out of the room, and even then we were right back where we'd started.

"What did you want me to do?" she demanded. "Those dates were specifically for damage control, damage that *you* caused. I wanted to come home, believe me. I missed my place, and I missed you, and you sounded so goddamned sad all the time. But Nate wouldn't let me off the hook, and I mean maybe he was right not to. I needed to get out there and make people forget about Toledo and Tampa. And you know what? It worked. *Swimmingly.* Things are hunky-dory again. And now you drop all of this on me, like I just didn't care about you, like you couldn't be expected to get on your feet alone? Did you expect me to throw all that out to come home and be your nurse?"

"No, of course not. I came to *you*, remember? I always come to you."

She shook her head at the ceiling, like she was imploring God for an explanation. "What does *that* mean?"

"It means that—" Too late I realized what dangerous ground this was. Tim was right: I really had suspected her of not loving me enough. And I had almost just told her that. But instead I told her, "It means that you don't seem to have really thought about what I've been doing here. I've flown literally all over the continental United States. I've thrown myself into a part of the world I've never even seen before. I've spent over a thousand dollars in just airfare." This was the unfortunately petty ending note of my argument. I hoped that we would be able to skip it. Thankfully, we did.

She nodded, leaning on the back of the desk chair, pulling her hair back over her ear. "I know. I know that you've done all that. And I appreciate it for what it is, I do. But how was I to know that you'd freak out in Denver? And how was I supposed to know what to do about it?"

"I didn't expect you to know what to do. I didn't even expect you to *do* that much. I hoped that you would have something a little more reassuring to say, something a little more like the way we talked to each other at Christmas. I hoped I could come up here and *not* have to fight for the slightest bit of time alone with you."

"All right, but again, you said it yourself. You signed on for this."

"Yeah, well—" For the second time I saw myself staring down the edge of a sheer cliff. But this time I knew, with the same sickening vertigo, that I had to jump. "Well, I didn't know what exactly I was signing on for."

Her eyes narrowed. "So, what, so you're backing out now? Two weeks later? Is that where this is going?"

"No, I'm not backing out, I—"

She shook her head and held up her hand for me to be quiet. "I shouldn't have let you come. I should have waited until I got home for us to sort this out. I have another meeting in the morning and then—"

"Lilly. *Stop.*"

I gasped quietly. At myself. Even Lilly's anger seemed to evaporate, replaced only with a kind of paralyzed shock. But this was a temporary lull. Now was my only chance, and I knew, even in my panic, that I had to take it.

"I know that this is hard for you to understand. I know that it is new and weird and you don't have answers for it. That this is not how Tim worked, how you were together. But it is how I work. This is what love is to me. Love is needing other people. And I mean that. *Needing* them. Love is when the world feels like a black-and-white movie whenever the other person isn't around."

She offered a little lopsided smile, trying to defuse me. "*Casablanca* was in black and white."

I scowled. And I was not a scowler. "Don't pretend not to know what I mean," I snapped, and this, too, was another small misstep, because her smile instantly gave way to anger again. But I was unmovable now. "This is a problem, Lilly. If you want someone who loves you like I love you, you need to have a better idea of what kind of love it actually is. Because maybe you think it's all the same, any man's love, but it's not. What I feel for you, what I felt when I was lying around wallowing in Denver, even what I felt in college, I feel it all very intensely. That's how I feel everything. Intensely. But you've gotten intensity mixed up with weakness, and I swear to God, if you do it one more time I'll be on the next flight out of here. You knew what this was in college, the whole time, and you know it now. If you're not ready for it, or not comfortable with it, or not... *whatever*, then that is your call and I won't burden you with it any longer. But now is the time to make that decision."

I had to take a breath after that. So did she. The room was so filled with silence that I had to sit down or risk being pushed to the ground by it. She just stared at me. I stared back, trying my best to look resolute and penitent at the same time. The silence stretched and stretched. She looked around at the walls, at the TV, back into the bathroom—the only light in the whole suite. I hadn't known until she turned her head to the side that she was crying. She had been hidden by the darkness.

"I'm sorry," I said, much, much more quietly than before. "I just—" I sighed. "Fuck. I just wanted you to understand."

She nodded and put the heels of her hands to her eyes. "No, I do. I think I understand."

"...Well then?"

She shook her head. "I don't know. I just didn't—" She gave a little huff of frustration. "I didn't know what to do with you. I haven't known this whole time. It's like one minute you're my prince, coming to sweep me off my feet, and the next you're this kid I have to babysit. I couldn't tell which one was really you. Not now and not in college. I don't even know if you're either one or something else entirely."

"And what about now? Can you tell now?"

She hiccuped, or choked, or something. "I—no. I don't think I can." She shrugged and tried to smile again, helplessly. She spread her hand around her throat, an old habit I recognized as her mother's. "I don't know."

I nodded, stood, and grabbed my coat from where I had thrown it across the desk. I was so close to her in that moment that I could have kissed her—and I wanted to. I would have wanted to no matter how angry or hurt I was by her. I would have kissed her if she had produced a large knife and thrust it right into my quivering gut as I stood there not looking at her. But I didn't. I took the coat and headed for the door.

"Well," I said on my way out, "you do now."

To be honest, I don't know if she said anything after that. To be even more honest, I wasn't listening for it. It didn't matter anymore whether she was slamming the door behind me or throwing herself down on her knees in the hallway and begging me to come back. There was only one way for her to know, once and for all, the man she had gotten herself involved with, and that was for me to leave the hotel, leave Seattle, leave wherever I needed to leave. All I could hear was the ringing in my ears and the sound of the elevator doors opening.

I was in the revolving door, struggling with my wheeled suitcase, when my cell phone went off. It was a number I didn't recognize, but the area code was 912, so I assumed my dad, from somewhere.

"Mr. Driscoll?" a poised, professional voice inquired.

I froze there, right there in that glass limbo. "Yes?"

"Mr. Driscoll, this is St. Joseph's Hospital. Are you Mr. Arthur Driscoll's son?"

My voice unraveled. The whole world had stopped turning. "Y-yes, yeah."

"Adin, I'm calling about your father."

I left the suitcase at the hotel. When Lilly got home to her apartment in Denver a day and a half later, I still wasn't there.

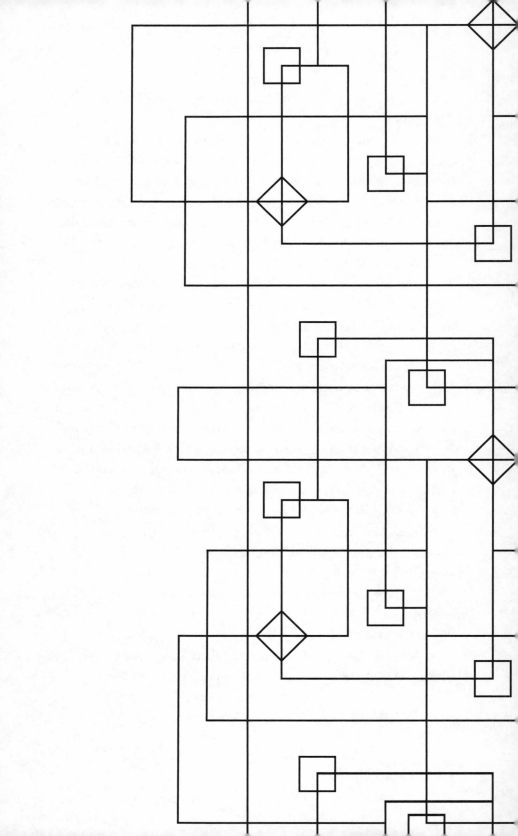

Part 2

March 15, 2003
Ohio University, Athens, Ohio

Lilly

"I THINK I'M GOING TO HEAD BACK!" I called out, glancing past the crowd for the door that led upstairs in the Sigma Chi house. The place was packed and someone had dialed up the bass on the main speaker system, making the whole house vibrate with sound. There was barely any room to move. Someone had turned the light out, and now only a cheap, plastic disco ball illuminated the room. The basement had become the place to be, as people slowly left the main floor to hang out where all the free couches were, along with two air hockey tables and a PlayStation with two controllers. Most importantly, there was also a boom box and a decent speaker system, which Jane and Tristan had been controlling for the last hour.

"You can't go back!" Jane said, climbing onto a chair. "Dance with me to one more song," she pleaded, her words slurring.

I ran a hand through my hair, wondering where Adin had gotten off to. I hadn't seen him since I'd gone to the basement to hang out with Jane and Tristan. I wasn't particularly crazy about walking across campus in a black tube dress alone at 2 a.m. Jason had gone upstairs to man the front door an hour ago, and I hadn't seen him since. He was gone a lot, actually, since he'd decided to rush Sigma Chi. I had tried to cut him some slack. I knew he wanted to pledge more than anything, and I was trying *not* to be the needy girlfriend.

I laughed. "That's what you said thirty minutes ago!" I took a step toward the door and heard something crack under my heel. The sound of broken glass and the smell of vodka wafted up.

"Careful! Broken glass!" Tristan said, raising the black boom box over his head as he made his way through the crowds, cranking the volume up on a familiar rap song and running around like a champion, high-fiving people. You had to hand it to him, he knew how to have a good time.

"Lilly, *come on*. It's nearly spring break!" Jane said, grabbing both of my hands.

"I have a *C* in Brit Lit right now. A *C*. I've got to ace that midterm. Plus, I have to work tomorrow afternoon." I knew Jane had no recourse there. She was at OU on a vocal music scholarship. My job was part time, but still.

"Are you going to walk back?"

"Yeah, I may stop at the cafeteria first."

She gave me a long look, and for a minute I thought she'd go with me, but then she quickly nodded and said she was staying. Tristan came to a stop near her, setting the boom box on a coffee table that had seen better days.

I leaned in and gave her a hug. "Be careful. Call me if you need anything," I said. Turning to leave, I slid a little on the alcohol and broken glass.

"Shit!" I said, surveying the floor that glittered with shards of glass.

"Careful, I got you!" Tristan said.

Before I could protest, I felt his hands around my waist, lifting me up like a bride. I shrieked, gripping his shoulder for balance.

"It's okay! Really, Tristan. I can walk." But he already had me in his arms, carrying me through the crowd, shouting for people to move out of the way (I believe his exact words were, *Out of the way, asshooooles!*). I wondered how much he'd had to drink. I was in four-inch heels and a little tipsy and Tristan seemed sober enough, so I relented. Guys clapped him on the shoulder as he brushed past them with me in his arms. Some girl from Health who never spoke to me winked as we passed. There was no telling what the campus rumor mill would dream up by Monday morning, I thought. Tristan carried me upstairs, through the foyer, and I tried not to feel completely embarrassed by all the hoopla.

He helped me to my feet at the front door.

"I think Adin's still around, somewhere," he said, breathless. "They've got Jason in the kitchen doing drinks."

I nodded and reached for the doorknob, feeling a cool rush of air hit me as I opened it. "Thanks. I'm okay to walk back."

"*Annnnd* that looks like him, right there, actually. Milling around with his camera."

I looked where he was pointing and saw Adin walking through the neighboring frat's yard, heading back toward our side of campus.

I said bye to Tristan and took off down the front steps, sidestepping a girl sitting in a guy's lap, an ashtray, and several discarded Solo cups. I slipped off my heels once I reached the grass so it was easier to walk. The ground was freezing.

"Adin!"

He stopped in his tracks, turning around.

"Oh, hey," he said.

I hurried to catch up with him.

"Aren't you cold?" he asked.

"*Freezing*, actually. I should have brought a jacket or something, but you know I always end up losing stuff like that at these parties."

"Here, you can wear my hoodie," he said, reaching to take it off. Without waiting for a response, he removed it. I caught a glimpse of his stomach and a few wisps of hair—it was a part of him I'd never seen despite all the times we'd hung out, even sleeping head to toe in each other's beds. I quickly looked away, rubbing my arms for warmth, and when I looked back at him, he was in a black T-shirt and jeans, his hair a little wild. I liked the effect.

Grateful, I put on the hoodie.

"Thanks. So, where you headed?" I asked.

"The dorms," he said, flashing me a look that was uniquely his—a soft smile laced with a hint of sadness or longing.

"Get some good photos?" I asked, pointing to the camera.

"I got one of Jason playing air guitar on an upturned crate," he said, flatly.

I laughed. "That sounds about right. Is it okay if we stop by the cafeteria really quick? I was going to get a coffee or hot chocolate. I wanted to get in a little studying."

He nodded and then looked behind me. "Sure. Is Jason not coming?"

I glanced back at the frat house. "He's managing the party," I said, smiling weakly. "He'll be there for hours, I'm guessing."

We walked in silence until we reached the cafeteria, both getting coffee, and then we went out and sat down on a wooden bench that faced the main quad. I laid my shoes on the cobblestone patio.

"I've *got* to get my hair cut," I said, gathering it all behind my right shoulder.

"You cannot cut your hair," he said, blowing on his hot coffee.

"Speaking of which, I thought I had a hair tie around here some place," I said, checking my wrist where I usually wore them like bracelets.

"Did you check the pocket of your dress?"

I looked at him and then squirmed a little to check my pocket. "What? Did I?" There it was.

"Huh. You were right about that," I said, putting my hair in a ponytail. "How'd you know that?"

He nodded and took a drink. "I thought you put it in there when we got to the party."

"Well, you were right." And it felt like there was more to say. Like the tiny moment that just passed between us was a turning point or a window into some question I'd struggled with. But I couldn't find the words. And I didn't want to say the wrong thing. I looked across the grass to the main library where a few small lights dotted the windows. Towering and regal, it was my favorite building on campus.

"Tell me why I shouldn't cut off all my hair."

"For one, it's amazing."

I laughed and took a drink. "Okay. I won't cut it then. *For now*. But this summer all bets are off."

"That seems fair enough. Still got to figure out the boat situation for our grand sailing adventure."

"Yes, we do..." I said, my voice trailing off. Our grand adventure seemed more and more like a fantasy. Where would the money come from? When I'd hinted at the idea to my parents, my father was quick to remind me that I'd need to work to help pay for school. "I've got to get through finals first."

He sighed. "They're only offering two photography classes next semester."

I relaxed a little, happy in the warmth of his hoodie. I thought I felt him shiver, so I scooted in closer. "The two creative writing classes were full when I registered. The creative writing program was a big reason I went to OU. Now what am I supposed to do?"

"Couldn't you just take a literature class?"

I hung my head. "I had to register for Children's Literature."

A smile spread across his face.

I elbowed him. "Stop," I said, trying not to spill my coffee.

"What?"

"I know what you're thinking!"

"It's just I didn't even know they taught that!"

I laughed. "My parents keep bugging me about the classes I'm taking. I had to send them my schedule I picked out for next fall. They wanted to *review it*. I feel like there will be some epic showdown when I get home."

"I'm sure it'll be fine. Maybe you'll like Children's Literature."

"You're lucky your mom and dad are so cool about photography."

"Speaking of which, my portfolio. I need to get a few pictures," he said, getting up and snapping a picture of the main building in the distance. It looked especially beautiful at night. I watched his silhouette move in and out of the moonlight. He took a couple of steps away and got a few of the library. I pulled the hoodie tightly around me and sipped on my coffee while he took a few more.

"You should come over this summer. Come down to Savannah," he said, settling back in beside me.

"You should come to Beaufort," I said. I knew he never would. My parents had met Adin, and although they liked him, it was immediately clear the three of them didn't have much to say to each other. Adin had been raised in Ohio. All of my family was from South Carolina.

"What would we do in Savannah?" I asked.

"We could hang out on the porch, get drunk, a little—"

"With your dad, of course. I love your dad. And your mom, too, if she wants to join in."

He nodded. "Right. Eat, drink, fall asleep in the swing. Wake up and do it all over again. I kind of love the South now," he said, an unmistakable bit of mischief in his voice.

I closed my eyes, imagining it all, relaxing my neck so it tilted toward him. "Can we just skip to the part where that's our life?"

He smiled that wistful smile of his, leaned forward a bit, and looked toward the dorms, holding the cup with both hands. "I'll skip ahead and you skip ahead. To the good part. To the part without finals, grades, having no money—we're imagining the future here." He turned to me. "Eyes closed!"

"Okay! Eyes closed. I'm imagining..."

"Tell me what you're seeing..."

I nodded along. I liked this dream. "When I skip ahead, I'm at the part where we live near the beach and have a porch, ideally..."

And it was only then that it occurred to me we were planning some dream life together. I opened my eyes. We were facing each other now, our bodies softly backlit by the tiny lights behind us. I could feel the mood had shifted to something tender and unexpected.

I looked away from him, focusing on the dark, silent quad. "So, in your mind, I'm spending the night? In Savannah?"

He nodded. "Yep, in my fantasy, you spend the night, so...plan on spending the night."

"Right! I'm sure Jason would love that..."

"He'll be in Michigan."

I burst out laughing and shook my head, amazed that he was saying all this. I nudged him, holding my cup with both hands and our eyes locked for a split second. It seemed like he was going to say something else, but he didn't, so I reached for his arm and we sat there, looking out over campus. It was a perfect night.

"Adin Driscoll, you are on fire tonight. First you tell me where my hair tie is, and then you ask me to stay *overnight* at your place."

"It's a good night," he said.

"Well, yeah!"

This made us both laugh.

Our laughter slowly died down and I was left with the uneasy feeling that came from living inside a shimmering moment you knew was ending and, when it did, you couldn't get it back again. How I loved our special bench, that tiny place in the world where we were free to invent our dream life near the water, on the front porch at the edge of the world. It was our greatest secret, that place—our meeting place. Or perhaps, I wondered, were we each other's greatest secret?

I hugged the fabric tighter around me, thinking about what he had said. I closed my eyes and breathed in the fabric, the pure scent of him. "A weekend in Savannah," I said, staring into the dark. When I glanced over at him, he had a look on his face that I'd seen before—one part longing, one part bliss. It was a look that I associated with a kiss—a look that might come before a kiss, perhaps—but Adin and I had never kissed. I was dating Jason. Others had seen the look, too. Jane had seen it. Tristan had seen it. Jason had definitely seen it. It said something Adin didn't have the courage to say. Or maybe it reflected something I couldn't say, something I couldn't admit.

But I wasn't sure, so I chose not to think about it, choosing instead to focus on how good it felt to be there with him, the sound of a far-off party dying down in the distance. I closed my eyes and leaned my head against his shoulder, watching the night come alive like a movie in front of us. Only there was nothing to see and everything to feel.

"This is one of the good parts," he said, leaning his head against mine.

"We won't skip it, then," I whispered.

❖　❖　❖

March 1, 2014
Seattle, Washington

Lilly

I TOLD MYSELF MAYBE HE'D LEFT SOMETHING DOWNSTAIRS. I sat there, convincing myself he'd be right back. It was as if the dynamics of our relationship had been reshuffled and I was still trying to play catch up. I dabbed at my eyes, occasionally glancing at the door, but it remained motionless. I realized that what I'd wanted to tell him hadn't come out right. I felt like I needed to apologize, and weirdly enough, I felt like he was finally starting to make sense to me. Like I was only beginning to understand who he was, which was odd, considering how long we'd known each other, but seeing his limit and hearing him out while facing that side of his emotional landscape helped me see the whole picture.

I needed someone to talk to. I knew Jane would be asleep. And so would Mom. I sat on the bed for a good ten minutes thinking about what Adin had said. I didn't want to lose him, but I felt like I kept crushing what was obviously there between us. Adin *was* needy. But he knew I wasn't used to what he was offering. Tim never seemed to need me the way Adin did. Since inviting Adin back into my life, it'd felt like I was slowly getting used to deeper and deeper water, wading out a little more each day. It was something that scared me, energized me, and tested me—all at once.

Was *this* the first serious relationship of my life? Why did the stakes feel so high? Why did I feel like my life was being defined by how I handled this? It had something to do with memory. There were many things about Adin that I cherished—he was romantic, sweet, and sensitive. But these were also the qualities I could only accept in small doses because I'd only received attention like that in small doses. Anything more than that was lost on me. It made me panic a bit. Anything more than that confused me.

I had always avoided needing someone the way Adin needed me, and I'm not sure what that said about me. I suppose the opposite was true, as well—I'd always discouraged that sort of behavior in my own relationships.

I sat on the edge of the bed, wringing my hands. It looked like Adin wasn't coming back. My mind drifted to mine and Tim's marriage, how it'd felt so vastly different. Tim and I had our own kind of fire—we were more like sparklers, dazzling in their own way, but never meant for anything higher or more grand. I knew what to expect. It was a tiny, beautiful thing.

Its smallness was manageable. Its smallness was what I understood.

But Adin and me? We were like a fireworks show you watch from a safe distance. By definition, we were never earthbound. But what happened up there in space among all that fire? I felt like I needed to know. But I couldn't know—that wasn't part of the deal. You get to see the explosions. You get to feel the heat on your shoulders and you get to witness the crackle of fire in the heavens. You can't know how it all works. You only know it does because you see it all around you. You see it in the air. The light spins and fights its way through the dark.

I was still fighting the voice in my head that was scared, worried, and nervous about us. I felt like I was on the high dive, frozen in fear, not ready to jump, but the adrenaline was there. I had trained for this. If I jumped, I'd make it.

If I jumped.

I put on my slippers and paced around my room. I looked at my cell phone to see if he'd called. (He hadn't.) I wanted to call him, but I didn't want to propose anything I wasn't ready for. I wanted to give him his space. I knew we both needed to calm down a little.

I'd wanted to ask him about Amelia Island. I'd wanted to ask him what he thought about moving closer to Savannah and Beaufort, since he seemed to hate the Rockies so much.

So much for that idea, I thought.

I picked up my phone and scrolled until I saw his name, landing on the text messages he'd sent in Tampa. After ten years of analyzing who he was and how he operated, there were still aspects of him that forced me to reconfigure my perception of him. He listened to his heart. Logic and reasoning took a back seat. He liked nature photography because he was among the few people in the world who had the patience, good taste, and purity to be a nature photographer, and he could somehow make it all sound fascinating. Being around him, you couldn't help but see his careful, clarified vision of the world as the one to aspire to. He was the most interesting person I'd ever met.

What Adin represented was perhaps the most intense, all-consuming romance of my life. He and I dwarfed every other relationship I'd ever been in. I sat there, trying to decide what to do next, quietly panicking. About twenty minutes had passed. It didn't look like he was coming back, and a whole new wave of despair rushed over me.

I remembered that Nate said he would be out late. I gave his room a call, and he picked up on the second ring. His speech sounded a little slurred. He said he'd just got to his room, but agreed to meet me at the hotel restaurant in ten minutes. I threw on some jeans, a black sweater, and my Converse tennis shoes. I walked downstairs and glanced around for Adin. He was nowhere to be found. Shaken,

I walked over to the restaurant and saw Nate give a little wave. I took a seat across from him. I noticed he seemed to be propping himself up on the table with his elbows. I wasn't used to seeing him without a bow tie.

"Christ. You need to eat something," I said.

"Ah, no, I'm good. Really. I'm actually on a diet. I didn't drink all that much."

"You are *not* on a diet."

"It's a cleanse. I meant *cleanse*."

"What kind of cleanse involves heavy drinking?"

"It was mostly hard liquor."

I shook my head. "You clearly *did* drink that much. Drink some water at least."

"Just don't order anything that will tempt me."

I ordered the mozzarella sticks and two waters with lemon. I turned back to him. "Well, Adin sort of just gave me an ultimatum. I think that's what it was. He left. He said I shouldn't confuse intensity with neediness."

Nate looked confused. "What? He just left? He left *the hotel*?"

"I guess. I'm just trying to figure out what to do. I feel like such a dumbass. I'm worried that I do think he's needy and, if I really think that, then that means we're doomed or something. Like, I'll never understand him. I mean, I messed up, didn't I?"

Nate sighed and ran his fingers through his hair and adjusted his glasses. He looked perplexed, as if I'd just delivered a philosophical discourse on existentialism in twentieth-century German literature— *in* German. The waiter brought us some water and then delivered the mozzarella sticks. I grabbed the first one, and then Nate sighed and reluctantly ate one, too. He relaxed in his chair. "Well, I think Adin needs to understand your career. Did he even congratulate you on what happened at the book auction?"

I shook my head and finished off a mozzarella stick. "No. That's not really on his radar, you know? It matters, but it doesn't matter."

He laughed. "It matters a hell of a lot, Lilly!"

I nodded along just to pacify him. Nate and I hadn't been on the same page since Grand Rapids. I felt embarrassed for asking about bailing in the first place, and he'd seemed irritated that I'd even propose such a thing. I'd felt like I'd gone from being one of his favorite clients to someone he had to keep a close eye on. But the auction had changed his tune, at least for the moment.

I picked my water glass up and looked away, not happy with where the conversation had gone. "He doesn't care about all that, Nate. He cares about everything but that. And I don't think I've been able to grasp that or appreciate it."

"Well, he ought to care about *all* of it, Lilly. He should be really proud of what you've done, not running away over some petty difference. I'm not sure he really...*values*...you."

I shot him a look. "You don't think he *values* me? What do you know about that, really? He moved across the country for me. He uprooted his life for me. He is the best friend I've ever had. And you don't think he *values* me?"

"*Lilly*," he said, motioning for me to lower my voice. "I didn't mean it like that. I'm just saying he should give you a little credit here."

I considered the idea. "He's given me all the credit I deserve, I'm afraid."

He raised a hand in the air. "Frankly, I don't think he has, but I'm just trying to be helpful," he said slouching in his chair, his eyes red and tired. "Jesus Christ, what time is it?"

"You need to go to bed. You're really struggling over there."

Nate shook his head and took a big drink of water. "I'm doing great. I just got a promotion. Did I tell you that?" he said, a sleepy grin spreading across his face.

"What? Really?" I asked.

"Associate agent!"

"That's amazing!"

"No, you're the amazing one. You kind of made my career. You helped give it focus. I knew your auction would be make or break for me, but it couldn't have gone better, Lilly. So, yeah, I had a couple past my limit."

"Only a couple?" I said helping him out of his chair.

"All right. Maybe a *little* more, but—it's been such a great week. And we're all *leaving* tomorrow. God knows when I'll see you again," he said, propping himself against a large column while I went to pay.

I walked by the table to make sure we hadn't left anything and noticed his phone. I picked it up and saw it was just after 2 a.m. The place had totally cleared out, and the lobby was now vast, spacious, and even more echoey. I draped one of Nate's arms over my shoulder and walked us to the elevator.

He laughed. "Don't you ever overindulge? You should be celebrating tonight."

I sighed, shifting his weight. "I'm ready to go home," I said, as we got in the elevator.

"You work too hard," he muttered.

"That's what they say."

"Are you on my floor?"

"Fourteen?"

"Yeah."

"Okay." I pressed the button for our floor. The doors closed.

I felt him sliding away from me, slouching onto the floor. "Oh, I really want to lie down. I think I'll take a little nap while we wait," he said, sinking onto the red carpet.

"No. Nate, come on." I bent down and grabbed his hands. I knew the time change had to be getting to him. I was trying not to laugh, but I had never seen him so drunk. And I *was* happy for him, despite how annoying he was getting. "Come on, seriously. Get up." I took both of his hands and he started laughing, swatting me away, reaching for the steel bar above his head.

"This is what happens when you leave me to my own devices!" he said, breaking free of me. "But Adin had to steal you away."

I rolled my eyes, assuming he was making a joke. I bent down to help him back up. But he pulled me to him, putting both hands on my cheeks and kissed me. *Hard*. It was not an afterthought kiss. It was not a peck on the cheek. It was more like the *I've-been-meaning-to-do-this-for-ages-and-now-I'm-drunk-enough-to-try-it* variety.

"Whoa!" I said, frantically going for his hands. I fell backward, catching myself with the palms of my hands on the floor. I scrambled to get up, trying not to trip on him.

"What do you think you're doing? Why would you even *try* that?"

"Lilly, I—" he reached for the bar to steady himself.

"I trust you, Nate—with everything. You can't just..." I felt the elevator slowing down. I got as far away as I could in the small space we were in and watched as he smoothed his shirt, clearly trying to balance himself and mentally grasp what he'd just done.

"Lilly, I'm sorry," he said, getting to his feet. "Jesus," he turned toward me. "I'm really sorry." But he was sloppy drunk. He tried to manage a thin laugh, but the flush of his cheeks told me he knew how out of line he was.

I got as far away from him as I could get, waiting for the elevator to reach our floor. He pulled a similar stunt two years ago, practically the same week we started working together. It had happened near his office in New York. Tim and I had been in town for the weekend for New Year's, and I had decided to drop by his office to put a name with a face. Nate was new to the job back then and had taken me out for lunch. During the course of the meal, he had put his hand on top of mine—a small thing, really, but at the time it had set off a quiet alarm. Yet it was not one I was willing to listen to because he was Nate Samuels, after all—an up-and-coming agent at a very prestigious agency. I was young, still trying to get a sense of what was normal behavior and what wasn't.

When I jerked my hand away, he had quietly apologized. The incident hadn't come up since. It was like we had decided to block it out, but something like that never gets blocked out entirely. It had become this weird moment between us, and I had never told Tim. Tim would have said, *Dump the douchebag*. But Nate was not a douchebag. He sent me flowers on publication day. He sent elegant, handwritten cards on my birthday. He had a PhD in American Literature from New York University, and he'd worked as an assistant for five years before getting this promotion. He'd been featured on magazine covers as the sort of agent other agents should emulate. In short, he was anything but stupid. I owed much of my success to his unique brand of genius. I knew that.

And so he had a few tragic blind spots.

I wasn't sure how to deal with the last two minutes. In all likelihood, he wouldn't remember it. He was drunk. And I hated him right then for that—for the awful shame I would inevitably feel whenever I thought back on his promotion and Seattle and the night Adin left me. There would always be the moment I'd wish hadn't happened—but *had happened* because of his carelessness. I didn't bother trying to understand where the idea of kissing me came from. Nate could occasionally act foolishly, but you'd never know it by his tailored clothes, his Italian suits, and silk bow ties. He was the portrait of a young New York Literary Hero. Truth be told, I wasn't interested in knowing whether he was attracted to me or not. I didn't want to know.

I had always been either deeply interested in a guy or not at all interested. There were very few exceptions, very little gray area. I either fantasized and imagined a guy constantly—(usually over the span of years), or I wasn't interested at all. As a rule, I never dated *anyone* I wouldn't consider marrying. I just felt like anything else was a waste of time. It didn't matter if the man was undeniably great looking (and yes, Nate was). I had never been interested. The idea of being anything more to him than a client never entered my mind.

I stared up past the large steel doors, fuming mad, watching as each floor became illuminated, mentally hurrying it along. "Nate. I don't know how drunk you really are, but if you say or do anything that could be remotely interpreted as an advance *ever again,* we're through," I said, glancing his way. The elevator came to a stop.

"Fair enough," he muttered. "I'm sorry, Lilly," he said, letting me pass him on the way out.

"Okay. Good night."

"Congratulations, again," he said as the doors closed.

I rolled my eyes. "Good night."

I headed back to my room in a daze and checked my phone. No missed calls. I put on my flannel pajamas and crawled into bed. Adin was right about Nate. He had reasons to be jealous and a little insecure. I imagined how I'd react if the situation were reversed. What was I doing? Why was I still debating whether or not I was ready to commit to Adin? I was already devoted to him. He was the first thing I thought about in the morning and the last thing I thought about before I went to sleep, but I'd never told him that, had I? I made a mental note to someday just let him know. He was the real thing. I kicked the sheets off my legs, flipped on the reading lamp, and sat up, propping my back against the headboard, thinking it all through.

I knew what I had to do.

from: Lilly Jameson
to: Adin Driscoll
sent: March 2, 7:15 a.m. PST
subject: Hey

Adin:

I am really, *really* sorry for the way I acted. You weren't being a child. You were being honest and speaking truthfully about your needs. I'm starting to think that I am the child in this relationship, not you. When you left me in that hotel room I expected you to walk back in, tell me we'd work things out, and that everything would be okay. I've basically been sitting around wondering where you went. I take it you're still in Seattle? Could we meet up?

I want you back in my life. I realize that it *was* your intensity that provoked all these same fears in me when we were at OU together. The way you looked at me back then is the same way you look at me now. And I suppose that eighteen-year-old me is still in there, still backing away from that cliff, but what's changed is that I'm ready to take the risk and allow myself to do the crazy free fall with you. I've spent way too long revisiting the *what if* question when it comes to you and me.

I say we go back to Denver together and pretend like the fight didn't happen. Do you think that's possible? I still have no idea what it's like to wake up beside you and just be… domestic and mundane for a second. Is that even possible for us? Somehow we've skipped that part.

Lilly

◈ ◈ ◈

Atlanta/Savannah, Georgia

Adin

I FLEW TO GEORGIA WITH ALL THE BAGGAGE in the world and not a single suitcase. The irony occurred to me before I even boarded the plane, but I couldn't take the time to laugh at it. I was entirely preoccupied with freaking out. I sat in my seat and tried to doze, failed, tried to read a *SkyMall*, failed, and tried to listen to music or to the German couple in the row behind me talk about EU politics, which really should have helped me get to sleep. But every time, the image of my father lying there on a hospital bed rose up before me and eclipsed everything else. I put my hand to my forehead and leaned against the window. I imagined what it would be like to climb out of it and fall, just fall for a while, get rid of all the mystery and the labor of keeping myself suspended a little longer, just bask in the certainty of a single outcome—*down*.

Atlanta was a tangle of metal and glass. Cars in front of cars behind cars wrapped around cars under cars passing cars, and all of them filled with incredibly angry people. But as soon as I was out of the city limits, I lost my anxious edge and found a sea of dull fatigue underneath. The drive to Savannah was around four hours, and I had to stop for coffee twice. Once the work day had begun, the traffic thinned nicely, but after that it was just empty, lonely road and scraggly pines and maples. My eyes were burning, my hands shaking. I thought I might have a heart attack, too.

Did I think about Lilly on the way, somewhere in that haze of terror over Dad? Yes, I did. A little. Mostly in anger or resentment, but occasionally with tenderness and longing. I hadn't wanted to leave, after all. But I knew, even now, that things with her would have been impossible if I hadn't. She needed to know exactly where we both stood. It was possibly the first time that I had done something in the exact moment I knew it needed doing, and I was grateful to myself for that. I had pulled through in the clinch. The rest of it was on her. It was her job, now, to do the proving.

But I still needed her, just the same. Desperate for something calming to think about, I allowed myself this brief fantasy where I walked out and she *did* come after me and convinced me to stay and led me back into her room and just stood there with her head on my shoulder, silent, weepy, exquisitely relieved. I would have crumpled in her arms like a marionette, I think, if she'd done that. But she didn't give me the chance, and I was grateful for that, too.

St. Joseph's made me think of Frank Lloyd Wright if he had built a theme park. I wound through a labyrinth of identical hallways, stopped to ask for directions three times. I ended up on the wrong floor once. It took fifteen minutes from the time I walked in the door to make it to my father's hospital room. I was breathless, sweaty in my coat, which was far too heavy for a heated building in the middle of the South.

The first thing my father told me when he looked up from his newspaper was, "Jesus Christ, kid, you look worse than I do."

The whole thing, I quickly learned, was not as dire as I had expected. He'd admitted himself for symptoms resembling a mild heart attack twelve hours ago. He'd gone into surgery before they ever called me, and he had insisted that they not bother me with the news until everything was okay again. But the hospital, thinking it was sidestepping a legal trap, would only tell me, "Your father went into surgery for a heart attack. He's still in intensive care." And that was it. I imagined him unconscious, breathing with one of those big pump things next to him, with that terrorizing heart monitor beep. Instead he was sitting up in bed with the curtain pulled wide and the sunlight pouring in. It was a startling change from the scenery in Seattle. He was drinking orange juice from a little plastic cup. He looked like he was having fun.

"You know Atlanta started spring training this week?" he asked, holding the paper out for me to see, as though I might want to come and read for myself. "I forget how early it comes, every year. Playing the Tigers on...Thursday." He put his glasses back on and went back to reading. "I got high hopes for the poor bastards. If they could have played anybody but San Francisco last year..." He shook his head, trailed off, and got lost in the article again.

"Dad," I started. He looked up, questioning. "I just flew here from Seattle. *Seattle.* I've been up all night losing my mind over this. Can we talk a little bit, before I leave you be?"

He nodded vigorously, folding the paper down and tossing it on the bedside table. "Yeah, yeah, sure. Sorry, I forget that you weren't here to see how small an issue it all was."

"Dad, it was a heart attack."

Shrug. Then he got this funny look on his face, like I'd offered him cat food for breakfast. "What the hell were you doing in Seattle?"

"I went there to see Lilly, try to keep things from falling apart."

"That sounds dramatic."

"It was, in fact, one of the more dramatic experiences of my life. I left her without saying goodbye."

He took the glasses off again. They were on a chain, the way old people wear them. I so rarely thought of my father as an old man, but here he was, sixty years old, staring down retirement. It made me feel old, looking at those glasses, at the deep jowly creases of his mouth, at his baldness, which had become impossible to conceal. He was the kind of man who had heart attacks now. "You did *what*?"

"She gave me a hard time about my reaction to Denver. She thought I was being a baby about it."

"You *were*."

"Yeah, but not the way she meant it. She was afraid of me for even moving there in the first place, I think, and when I told her that I needed her there with me to make it all real, make it all make sense, she tried to shrug me off for work. So I followed her to Seattle. She mostly ignored me the whole time, and then she went off on me for asking her to actually appreciate how much I was giving up for her. I told her that she had me confused with some kind of weakling, when in fact my only weakness was her. And then I walked out. And then the hospital called."

"And you left. Without telling her." He looked gravely disapproving.

"Yeah. I'm not sure she knows whether I'm still in the same city as her."

There was a knock on the door. I turned, realizing for the first time that I was still standing there in my coat. A young nurse came in with a clipboard and a stethoscope. "Good morning, Mr. Driscoll," she sang, in that lulling Southern drawl my dad was always so nuts about.

"Morning, Therese," he greeted her, and I was embarrassed to hear a little bit of the flirt in his voice. "You do me that favor yet?"

Therese grinned, and he grinned back. They grinned together, like longtime friends and conspirators. "I talked to Dr. Jackson," she said, "but they're very adamant. Heart surgery patients don't get morphine."

"Oh, come on. I know they're probably sitting on a ton of that shit. They can spare a few drops. My insurance is probably paying for Jackson's new kitchen."

"Rules are rules are rules, Arthur."

"Yeah, yeah." He suddenly noticed me again. "Hey, Therese. This is my son Adin. He flew across the country at two in the morning just to find out I'm not dead."

Therese turned and shook my hand. Her eyes were big and brown, and her smile was like a toothpaste commercial. "It's good to meet you, Adin. I promise, we're all just as relieved as you are."

"I appreciate it." I sat down, finally, and waited for her to finish checking him out, prodding and asking questions and counting seconds on her watch. He overacted when the stethoscope was cold against the flesh of his chest. Therese shook her head and gave me this look like, *Do you know what to do with him?*

When she was gone, he shook his head wistfully after her. "The women are better in the South. Don't let 'em tell you differently." This was a strange thing to hear out of his mouth, considering he had moved here to be with Mom. But that was my father. Deep down, under the gray hairs and the plaid dress shirt, beat the lucky, lucky heart of a frat boy. "You should call her," he said.

"Who? Therese?"

He nearly spit his orange juice. "Ha! You wish. Lilly, you ass."

"No. She calls first."

"What is this, high school now?"

"Call it what you want. But she knows she pegged me wrong. She knows what she means to me. It's her turn to make the effort. She needs to figure out whether that's important enough to give up a little security for." I was suddenly incredibly thirsty. I hadn't had anything since the wine at dinner and the coffee on the road. "You got a Coke machine around here?"

He offered me his orange juice. I'm not a big fan of drinking after people, but I was desperate. I took a sip. It tasted like the hospital. Everything you eat or drink in a hospital always does. "So I'm guessing you need to stay with me for a little while," Dad said, watching me choke it down.

"No, no, no," I said, palms up in protest. "You don't need me taking up all your space."

He regarded me with a hint of irritation. "You've seen the size of my house. I'd barely notice you were there."

"Thanks a lot, Dad."

"You know what I mean."

I nodded, smiling. "I do. I'll think about it."

I THOUGHT ABOUT IT, AND IN THE END I couldn't quite convince myself I didn't like the idea. Dad had over the last couple of years hinted, in his proud way, that he was lacking for company these days, and besides, I missed the warmth. Until I visited Lilly over the Christmas holiday in Beaufort, I hadn't been this deep in the South since I was a kid, when he and Mom and I took trips here every summer (coming to see her before she died didn't seem to count). That week it was sixty-five degrees in Savannah, and I wanted to feel the air on my forearms again. Plus, I needed to be close to someone for a little while. I couldn't face what was going on inside me in a hotel room.

So, at twenty-nine years old, I moved back in with my father. I slept in my old bed, which he had moved into the third bedroom along with all my other old stuff. I woke up every day for the next week feeling like I was a college freshman again, home for spring break. That first afternoon I texted Lilly to let her know where I was and why, but after that I tried to put her out of my mind. And for the most part, that's exactly what I did.

The mornings were all nearly identical: I got out of bed and went downstairs where Dad was already having breakfast and watching TV. I had two cups of coffee with him, gave him a daily installment on my life in the past several months, mostly Lilly, and then I went upstairs and showered. I put on jeans and a T-shirt, the same ones I wore ten years ago, and maybe a windbreaker, some sneakers. And I went outside and took a walk around.

Up Juniper, across Windsor over to Bridlewood or King Palm.

It was so *alive* everywhere, so warm—not just the temperature but *everything*. Not like Denver. Everything was smaller. Here there were more trees than people. Everybody was dressed like me, and some of them told me hello with that same slow honey sound as Therese.

What happened to me in those few days happened slowly, but by the end it felt like it had come on all at once. For the first time in God knows how long I was bound by nothing. Not by Columbus, not by Family PhotoWorks, not even by Lilly. It was like she and I were both divorced now, she from Tim and me from the nagging conviction that I was *doing it all wrong*. For Savannah, for my dad, there was no wrong. There was no right, either. Both of them just let me be.

Which, of course, was exactly what it took for me to realize that I was, in fact, kind of sort of to blame for everything after all.

Sure, it was shitty of Lilly to leave me to stew in my madness for two weeks. It was a terrible decision. But not a cruel one. And was I any better? I had expected her to single-handedly cure me of my ennui, but what was she supposed to do, really? It was my brain, my life. I could have done more, with or without her, than lie around hopped up on coffee and sugar and nicotine, debating the merits of a decision I'd already made. I could have gone out. I could have attacked that city, made it my own. I could have gone after that new life the way I went after Lilly herself. I could have taken some fucking pictures. But I had needed time to catch up to myself first, to catch up to what I had done and what it really meant. Time that I was only really getting around to taking now. I had discarded an entire life, from the apartment in Columbus right on down to the suitcase in Seattle. It was only here, in Georgia, that I was finally letting myself take a hard look at these facts.

On the fifth day I woke up with a single overwhelming impulse. I pulled all the boxes out of my two closets and emptied them on the bedroom floor. I checked under the bed, in all the dresser drawers. I ran downstairs in my boxers and bare feet. Dad was sitting in his recliner watching a network morning show and complaining about the female anchor's hair. "Did you put any of my stuff in the attic?" I asked.

His head turned a little. "Um, yeah, I think so. Couple boxes up there, probably. High school books, other junk. You looking for something?"

"Yeah." But I was gone before he had time to ask what.

The attic was small and filled with air almost too heavy to breathe. Even in early March it was uncomfortably hot. I had to shove past the bones of an old treadmill and several crates of children's clothes before I found the boxes with my name on them. I yanked them toward me, tore them open, and threw the unwanted contents all over the attic floor. At the bottom of the second box, in quite literally the last place I could have looked, was my Nikon D1, gray with dust. I wiped it off carefully, removed the lens cap. The lens and the viewfinder were intact. Everything looked okay.

I left the rest as it was, ravaged and messy. When I came back down, I had a grin on my face so wide it could probably cart a mobile home up I-75.

"What the hell are you doing?" Dad asked, and I imagined myself as I must have looked to him—half naked, hair plastered to my forehead by sweat, beaming like an eight-year-old on his birthday. I thought about saying something good and trite, like, *Only what I should have done a long time ago.*

Instead, I ran upstairs and leaped into my jeans from yesterday. I didn't even bother to put shoes on. Then I came back down and said, "I'll be back," and just like that I was gone.

I started taking my camera with me on those walks every day. It had been a lot of years since I took a picture of anything more complicated than a metal-mouthed Columbus middle-schooler, and I expected the initial results to be embarrassing. But they weren't. They were kind of good, actually. There was one of an abandoned house at the corner of the subdivision. One of a car with "Seniors 2014" soaped into the rear windshield. One of a little park at the corner, just at the moment the rim of the sun slipped from the tops of the trees. I needed a better camera, for sure, needed to buy some new lenses and maybe a matte box, *definitely* a tripod and a mount. But what I was doing wasn't terrible.

I hadn't forgotten how composition worked. I could still navigate the camera's menu like the hallways of my own home. It was like riding a bicycle, except that the bicycle was some distant, untouchable corner of my whole being. The one sad attempt I'd made in Denver started to evaporate like a bad dream, those too-dark shots replaced by a growing collection of better quality work. Whatever had lived inside of me when I was a kid, it was still there. And it still wanted out.

When I finally got around to checking my email, I saw with a leap in my chest that Lilly had written me. I read it. I read it again more slowly. And then I went downstairs, just like I did every morning.

Maybe this was what was missing, I thought. Maybe the reason Lilly had thought I was asking too much of her was that I was. And maybe, probably, it was because I had funneled myself into a place where she was all I had, the only lifeline. I didn't regret going to Denver, not for a second, but I knew now that it didn't mean what I had wanted it to. It was romantic to believe that I had given up everything for her, but it was also self-indulgent and not entirely accurate. The truth was, what did I have to give up? Nothing. I was drawn to her because she was the absence of nothing. I'd pinned all my hopes on her and then scolded her when she groaned beneath their weight.

But I knew now that I didn't have to. For her sake and mine, I had to build my own house before I asked her to come live in it with me. So I went out, every day, and started laying brick.

One evening I came in from a long trip, three hours at least, and Dad was standing at the kitchen island, riffling through something. The nylon strap of his glasses trailed up from his neck. I glanced down as I was working out of my tennis shoes and saw that they were some photos I'd had developed that morning. Shots of Pulaski Square, green lawns and a marble monument, the steepled fingers of oaks.

"You've been busy," he said, still perusing, flipping the photos one by one over the stack, like a deck of cards.

"I have."

He glanced up, removed the glasses and let them fall against his chest. "You know, the day I found that camera here, stuffed down at the bottom of a box like some goddamned teddy bear, I honestly wondered if you'd ever pick it up again."

"So did I," I said, nodding.

"I was mad, too. Let me tell you. That camera was your mother's shining moment. She was so proud to be able to give it to you. And some parents spend less on cars for *their* graduation gifts."

I grinned down at my feet, a strange mixture of amusement and shame. "I know. I'm sorry."

"May I ask what precipitated its resurrection?"

The Nikon still hung from its strap at my neck. I glanced down at it. Dad and I were like mirror images, each with his own apparatus. "Honestly, I'm still figuring that out myself," I said, running my thumb over the shutter button. "But I know it couldn't have happened anywhere else. God knows I wanted it to. I tried in Denver. But there was something about being here, with everything else that's gone down in the last few months. I think I needed to go through all that. And I needed to end up here afterward."

Dad was quiet for a second, watching me. He picked up the pictures again and settled them into a neat pile against the counter. "These are good, kid. But sooner or later you gotta stop working *pro bono.*"

"I know."

"I don't mean that I mind having you here, of course. A second pair of hands is nice, especially when I've got a deadline coming up. But you're sitting in the corner right now. Sooner or later you'll have to get back in the ring."

I glanced out the sliding glass door to the porch, where the Georgia spring poured down like liquid gold over the yard. It had been a long time since I had given the world such a casual glance and found it thrilling, inspiring. I didn't shrink back from it; I wanted to go out and grab it up in big handfuls. "I will," I told him. "Soon. I can feel it."

⟨•⟩ ⟨•⟩ ⟨•⟩

December 15, 2002
Ohio University, Athens, Ohio

Adin

I THINK I KNEW BEFORE I EVEN ANSWERED the phone that she would be crying. She texted me, *can I call you*, and all the alarm bells went off. She rarely called, certainly never asked permission. It was usually me who called first. If she was asking, it meant she needed something. And if she needed something...

"Adin," she choked. "I'm sorry, it's just—Jason and I got in this big fight, and he went off with some other guys to..."

After that, all I could hear was the cadence of her tears and the sound of my own conscience yelling at me. Don't go see her, it warned me. You are better than that. You do not take advantage of vulnerable people. You also don't get taken advantage of when *you're* vulnerable. But it was the last day before Christmas break, and there was a sense of possibility permeating the school. All but a handful of us had already left for home, and the *rules*, whatever they were, seemed to have left along with them. The grounds were quiet, the halls darkened. The spell of the last semester, rather than being broken, was for one night amplified to the level of a lucid dream.

And so I grabbed my coat and hustled four blocks to her dorm. The doors were locked, and she had to come out through the lobby to let me in. Her face was still colored and puffy with tears, but she smiled when she saw me, and the smile was of the kind that made my chest collapse like rusted scaffolding. "Thanks for coming," she said, and I marveled at how anyone could conceive of this as a favor to *her*. When she hugged me, all sweater wool and hair, I closed my eyes over the top of her head.

Her room, a girl's room: great big cozy comforters, in white and pastel; photo collages of friends, many of them from that unknowable era of pre-college adolescence; scarves thrown over the arcing branches of the floor lamp; the thick, permeating scent of vanilla. Lilly's room was always darker than mine, always smaller, somehow, with the density of its objects crowding in. She covered up the concrete bricks with posters, tossed thick rugs over the tile, took down the Venetian blinds, and put up curtains. I envied her that ability, to make a home out of what usually felt to me like a jail cell.

There was music playing when we came in. I struggled to identify it—something moving, but not familiar. The half-intimacy of other people's favorite songs. "What is this?" I asked, and Lilly, sensing immediately what I meant, said it was "High and Dry" by Radiohead. I'd brought my own music, part of the duffel bag survival kit I now routinely took to her place. Toothbrush, deodorant, a book, some homework (ever the optimist, was I), camera, and a scuffed black Sony Discman. All these I lifted up onto the end of her top bunk, unhooking the great big headphones from the bag's handle.

"What did you bring?" she asked, and I, sensing immediately what she meant, said, "Ryan Adams."

"Demolition?"

"Heartbreaker."

She smiled. "Good."

We sat together in her bed, backs to the wall, shoulders brushing, burrowed beneath her covers (maintenance staff controlled the thermostat, and they'd yanked it down to 65 in anticipation of everyone's leaving). When she reached over me for the bag, to get out the Discman, to see what book I'd brought, it was like her body was everything I could see and touch for one moment—and then she was gone again, just a girl I knew, untangling wires.

I didn't ask if they were breaking up. I didn't want to know. And I also didn't want to give myself away. Not that she didn't know—how could she not know? But this was the sort of boy I was. Like a famous actor afraid of being caught on camera. In the end, she brought it up. "I don't know if we can even stay together," she said. "Not if he's going to be this way all the time."

"Yeah," I replied. Cool, noncommittal. The hazy solace of the unrequited lover.

"I just—I was in this really weird place, you know, and you were the first person I thought of."

"How come?"

She pondered this, lips pinched up and off to the side. "Because I knew I wanted to be alone and listen to music," she said. "And you're the only person who loves music like I do. And you're the only person I can be with where I can feel like I have company without having to put on a show."

I thought of Tristan, how he'd tried to berate me out of this vicious cycle I was in. I had told him about this, the last time Lilly had told me something to this effect. *That's not a good thing*, he'd insisted. *You only want to be with someone who will fucking try for you.* But I wasn't sure about that. I didn't feel obligated to put on a show for Lilly, either. It was one of the most valuable things we had going.

We sat in comfortable silence for a minute or so. Then Lilly hit the remote for her stereo, plunging the room into silence. She put the headphones on, and kind of left me behind for a little while. I leaned over and checked the display, saw that she was on track 14. "In My Time of Need." Naturally. It was an odd experience, being stuck out here in this quiet room while she was swimming in the music, eyes closed, chin bobbing. But it was pleasant, too. Like watching someone through a one-way mirror. Lilly, with all the barriers torn down, all her public faces wiped away like too much makeup. I wished I had the sort of headphones where we could each take one.

It was almost the end of the song before I got the idea to take a picture. But I had to be fast, had to catch her off guard. I took out the camera and left off the flash (eyes still closed—I could totally get away with it). But she must have sensed my movement, because no sooner had I snapped it than she opened her eyes and gave me that look, that head-tilted, eyebrowsy look. I grinned bashfully, made a palms up gesture—*You got me!*—and returned the camera to my bag.

She took off the headphones. I thought she would say something angry, something about how now was a bad time for that shit, but instead she said, "Why do you think music does this to us?"

"What?"

"Why do you think that on days like this it feels like there's nothing I can feel on my own that's not better with music? I just feel *more* if I mix it up with a song, like a big fancy cocktail."

I stretched my legs out over the edge of the bunk, staring up in thought at the ceiling tiles. What I wanted to say but didn't was, actually, that was more or less every day for me. "I think music is just someone else's feelings distilled. Like, boiled down to some essential essence, this crazy dense little ball of a person's life. Whole years made into three and a half minutes. And the best songs are the ones where the feelings you're balling up are the sort everyone else has had. Anybody can listen to it and know exactly what it means. It's like it's plugged straight into their own heart."

"Okay," Lilly said, shrugging. She was running her finger along the hard plastic arch between the speakers. "So why do I feel like this when I listen to it?"

"Because—because being sad is one of the few times in your life that you don't feel obligated to rein in whatever you're going through. Usually we all think we have to keep our emotional shit in line, our excitement or anger or—well, our love, I guess. Except when we're desperate. Then all that time spent holding ourselves back has to be made up for. Then we can't possibly have *enough* feeling. We could just pour as much of it into ourselves as possible and never be full. And then along comes music, which is basically built just to pour in a lot of emotion really quickly. It's made by people like that, for people like that. It's a big glass of water in the desert."

She stopped, turned to look at me. Her eyes were still shot through pink from crying, but in the near dark they seemed to glow like tiny lamps. "Yeah," she said, nodding. "Yeah, that's exactly what it feels like. Water in the desert. Like being filled up."

"Yeah." I wanted to reach for the stereo remote, so that we could have that feeling at the same time again. But it seemed wrong to even move in this moment, to break whatever fragile sensation was hanging in the air between us. Also I would have had to reach into her lap.

Lilly's head fell down toward the headphones in her hands. She got this look on her face, like she was about to say something but only with great reluctance. "I feel that way with you, sometimes," she said. "Filled up."

"Y—you what?"

She glanced away, grunted in frustration. "I don't know. That's just the only way I can think of to say it. I know it doesn't make any sense."

"No, I mean, it—it made sense, I just..." If ever there were a time in my life when I should have said the things that needed saying, this was it. Or maybe not. Maybe this would have been exactly the wrong time for it. Because as incapable as I was of telling Lilly that I knew exactly what she meant, that I had felt that way every day that we had been in each other's lives, I think she would have been just as incapable, that night, of hearing it. But there's no way to know. There's never any way to know.

Somewhere in that irrelevant sea beneath our perch, her phone went off. And that expression she'd been wearing a second before was gone so fast I was immediately unconvinced it had been there in the first place. She was scrambling to climb down, to snatch up the phone from her desk. She checked it, and there were a few terrible breathless moments in which I waited for the inevitable. Finally she looked up at me, with a face that, for once, was entirely indiscernible. "It's Jason," she said. "He wants me to come over and talk."

And I, sensing immediately what she meant, packed the Discman into my bag again.

⌖ ⌖ ⌖

March 7, 2014
Savannah, Georgia

Adin

from: Adin Driscoll
to: Lilly Jameson
sent: March 7, 11:00 a.m. EST
subject: A lot of things

Lilly,

Where to begin. Beginning is always the hardest part. I sit here in my boxers, drinking coffee like water, getting distracted by the breeze because I didn't think to close my window before I sat down. There are so many parts to this puzzle and I am struggling to find a way to get all of this to make sense to you.

Okay. Here's a good place to start:

Yesterday I took a picture of a garden here in Savannah. People are planting gardens already. It's unheard of to someone who's spent his whole life in a place where the ground is frozen until the last weeks of April. But here they are. It wasn't a garden like you're thinking—pristine circles of gardenias, the smell of cut grass. They just started, so everything is mostly underground. There are a few green buds, but for the most part it's just a whole lot of the "before" image. It still gets below fifty sometimes at night. But today it's almost seventy.

The garden was just a lot of pine straw and wood chips and grass struggling up from the cold snaps. But it was still beautiful. Not in the normal way, not colorful or vibrant or cheery. But filled with hope. Aspiring. Ready to give it another go. I took a picture of it because that's how I feel right now.

A few months ago I was twenty-eight years old and I'd

never done anything risky in my whole life. Then, all of a sudden, I was doing risky things all the time: kissing you, punching a stranger in a hotel lobby, moving to the Rockies. And then the biggest risk, the one I never would have thought I could take until the opportunity came: walking out of your room knowing full well it might be for the last time. All of these things were equally terrifying to me, and yet, somehow, I lived through them all, like the sole survivor of a plane crash. I amazed myself with my tenacity, my growing level of comfort with the bleeding edge of my own life. And now here I am, in my father's guest room (really just a reenactment of my old bedroom), holding a camera without feeling disgusted at it for the first time in years. I'm not dead. I'm not even unhappy. I am the opposite of these things. And I'm doing it without you.

I don't mean to sound harsh. It's not as though I'm trying to get back at you or anything, I promise. Do I still love you? Of course I do. Stopping that would be like trying to halt a freight train with a pillow fort. I love you every bit as much as I did at Christmas, or in that bed in Tampa. Do I need you? Well, that's a more complicated question. I *don't need* you in the sense that I'm starting to learn how to be happy here, to walk around and not feel like I did in Denver that the sky is leaning on my back, without having you with me. But when I lie down at night, there's still an empty spot in the bed. When I sit in a restaurant booth, I look across from me and imagine you sitting there, telling me (with your mouth full) that I should try this. I've dreamed about college twice since I've been here. Both times it's you and me in the East Green, where we used to sit and talk after dinner, and I'm kissing you and you're slinking your arms under my coat and around my waist. That never happened when we were in college, but my brain doesn't seem to mind this so much.

Dad's fine. Don't worry. He acts like the hospital didn't even happen, because he's Dad. He offered to take me in for a while, and I couldn't deny that it would probably be good for me. And it has been, Lilly. I mean God, it's been like a miracle cure. All this sunshine, all these kids and their dogs. I don't know which is the dream and which isn't, here or Ohio, right now or everything else.

I'm not sure what's going to happen after this. I mean, my car is still sitting in front of your apartment, so obviously I will be back in Denver at some point soon. I'm sure I also left something of a mess in your kitchen, thinking I'd be back the next day. I owe you some cleaning, and I need to take all my crap off your hands. But I can't stay there in Denver, Lilly. It's your home, not mine. You chose it before we tried to have a life together. Being there makes me feel like a guest, or an intruder even. I would have loved being with you, but I never would have been happy there.

I'll be here a few more weeks, probably, while I figure that out. But I know whatever I end up doing, it has to be photography, and not suburban family photography, either. Somehow, during all those years when I was struggling to get out of bed in the morning, I managed for the sake of my survival to force myself to forget how much I love taking pictures. I probably put down the camera and started on the task of forgetting pretty much the day I graduated from OU. But I remember now. And I have the savings to do something about it. I want to try to move somewhere close to Savannah, get a job as a photographer with a Southern magazine. I want to wake up every March and go out jogging in shorts.

But—and here's the rub—I don't want to do those things without you. I can't stand to picture it happening that way. That's hard for me to admit, because I'm still a little hurt about what you seemed to think of me in Seattle. I'd like to keep pretending I'm this emotional powerhouse. And in some ways I guess maybe I am now, or at least I will be someday. But you're still like this bruise that won't heal. So where does that leave us? I don't know. Dad's been nagging me to get back to you, especially once I read him that email you sent, but I can't decide what we should do. I hoped that writing you this (absurdly lengthy) email would help me fumble my way to an answer, but I'm no closer than I was two hours ago.

What I do know is this: I haven't been this happy in an extremely long time. It's a different kind of happy from those two days in December or from Tampa, and *very* different from freshman year. But it's happiness just the same. And I know that I still love you, Lilly. I know, in a way I didn't when all this started, that things can change in ways you never believe they will until they do. I *don't* know what to do with all these things that I know. But for now, I'm glad just to know them.

Adin

An hour after I wrote this, something so obvious it embarrassed me popped into my head. I went downstairs, where Dad was folding laundry like a military man, although he had never been one.

"Dad," I asked, and he looked up at me through his reading glasses, which he had forgotten to take off, "you never told me if that was you at Lilly's reading. In Atlanta."

He grinned and held his hand over a pair of screaming-loud orange shorts to make the first crease. "Yeah, that was me." He said it like it was something so casual, like I had just asked if he was the one who drank the last of the milk. He made two neat folds and carefully placed the shorts on the arm of a neighboring sofa.

"Well, why the hell didn't you tell me? Or her?"

"I didn't think it was important." He shrugged. "And I didn't want it getting back to Lilly."

I gave him a look that made it clear he was not allowed to stop there. He sighed and, seeming to finally notice them, removed the glasses.

"I didn't remember her so well from when you two were kids. But you were making this big deal about her, so I thought maybe I should get an idea. You said she was on a book tour, so I looked up her schedule and showed up. It was close, I didn't work that day. I needed to see what all the fuss was about." He leaned back in his chair, which still smelled like cigarettes even though he'd quit eleven months earlier.

I came into the room with him and sat down on the end of the sofa not occupied by shorts. "Well?"

Dad grinned. He knew I wouldn't have asked this under normal circumstances. I would have been too proud to admit that his opinion mattered that much to me. But this was a special case. I was a rapidly aging adult tossed deep into the kind of love that only teenagers are supposed to swim in. I might have been more bothered by this, more embarrassed, revealing this kind of vulnerability to my own father. But I wasn't so much, because the only other person I'd ever known to struggle with that kind of love was him. He had wilted when Mom died. He had spent years in this house after she was gone, living with her pictures and her clothes. It was only by the grace of the few friends they had made that he got back out again, started writing again.

"I realized once I got there that I hadn't forgotten as much as I thought," he said. "Because she hadn't changed all that much. Her hair's a different color now, and she dresses like a grown woman. But I remembered her voice and the way she puts her hands together when she's answering a question."

I blinked. "She does?"

"Yeah. She does. And she puts her chin down when someone says something nice about her. And she's still oblivious to the advances of men."

"What? What does that mean?"

"Oh, she had some guy with her, hovering over her the whole time. I guess it's a guy she knows professionally, but that's not his game, I'll tell you that."

Jealousy washed over me, made the skin on my neck crawl. "That's Nate. Her agent. We've argued about him before. I gave him a black eye in a hotel in Florida."

"You did *what*?" Dad has always been one of those dads who tells you to stick up for yourself, don't take any shit from anybody. But I'd never been good at taking his advice. I was bullied a lot as a kid. I never got in trouble for fights. In fact, I don't think he'd ever known me to hit anybody before.

"Yeah," I told him. "We had a, uh, dispute in a Hyatt lobby."

"Boy, kid, you got it bad for this girl, don't you?"

I smiled and looked down at the floor. "Yeah, I sure do."

"So, what? You asking my advice? Is that what we're really doing here?"

"Well, that wasn't my plan when I came downstairs. I just wanted to know why you went to see her. But...I guess that's what it is now."

He did his ragged old-man cackle and stood up with surprising ease. "She's a good writer," he said, passing me on his way to the kitchen. He opened a cabinet, plucked out a filter and put it in the coffee maker. "Not my usual genre, but..." He poured the water and hit the button. Small gurgling sounds drifted through the house. "She's beautiful, too. And very sweet, good-natured. And she cares about you quite a lot."

I stood up and followed him. "How do you know that? I wasn't even there."

"No, but one of the kids asked her if she had a boyfriend, and all the other kids went '*Oooooooh*,' just like that. And she looked down at her podium and said..." He paused to search his memory, one hand still up in the cabinet for a mug. "Oh, what was it. It was something like, 'I think I might,' or 'I hope I might.'"

"Which one? Because those are very different."

He shrugged. "Both. Neither. I don't remember what she said, exactly. I just remember the way she said it."

"And how was that?"

Before he could answer, my phone was ringing. I checked, knowing already that it would be Lilly. It was. I stared at it for a few seconds, fighting, fighting. I let it go to voice mail, put it back in my pocket.

"Who is it?"

"Nobody. Unlisted number. I'll let them leave a message." I leaned against the kitchen table, arms crossed. "So. How did she say it?"

He turned the mug around in his hands, trying to marshal his eloquence. Then he said, "Like someone had just run over her new puppy. Or she had crashed her car the week she got her license and she had to tell her mom and dad."

"What?" I shook my head, gaping. "And *that* makes you think she's in love? That's what love sounds like to you?"

Dad laughed very loud then, so hard he almost dropped the mug. "Oh, look at you," he said, scratching at his bald spot. "Still such a kid."

[✦] [✦] [✦]

Denver, Colorado

Lilly

In a week's time I had packed up my things—and his—and headed back to Denver. The tour, the marathon was over. I kept looking at my phone, checking my voice mail, hoping to hear something more from him. After a couple days of not hearing from him, I began to fear the worst. I suspected he was through with me. I was pretty certain I'd fully decimated the last chance I may have had with him. That's what being scared of love gets you: the absence of love. But the silence was unbearable. I cried and got mad—at him for leaving and at myself for being such a coward. It was not unlike Tampa when I heard nothing from him, only this time I worried there'd be no reappearing at the last minute. And that's what I feared the most—that he was gone from my life for good. On the plane from Seattle to Denver, I still hoped he was waiting for me...somewhere.

By the time the plane landed, I'd convinced myself he was back at my place in Denver. He'd have coffee brewing. He'd wrap me in his arms and hold me, erasing the fight, forgiving me for how I'd acted in Seattle. We'd begin again.

I was way off.

I unlocked my condo and the coolness of the March air, coupled with his disappearance, hit me all at once. He had turned the thermostat down to 60—something I would never do—so the air was chilly. He had left a mess and I thought back to his email. How he'd felt untethered. How he'd rarely left. How he wasn't sure what he was doing there, waiting. Waiting for his life to begin. I absently straightened the kitchen mat and felt crushed all over again, as if I was witnessing the illustrated version of what he had confessed in his emails, said and unsaid.

This is me not doing great.

This is me trying to be okay, Lilly.

This is me, here, without you.

I turned on all the lights and opened the blinds. It was his brand of mess that left me so heartbroken. It was the sort of mess I'd wanted us to make together—white dress shirts discarded outside the bathroom door; a lone, half-finished vanilla soy milk carton in the fridge; a cast aside issue of *The Atlantic* on the floor in front of the sofa; two white ankle socks hugging the edge of the bedpost; and a crinkled, wallet-size picture of us by the alarm clock. The photo looked like it had spent the better part of a decade in a leather wallet. It was a picture of us back in college—me dressed up for some event, him gallant with his arm around me in a dorm hallway. I pocketed the picture and picked up each thing, imagining him moving through the rooms without me, trying to be patient. I wiped cigarette ashes into my palm, and I got out the picture of us again—we looked about eighteen. I put it back in my pocket and moved his loose change into a spare ashtray and then dabbed my eyes with the cold, wrinkled shirt I'd picked up off the floor and tossed it into the laundry hamper.

The next few days I spent catching up on email, doing laundry, and restocking the fridge. I'd barely heard from him. All I knew was that he was in Savannah. Maybe I had really misjudged the fight. Maybe I had not only destroyed any potential romantic relationship but also ruined our friendship in the process. I grew more and more uneasy as each day passed. For so long he had been a fixture in my life, not a constant presence, exactly, but more of a planetary one. We took turns orbiting each other. We took turns being each other's moon. That pull, that closeness, had informed and shaped me. He was in my DNA. I liked to think that, after all this time, I was still a part of him, too.

After so much work and effort, was this really it? Was this his way of saying goodbye? To fade into the ether? It felt more and more unacceptable.

By March 6, I couldn't concentrate on anything or think straight. I was desperate to talk to him, which is what led me to locate Arthur Driscoll's phone number in Savannah. I had never done anything quite so sneaky in order to simply talk to a person, but I felt like I had no choice.

Number in hand, I grabbed my phone and dialed Arthur Driscoll's home telephone number, repeating each number slowly as I entered it in my phone, my stomach doing panicked, nervous flips the whole time.

Arthur picked up on the first ring.

"Hi, is this Arthur Driscoll?"

"Hello! Is this who I think it is?"

His comment gave me pause. Was he messing with me? Had Adin even *told* him about me? Or was Arthur simply assuming I was an insurance saleslady? I tried to remember what I had planned to say, which wasn't much of anything. Let's face it—I was secretly dialing a boy's number because I was scared they didn't like me enough.

I stammered, "I'm sorry. Do I have the right number? Is this the *Driscoll* residence?" I wanted to sound classy, purposeful.

"Lilly? This is Arthur! I recognize that voice. How are things out your way?"

I relaxed a little. This was the Arthur I remembered. "God! How did you know it was me?"

"I was in Atlanta. I was at your reading."

"Oh yeah?" I shifted uncomfortably.

"No, it was good. But I know why you're calling. Adin, right?"

With one word, I felt like I was sixteen again, trying to cleverly extract information, shaking down anyone to get a firm yes or no on someone's emotional barometer at that given time. "Yeah, that's right," I ventured. "Thing is...I haven't heard much from him."

"I know, I know. He's out with a camera right now."

"He is?"

"Yeah, he's hard to keep track of these days. I was in the hospital for a little while for my heart. I don't know how long he plans to stay. I've been telling him he needs to call..."

I tucked my legs underneath me and looked at my front door. "Yeah, I wouldn't have called the house, but I wanted to know how he was doing. I'm so sorry to hear you were in the hospital! And to be calling you like this, but...is he at least *okay?* And you don't have to answer that, but, we got in this fight. In Seattle—"

"Oh, he's doing well. I know he's enjoying being here. I think this is a good place for him right now. But, I think..."

"I'm coming to see you both." Before I even realized what I was saying, I'd already said it. "Is that okay? Do you think that would be okay?"

"Good. I was just going to suggest that," he chuckled.

"Good!"

"Yeah, come on!"

I laughed. "Really? It's not a bad idea?"

"Oh, no..."

"Hey, Arthur?"

"Yeah?"

"I want to make this a surprise. Can you keep a secret?"

"We can do that."

from: Lilly Jameson
to: Brenda Jameson
sent: March 6, 8:35 a.m. MST
subject: Checking in...

Mom,

Just wanted to give you a heads up: I am going to Savannah for a couple of days. Adin is there visiting his father who apparently was in the hospital for a heart problem and I'm going to take the opportunity to look at some properties on Amelia Island. I'm just not sure about my place in Denver—I feel so distant out here. I'll try to swing by and visit you. Also, not mad at you about Atlanta. Tell Dad hi for me.

Lilly

I'D BEEN TO SAVANNAH SEVERAL TIMES, BUT ONLY twice with Adin. It had been the summer after sophomore year while we were in college. We had both gone home for the summer—I to Beaufort, he to Savannah, and we'd met up a couple of times to go to a local bookstore and walk around the waterfront. But things had been quiet, laced with sadness both times, from Grace passing away. Our time together had felt strained—me trying to be a good friend and say the right thing and Adin trying to feel okay again. I felt like nothing I said was helpful or adequate. I remember arriving at his house one afternoon that summer and, when I asked him what he wanted to do, he replied, *Just walk*. And so we had. We walked to the *Waving Girl* statue and just sat by the water for a few hours. We barely spoke. But we were together.

I always liked going to Savannah. The shadows cast by live oaks seemed to amplify the strange, gothic beauty of the place. I liked the mystery of it, its exotic aura. It was part of the reason I wanted to look for properties on Amelia Island. It was close but not *too* close. In college, we'd joked about someday renting a boat in Beaufort and taking it down the coast, hitting the main ports before arriving in Savannah. We'd talked about it the way some people talk about cross-country road trips.

Savannah, Georgia

I ARRIVED IN SAVANNAH ON THE MORNING OF March 8, thinking about Adin's email that'd I'd received the day prior. I drove my rental car over to the Driscoll house, hoping to find Adin there, but he was out. Arthur told me he was taking pictures of a *fancy pants* home and garden show that he'd seen advertised downtown. Arthur insisted I come in for a bit. Apparently Adin really *was* trying to get into photography. Some of his photos were scattered on the kitchen table. Arthur handed me a couple of 5"x7" black-and-white prints that Adin had recently developed. There were pictures everywhere, as though Adin's proclivity for photography had taken a turn for the obsessive. But it aligned with his personality—if he was passionate about something, you knew it. You could see it.

I remember taking a poll in college: I asked all my friends what their book title would be—if they could choose a title, anything, what would it be? I wrote down all the answers. One night I asked Adin, and his response, without thinking, was *A Blind Man Could See How Much I Love You*. He'd said it in front of Tristan, Jane, and, worst of all, Jason. We'd all been in someone's dorm, drinking during dead week. But the tone of the night shifted once he said that. Embarrassed, I nodded once, pen in hand, and scribbled down his answer, panic washing over me. No one said anything for a little bit after that, and

Jason grabbed a beer and left the room. An hour later, we had one of our biggest fights ever—about Adin.

I moved the pictures around on the table, looking at each one. There were some small groups of prints, too, as if Adin had been trying to pick and choose pictures for a contest. Lots were of flowers. Some lilies, even.

I studied the prints. "He was always so talented. This is what he was born to do."

Arthur lifted a thin, black portfolio from a chair on the other side of the table. He handed it to me and asked if I'd ever seen it.

"What?" I asked, accepting it. "What is this?" I asked.

He smiled, knowingly. "You mean to tell me that, after all this time, he never showed you his freshman Humanities portfolio?"

I shook my head. "What? No." I glanced down at the dusty portfolio. It seemed as if it had spent the better part of a decade in an attic. "That's his portfolio? From OU?"

He nodded. "It's something he brought downstairs the other day. Open it."

I unsealed the top and opened it to find a small piece of notebook paper taped to the inside cover. Across the front line, he'd written CALLA LILIES in a block font, as if that was the project title. It took up the length of the top line. *Callalily* had always been a screen name of mine. There was a grade written on the same sheet: *98%. A. Excellent work, Adin. I'm sure your subject (ahem) would like to see these. Cheers.* Then a signature I recognized as belonging to our freshman year Humanities teacher. My hand trembled as I moved the sheet of notebook paper to the side to find an assortment of pictures. They were all of me—all in black in white.

There were maybe ten of them, roughly 8"x10" in size. There was one of me sitting on a bench near the main quad, blowing on a cup of coffee, wearing a hoodie that belonged to him. In another photo, I'm sitting at my desk in the dorm looking at the camera as if I'd been pleading with him to stop something—probably taking pictures. There was one of me with his big black headphones on, my eyes closed. The last picture I remembered too: freshman year spring formal. In the picture, I'm in a white halter dress wielding a long-stemmed rose like a sword, challenging him to a duel.

"These are..." My mouth felt dry. My palms were sweaty. I scanned the other photos in the portfolio.

"They're all of you," he whispered.

"They're all of me," I said, my voice catching in my throat. "He never told me..." I looked up at Arthur. A thousand memories rushed back. The puzzle began to assemble itself.

"He told me his theme was *education*," I said. "He wouldn't tell me anything more than that." I flipped back through the pictures, trying to pin each one to a moment in time. "I remember him taking a lot of pictures that year."

"*Education*?" he asked.

I nodded, lost in thought.

Arthur considered the idea for a moment. "I suppose it was. You were all he seemed to talk about. You and photography." He turned to wipe down the countertop. "You and that camera were his education. So I'm not sure he was lying."

I felt a rush of heat and sweeping energy shoot through me as I reluctantly handed Arthur back the portfolio. I felt like some secret vow between Adin and me was coming into focus. Somewhere along the way, without ever saying the words, I'd asked him to never let me go. And he'd agreed to that. He never had let me go. Never would. And I would never let him go, either.

What had he meant by telling me his theme was *education*? What could I have possibly taught him? I wished I could see Adin in those pictures and understand what was passing between us. How many pictures must he have taken to arrive at these perfect 10? I didn't remember him taking most of the ones in the portfolio. He'd been an invisible presence, sewn into the fabric of my days.

Adin could see to the center of a thing. He could be alert to the quiet moment that a thousand other people would overlook because, to them, it didn't exist. It was the quality of stillness that was developed through patience. Through the aperture of a lens, he could make a loose strand of hair reveal a higher purpose or a hidden intimacy. He could transform a girl simply holding a cracked maple leaf up to the camera into something noteworthy and even deeply metaphorical. He had managed to record my life without me knowing it. Not the headlines—everyone knows your headlines—but the *real* story. How I struggled to articulate things, how my mom and dad didn't understand—or even seem to want to understand me. How I kept things in and how I sometimes let my anger get the best of me. And, worst of all, how I could deceive myself and run from things that scared me instead of facing reality.

Arthur gave me directions to where I could find Adin. I got in the car and sat still for a moment, my mind sorting through the images and memories.

I drove around the ancient squares, lined with oaks and dotted with small fountains. I rolled the window down to get a better look at everything. I remembered some of the homes from visiting Adin when we were in college—the bright ones. They were the easiest to keep track of. I drove for about ten minutes, following his directions, until I spotted a large white banner flapping in the wind, adjacent to an enormous flower garden. There were people milling around—women in clothes I thought my mother would approve of and men in seersucker pants.

I parked a block away and grabbed my phone off the car charger. Head down, I glanced around for Adin. Nothing yet. I walked past the banner and over to a large crowd that had gathered around a woman in a khaki-colored outfit who was telling them something about the *local community efforts of heirloom preservation*. I don't know. I tried to watch her and blend in. That's when I saw him.

He was all business, making his way down a gravel path between two raised flower beds several feet apart. He was wearing a black T-shirt and khaki cargo pants, a large black camera hung around his neck. It looked exactly like the one I remembered from college. He had a determined look on his face—something I'd glimpsed in Seattle. He looked like he was in a hurry, off to capture something only he knew about. Seeing him like that—so focused, camera in hand—made me understand what he hadn't had in Ohio and what he'd needed to find. People were milling around, and the crowd was getting bigger. I worked to extricate myself from a large group of teenagers wearing Future Farmers of America caps.

By the time I got away from the school group, I'd lost sight of him. I glanced toward where I'd last seen him and took off, not caring if I blew my cover. I jogged past a bird bath, past ladies in white, large-brimmed hats, and past a local perennial bed with a gravel path snaking through it. I was racing past each exhibit now, searching past large rows of shrubbery, when I finally spotted him. He was secluded, crouched in the gravel with his camera, zooming in on something I couldn't really see. Whatever it was, it was all he was thinking about. I smiled to myself, seeing him so focused, so unaware of how close I was. I thought about shouting out his name or just going up to him, but I hung back.

I got my phone out and sent him a text:

Lilly: Adin, you and flowers
Adin: What?
Lilly: Remember in college. All the flowers?
Adin: Wait. Are you…
Lilly: I'm near the pine tree. Black hat.

⟨•⟩ ⟨•⟩ ⟨•⟩

Adin

As THOUGH SHE WOULD EVER HAVE TO TELL me which one she was.

I was stunned. I'm glad, in retrospect, that my camera was on a strap, because I dropped it when I saw her standing there. She started walking toward me, legs like silken pistons under the fabric of her dress, but I couldn't move, couldn't push myself forward to meet her. I just stood there, gaping, the eye of a storm of tourists and Garden Club members.

There was something subtly but wildly different about the sight of her, something that was so unlike the way I had come to envision her that at first I thought she had made some kind of major change in her appearance, like cutting off all her hair or something. I think it had to do with how I had only seen her in cold places, bundled up under gray skies, with the color of her eyes and lips and skin muted and flat. Here she was now, vibrant and elegant and unfettered. Her bare shoulders were practically lit from beneath. Her face dazzled. She seemed larger and smaller at the same time. The girl she was in college and the woman she'd become, for the first time, coalesced before me into someone more beautiful than both.

I stayed rooted as she came to a stop in front of me, still holding my cell phone out. I must have looked like I thought she was a ghost. She smiled, and all my worry, all my lingering anger, all my uncertainty, melted like Southern snow.

"I know you didn't ask me to," she said, "but I did it anyway."

I pocketed the cell phone. I knelt and put the camera back in its bag. I didn't say a word. She watched me, one thumb hooked through the strap of her purse, waiting. All around us a hundred strangers passed like the figurines in a giant clock, noticing everything around them except the man and the woman at their center, who were both shaking a little now, like there was a stiff, late winter wind that only they could feel.

I stood up, shouldered the bag. I took her hand. And off we walked, away from the crowds, from the noise and the confusion of movement. Away from everything. Just away.

⊠ ⊠ ⊠

January 4, 2004
Ohio University, Athens, Ohio

Adin

I CAME BACK TO ATHENS FROM THE BREAK with a Lilly-shaped hole in my heart. Every day I was away from campus, I woke up and lay down with her on my mind. She walked through my dreams like an extra on a movie set. I guess a lot of this was because of Mom and Dad—the sudden move to Georgia, the way that they acted like everything was fine when it was very clearly *not* fine, in ways I was left to guess about on my own. I suppose I needed something to occupy my worried thoughts anyway. It was just that Lilly would have been there no matter what. If anything, my need for distraction only rooted her more firmly at the base of my brain.

When I got back, something had changed. Lilly wasn't thrilled to see me. She wasn't unhappy—we hugged, caught up, went for soft serve at Nelson Hall. But I'd always had a sense that somewhere underneath her dense obliviousness to my affections lay a secret knowing—and maybe, though this was far less certain, a secret agreement.

Not this time.

"Jason and I are going to Austin for spring break," she said proudly. "It took two years for him to agree, but it's on the books now."

"Cool," I told her. Meanwhile something in my chest tightened, kind of like when you twist a screw too far and you think, *Oh shit, that's not coming back off*. I think I'd finally realized over the break just how far my feelings extended, which is to say endlessly. I think a part of me thought I'd tell her so when I got back, consequences be damned. But that had felt impossible at the time.

"I don't think he'll appreciate the music scene like I do," she went on. "Not like you would. But he'll like the food."

Is she doing it on purpose? I wondered. The screw in me tightened again, threatening to strip.

We spent all of that Saturday together making a hard go at doing nothing. Sitting on benches, watching TV in my room, waiting for the next mealtime at Nelson. Lilly would look at me sometimes, in these moments, and it was like she knew that things weren't okay. I was having this sick, tingly feeling, like I might throw up. Except that throwing up wasn't what this feeling was leading me toward. Something, I knew, was making its way up my throat, ready to escape me, but not that.

For a year and a half now I had been part of this person and she part of me. I had watched her get her heart broken and had been the one to fix it, multiple times. I was her mix tape, her burn lotion, her lockbox, her pacemaker. Lilly had said things to me, about her need for me, that I could swear she had never said to Jason. And yet, still, it was Jason who would be rolling his eyes through the concerts in Austin. At the end of the night, at the end of *every* night, Jason would sleep with his chest to her back, one arm draped across her shoulders. The injustice of it, the existential weight, was crushing me like a rock. I couldn't be home, not with the long mysterious silences between my parents that gave me a strong whiff of divorce—or something worse. But now I couldn't be here, either. There was no place for me. What little square footage of the world I could call my own had closed up.

I didn't know what I was going to say to her, but I knew two things. One, it would change everything between us forever, and two, I was going to wish that I. Had. Not. Said. It.

Lilly looked beautiful. She was wearing the black fleece hoodie I'd bought freshman year, the one that, at this point, was more hers than mine. Her hair was wind-tossed and settled in ribbons around her shoulders. She moved her head to watch the kids passing us, and I got quick fleeting glimpses of her reddened cheeks. I had never wanted her like this. Maybe it was the stress I'd just come from or the stress of having to start a whole new semester, full of nights spent sleepless and desperate and euphoric with the thought of her. Every new moment was a risk that I would grab her and kiss her.

She turned, turned back—turned again. "You okay?" she asked, the way that everyone asks that when they know the answer.

I stopped walking. I felt like I was having a heart attack, like the world might shatter around me. I reached up and gripped the hair at the back of my head, hard, like I could pull myself out of it. "Lilly, I...," I started, but the dizziness made it hard to talk. "I just—"

Now we had both stopped. Lilly had turned to face me, and I could see what had to be—*had* to be—recognition in her face. Of what this moment was about to turn into, of what I was about to inflict on it.

"Adin—"

"Lilly, look, I have to tell you something, and I—"

My phone buzzed in my pocket.

Lilly and I both stopped.

I reached in and pulled it out. In the two seconds it took me to do this, I was overtaken by a premonition, as though a voice inside of me was telling me, gently but firmly, *You will never forget the thing that is happening right now.*

Arthur: kid, call me ASAP

Adin: what why

Arthur: Emergency. Find a phone. I don't want to text.

Somehow I knew. I did. I started walking away from Lilly. I didn't say anything, and neither did she.

Adin: i'll be to a phone in five. what is it

He didn't answer. But he didn't have to. Maybe I'd figured it out a long time ago—the sudden relocation; Dad being the one to call instead of Mom; that one moment, right in the middle of Christmas, when Mom started crying and she wouldn't tell me why. I was nineteen. Not an adult but not enough of a child to let these things pass me by.

I broke into a breathless sprint toward Adams. For the first time since our first semester at OU, I didn't think of Lilly at all.

❖ ❖ ❖

March 8, 2014
Savannah, Georgia

Adin

ON MY FATHER'S BACK PORCH WAS A SWING for two, with a little red pillow and a small oak table for glasses and newspapers and vases. We sat in it until it was dark, sometimes talking as we drank our way through half a bottle of wine and a couple of mint juleps (of which my father had become quite the craftsman since he moved down here—he insisted that no Southerner should be without the proper makings of a mint julep at any time), but mostly staring quietly at each other, our breaths coming slowly and then quickly and then slowly. Every time one of us leaned forward to kiss the other there was a blooming heat in my face and chest and a sensation of being caught in a blast wave, as though a large bomb had gone off in the neighbor's yard.

I was in love with her this time in a way I had never been the other times. Before, I had expected that she would walk right back out at any minute. That all this was a cruel and elaborate hoax perpetrated by the universe. I'd kept myself safe, well guarded. I had been the one to walk out, in the end. But here she was now, the one to fly cross-country to make it right.

As I drove back to the house, a voice inside me was screaming, *Don't crumble now! You'll be annihilated by this woman! You were so close to getting away!* But I didn't care. I had spent the last ten years listening to that voice, always on the run from the people I thought could damage me like Lilly had. Here, at the end, all I wanted was to just get caught.

For the first time since I had arrived in Georgia, the temperature dropped to the mid-fifties and I brought out two jackets. To Lilly I gave the old one, fleece with a black hood. I wasn't sure she would remember it, but she did. "Oh no you *didn't*," she said when she saw it. "Tell me this isn't what I think it is."

"It's not what you think it is."

She glanced up at me with a lopsided frown that meant she was trying to hide her laughter behind disapproval. Then she took the jacket and threw it over her shoulders. The image was surreal: Big Lilly in Little Lilly's clothing.

"Another drink?"

She nodded. I disappeared through the screen door and into the kitchen, where Dad was making pigs in blankets. He often complained that he was never a good cook, despite being a seasoned eater. But he had picked up a handful of things in his travels through the culinary realm, and this recipe was an oldie but a goody. I started to pour two more glasses of wine, putting on my best show of being steady and sober. I was always embarrassed to let my dad see me tipsy. "I can't believe this is happening," I confessed to him quietly.

He grinned and pulled on an oven mitt. "I almost can't, either. She sure took her sweet time getting here."

I stopped pouring, glanced up in surprise. "Wait. You knew about this?"

He tilted his head toward me, with that don't-be-stupid expression. "How do you think she knew where to look for you?"

My brain was sluggish with alcohol. I tried to work my way through this new puzzle. "Wha—? Well how long did you know?"

"She called a couple of days ago. Swore me to secrecy."

"So when I was asking you about her, and you were telling me that she still cared about me—as though that was merely your *manly intuition*—this is what you were hiding."

He shrugged coyly.

I shook my head. "So, what, did you make up the story about the kids asking her if she had a boyfriend?"

"Oh no, that really happened. Just consider it Exhibit B."

I stared at him, holding a glass of red in each hand. He patted me on the shoulder with the mitt and said, "Get out there. Don't waste that healthy buzz on me."

I blushed and fled back outside.

"Thank *you*," Lilly chirped merrily, as I handed her the wine. She had her legs up on the swing. The hoodie was wrapped around most of her tiny frame. I sat down heavily beside her, let my head fall back against the headrest, and let out a long breath. "You okay?" she asked.

"You and Dad conspired against me."

She laughed, looking away toward the yard. It was entirely dark now, but the sky was still gray at its edges with the lights from downtown. We could see the outlines of the trees against it. "You're wrong there, Honeypie," she cooed. "We were conspiring *with* you. You just didn't know about it."

"That's the definition of—"

She kissed me to shut me up. It worked extraordinarily well.

"So," she said. "Let's start over. All over."

I smiled. I couldn't help it. Happiness was staging a violent coup. "Okay."

"Tell me about Tristan's wedding."

"It's in May, in Vegas. He and his girlfriend Viv want a Vegas wedding, but they want the wedding itself to be normal. So tuxes and dresses, corsages, wedding presents, and a long, awkward reception where the women all line dance and the men all sit and get toasted. The whole shebang."

"That sounds dreadful."

"It's a wedding. Of course it's dreadful."

"Hey, now," she teased, ribbing me, "*I'm* the one who had to wear the damned dress once already. You don't get to talk about weddings that way until you've seen one from the other side of the looking glass."

"Fair enough," I replied. "But I assure you, being a guest is *pretty* bad. All that excruciating small talk, and even in winter the tux is too hot, and there's all these freaking kids everywhere. All the inconveniences you'd have to deal with, except that I don't get to leave halfway through and fly to Bermuda to have marathon sex with a gorgeous new spouse."

She shook her head and threw up her hands to God. "Oh, the naïve ramblings of the uninitiated."

"Quiet, you." I leaned over and kissed her, and she held my head in both hands and leaned back. She tasted like wine and smelled like perfume—the same kind she had worn in college.

"So here we are," she said, settling my head against her chest. "Finally."

I took in a deep breath, feeling her heartbeat in my ear through the fabric. "Finally, indeed."

From inside, I could hear the scrape of a pan as Dad pulled it out of the oven, the tinny rise and fall of NPR. Somewhere a few houses down, a peal of laughter echoed toward the sky. Lilly put her arms around me, one slung back behind my neck, one down over my hip, and I had a moment so surreal it almost made me pitch forward with vertigo, like those times you suddenly become lucid in the middle of a dream. I'd rubber-banded back to the past, to that that week I had spent pining for Lilly harder than any week before it, and then bounced forward to the present—the here and now, sitting in this porch swing with Lilly in my arms.

This is time travel, I thought. *This is the place where all roads meet.* But what I said was, "I'll be right back."

I untangled myself from Lilly, rushed past Dad inside, and leaped up the stairs two at a time in my half-drunk exuberance. A minute later, I ran down, burst out the screen door, and held out one half of a pair of earbuds to Lilly.

She laughed as she took it and placed it in her ear. "What are we, nineteen again?"

I sat down and gave my phone a few taps, while I fiddled with my own bud. "For the next hour," I said, "yes. Yes, we are."

from: Adin Driscoll
to: Tristan Rawlings
sent: March 9, 10:07 a.m. EDT
subject: You won the bet, I guess

Dear Mr. Rawlings,

There has been an astonishing change of plans. You will recall that I left Seattle in a tizzy, uncertain about my future, to put it mildly. I will recall that you did the online equivalent of an eye-roll and told me, "I'd give it two weeks."

Well, you overshot it. Lilly showed up in *Savannah* yesterday, ready to make amends. And I didn't even try to play it cool. I was powerless. I'm ashamed of my weakness, I guess. But I would have been more ashamed if it had ended up any other way. It's been too long coming.

Unlike last time, when she really just gave me a cursory nod and then went back to talking about royalty rates, last night Lilly asked me all about the wedding, and I told her as much as I could. She's in for real now. So I guess we'll be there on May 17th. I can tell you congratulations, and you can tell me you told me so. I'll make it your wedding present. Don't worry, though, I also have my eye on this twenty-five-piece silverware set where all the handles are roosters and hens. It's magnificent. You guys will loathe it.

I would write more, but Lilly and I are getting a hotel room for the day so we can make it like shipwrecked adolescents. We're not so pumped about consummating our reunion with Dad reading the paper downstairs. I'll write you again from the other side. I won't bother to check for a response, so I will simply imagine that you're wishing me luck.

All my love,
Adin

◆ ◆ ◆

March 10th
The Dew Drop Inn, Savannah, Georgia

Lilly

ADIN AND I FOUND A B&B CALLED THE Dew Drop Inn to stay in so that we could have some privacy. So far, Savannah was turning out to be just what I'd thought it could be—a calm little oasis in the South, perfect for the two of us to decide where our relationship would land.

I woke up an hour before Adin that morning, which wasn't that uncommon. I left him in the room to get ready while I went to the main house, where I'd been told the ladies who owned the B&B served homemade breakfasts for the guests each morning. I walked from our room to the main house and pushed open the heavy front door.

The room was one of those sprawling Southern living rooms, equipped with deep chocolate hardwood floors, Persian rugs, a grand piano, massive mirrors on the walls, and a large fireplace in the corner. I walked through the living room and passed a little old lady sitting near the foot of a stairwell, manning the front desk. She glanced up at me when I walked in and asked which room I was staying in.

"I'm sorry—which *room*?"

She nodded. "What was the *name*?"

"Um, I guess I'm not sure. It's painted red, if that helps."

She scanned the ledger in front of her. "Ah ha! *Honeymoon suite!*" She smiled up at me. "Good morning, Mrs. Driscoll!"

I was taken aback for a moment. I opened my mouth to correct her, but she seemed so pleasant, so eager to please, that I decided against it, and honestly, it was a little thrilling to just go with it. I'd never really let myself consider life as Mrs. Driscoll, and here was my chance. I nodded along, busy untangling the mystery of why she'd call me Mrs. Driscoll in the first place. I hadn't been with Adin when he checked us in yesterday. I'd been outside putting money in a parking meter.

I headed into the dining room and spotted a couple sitting at the table. They'd each found two boxes of Frosted Flakes somewhere and had each opened one and dumped it into a bowl of milk. Neither one smiled at me. I breezed past them and heard several women's voices coming from the kitchen.

I walked into the kitchen and grabbed a plate from a metal rack sitting by the large coffee area setup. I was feeling right at home— Mom had a similar set up at our B&B. The place was clean, no coffee drips anywhere, no sugar sprinkled on the counter. And there was the smell of pancakes. *This place is heaven,* I thought. *I could live here. Adin and I could live in the red room, and the ladies would cook for us and the coffee would just be ready every day at—*

"Hi, good morning!"

I turned and there was a small older woman beside me, taking down a coffee cup.

"Hi, good morning!"

"You're an early bird like us, I think!"

"Oh, maybe so. My boyfriend's still getting ready."

The lady looked slightly bothered. "Oh? You're not Arthur's new daughter-in-law?"

"Sorry, what?" I asked, genuinely surprised by what I was hearing.

"I thought you were *Mrs. Driscoll.*" Her voice seemed to be getting louder, as if she thought that my hearing was the problem. "I worked at the paper with Arthur. I saw the sign-in sheet," she said, a twinkle in her eye.

The sign-in sheet?

What did he write on the sign-in sheet? I wondered. "Oh, I'm just so used to calling him that you know, we were together for a long, *long* time. I just can't get used to calling him anything else!" I couldn't believe what I was saying. I was still trying to sort out why the whole place seemed to think Adin and I were married.

"Bless your heart!" The lady chuckled, nudging me in the ribs. "We know Arthur and Adin. They are the *sweetest* people."

"I saw you two at the Garden Club. My friends from Galveston came up this week." The lady sat her cup of coffee down and poured some sugar into the black coffee. "How is Arthur, by the way? I haven't seen him in a long, long time."

"Arthur is doing great. Still a great cook and I think he still writes some." I picked up my coffee and was about to go in search of pancakes when I realized I didn't know her name. "I'm sorry, I didn't catch your name."

She sat the dainty half-and-half pitcher back on the counter. "My name is Mrs. Amandine Walters. They call me Mandy. I kept the Walters." She picked up her coffee cup. "You tell him I said hello."

I nodded. "Okay. I'll do that."

That's when Adin burst into the kitchen. He spotted me and smiled, no doubt still thinking about the night before. I smiled back, watching him over the rim of my coffee cup. His hair was still slightly wet and wavy as if he'd just had a shower. For a second I wondered if he thought he'd lost me. He'd looked a little panicked.

"There he is! The *groom*!" Mandy called out. She took a sip of her coffee. "Good morning, *Adin*!" she called.

Groom?

I turned, nearly choking on my coffee. *What had he done? Announced to the place we were newlyweds?* He walked over and put his arms around my waist as I stood there, trying not to let anyone see how that word had sent the blood rushing to my face, how that word had turned my black-and-white reality into a full-color version. Needing to distract myself, I turned to place my breakfast order to the cook.

He relaxed his grip and I took hold of his hand and squeezed it, trying to play normal. I sat my plate on the counter and turned to him, waiting for him to say something, staring him down on this one.

As if sensing that I was not okay with what he'd said, he pivoted to the others, blushing. "*Groom*, huh?"

Mandy picked up her plate filled with berries and yogurt. "I saw the sign-in. You two have done *done* it!"

Two of Mandy's friends walked in. She turned to the women. "Newlyweds!" she said, pointing toward us. "Arthur Driscoll's boy."

I cleared my throat. "You know, *Honey*, I think I was supposed to check a box on that sign-in sheet for our lunch option for the day." I detected a look of terror pass over his face. I handed him my plate and smiled sweetly up at him. "Hold on to that for me. This won't take but a second. I just need to find our names."

I turned to go and, within about two seconds I could hear the sound of dishes being passed and shuffled, chairs being shifted. Soon he was right behind me.

"Whoa, Lilly," he said, taking hold of my arm. I was standing about three feet from the front desk. Adin turned to the sign-in sheet. "Let me handle this," he whispered.

"No, you signed us in yesterday." I walked over and picked up the sign-in sheet and flipped a page. I scanned the sheet and zeroed in on Adin's weirdly angular handwriting. He'd signed us in as *Mr. and Mrs. Driscoll.*

I stared at the words and gripped the edge of the desk, leaning closer to the sign-in sheet, making sure I was reading it correctly. I was stunned. That was the difference between us—he could go out on a limb like that, make himself (and his intentions) completely transparent and stand behind them, whereas I kept my cards close to my chest. It was something about him I loved, but it infuriated me at times. He declared what he wanted. Hell, these days he practically broadcast it. All my life I'd been the sort to keep my own desires hidden, like rushing water that lay just underfoot.

I handed the ledger to him. Maybe a little too forcefully.

"Why did you sign me in as...your *wife*?"

Adin looked back to the table and then at the paper. "To save... space...for the other guests. I didn't want to take up two rows."

I tried to rein in the sarcastic remark I was ready to launch at him. "You didn't even give me a *name*. Not even *Lilly*. Nothing. And that is...*not us*."

He took a step closer to me, lowering his voice. "But, I mean, what's wrong, exactly, with me writing that?"

I looked at him and felt my life go blurry, as if the sea had risen up and dissolved the path I'd been following on the shore. In one way, he was right. It was the truest thing in the world—in some distant universe my life got braided with his. I had been bound to him since I'd known him, but it was preposterous to me that he would have the audacity to write something like that.

I looked right at him. "We are *not married*, Adin. You can't just... words matter!" I said, looking back at what he wrote, feeling myself nearly buried by the enormity of it and what it said about him and his intentions. I reached for his hand. "Adin, you have to understand I just separated from someone. I can't just..."

Adin took the ledger from me and led me into the foyer out of sight from the others.

"I didn't think that the entire B&B would have the damn thing memorized by morning. Seriously. I...don't know why I did that...it was a split-second thing for me." His voice was picking up speed, getting slightly high-pitched. "I guess I can see why that would bother you, but I'd be lying if I said I don't intend for this to...go there...*someday*."

"What?" All of a sudden I was acutely aware of how I'd had zero cups of coffee. My head was spinning.

Adin propped himself up against the grandfather clock. "Lilly, I *want* to marry you someday. That's my idea of happiness. Remember in college, that French phrase you taught me, what was it, *vision du bonheur*? Vision of happiness? Well? Mine is waking up next to you for the rest of my life. It's making *this* official. In front of everyone. And...being with you until you look like, well, her." He pointed to a woman using a cane to get around. Someone was helping her get situated at the table. Her short-sleeved, button-down denim shirt had a large sunflower sewn on to the pocket.

I looked from the woman back to Adin. "Adin, I just...*cannot* use the *M* word with you. Not today. Not tomorrow..." I took a deep breath. "Not for a while."

Adin crossed his arms. "What? Is it me? Or is it the word?"

I shook my head. It was not him. In fact, the only other person I would ever consider would be him. But marriage was the last thing on my radar. Did he not comprehend the fact that seeing him so soon after my separation was a marvel to me and my family? And he was already thinking about the next step?

"It's just I am still...in this...foggy post-traumatic...divorce stage, and so when I hear that word, I just freak out. It feels like a bad idea... it makes me feel the opposite of relaxed. I don't know what the opposite is—"

"How about what you look like right now, 'cause I could take a Polaroid." Adin ran a hand through his damp hair. "You're acting like I just asked you to move with me to fucking Iran for a year."

"No, no it's just...I'm *fine*. Just, please don't use that word with me."

Adin exhaled loudly and did something with his body that made him look like he'd been deflated. "God. I don't think I've seen you this nervous." Adin relaxed a little and shifted his weight. "I've seen you speak to rooms full of people, and you're not like this." He paused for a moment. "So you're saying, don't use that word with you—but is there an expiration date I should know about? Because I love you, and I don't mean to beat a dead horse here—"

"Adin, *please*. This is not a conversation we should be having."

"Lilly, I don't want to do the goofy, noncommittal civil union bullshit," he continued.

"Adin—"

"Well, are you saying you'll *never* get married again?"

Oh boy.

I lowered my voice. "It's just that it will be...a *long time*...maybe a *very long time*, before I can take that next step."

Adin seemed to visibly clam up as if my words were actually eating away at him or, at the very least, making him less of a person.

I took his hand, hoping to temper what I'd just said. Because I did love him. And I did trust him and what we had. I knew what we shared was rare and worthy and worth saving. But I couldn't promise him I'd want to get married again. I just couldn't wrap my head around something like that, even if it might happen someday. I wasn't willing to lie and say I'd want that.

"Adin, I know what your idea of happiness is. And mine looks a lot like yours, but I'm trying to be honest with you. This is how *I* operate these days. I just can't even think about...*marriage*. It's not a game to me. Hell, I can't talk about it. And that's okay, right? We have *time*. We're not even thirty!"

Adin nodded, still shrinking in front of me.

"Hey," I said, lifting his chin. "We're here. Together. *Right now*. We're staying in the *honeymoon suite*, of all things..."

He smiled half-heartedly.

I took his hand and kissed his knuckles. "How do I explain it? It's kind of like the concept of jinxing something. I just don't want to jinx this. And I don't want to tempt fate. And I feel like you're doing that."

His smile brightened a little. "Okay then, Mrs. Driscoll. I'll never tempt fate again."

"Adin!" I shot him a look and pushed him toward the mahogany stairwell. I gave him one of the better kisses mankind has ever known. I fell on top of his lap and wrapped my arms around him. Our kiss turned into a make-out session. Before long, he was in good spirits again.

I got up and he held on to my hand, as if requesting another love fest on the stairwell.

"Are you ready, Mr. Driscoll?" I asked, after standing there holding his hand for what seemed like a long time. But he held on, taking me in with that fully present way he had of looking at me.

"I'm ready, Mrs. Driscoll. Whenever you are."

I didn't even bother to correct him.

⧆ ⧆ ⧆

Adin

So I GET TO THIS PLACE AT FIVE-THIRTY the previous day. Lilly is out in the car, taking a call from Nate about one thing or another (and I feel just a little guilty for thinking, *Good—they have* lots *to talk about this time*). I'm in this short-sleeved dress shirt and a pair of cargo shorts. I look like such a tourist. The only thing I'm missing is sunscreen smeared across the bridge of my nose.

I get to the desk, and before I can say anything, before I can put my damned suitcase down, the old lady with the colossal trifocals looks up and says, "Well, good evening there, Adin!"

I freeze. I've never met this woman before. How the hell does she know who I am?

As if reading the question in my face, she squawks, "You're Arthur Driscoll's son, ain'tcha?"

"Yeah, that's me. I'm really sorry, but—do I know you?"

"No, of course you don't, Honey. But *I* know your dad. Everybody does. He's a local celebrity. The Ohio boy come down to write beautiful poetry about Southern food." Poetry? *My* dad? "He's got a picture in the front hall. We all pass it when it's his turn to host the potluck." I am certain now that she has my father confused with someone else. Except that no other strange, potluck-hosting father in Savannah would have that ridiculous shot of me in my last year of college, struggling with a giant fish I didn't catch myself, grinning at the camera under a big dopey bucket hat.

"You look a little older, a little more handsome, maybe," she tells me, "but you ain't changed much. I could spot you a mile away. Arthur Driscoll's boy. We heard you were in town, but I didn't expect to see you *here*."

"Yeah, well...," I shrug. I'm blushing like I'm on fire. I'm so confused I've forgotten exactly what I was supposed to be doing here at this desk, talking to this little old Southern lady who may or may not be hitting on me.

"Well, you're in luck," she says, lugging a laminated photo album up and into my hands. "The Azalea Suite just opened up two days ago. Had a nice couple from up in Vermont in there for about two and a half weeks." She leans forward confidentially and murmurs, "Honestly, thought they'd *never* go. We just about had to shove them out the door by the end."

I flip to the room in question. It's actually its own little guest house, separate from the main building, off in its own little corner of the modest gardens. The interior is plush, elegant, sublimely Southern, decorated in dark crimsons and bright, clean whites. I'm surprised to find that it's exactly the sort of place I was imagining when Lilly and I decided to come here. "This I beautiful," I say, and she smiles, looking satisfied. "But I—well, I gotta be honest. What made you choose this one for me? You didn't even know I'd be coming."

"Well, hon, Arthur wrote a whole column about it in the Sunday *Morning News*. You and Lilly both. I hope you two didn't think to honeymoon here hopin' for a little privacy, 'cause you're gonna be hard up to find anybody around here who doesn't know who you are."

Wait. Did she say *honeymoon*? She *did* say honeymoon. She—
Oh God.

"Uh, well, yeah, we were kind of hoping to fly under the radar," I
confess, trying to buy some time. My mind is racing in a panic, trying
to stay a step ahead of my mouth. There are a lot of very important
calculations to make before I choose my next words: Everybody knows
Arthur. Arthur, without telling me anything about it, has spilled
something of our story to the whole damned town. It's the South,
and so naturally a man having a woman come stay with him and
then booking a bed and breakfast with her must necessarily be that
woman's husband. At least, among the circles Dad apparently runs in.
(Dad has circles, though? I still can't get over that part.)

If I clear up the whole thing now, there are some unfortunate
possible implications for the Driscoll clan in Savannah. Implications
which I, in my frantic state, am not willing to risk conjuring. I stuff
my hands in my pockets, before she has a chance to check for the
ring. "Boy," I chime merrily, "you guys are really great. You had
my room for me before I even knew I wanted it. My wife will be
ecstatic." *Wife? Did I say that? Did that come out of me?* I have
to admit that, even as I'm panicking about going along with this
horrendous lie, the sound of it on my lips thrills me in a deeply
secret and awful way.

She beams and gives me a pen. I write in the sign-in log with a
shaky script: *Mr. and Mrs. Driscoll*. And this, too, excites me.

"If you want," she offers, "we can send somebody out to help you
with the luggage."

"Oh, no, that's fine," I quickly reply, imagining the horror of this
getting back to Lilly in the parking lot. "We'll be fine. Thanks."

She looks ready to make more small talk in that aggressively nosy
Southern way, but I'm moving away from her now, making a hasty
tactical retreat, so she simply calls after me, "Dinner's in the dining
room at 7:30! It's baked flounder!"

So I FELT REALLY BAD ABOUT THIS. I did. I had panicked in a bad way, and now, everywhere Lilly went, people were going to be asking to see her ring. But I wasn't ready to besmirch Dad's good name here. If I ruffled all the biddies' feathers, he could lose his readership. At least, that was the argument I was prepared to make to Lilly. Maybe. If she asked. I had no idea what his readership was, or why he was publishing columns on topics other than food. He was always this kind of guy—like I needed a security clearance to get the details of his life.

We had lunch with him the next day at a little burger shop downtown. Dad was a burger guy. The more patties the better. People were always shocked by this—I guess they expected more refined tastes from a guy who wrote so well about cuisine. But nope. He was a burger, pizza, and macaroni kind of eater. Everything else was just to make a living.

When Lilly left for the bathroom, I tried to get it all out of him as fast as possible. "What the hell, Dad? What did you write in the paper about us?"

He nearly choked on a french fry. "What?"

"Everybody at the hotel knows who we are. I had to tell them all I'm married just so they don't think your kid is running around—" I couldn't finish this sentence. Not in front of my father. But he got it.

"I was kind of hoping to get away with that. But you didn't have to lie about it."

"But I mean what would people *think* if I said she was just my girlfriend? What would they think about you?"

Dad cocked his head at me, smiling in that way that gave me time to brace myself for embarrassment. "Adin, I know you don't have much experience with the South, but even you have probably figured out that time moves just as fast here as it does everywhere else. It's not the 1800s. People would get that you're—" he couldn't do it either, "doing what you do outside the sacred confines of marriage."

"Okay, fine. I guess I'm just old-fashioned. But I actually needed to talk to you about the other part of it." I glanced toward the back of the restaurant, checking to see that Lilly wasn't on her way back. "Look, she found out this morning. The desk lady said something to her and she saw where I'd written *Mr. and Mrs. Driscoll* in the registry log. And she com*pletely* freaked out. She was saying all this stuff like she's not going to be ready for marriage for a long, long time and she was really uncomfortable with the whole thing."

He shrugged and went for his pickle. "That seems reasonable. She just got divorced. You started seeing each other only a few weeks ago."

"Yeah, but the thing is, I *do* want to ask her to marry me someday and it worries me she feels this way about it now."

This time it was Dad who checked for Lilly's impending return. "Boy, are you *crazy*?" he asked, his voice a harsh whisper.

"Yes, Dad, I am. I'm utterly out of my mind. But I can't help it. I've been in love with this woman for *ten years*. And we've at least had feelings for each other since we started talking again, and that was months ago. And May is still a little way off. I'm not buying the ring today, for Christ's sake, but don't you think it's something to at least start thinking about?"

"No. I don't. And neither will—" He straightened. I looked over and drew a sharp breath. Lilly was coming back toward us. We both tried to smile, and I was sure for a second that she would see our identical awkward looks, but then she got waylaid by a waitress who had been itching for a chance to fawn on her, the new wife of Arthur Driscoll's kid. She glanced from the waitress to me with this look that said she was going to kill me for it later.

"Look," I whispered to Dad, "I know that Lilly went through something hard with Tim. I know that must make the institution of marriage seem a little more daunting. A lot more daunting, whatever. But why should *I* be punished for that? I haven't been married yet. I haven't done anything wrong. Why do I have to pay any penance for it?"

He looked back from her to me. He suddenly seemed very grave. Earnestness was not something my father dealt in frequently, so it was always a little frightening when expressions like this overtook him. "Because," he rumbled, almost scolding me now, "that's part of the package, kid. You chose to fall in love with a recent divorcee. If she says wait, you say, 'How long?' That's the price you pay."

I was about to protest that I hadn't *chosen* to do anything, that love, in fact, did not ever work that way, but then Lilly had made her escape and was sitting down with us again. "Adin, if anybody figured out I was Lilly Jameson, not Lilly Driscoll, I'd have to get a bodyguard and a publicist." She picked up her fork and then added, "Well. Another publicist."

from: Adin Driscoll
to: Tristan Rawlings
sent: March 10, 7:11 p.m. EDT
subject: WTF do I do now

Hey,
I have a problem. My problem is this: Dad wrote some column in Savannah's paper about me and Lilly. Now everybody in town knows who we are. This woman at the place we're staying actually assumed we had gotten married, and I went along with it, thinking a bunch of old Dixie matrons would run Dad out of town if they found out his son was having premarital coitus with a recently divorced woman. Turns out Dad thinks the South is a lot more progressive than I gave it credit for. So now I'm stuck in this lie, and she knows about it, too. Lilly saw the register: Mr. and Mrs. Driscoll *in my handwriting.*

The other, bigger problem is that she insists that marriage is not something on the table for her right now. Which is kind of a big problem, because sooner or later it's going to be the entire contents of the table for me.

Dad thinks I'm being an insensitive prick and she'll just shoot me down if I try to move too fast. But like I told Dad, I've been in love with her for so long, marriage feels totally right to me. I don't want to be her *boyfriend* when we're forty. I get that she just got out of the last marriage, but I mean, if we're the sort of couple that is going to be successfully married at any point down the road, what difference does it make when that happens?

I know that I'm probably getting on your nerves by now. I know I sound like some ridiculous anxious teenager. But I'm almost thirty, man. How often do people let themselves fall this hard past thirty? Hell, past twenty-two? Lilly is giving herself over to this in a way that no aging, jaded woman in a bar ever will. Our shared past is our only saving grace. It feels like my last chance at the kind of whirlwind romance I've spent my entire youth waiting for.

Adin

· · ·

from: Tristan Rawlings
to: Adin Driscoll
sent: March 11, 6:48 p.m. EDT
subject: Re: WTF do I do now

Dear Mr. Driscoll,
You, sir, need to simmer down. You are so wound up I could use you for a watch. I actually read your email out loud to Viv while we were in bed last night, and we both laughed at you. Hard. Take that as a sign of the gravity of the situation. Or maybe the antigravity, I don't know.

Personally, I think going around calling your woman "Honeypie" in front of a bunch of old people is hilarious.

You should really be enjoying that more. It's pretty priceless. And I feel like I should remind you that Viv is one of those bar chicks you're so uppity about. Maybe you would have been better off spending your 20s in a library, with your own kind.

You have been coming to me bawling about this great, epic love of yours for months. And now you're worried that she's going to bail on you if you propose? What the fuck, man. Either you were totally delusional when you were making me suffer through all your OTHER disasters with this chick, or you're just being a wuss now. Being that she's put up with you through all this already, and that you've set a magnificent precedent for being a wuss in most other things, I'm voting for the second one.

You know what the worst case scenario is? She says no, maybe later. Or even no, I don't want to ever get married. But so what? You're still waking up every day with her, probably calling her by disgusting cutesy names that Viv and I would have to slap you for. Buy her a big white dress, dance with her in your living room, and then take her to some island where the natives have all forfeited their land for souvenir shops and screw her until you both can't move anymore. It's that easy. Ask her, if you want to, if that's your deal. But it's not the end of the world, either way.

I swear to God, I will start charging you for this. What kind of perfect love story includes so much fucking up?

Tristan

❖ ❖ ❖

March 12th

Savannah, Georgia

Lilly

from: Nate Samuels
to: Lilly Jameson
sent: March 12, 1:20 p.m. EDT
subject: Something to tell me?

Lilly—

Well. You're never going to believe who just called—your ex, of all people. Yep. Tim Beals just called me at work because apparently you've been ignoring *his* call so he called the receptionist and asked for me by name. He read in *The Denver Post* something to the effect of "Local Author Marries College Sweetheart."

My response to him was basically a very inarticulate *whaaaat*, while I frantically started going through my email, googling, and sorting through mail trying to figure out if I'd just overlooked some urgent correspondence.

Then I checked *The Denver Post* online.

Some lady in Savannah is saying you've gotten hitched— something about you and Adin honeymooning in the area. They named a bed and breakfast, in fact. Is this true? Do we need to rearrange your schedule? (You are still planning on going to the Writers in the Schools event in Vegas, right?) I think we need to talk about this—I'm not a fan of a potential name change—just throwing that out there. It would just lose and confuse your audience.

Anyway, I didn't know you and Adin were getting so serious. Just thought I'd let you know Tim is looking for you.

So did you both elope in Savannah? Care to call me when you get a sec?

Nate

• • •

from: Lilly Jameson
to: Nate Samuels
sent: March 12, 5:15 p.m. EDT
subject: Re: Something to tell me?

Nate:
Adin and I went to a B&B in Savannah and he mistakenly (don't ask) checked us in as Mr. and Mrs. Driscoll to speed up the check-in. Apparently some locals saw this and I suppose they told people and somewhere along the way someone connected the dots.

I'm sorry Tim called you. He said some things to Adin a few weeks ago that really pissed me off, so I've not been taking his calls. I'll call him back though. I'm sure he must think I've lost my mind or something.

I'm leaving Savannah tomorrow to look at a place on Amelia Island, then I may go to Beaufort to see my parents for a few days. I'm still planning on going to the Vegas Writers in the Schools event. You have my number if you need anything. I'm sorry about all the confusion.

Lilly

AFTER I LOOKED AT A FEW PROPERTIES WITH a realtor, I walked around Amelia Island all afternoon by myself, mostly thinking about the last week. I ended up at the island's one convenience store. I bought a Coke and went outside to sit on the wraparound porch and took my sandals off.

Adin and I seemed to be out of step. I didn't like that there were a lot of people out there who thought I'd remarried so soon after my divorce. And I didn't like that I'd freaked Tim and my whole family out. Many people had seen the news and a steady stream of congratulatory cards had started coming in, arriving at my place in Denver and at my parent's place in Beaufort. The whole thing was embarrassing because people hadn't just read that we'd gotten married, but they read about our history, too, which *was* real.

Arthur's piece began to circulate online. Readers wrote to me touching letters about fate. Fans began posting stickers of wedding cakes on my social media pages. Old college buddies confessed to me that Adin had always had a thing for me, and OU's alumni network wanted to do a story about us. It had put me in an awkward spot because, on the one hand, people thought it was a great love story and were genuinely happy for us, but I had to be the one to limit that love story. I had to be the one to correct everyone. Going to Amelia to check out some properties by myself had been my way to get some space. I needed to think. And I didn't want to blow up at Adin, which I knew was coming if I hung around Savannah.

The story in *The Denver Post* got picked up by two other large news outlets, and my email and social media accounts began to explode with messages of congratulations. That's what you get for tempting fate, I'd told him, handing him my phone so he could see the outpouring of well-wishes on my Facebook account.

I'd overheard some of the conversation between Adin and Arthur in the restaurant. I'd stopped to look at some framed photography from the *Midnight in the Garden of Good and Evil* movie while Adin had been talking about marriage again.

Adin was already trying to find the right time to propose, and it scared the crap out of me. Had he not understood what I'd been trying to tell him? I felt like he was trying to slowly push me into something and right then the last thing I wanted was to feel pushed into anything.

I'd listened to Adin explain why he'd done what he'd done at that B&B, but part of me still suspected there was more to the story. It felt like there'd been a rip in the fabric of who he was and when I looked through the tear I saw the real Adin, perhaps the person he wished he could really be around me. He really did want us to get married, and writing my name down as Mrs. Driscoll was his giving that *other Adin* room to breathe. He was chomping at the bit to take the next step and I felt guilty because I knew I was letting him down, not willing to go there. When I told him I might be ready again, *someday*, it was presuming that how I truly felt would change pretty dramatically. I knew that my qualifying the whole thing was mostly an attempt to play it safe and not lose him.

And so I left. I needed to be alone. I needed some time to think about what I could and could not offer Adin.

I drank the last of the Coke and slipped my shoes back on. I knew myself well enough to know that I would make a mess of this if I wasn't careful.

And one thing continued to nag at me: When I had told Adin that the B&B mix-up had gotten out and that *The Denver Post* had run an article about us honeymooning in the area, I'd seen a split second of something like delight cross his face (again, a rip in the fabric). I'd wanted to point out that he was to blame for the confusion, but I held back. I was angry that his oversight felt careless. This was *my* life, and now a lot of people believed something that was not true. *His* carelessness made *me* look careless. But I knew I was witnessing the unsaid thing he wanted—he wanted the *love show*. He wanted the spectacle, and he wanted the clarity that came with an official title applied to us.

I'd put the last of my things in the rental car and left without saying much. I was beginning to think that I was leading him on since I had no desire to get married and marriage was clearly a very big deal for him. I couldn't ignore what he would eventually want me to commit to. Still, as I left him, I could feel my life getting darker, dimmer somehow. And then I understood what it was: I was submerging myself (again) in that grayness that characterized my life without him. When did his affection and proximity become the central, steadying force in my life? Yet it felt like we were speaking two different languages, some days, linked only by what went unsaid and by the gravitational pull of our bodies.

But I couldn't do the love show. I couldn't play that kind of game. And I couldn't tell that kind of lie.

Before I left, I told Adin I would see him in Vegas for Tristan's wedding. I told him I needed to get back to things in Denver and, while standing in his driveway, he gave me a look I'd seen before—a mixture of apprehension and fear. I'd walked to the edge of that cliff with him, hadn't I? But I wasn't ready to fall with nothing but my back to the wind. I felt foolish. I felt like I was losing sight of myself. I wasn't ready to take this any further, no matter how right it all felt. Or how many nights I'd gone to sleep wondering where he was or what he was thinking about. I was not going to lead him on. And so I began to do the one thing I swore I would never do again—put distance between us.

⬖ ⬖ ⬖

October 11, 2004
Ohio University, Athens, Ohio

Adin

I WAS ON MY WAY OUT THE DOOR of a coffee shop on Union Street when I heard Ryan Adams drifting from the window of a passing car. Not the old stuff but something from his new album, maybe "Answering Bell," maybe "New York, New York." I stopped short, like I'd caught a whiff of a strong scent, and turned, seeking out the source. This was a college town—just about anybody could be blasting Ryan Adams that fall. I guessed it was the El Camino rounding the corner to Court, the one with the four different Kerry/Edwards bumper stickers and the peace sign hanging from the rear view, but who could say? As it disappeared from view, the song faded and only the chill on my neck remained.

"You okay?" Corrie asked, blowing steam off the rim of her cup. I glanced down at her, and she looked back, her small brown eyes crinkling at the corners. She was in her wool coat and scarf, bundled up like it was January, both hands wrapped around the paper sleeve for warmth. This was how she was—thin-skinned, like me.

"Sure. Why?"

"You just had this look on your face."

I winced, but tried to hide it, being as I was now under scrutiny. "A look. Huh."

"Yep." She took a sip, grunted, held it in her mouth for a second. "Hot?"

She nodded.

This was a fairly standard-issue conversation for us.

Athens was deep in the throes of autumn, long rivers of color like a moat around the campus, bare ends of branches poking at the belly of the sky. Corrie and I crunched our way back toward Boyd, she firing off texts one-handed, a skill that would forever escape me, and me trying my damnedest not to dwell on what it was about that music that had so enthralled me. I didn't want to believe the real reason, and so I satisfied myself that it was just nostalgia for freshman year, a topic that had, in fact, been on my mind fairly often lately. I had watched Corrie's own initiation into her new circle in the weeks since we'd started going out, observed from an outsider's perspective the way that she and her little coterie had started to set, like handprints in wet concrete. They were good people, and I'd hung out with them on a few occasions, the same way she'd hung out with me and Jane and

Tristan and Julianna. But they weren't *mine*, those friends of Corrie's. And I should have been able to realize, right off the bat, that Corrie wasn't mine either.

"I've got to do some Euro History when we get back," Corrie informed me in half-monotone, still thumbing away at her keypad. "Some outlining for a paper."

"That sounds intense. You telling me to piss off?"

She glanced up, smirking, and then lifted herself up on her toes to kiss me. "You're cute when you use profanity."

"I think I'm *roguish* when I use profanity. I'm *cute* the rest of the time."

"Thankfully you're also modest under both circumstances."

"That's how I make the cute part work."

We kept walking for a minute or two. She was still working her coffee down to room temperature, and I was shuffling through the ankle-high leaves, kicking them up in that way adults can't ever seem to restrain themselves from (or, at least, not this adult). "No, really though," I said, after a bout of silence. "You want me to give you some time alone to work?"

"Um," she glanced up at me and then back down at the phone. After a split second of deliberation, she slipped it into the pocket of her very, very tight pants. "You don't *have* to go."

"But it would be better."

"I didn't say th—"

"Hey." I stopped and turned, laid my hands across her shoulders. "It's okay," I said. "I'm not delicate. I can live somewhere else for a day. I'm not a dude who needs to be needed all the time."

I had hoped that this assurance would soothe her, that maybe she'd even be a little relieved to be dating a guy who could say these things clearly and out loud. But instead it seemed to make her mildly uncomfortable, and I sensed right away that I had made too much of her protest, turned this into a more serious moment than it deserved to be. I liked Corrie—a lot. It was easy to forget that we'd only been together for five weeks. "Okay," she said, eyes down, thumb fidgeting against the side of the cup. "That's cool. I can just text you when I'm done. Meet you back at Boyd for dinner?"

"Mass-produced meat loaf. I can't wait."

She smiled again, but it was just a little bit less enthusiastic, a little more for my benefit. "Miss you," she said, and gave me another small peck.

I kissed her back. "Miss you, too." Which, in fairness, was only half a lie. I would miss her, in those next few hours. Her little blond spirals; her high, lilting voice; the way she would sit with her legs bent at the knee and crossed at the ankles, book huddled against her chest. But I wouldn't miss the constant, exhausting effort we were both sustaining. Being alone, even if it meant being away from her, would hit me like a cool washcloth to the forehead.

TRISTAN AND I HAD MICROWAVE BURRITOS AND A few shots of Kamchatka vodka back in my room. Tristan was multitasking, getting in his Poli Sci reading during commercial breaks of *Jeopardy!* I was mulling over a series of photos I had taken the day before, black-and-whites of some older Athens storefronts, hardware signs, and working-class bars. I also had a bunch of shots from a week ago, places along SR 32 where the trees had gone bare early. But nothing jumped out at me. Nothing seemed worthy of portfolio placement. There was something so drab about it all, so commonplace. Everything just screamed, *This is the shit that photography students put in portfolios.*

"Womp, womp," Tristan said. I looked up, and he was staring at me with an exaggerated look of woe, bottom lip jutting out.

"Yes?"

"You have this *look*, right now. Such a look as I haven't seen since...I don't know. Tuesday."

I sighed, turned away from my computer screen, crossing my arms over my lap. "You're the second person to say that to me today."

"I'll accept that. I'm probably the first person most days." But when I didn't laugh, he rolled his eyes and grabbed the remote, muting the TV. "Fine. I will console you for the next five minutes. *Double Jeopardy!* is always less fun than single jeopardy, anyway. But at *Final Jeopardy!* I'm turning Alex back on, and all your problems better be solved by then."

"I didn't ask to be consoled, man. I'm just doing my homework over here."

"You never ask. It just sort of happens. Also, you've gone out like four times in the last two weeks to take a butt-ton of pictures, but then I just watch you clicking delete, delete all the goddamned time. So many clicks, I feel like I'm in a fucking watch factory. Also—"

"I miss Lilly." I looked up, and for once I'd managed to stop Tristan in his tracks. He'd all but left his mouth hanging open. "All right? You want to play shrink, there it is. I fucking miss her. She left, and she didn't come back, and she hasn't called *once,* and I might never see her again for all I know, and I can't even so much as hear a single song without it reminding me of all of these things. I miss her. And I miss everybody else, too. I watch Corrie with her little group, and I'm so jealous of her it makes me feel sick. She makes me happy, and I really like her, but shit just feels *different* this year. It feels broken in a way that can't be fixed. Everybody—you, and Jane, and even Jason, that son of a bitch— we're just these pieces scattered all over campus now. Except Lilly. She is halfway across the country. And it bothers me. A lot. I don't know why it doesn't bother you guys, because it should."

I turned back to peruse my photos again, mostly as an excuse not to look at him. But I could feel him still looking at me. Between us, a muted Alex Trebek performed his hosting duties in pantomime. Outside in the street a passing car, the whooping cries of men who were better than me at being young.

"It bothers us, dude. Trust me." Tristan sounded serious now. I could always tell when this happened, because he lost the affectation. His voice deepened, his words got rounder at the edges.

"Well, you're just handling it better than me, I guess."

He sat there for a minute, leaning forward, hands folded between his knees. Then he slumped back. The chair groaned beneath him. "So then what if Lilly did come back? What if she were here, and she was as different as everybody else is now? And she saw that you were different, saw you and Corrie together. Would your life be any easier than it is, if that happened?"

I shook my head. "No. But I could say to her, God, this isn't easy, is it? And she could say, No, it's definitely not. Let's go lie in Bicentennial Park and listen to terrible music and talk about it."

Tristan was quiet for a minute or two. I glanced over at him a few times, but he was looking away, troubled, though I couldn't tell exactly why. Then he hit a button on the remote, and Alex interjected, "Legend says this musical was inspired by Lunt and Fontanne's backstage bickering before a Shakespeare play."

"What is *Kiss Me, Kate*?" we both asked in unison.

LATER, AFTER ANOTHER HOUR OR TWO SPENT DISCARDING photo after photo ("Careful," Tristan warned, "or you won't have any darlings left to kill."), I called Corrie and said I wasn't feeling well. As usual, it wasn't entirely a lie, but it was close enough that I felt queasy saying it. I wanted to text her, but that would have made me feel even worse.

I took the camera out, with no particular plan except to find *something* I could take a picture of that wouldn't disappoint me later. I did some experimenting with street lamps in the low light, different shutter speeds, higher ISO. I took some shots of the residence halls (but stayed clear of Boyd). Eventually I wandered over to the East Green, to the bench out in front of Jefferson. It felt strange to be there, like wandering into a house your parents sold years ago. I stood there, looking at it, camera hanging heavy at my neck. I thought about taking a picture of it, but that felt impossible somehow. I may as well have taken a picture of freshman year itself.

Twice I took my phone out while I was walking around, brought up Lilly's number. My thumb hovered over *Call*. One button, one minuscule gesture, was all that separated her from me. But that wasn't true—there were also five hundred miles, and Jason, and my own simmering rage and fear, and the colossal, insurmountable truth that you can't have your own past back, not the way you want it. You can only hope for some version of the future that's just as good.

It was almost 11 p.m. by the time I stumbled back to my dorm. I stood in the doorway, looking through the bleak, desperate selection of shots I'd taken. For some reason, stopping here on the front step made me think of how Tristan and I used to have a cigarette after dinner a couple years ago. Menthols, naturally. Smoke in the darkening sky, cool fire in our throats. Now Tristan spent every evening at the gym, and his only vice was booze. So much that we could never have back. So many small moments. So much time piled up in some cosmic landfill somewhere. It seemed pointless to try to take pictures of anything. If all it would do was remind you of what you couldn't have, like items in the window of a closed-down shop, then why do it at all? Why pour so much of yourself into clinging to a single second, a single point on the line? I was finished with all that, finished with my own unreachable, unknowable history. I didn't want to capture the present—I wanted to live in it.

I called Corrie back, and I went over. The camera I left in my room. It could wait, I thought. The pictures weren't due till December.

⧫ ⧫ ⧫

March 20, 2014
Savannah, Georgia

Adin

WHY DID SHE GO BACK TO COLORADO? I couldn't guess. Sure, she had to get back to what was, at the time, her regular life, her own home and her job. But a lot of the book stuff was dying down; there was nothing for her there. And still, here we were. No talk of when we would see each other again. It was a wait and see, the way people part ways after a second date. Except I thought that we had skipped that part. I thought that, after all the years of history and after these past couple of tumultuous months, we had bought the right to get straight to the *being in love* part.

Imagine my surprise, thinking this way, when she announced she was going. "Going?" I asked.

"Yeah," she said, picking hairs from the shoulder of her blouse. "I still need to go see my parents in Beaufort, and I have stuff to get back to at home, and I figured, you know, since I'm already packed and everything..."

The way she said it reminded me of in the movies, when people say, *Well, I'd make you breakfast, but I gotta get ready for work. I'll call you, okay? Yeah, sure. I'll call you.* Why she didn't just tell me I'd scared her off with the marriage stunt was bewildering to me, because she had to know that we both understood that's what it was. She stayed for dinner, a quiet leftover pot roast Dad had brought home from the grocery store the day before, and then I saw her off in her rented car. She looked especially beautiful, in the way that leaving people do. She had her hair up with sticks, like she had worn it in college.

"I'll call you when I get there," she said. And then she didn't.

Two days later I got a call from Enith Higgs.

"Who?" I asked. I was out for a walk, trying to negotiate an intersection by the highway. The sound of chrome-ribbed Fords roaring by made it hard to focus.

"Enith, honey," she said. "You stayed at our little getaway earlier this week."

"Oh!" I said. "Right. Yes."

She had a proposal for me. I was a photographer. The Dew Drop Inn needed its website updated somewhat urgently. Would I be willing to take some pictures? They could pay, of course. Word on the street was that I was looking for work. "Sure, Ms. Higgs," I relented, grimacing at the idea that my career stall was somehow public knowledge. "Of course I'll take some pictures for you."

"Oh, Honey, you're makin' me feel like an old lady," said the old lady. "Call me Enith."

"Yes. Enith. Pictures. I'll be there tomorrow."

I showed up at eight-thirty that morning. I was eager to be done with this job. The sight of the place, especially the cozy little suite at the back of the courtyard, was kind of sickening to me now. It made me think of hairs picked from a blouse, hands disappearing into a driver's seat. I started snapping almost at random, thinking they'd never notice if the work was awful or not. As long as it was their little project in the frame.

It wasn't until about twenty minutes into it that I started trying. Once the shock of seeing it all again so soon had worn off, once I had settled into a groove of scout, pose, frame, click, something switched over inside of me. An old instinct kicked in. I stopped being an anxious, heartsick kid and started being a hired lens. I was in the courtyard, facing this big, white Spanish colonial revival, looking down a corridor of Roman arcades toward the front, past a stone fountain with moss on its lip and up the back of its demure cherub. I took a long, deep breath. I raised my camera. I searched for the shot like I was looking through a periscope. I took the picture.

A moment passed, but it was more than a moment. I lived inside it for a little while, made it my home. I took long, gulping breaths, as though I'd just come up for air. And I felt, at some layer of my being too deep to be scanned or painted or written or even properly conceived of, a distinct sensation of release.

I went back to the car for my tripod. I moved on to the narrow, tidy fenestration, the awnings, the stucco. The Dew Drop became the whole world for a little while, and I moved about it boldly, like an explorer. I barged into unoccupied rooms, climbed ladders to shoot over the tops of light fixtures, dirtied my elbows in the grass. I took over a 150 photos. At one point, about halfway through, I went back to the car again. This time I got my phone and a pair of earbuds. I did the rest of the shoot listening to *Heartbreaker* on repeat.

Two hours later, I brought the camera inside to show Enith. She was in rapture. "Oh, honey," she sighed, "these are *gorgeous*. These are *just* what we need. I'll have Betty's grandson put these up right away." She took out a big binder from underneath the desk. "You workin' for anyone, or should we just make the check out to you?"

"Oh, uh," I stammered. I was always uncomfortable talking about money. "I guess, uh, just to me."

She pulled a pen from a coffee mug by the register. She licked the tip. "How is two hundred?" she asked. "That sound fair?"

The room seemed to buckle and sway. "What?" I replied, a little rudely. "But I was only here for two and a half hours."

Enith grinned. "Well, it was two and a half well spent, hon." She made a few shaky chicken scratches, and I was suddenly two hundred dollars richer. "I knew you did this for a job," she went on, "but I had no *idea* you were *this* good. I'll have to let the girls at The Newton Ridge know about you."

I shrugged helplessly. "What's The Newton Ridge?"

"Oh, it's a place over in Bloomingdale. I have friends there. We were talking about how we all needed new photos. That's how I remembered you. I'm sure once they see these, they'll just fall all over themselves for you." She glanced around and then leaned forward secretively. "And they've got a lot more money than we do. Just don't tell anyone I said that."

I had to focus on keeping my breathing steady until I was back in the car.

from: Adin Driscoll
to: Tristan Rawlings
sent: March 20, 6:04 p.m. EDT
subject: Re: Re: WTF do I do now

Well, I decided what I'm going to do. I'm not going to ask Lilly to marry me. Maybe this is weird, but I guess I just realized that I have other things to make me happy now, not just the promise of epic true love.

The craziest damn thing has happened: I'm actually making money taking pictures. This lady called me from the place where Lilly and I stayed, saying she'd pay me to take a few shots for their website. I figured she'd just give me like forty or fifty, as a favor to my dad. Instead she gave me two hundred, and a referral to some friends in Bloomingdale. The friends gave me the same job, this time for four hundred. I don't know what makes these women think that they need to pay me so much; it's like they're just itching to get rid of the money. But they sent me off to friends, who sent me to more friends. I've done two motels, a nursery, and a little plantation house this week. I've made over $1,500. That was how much I made in a whole month at Family PhotoWorks. And I LIKE this job. I can take whatever pictures I want, and everybody seems cool with it. I can pick my angle, my lighting, my zoom, my composition, anything, and they pay me through the nose for it.

I'm looking at apartments on Tybee Island, so I can stay close to what looks like it might be steady work. I've got another four jobs lined up next week alone. I think someone might want me to do their wedding; I had this picture of two guests in a porch swing that they just wouldn't stop talking about. What happened to me, man? A few months ago I was a miserable Yankee drone, with no plans and no motivation to make them. Now I'm a few hundred miles away, taking pictures of stone gargoyles for a hundred bucks an hour, getting an apartment in a place I actually like.

The fact is, I was clinging to Lilly because she was all I had, and I was ready to claim her for the rest of my life just to make sure I'd never have to worry about having nothing again. Now that I'm starting to see what she saw, how you can fill all the holes yourself, I understand why she was so scared of the pressure I was putting on her. So I'm just going to let it ride, see where it goes. I love her, and she doesn't need me forcing her into something she's not comfortable with. I won't see her again until we come to the wedding in May, and I think when that time comes I'll have the sense to man up and finally be the version of myself that she's been waiting for.

Good news for you: maybe you can stop playing therapist now.

Adin

⊠ ⊠ ⊠

March 30th
Amelia Island, Florida

Lilly

from: Lilly Jameson
to: Tim Beals
sent March 30, 8:30 a.m. EDT
subject: Hey Tim

Hi Tim:

Thanks for the birthday card and flowers. I did sort of have a moment where I was like *oh my God, I'm 29 now...next comes...scary!*

I just want to say how sorry I am, again, for that thing in *The Post*. When I heard about it I just felt like the most insensitive jerk, ever, even if none of it was true. I can understand you being a little freaked out by the article. I'm sure you thought I'd lost it for good.

On a happier note, I just bought a place on Amelia Island. For the first time ever, I'm a homeowner. I looked at the area you mentioned, but I chose the more family-oriented part of the island. It's not too loud. And it feels safe. It feels like home. When I saw this group of little girls riding horses on the beach, I just sort of fell in love. I sign the contract tomorrow morning.

Tomorrow I'm going to Beaufort for a couple of days—it's Dad's sixtieth birthday and I can't miss that. Also, Mom said she had something in mind for my birthday—I'm guessing it's one of her famous B&B breakfasts with all my favorites. I'm looking forward to it. Then it's back to Denver. I have a ton of work to do on the series before jetting off to Vegas in May—I'm going as Adin's date to his best friend's wedding.

Lilly

Jane: Oh my God. There you are! Where have you been?

Lilly: everywhere!

Jane: saw you on YouTube in Atlanta. You looked so cute. and very bright!

Lilly: no. that wasn't cute. That was a travesty. Mom bought those pants. It was an emergency situation.

Jane: lol. I thought you didn't look like yourself. You had this deer in the headlights look on your face, like you were spacing out.

Lilly: something like that. how are things out there?

Jane: Harlow likes your books, I think. So you have a new fan. Trying to be ok w/ this stay-at-home thing. I feel a little out of touch w/ the world. I think I'm going to do the daycare thing—I have to get out of the house for my sanity.

Lilly: wow. You don't have to do that, though, right?

Jane: oh I know. You can't win, lilly. Just can't. you should have seen the look philip's mom gave me when he said I was going to try to get my old job back. Kiss of death.

Lilly: try to ignore her. block her out. She can't really know what you and your family need.

Jane: exactly. That's what I keep telling myself. So, you're moving back to the area, I hear. where is adin in all this?

Lilly: well, Amelia Island. Adin and I are…

Jane: don't tell me you two broke up

Lilly: no…I don't think so. I overheard him and his dad—adin was talking about proposing TO ME of all things. And I am nowhere near ready for that. So I left. I kind of bolted…just to put some space b/w us. We've not broken up. I like to think of this as giving each other space.

Jane: just remember what we talked about. I'd hate to see either of you w/ anyone else. I was actually really happy when I heard the wedding rumor.

Lilly: but I don't want to get married and I feel like loving him isn't good enough.

Jane: well…imagine him w/ anyone else but you. How does that make you feel?

Lilly: Don't even say it. Believe me, it's occurred to me how miserable I'd be. I'd be a festering little mess about it. And how stupid is that? Maybe I'm the impossible one.

Jane: I've thought the same thing. I have the option to stay home, raise my kid, oversee everything, etc. and yet I can't. that's just not me. I have to have a career—for my sanity. in order to live with myself otherwise I start feeling out of touch with everyone. But you and adin? I think you're both fairly ridiculous for different reasons.

Lilly: I told him we can be together, but I can't talk about marriage now. I just can't consider it. It scared me that much.

Jane: fear of entrapment? Are you scared of commitment?

Lilly: maybe, oh I hope not. I think I'm scared of making a mistake. Some people seem so much cooler about their mistakes. They can make mistakes all day and have this *whatever* attitude about it. To me, that's messy. That's NOT ME. I like getting things right. I like making sense. I don't like messes.

Jane: well adin doesn't seem at all concerned with you…

Lilly: being a mistake? for him?

Jane: Yeah. Just saying.

Lilly: I know. His confidence in me *not* being a mistake also worries me a little. Sometimes I wish I sensed more hesitation, more…I don't know, deliberation on his part. He's so certain about everything, and here I am…full of uncertainty. Full of fear.

⊠ ⊠ ⊠

April 1st–May 1st
Fort Collins, Colorado

Lilly

So what happened between April 1 and May 1? Not a lot, really. I flew back to Denver and made a lot of progress on my book series. I made fires in the fireplace and watched the snows begin to melt on the Front Range. Toward the end of April, I moved to my new home on Amelia Island. But before I moved anywhere, I had a long overdue dinner in Fort Collins with Tim.

He had made reservations at an Indian restaurant that had opened a week earlier on the edge of the University of Colorado campus. I hadn't seen him in over a month and my impending departure, as we both knew it, was permanent. I wasn't just leaving to go on a book tour—I wasn't coming back. This was me closing the book on us. I was really leaving this time. I realized it could be the last time we saw each other, and my stomach went into knots.

I walked into the restaurant at 6 p.m. The place was dark except for small lanterns that had been lit at each table. I saw Tim sitting near the far end of the room at a small, circular table for two, his back pressed firmly against the back of the chair.

I flashbacked to when we'd first met: I was a junior at USC, lost in a sea of other people. I'd been sitting at a rickety circular table in a coffee shop on campus one day in January, editing a short story and catching up on some assigned reading. He'd walked by and, seeing my tattered copy of *Lolita*, asked me how I was liking it so far. "How long you got?" I asked, looking up at him. He laughed and ended up taking a seat. We started talking. I was shocked when he told me he was a law student. He could easily talk about Leibniz, Nabokov, and French surrealist poetry. He was smart and funny. Smarter than about anyone I'd ever met. He got up at one point and ordered us both the same sandwich— peanut butter and banana. I'd never had one, but it was delicious. We talked for hours. He told me stories about going to undergrad out East. How he was interested in Environmental Law. How he'd decided at the last minute to go to USC for law school because it was closer to his family back in Charlotte and how he'd hated New England winters. I told him about the guy who wrote music lyrics in my Fiction class and turned them in for critique. How I had transferred from OU to USC. How I'd walked in on one of my roommates pleasuring herself in the shower. How my French class had me thinking about going to France someday. How my dad would hate that.

We laughed and talked, ate our sandwiches, refilled our coffee cups, got some water, got more water. And then I realized the sun was setting.

We ended up getting dinner together at the same cafe. He'd asked me to go somewhere off campus, but I didn't really know him, so I made up an excuse for needing to stay close by. When he asked for my number an hour later, I happily gave it to him. And he called the next day. And the day after that. What he didn't know at the time was that my life had become a dark, quiet space, devoid of friends, parties, and laughter. I had a 4.0, but I hadn't been living life, exactly. He changed that.

And there he was—waiting for me now—the one alone, lost at sea.

He gave a slight wave and I headed toward him, noticing how chilly the restaurant was. I wore a black leather bomber jacket over a tight-fitting white T-shirt and jeans with an aqua scarf around my neck. I tossed my bag onto the floor beside me, wishing I'd worn more.

"Hey, new scarf?"

"Um. No, not really. Well, sort of. I borrowed it from mom's closet last time I was home."

"How are they?"

"Dad's still puttering around the farm and letting mom run the B&B. He pretends to hate it, but he talks to the guests more than she does," I smiled, sitting down across from him.

"The company's probably good for him," he said.

"Oh yeah," I nodded. "I like to think it broadens him, all these guests coming and going. Maybe it'll open his mind a little. I'm still waiting on that part." I shifted in my seat and glanced at a large mirror on the opposite wall that made the whole room feel like it was twice as big as it really was.

"So tell me how you found out about this place."

Tim crossed his arms and leaned in. "Oh, one of our clients told me the place was good." He glanced at the mural and then back to me. "I know you love Indian food." He fumbled for the menu, slightly pushing the lantern against the wall. "You'll probably order what you always order, though, right? You like to stick with what you know," he said unfolding the menu.

"Oh, I don't know. Maybe I'll get something different."

Tim cleared his throat, looked at the menu for a moment and then set it aside. I could tell something was bothering him. He seemed agitated. A little fidgety. He touched his tie and stared at the lantern's wick. I realized the tie was one I'd bought him at Brooks Brothers years ago on our first (or was it second?) Valentine's Day.

"Nice tie," I said, reaching for my water glass.

He glanced at the tie and then smiled. "I thought you'd appreciate that."

"I do."

He relaxed a little. "So tomorrow's a big day. Are you looking forward to getting down there?"

"I am. I'm ready for a change. For the next chapter. You know you're always welcome to visit me or mom and dad."

"Well, I'll get in contact with you when I'm in the area. But your parents? They hated me," he said. "You know they never liked me much."

"Oh, I don't know about that."

"Lilly, your dad showed me his gun collection, for God's sake. First time you introduced me to them. He shows me his *gun collection*. You don't think that's sending a message?"

"He's genuinely *proud* of that gun collection."

"All I'm saying is that I'm sure I'm no great loss to the Jamesons."

I looked away from him. "They don't hate you. *At all*."

Tim laughed and leaned back in his seat. "Are you kidding me? They despised me. The minute he found out I went to Yale, I was a goner."

"No, the minute you said *no* to a *tractor pull*—that was the minute you were a goner."

He laughed. "Well, there was no way in hell I was getting on that thing."

"Adin did. Adin wore a helmet."

Tim choked on his water. "What? At a tractor pull with your dad?"

I shrugged. "I think he thought that was protocol."

"Did you get a video of that? I would love to see it," he said, still chuckling to himself.

I shook my head. "No, no. I wish I did. I think I was in shock that he was there at all."

"Oh yeah?"

I nodded. "He just showed up, and the next thing I know Dad is giving him the lay of the land and then they're both up there on a tractor. He was the last person I thought I'd see."

"Well, then he already has me beat. He did a tractor pull."

"Honestly, Dad seems to always be on my case about him now, if that's any consolation. If Adin and I broke up, then I'm sure dad would start liking him, too."

"Adin would never break up with you," he said flatly. He sounded like an exasperated teacher, repeating for the hundredth time that $2+2=4$.

I opened my mouth to say, *Don't be so sure about that*, but right then the waiter came and took our orders. I ordered something completely unfamiliar (because I felt like doing this would prove something important to Tim, though I wasn't sure what) and Tim ordered my old standby for reasons which I'm sure he had thought deeply about but which were lost on me. We sat there quietly for a moment, trying to speak to each other.

I unrolled my silverware from my napkin and began fiddling with the lantern, making the flame grow bigger and then smaller.

"Well, I'm glad your dad doesn't think I'm a douchebag," he said.

"No one thinks you're a douchebag, Tim," I said lowering my voice.

"Well, *you* seemed to think that I was—"

"I *never* called you a douchebag." I sat back in my chair and looked squarely at him. "That's not how I talk."

Tim rolled the sleeves up slightly on his maroon sweater, becoming instantly businesslike, re-dignifying himself by sitting up even straighter. I thought that this must be what he looked like in the office, working with clients. And the person he presented was polished, clean, capable, and professional. And I'd always loved that steadiness about him. But it was almost boring, how well he did at life. Or how easy life seemed for him, and I hated myself for thinking that because I had loved him. And I still did, in a way.

"Well, no...you didn't call me that, per se. That's not your style. I thought I was supportive."

"You were supportive, Tim. But you took on way more when I asked you not to. You worked all the time. You still do. You always will."

"This is my life, Lilly. I saw an opportunity—"

"Yeah, you did, Tim. You *did* see an opportunity."

He sat there, silent, daring me to say more.

"Did you really think I wouldn't catch on to what was going on, Tim?"

"Lilly, you and I hadn't—"

"I know we agreed not to talk about it anymore, but don't try to put the blame on my shoulders. Not the day before I leave. You checked out and then I checked out. It's really...as simple as that." I scooted back from the table and looked at him.

"Okay. Fair enough..." he said, trailing off.

"That's not a revelation to you."

He raised his hands as if he would no longer have anything to do with the dispute. He took a drink of water, and the way he sat there, so calm and square, irritated me. Emotion needed a way out, didn't it? Didn't you sometimes need to slouch, to get angry, to lean in, to wring your hands? To pull your hair a little bit? To get a little uncivilized? Why did Tim never let himself just be a little wrecked by feeling? And as soon as my mind asked the question, I knew the answer. *It was a lack of feeling.*

"Would you like for me to order us a pot of tea?" he asked.

I took the napkin from my lap and sat it on the table. "Sure. That sounds good."

"Jasmine okay with you?"

I took a deep breath. "Yes," I said, not looking at him. I was thinking about what it was like right before we separated: I could tell him I'd be gone for three weeks, and he'd respond with the same level of interest as me telling him I was picking up sushi for dinner.

Tim flagged down a waiter and placed the order then looked back at me. "Lilly, I know this is probably the last time I'll see you for a while, so I just wanted to clear the air a bit."

"Clear the air? What do you mean?"

"And this is just me getting some closure," he said, prefacing things. "Was there ever anything between you and Nate?"

Nate? This is what he's thinking about?

"No, Tim. I told you nothing has *ever* happened between me and Nate."

"I just know you two talk a lot."

I waved the idea away. "I don't even know why we're talking about this."

I couldn't help but notice he chose to fixate on Nate, never paying much attention to Adin, as if Adin was nothing more than a blip on the radar, and this made me angry. I sat there wondering why he didn't seem to expend the same amount of worry and anxiety there. No, it was Nate that he was secretly either envious or jealous of. Probably his bow ties. His expensive glasses. His high-profile career in New York City. I was all but certain he'd found a way to start looking into Nate's background. He'd probably found a way to get a criminal background check and a credit report run on the guy, just to satisfy that jealous little itch.

"Okay, then. What's the deal with Adin? Is this new house of yours a joint venture?"

I reached for the scarf and began looping it around my neck. "No, it's mine. I don't really know what's going on with Adin. He's working as a photographer in Savannah."

"So he's in Savannah, and you'll be on Amelia Island? How far is that? Three hours?"

"It's just shy of two hours," I replied, a little too quickly.

He crossed his arms and stared at me, a self-satisfied grin forming. He took another drink of water.

"The self-employed thing is kind of a red flag," he said, leaning into the table slightly.

I eyed him carefully. "*You're* self-employed."

"I think we both know my situation is a little different from his."

I took a deep breath. "Tell me what you're getting at."

"This economy and all. People can't afford *nice* pictures. That's kind of a luxury these days."

"He's not a hobbyist, if that's what you're getting at. He does professional-level work."

"Lilly, I'm just telling you what I know. If you want my opinion on the Nate versus Adin thing—"

"I really don't!" I said, just as our waiter appeared with our meals. "I really *don't*, Tim. And it's not even a competition," I added.

Tim pursed his lips. "Fair enough," he said, lifting both hands at exactly the right time for the meal to be placed in front of him.

⟨⟩ ⟨⟩ ⟨⟩

May 16th
Las Vegas, Nevada

Adin

VEGAS IS A LARGE PLACE. STRANGE LOOKING TOO, like a great big Jackson Pollock painting for the sky to look at. It's always unsettling to be in a city that is built specifically to not look like other cities. Especially when you're there for a wedding. And especially when you and your date have spent the last month only talking about once every week and a half. And you spent her birthday in rural Georgia, with no cell reception or wireless internet. And you missed picking her up at the airport.

We agreed that since I was there a day early for the bachelor party (which would take a book to get into—except to say that Tristan was both dismayed and delighted), it was my job to pick Lilly up at the airport. This would have been easier to do if I had a car, but Tristan and this other guy, Fuad, snuck out of my room at 3:30 in the morning and took the car to Battle Mountain so they could weather their hangovers drinking a six-pack of Sierra Nevada (not, in spite of their insistence, brewed in Nevada) in the middle of the desert.

I tried taking a cab, but taking a cab through Vegas is like taking a horse through a horse trailer. I did not, of course, arrive in time. In fact, she called when I was halfway there to say she was renting a car and coming to the hotel alone. She got there a full hour before I did.

I rode up to the twenty-second floor fidgety and hot, fingering my tie and the metal bar snaking the elevator's midsection. I hadn't seen her since she sped off from Savannah into the Western sunset. I hadn't talked to her since the beginning of the month, when we finalized our plans for the wedding weekend and I told her I had become successfully self-employed. "That's great," she said. "That's good to hear. I'm happy for you." This, I thought, was not the language of lovers. This was the language of once-coworkers who call each other once a year to offer updates on the kids.

She told me she had had dinner with Tim, which made me cold all along my neck and forehead.

"How did it go?" I asked.

"Ugh. Terrible," she replied, and I was secretly pleased to hear the disgust with which she said it. "He was being an asshole. That much was established."

"I see."

There was a fairly lengthy silence, and then she said, "Well. I have to let you go. I've started on this first book, finally."

"Okay."

"I'll talk to you later. Okay?" It sounded like a legitimate question.

"All right. Talk to you later." And the matter was settled.

The doors dinged open. I had to take a second to fan myself in the flower-urns-mahogany-tables mini-lobby. I stood there with my hands on my hips for a second. I took a deep breath.

I walked down the hall. I put my key in the door.

I came in.

"Hey," I ventured cautiously. No answer. I ducked into the bathroom, checked the beds for a sleeping body. Checked the balcony.

She wasn't there.

⊡ ⊡ ⊡

Lilly

SOMETHING WAS WRONG. I HAD SPENT NEARLY THE entire flight from Charleston to Vegas in the bathroom nauseous. I thought maybe I had been poisoned, just lightly poisoned somehow. Maybe Tim did it to me. At the time I attributed it to stress and nerves—after all, I was finally seeing Adin after a month apart and I didn't know where we stood. Thing is, I'm never sick and I've always loved to fly. So, when we landed in Vegas, I was feeling pretty rough—and I kept having to pee from all the ginger ale I'd been drinking trying to ease the nausea. What was wrong with me? Was this just some freak twenty-four-hour bug that was going around?

At the airport, I waited for Adin but he never showed up, which pissed me off, but I was mostly preoccupied with trying to figure out what was wrong with me. I sat on a bench, glancing around, hoping I'd spot him. I got out my hand sanitizer and spritzed away. When he never showed up, I rented a car to get to the hotel. Standing at the Budget counter, I felt a little light-headed. I was initialing my name beside the date on the contract when I paused, rereading the date.

When was the last time I had my period?

Can't be right, I thought, pushing the signed contract across the counter.

I got out my phone and looked at the calendar, scrolling between the different months, trying to remember where I'd been and when I'd been there.

Then the terrible math hit me: it had been months, *months* since I'd had my period. I felt a very intense panicky heat break out in me. A rush of adrenaline shot through my body, making my hands shake as I reached across the counter for the keys. I left the airport with my mind racing.

I tried to remember each and every time I'd been with Adin, speeding through each memory, only slowing down for the important parts.

One memory stood out to me, with its glaring omission. There was one night that I hadn't been as careful as maybe I should have been.

It was right after *The Tampa Incident* on Valentine's Day, and I had stopped taking my birth control pills that same week. And so we'd had unprotected sex. We'd had unprotected sex about six times in Tampa.

I entered the address for the MGM Grand into my phone and headed toward the hotel. There was no way I could let Adin know. We'd barely spoken lately and, for all I knew, he had lost interest in trying to make our relationship work. I'd noticed how our communication had dropped off. One minute he wanted to take things too fast, the next minute it was like there was nothing to take anywhere in the first place. I had to get to the room, dump my stuff off, and buy a pregnancy test.

According to the GPS there was a Walgreens on the same block as the hotel. I dropped all my stuff off without running into Adin, dashed over to the Walgreens, bought the test, went into the lobby restroom at the MGM Grand, and took the test. I didn't want to risk him finding me fretting over whether or not I was pregnant in the room he'd booked us. I knew if he was around right then I would have an all-out panic attack or a breakdown of some kind. I tore into the wrapper and followed the extremely tiny square of instructions. I walked out of the stall and carefully set the test down near the paper towels on the far side of the marble counter and waited for the results. Sixty seconds.

I could wait sixty seconds.

I propped myself against the wall closest to the test. I kept glancing at my watch. I was in the process of rereading the directions when about ten girls all wearing Beta Club T-shirts and black leggings walked in. They looked like middle-schoolers. I uncrossed my arms and turned so that my back blocked the test from view, aware that I was maybe not the best example for young women right then.

"Hi!" a young Asian girl with pigtails said.

I reached for the pregnancy test and sat it up high on a paper towel dispenser to get it out of view. There were five stalls in the bathroom, and they were all suddenly occupied. It was like a school bus had dropped them off for the weekend.

I swiped my hand under the faucet to get it to turn on and pretended like I had been washing my hands. "Hi! Are you all here for a...convention...or something?" I glanced at myself in the mirror and shook the water off my hands.

The girl took her phone out of a tiny black purse. The phone was covered in small, pink adhesive beads. "Oh yeah. We have to do our stage performance in like, an hour. Some of us are super nervous about it, but we've been working on it since March! I think it'll be fine."

"Oh yeah? Well, that's cool," I said, idly glancing at the pregnancy test to make sure it hadn't fallen into a trash bin or simply vanished.

The girl was doing something on her phone. "It is! We're doing this James Bond dance. It's only five minutes long, but the choreography is insane. It's amazing."

"I bet you'll do great!"

One of the stalls opened and the Asian girl practically skipped toward the stall.

I glanced at my watch. Time was up. Time was up two minutes ago. I pulled the pregnancy test down from the towel dispenser and reached for the directions one more time to compare the two.

I heard one of the toilets flush. A girl walked out and washed her hands. I focused on the test, reread the instructions, and stared long and hard at the color. Then I read the instructions again. I looked at the test one more time. A girl ducked by me to get a paper towel. Leaving, she called back, "Well, I hope you enjoy Vegas!"

I looked at her and smiled. "Good luck," I said, but it felt like an effort getting those words out and making them travel from me to her. It took too much energy. Words didn't do enough. Words didn't work hard enough anymore. I walked into a stall and locked myself in, grabbing some toilet paper and dabbing my face with a big, angry cloud of it and then flushed the whole thing. I walked out and buried the pregnancy test in a trash can. I could feel myself choking up.

"Thanks!" she said. She tossed her paper towel in the trash can and headed for the door. "Don't need luck! I am ready for this! *Ready!*" A few of the girls started clapping as they left, and before I knew it, they were all chanting some peppy cheer down the hall. I wondered if I could feel a little something like that, if I could feel just a little bit like that.

⟨⟩ ⟨⟩ ⟨⟩

Adin

I WAS WATCHING *AMERICAN IDOL* WHEN LILLY BARRELED a little clumsily into the room. She saw me and got this deer-in-headlights look and then ducked into the bathroom.

I had imagined a lot of ways that we might greet each other, but nowhere on the list had I put, *Um...you okay?*

"Fine," she chirped. I could hear generic bathroom rustling. "How have you been?"

I slid from the mattress to my feet. "Fine," I replied, in a slow imitation of her hasty assurance. I was waiting for the cold silence or the hot shouting, extreme emotional weather of some kind, to punish me for the airport incident. Instead she burst back into the room, reddened and vibrant, and threw her arms around me.

"Hey," she said. She smelled like sugar and vanilla. I wanted to press my face into the crook of her neck, but I felt like now was not a good time. She fell back from the hug and stood there, running her arms up and down my shoulders. "I missed you."

"I missed you, too." It was terrible, the way I wanted her, wanted to lock the hotel room door and just lie there entwined with her in the bed, trying to get our bodies to grow into each other like ivy. It was coming on like nausea, a sudden, overwhelming loss of control. We hadn't gone this long without seeing each other since Christmas, and while my life had taken a turn for the brighter, had become full and busying and filled with distraction, I still missed her.

"Well," I said, stepping away. I straightened my tie, classic man tic, but she didn't seem to notice. "What do you feel like for dinner?"

She shook her head, placed her hand to her gut. "I'm not really hungry."

"Oh." I was starving. I hadn't eaten since the night before; air travel always makes me sick.

She seemed to catch my disappointment. "We can go out if you want to."

"Oh, no, that's okay."

"Aren't you hungry?"

"Well, I mean. A little."

"Then let's go out."

"Well not if you don't want to."

"I want to if you're hungry."

"Well, I don't want to if you don't feel well."

"No, I feel okay."

"But you're not hungry?"

"I ate on the plane. It was a long flight."

"I know. I flew it too." I didn't mean for this to sound bitter or irritated, but I was thrown off kilter. She was supposed to be mad, or distant, or something. Why was she being so nice? It was freaking me out. I had come prepared to be as cool as she wanted me to be, to just let this be what it was and not try to fly at her like a love-struck assailant. I turned my back to her, tried to embrace the cityscape instead.

"Is something wrong?" she asked.

"No," I said. "No, everything's fine."

"Well, let's go get dinner. I'll get a little house salad or something."

I had worn a full suit because I wanted to look good for her. I wanted to wear something that felt like a second, better-looking skin, something that would make me feel silky and confident in her arms, something that, deep, deep down, I hoped she would tear off of me with desire. Now, in the middle of May in the desert, I was just feeling hot. I resented my tie. "Are you sure you're up for going out?"

"I better be," she said, glancing over the laminate of TV channels. "I'm here for a wedding."

Dinner was fine, okay by most normal people's standards. I had fried oysters; Lilly had a glass of water. "You want to get some wine, at least?" I asked. She shook her head no. "I thought you liked wine," I said. I was hoping we could plow our way through the weekend by oiling ourselves up with booze.

"I do like wine," she said, running her fingers along the tongs of her fork. "I'm just not in the mood for drinking."

I smiled, reached tentatively for her busy hand. "Maybe I should revoke your writer's card, in that case."

She grinned, let me take the hand. But she was still and reserved under my touch. I was sliding into panic—something was way, way wrong at this table. I knew that things had been shaky after the marriage debacle, but it was something that our reunion would smooth over, wasn't it? We loved each other, and people who love each other surmount such minor hiccups with laughing ease, don't they?

"When do we need to be ready tomorrow?" she asked.

I leaned back. I retrieved my hand. "I'm a groomsman, so I need to be there at one o'clock. You don't have to be there till three."

"You're not the best man?"

"No, his brother's the best man. I didn't have time to plan a coup." We were both smiling now, but it was like building a house on swampland. I knew that, at some point soon, all our hard work would only sink.

⟨⟩ ⟨⟩ ⟨⟩

Lilly

MUCH LATER THAT NIGHT, ALONE IN OUR ROOM, I pictured the future Adin, the father Adin. After I found out I was pregnant, the world had felt tilted or maybe it had been set right. That knowledge created this undeniable connection between us that I'd never experienced before. It was better than Tampa, what we shared in that room, backlit by the Vegas cityscape. I felt like a wave of acceptance had come over me. No matter what, we would forever share this one thing together. This one incredible thing.

He made a dream come true for me. But he didn't know it yet. I wondered how he would take the news. Would it matter to him that we weren't married? Would it matter to him that this wasn't exactly the right time? It was almost dawn when we decided to get some sleep, but not before he managed to give me a hickey that would be difficult to cover, considering the dress I brought to wear at the wedding.

I decided not to tell him about the pregnancy. Not for a while at least. What we were was still up for debate, and I didn't want the pregnancy to impact whatever decision we arrived at. As elated as I felt, I was also scared to death. I had always wanted to be a mother, but it had been in the vague future. It had never been in my immediate plans because I'd never felt like I'd found the right partner. I still felt like I wasn't ready. Every word that passed between us and every look now carried an absurd amount of weight. I found myself mentally tallying his good qualities verses his bad qualities, stupidly trying to decide if he would make a good father and if this was anything he'd want in his life.

Earlier that evening, when he went out with the guys, I ordered a fruit platter from room service and got the small picture of us out of my purse. It was the one he'd left at my place in Denver, but I'd held on to it, keeping it close. I did a little shopping for baby books online and then I parked myself on our king-size bed and made some notes while *Beaches* played on the flat-screen in the background.

Here's what I came up with—*a daddy potential list*:

Daddy Potential List

Pros	Cons
Decent height	Forgetful (forgot bday)
Artistic	Can be tediously insecure
Sensitive	Passive
Sweet	Takes a while to get around to stuff
Loving	
Funny	Fickle
Good taste in music	Messy (i.e., clothes heaps, dishes)
Good taste in movies	
Arthur is great	illegible handwriting
Faithful	Does he even want child (right now?)
Stable (?)	
Likes CBS Sunday morning	Dad thinks he's a bum
Likes books, likes what I do	Tim thinks he's a bum
Romantic	Child now would scare him away
Optimistic	Child would lock him into something?
Loves what he does— photography	

Maybe the list was dumb, but I was panicking and my mind was all over the place. Making lists had always helped me. Sure, we were great together, but I didn't even know what we were and, all of a sudden, I *needed* to know. But how would I figure something like that out without coming across as pushy? Or suspicious? The last thing I wanted was to make him feel entangled in a life he had no interest entangling himself in. I wanted the magic to stay this time, but I was trying to prepare myself for the worst-case scenario, which was that he had lost interest in me and wanted to live his own life in Savannah and leave me—and the future child for me to raise.

I put the cap back on my pen, reread my list, and nibbled at the few remaining grapes on the large, white plate. I picked up my cell phone to call mom when I heard a key in the door. I knew it was Adin back from the bars with the guys. I scooted the fruit tray off my lap, frantically wadded up the list, tossed it under the desk on the other side of the room, and reached for the remote.

✦ ✦ ✦

Adin

LET ME TRY TO PRESENT THIS AS IT appeared, as it felt, to me:

10 p.m.: The whole group, sans groom, invites us out for drinks. Lilly declines, citing her stomach trouble. I waffle, guiltily—I haven't seen these guys in a very long time. Lilly insists that I go, saying she has work to do and she'll be boring company if I stay in. Grateful to both her and them, I accept.

11 p.m.: I get roped into drinking a whole lot. I am not a drinker, at least not after this fashion. For better or worse, I do my drinking in solitary marathon sessions—I don't front-load shots in the company of a legion of screaming adult men. I definitely never drink in Vegas, where the cocktails are twice as strong and three times as expensive. Maybe it's that I'm so flush with cash from my newfound success. Maybe I'm just on a high now that I can return to my group triumphant,

The Guy Who Found His Calling. I'm not sure what seduces me, only that I am seduced.

1 a.m.: We hit the last bar. I texted Lilly, to tell her I love her. I get no response. I get antsy. It's obvious that she just didn't hear it, or she's busy, or she's sleeping off her bug. There are a thousand very good reasons why she is not shooting me back a fake digital peck on the lips. But I, in my stupor, disregard them all in favor of the one very bad one.

2 a.m.: I stumble across the too-bright lobby and into the elevator. I hold my breath and wish like hell for the trip to end so I can stop feeling giddy from the rise. I stumble a little more down the hall and into the door, where I spend three minutes fishing the card key from my wallet. The hall, not unlike the lobby, is very goddamned bright.

2:05 a.m.: I walk into the room, which is blessedly dim, intent on pretending that I am still sober. Yes, hi. I'm sober Adin. Sober Adin had a pleasant evening, yes, he did, thank you for your concern, but really we have a lot to do tomorrow, so time to turn in. Good night.

Lilly, sweet luminous Lilly, is sitting cross-legged in the middle of the bed, with her soft, white hotel robe kind of flowing out from her majestically. I stand there, just inside the room, leaning heavily on the corner of the wall, and I breathe, "You love me, right?"

Just like that, I have blown my own cover.

She puts aside her pad and pen and smiles at me, indulgently. Oh yes, she can see it in my face: I am toasted, toasted, oh my God, what if she wants to have sex? I've heard that being drunk makes it hard to, um, function. That is the grist at the rumor mill. "Of course I love you," she says, and I search this gentle assertion for subtext, I comb it for traces of a well-meant lie. What is wrong with me? I'm drunk, and I still can't—why the hell am I worried about being forced into sex and not loved *at the same time*?

2:06 a.m.: Lilly is suddenly amorous, and my "hastily removed-suit" fantasy is fulfilled. We go at it like we haven't seen each other—or anybody else—in five years. I feel like I'm having sex with a Platonic Form, probably the one for sex. To my intense relief, I function properly.

2:38 a.m.: We're semi-reclothing, and Lilly asks, "Do you love me?" I'm yanking my boxers back on, concentrating very hard on not falling face first into the mattress, and I glance up at her, a little confused.

"Yeah, of course I do. Why?"

"You asked first."

I blush and start searching for my undershirt. "I just—it's just I texted you earlier, and you didn't text back that you loved me so I was worried."

Her head falls back against the headboard. "I wonder sometimes just how old we really are." I think for a minute that a fight might be starting, but I look over and she's still smiling at me.

"Why did you ask me, then?" I insist. I feel a little steadier; I've just spent half an hour sweating out my drinks. I float across the room toward the bathroom for a little plastic cup of water. I am dreading dealing with the plastic covering.

"I just," she begins. I switch on the bathroom light, and I want to hiss like a vampire. "It just seemed like you were being really...I don't know."

"Really what?" I didn't know how thirsty I was. I forgot how much I love water, the endless expanse of quenching that fills me like love.

"Really...I don't know. Not loving."

The needle skips on the record of my life.

I leave the cup by the sink. I come back out into the room. Lilly is lying, is strewn, across the bed, looking sultry and vulnerable. "What does that mean?" I ask, and then, almost without a pause in between, "Hey, did I put a condom on or did we just start? Why didn't you tell me to wear a condom?"

She shrugs. "I don't know, Adin. Maybe we should just talk about this in the morning."

"No, but, I mean, why would you think that I'm not being loving?"

"Because you haven't been. You've been nothing like your normal self since I got here. You've been so...held back."

"Well, I mean, you haven't been normal either. You've been so...nice."

"Wait, so I'm not nice now?"

"No, I mean, not like that. Fuck." I run my hands through my hair, I breathe in, I try to hit the sober button. "Yeah. Yeah, this is morning talk right here."

"Too late now," she says. "Do you think I'm not nice?"

"Do you think I'm not loving?"

She pulls herself up, wraps the robe around herself like it's for protection. Fuck, why did she not answer my condom question. "It's just that you're normally so unreserved, so, I don't know, so *right there* with the way you love me. It's part of why I love being with you. But today you haven't been like that."

"Well, I mean, I thought you didn't want me to be like that."

"What?"

"I thought you wanted me to be less, like, right there and all. I thought I was scaring you a little, trying to take it too fast."

She gets out of bed. She's upset now. "God, Adin, why can I never know where I stand with you. First you're the most passionate guy I've ever met, and then you're jetting off to find yourself, and then you want to propose to me, and then you want to slow things down—"

"Whoa, whoa, whoa," I hold up my hands. "Back that train up. When exactly did I want to propose to you?"

Why I ask this question is a mystery to me, drunk or otherwise. But somehow she knows, somehow she has figured out my dark secret. Why am I acting indignant, like she's making it up? It's too bold to be a bluff. She knows. And then I feel a sickening plunge— *she knows.*

Lilly sighs, crosses her arms. She has to tell the floor, because the floor will take it better than I will. "I overheard you. Talking to Arthur. I heard you talking about wanting to propose to me."

For a second, I think I'm going to puke, for any number of reasons. Then it passes, and as soon as it does I want it back, because I will take any excuse, *any*, to get out of this room.

❂ ❂ ❂

Lilly

"LILLY, YOU WERE NOT, I REPEAT NOT SUPPOSED to hear that."

"I know! I shouldn't have said anything. I just thought we were, well..." I shoved my hands into the plush pockets of the robe, looking for the right words, and turned away from him slightly. "Just...not the sort of couple to not speak for so long. I mean, would you call this dating? This to me is a fucked-up limbo state. Some days I think we're together, some days I really don't know. I don't know what to tell my friends or my parents, and that bothers me."

Adin nodded.

"I mean I'm not saying I want you to propose. I don't want that. Not...like...this, anyway. Oh my God, I need to shut up. I feel like I'm scolding you or something. Jesus, I'm sorry. I shouldn't have even mentioned that."

He looked away from me. "No, no. You heard right."

I thought he might say something else, but he didn't. I took the robe off and climbed into bed. Adin said nothing, only nodded his head once as if putting an end to the conversation. He turned and went into the bathroom and seemed to be brushing his teeth. I heard the toothbrush hit the vanity, then the light flicked off.

"Lilly, I don't want you to think for a second that I didn't miss you while you were away. I was trying to give you some space."

"I missed you, too," I said, resting on my side to face him.

Adin settled into the bed beside me. "I just don't know how fast or slow you want this to go. I'm trying to find the right speed. I think you know the speed I tend to go when it comes to you. You can rest assured that I'm right here with you. I am in this. Deep."

I'm in deep with you, too, Adin, I thought. You have no idea how deep.

I took his hand and began outlining his fingers. "You're right here with me, huh?" I scooted up to him.

"Oh yeah."

And before I had time to say anything else, he turned the light out. I ran my fingers along his chest, wondering just how *present* he was, how ready to get in my life.

❖ ❖ ❖

May 17th
Las Vegas, Nevada

Lilly

THE NEXT MORNING, ADIN AND I SLEPT IN and then ordered room service. The morning was a lot like Tampa—tangled sheets, heavy petting, and lots of wet kissing. It was like a honeymoon, only better than any honeymoon because we weren't concerned with travel logistics or blowing obscene amounts of money or whether or not we were having enough sex. At around 10 a.m., we took our coffee out to the balcony and looked out over Vegas, which was mostly traffic and billboards.

We stood there in silence for a little while, content.

"I want us to be able to do that every day," he said, leaning over the balcony.

I smiled, assuming he was referring to us spending two hours in bed scanning TV stations between making out, having sex, and eating yogurt parfaits.

I sat my coffee cup down and walked to the edge of our balcony. Looking down, I felt a small wave of nausea. I took a step back.

"So how's Savannah lately? How's the photography going?"

Adin exhaled loudly. "Well, a lot is going on. I'm taking pictures and getting paid for it. I'm sort of a businessman now."

I glanced at him. It was an odd word choice for him, *businessman*. I didn't love it. "What? You? A businessman?"

Adin smiled and reached for his coffee cup. "I know. Seriously. I'm loving it. I'm making lots of connections in the area, too, and it's paying off."

I reached for his hand to steady me and felt the wind kick up a little. I was hot and the breeze felt really good. "Well, I'm glad to hear that. You have a gift, and Savannah, well, what a place to be a photographer! I'm glad you've found something that makes you so happy."

Adin turned from the city to me. "Yeah, well, it is pretty great. And you're not far from me now. Are you liking Amelia Island?"

I nodded. "I love it. It's quiet. There are lots of families in the area. Lots of kids," I said, my voice trailing off. "It'll be a great place..." but I caught myself. "It'll be a great place to get work done."

"Right. All those kids. You can observe them in action. That'll be good for you. I could see you on the weekends, or you could come to Savannah?" he said, his voice rising at the end.

I thought about what he was saying. It felt like we were doing this carefully choreographed dance of what we could and could not demand from the other, privately wondering how perfect things really were and if there was anything, *anything*, the other was willing to cede.

I was ready to offer him anything if he was the slightest bit unhappy with his situation in Savannah, but I couldn't detect a hint of unhappiness or dissatisfaction.

"Yep. Those kids," I said, distracted by how happy I felt just being there with him. "Hey, can you hold on for just a second?"

Adin nodded.

I went in and poured a glass of water and met him back on the balcony.

"Sorry about that. I just feel kind of warm out here."

Adin gave me a searching look and got his phone out. "Really? You're hot out here?"

I took a sip of water. "Well, we're in a desert, so..."

"It's not even seventy degrees. You've always been so cold natured."

"Hmm. Could be the dry heat," I said, looking away. I felt like I was revisiting that class I'd taught in Tampa, lying about having allergies. There were a few things I'd learned I was really, truly incapable of— small talk and elaborate lies.

Adin sat his phone down and looked at me. "I've noticed you've not been feeling too great lately. What's going on? Anything I need to know about?"

I stared off into the distance, wondering if he knew. Maybe pregnancy was something the father in the equation could sense. Kind of like maternal instinct. Adin knew me better than anyone, but still... how would he *actually* know?

I took his arm and leaned against him. "No, seriously, don't worry about me. I think it's just the move, you know...moving from high elevation to sea level. Then, well, I flew here to the desert. It's just a lot to get used to."

"Well, I can understand that," he said, sounding tentative. "I didn't feel too good when I went to Denver."

"Right. There you go. You know what I mean," I said, glad that we were moving the conversation ahead, to something easy.

I stepped back and picked up our coffee cups and turned to go back into the room.

"Lilly."

I stopped in my tracks.

"Yeah?" I turned back toward him. He was facing the city again.

"You've not had a drink since you got here and we've not been using anything."

Just then I thought of another positive attribute to add to the *Pro* column—*observant.*

⊠ ⊠ ⊠

Adin

WHAT, EXACTLY, STEERED MY THOUGHTS IN THE direction of pregnancy, I can't tell you, except to maybe chalk it up to male intuition. And, when I say *intuition,* I of course mean *paranoia.* The picture was kind of resolving itself in front of me: Lilly is avoiding alcohol; Lilly is sick to her stomach; Lilly is getting a glass of water when it's 68 degrees; Lilly doesn't feel like going out; Lilly is suddenly not so hostile to my aspirations to a serious relationship. A man is oblivious to a lot of things, it's true. But the possibility that he might be a baby daddy is not among them.

Lilly gaped, in much the same way that she had when she walked in the previous day and saw me lying there laughing at some poor kid mangling "Paradise City." Gaping, by the way, ladies, is not the appropriate way to answer a veiled accusation like this one. It did little to calm my nerves. We were on the brink of something, both looking over together. Her sickness was proving a little contagious. That we were suspended twenty-two stories up in the air did not escape my notice.

"I—" Lilly began, and then from inside the room, from last night's discarded slacks, came the sound of my cell blasting M.I.A.'s "Paper Planes."

Tristan.

I glanced at it and then at Lilly. "Hold that thought," I ordered her, a little too sternly, and then I rushed in to answer.

"Morning, comrade," that nasally voice greeted me. "Listen, photos are starting early. It's supposed to get up to, like, eighty-something or whatever, and I don't want to be swimming in my superfly tux. Think you can be here in an hour?"

I loved him and hated him for saving me and stealing me from this situation. "Yeah," I said. "I can."

"Well, don't sound so happy about it."

"Sorry. I don't mean to."

Pause. "Adin," he said, suddenly very serious, "if there's something wrong, you know you can come to me—"

"No, don't worry about it."

"Let me finish. You know you can come to me *on any day but this one*. Today, you keep it to yourself. I hope I'm making this abundantly clear."

"Yes, sir. Clear as the day."

"Good. Now suit up!"

Click.

"I have to get dressed and leave right now, apparently," I called to her, as I started back for the balcony. Outside it was getting brighter. Lilly was chugging her water. "But, real quick—what's up with you? You know what I mean."

She swallowed hard and then shook her head. "I'm fine."

"No. Really."

"Really. I'm fine."

I gave her this look, this really grave look, like, *I know what you did, so you may as well tell me now*. She smiled, took another sip. I let my shoulders sag, defeated, and then went to squeeze into three layers of thick clothes.

FINALLY, AFTER MUCH FANFARE, TRISTAN AND Viv got married. The service was such a comic gem that Lilly and I were both more than happy to forget ourselves in their honor for a few hours. They were ostentatious. They invited participation. Everybody drank and sang '80s hits. Viv threw a riding crop in place of a bouquet. And yet it was sweet, too, watching them. They dressed elegantly, vowed earnestly, and accepted all our trite compliments with grace and magnanimity. It was that rarest of rare surprises—a fun wedding.

We were swarmed at the reception, mostly by friends whose kids had read Lilly's books, but occasionally by the guys, who wanted to congratulate me again on cutting the cord with Family PhotoWorks while they stealthily checked Lilly out. She was, after all, stunning in a classic black dress and heels, her hair a fancy bouquet all its own, as though it were the prom or something. She seemed much improved, deigning even to eat a few cocktail wieners and a slice of turkey. She did not, however, touch the wine. I wanted to go after her about it, but we were having fun, unalloyed fun. We were really laughing with each other and enjoying fielding questions about ourselves. I didn't have the heart to ruin it for either of us.

Tristan stopped to give us an obligatory send-off before he and Viv descended the steps to their pink Cadillac convertible and sped off toward San Diego, where they would stay for three days before they flew to Okinawa. His bow tie was purple. His hair subtly glistened with gel. "So," he said, taking a seat across the reception table from us, "this is that Amy girl you told me about, right?"

I offered him a lopsided smile. "Ha ha. Tristan, this is Lilly. I'm sure you remember her from college."

"Of course I remember Lilly, you bum. I gave her a bear hug at the buffet table. She promised to dedicate her next book to me."

Lilly shrugged at me in mock helplessness, toyed with the back of her tower of hair. "He was too charming. I couldn't resist."

"You watch out, man," Tristan said, "or I'll marry her next."

"You'll have to fight me, kid."

Tristan was a lanky 5 feet 8 inches and looked years younger when he shaved. He could have been my nephew.

"Yeah, yeah." He took a healthy swig of wine and then asked, "So when are you two tying the knot?"

Lilly coughed. I wished my own glass weren't empty. "Well, you know, I mean it's a little soon to be wondering about that."

"Well, she didn't catch the riding crop, that's true. But do you guys have any plans?" He turned to Lilly. "I've only gotten his whiny side of the story. I don't actually know any of the important stuff."

She laughed, but her expression was uneasy. I watched her carefully, waiting to hear the official story, which we had not yet begun to discuss. All we had agreed on was that we hadn't agreed on anything. To me, there wasn't anything to discuss. I had just gotten a place of my own, but if she had asked I would have gone straight to Amelia Island and thrown up the white picket fence myself. I didn't care where I called home, so long as when I came to it, she was there.

"Well, we're still figuring things out," Lilly said, nibbling at a croissant. "I mean we've only been going out a few months, you know, and it's been so many years since we first really got to know each other. We each just got our own place, pretty near each other, so there's no reason to make any big leaps just yet. We're just concentrating on having fun, working out our careers."

Tristan nodded through all of this, and it went on, too. The whole time it felt like he had one eye on me, to see how I was taking this. Which, it must be noted, was not well. I knew that I had no right to expect Lilly to deviate from a neutral public stance; our various obstacles were no business of the masses. But it still stung to hear it, the matter-of-fact way in which she dismissed any next steps, the way she talked about it like we were a couple of kids going to the movies every weekend. I rolled a wiener across my plate and smiled at all the moments where I was supposed to concur.

"Well, that sounds like a solid plan to me," Tristan said, clearly ready to make a swift getaway. "Good luck to you two. I'm glad you finally figured out your decade-long epic drama." He rose, too quickly. "Me and the missus are off for the coast. Wish us luck."

We wished him as much. Then he and Viv trickled out the door into the night, trailing a crowd of suit coats and silk dresses behind them.

I watched them for a long time, like a departing plane, dreading the moment when I would have to look back at Lilly. Then, finally, when I couldn't put it off anymore, I turned around. She was sitting back down with another slice of turkey.

"If you haven't had some of this," she said, "you should before we go."

[∘] [∘] [∘]

May 18th–20th
Amelia Island, Florida

Lilly

from: Lilly Jameson
to: Nate Samuels
sent: May 18, 8:08 p.m. EDT
subject: A Crazy Idea? *attachment*

Nate:

Hey, I hope all is well in New York. I just returned to Amelia Island from Vegas. The Writers in the Schools event went really well. I'm sure you probably heard about Adin showing up and having a mini-class on photography and the arts. It wasn't on the roster, but when he presented the idea to me, I just knew the kids would love it—and they did (see attached photos).

But I'll be honest. There were other reasons I wanted to see how Adin would interact with a room full of eight-year-olds.

I'm pregnant, and I wanted you to hear it from me first.

Also, the fact that I'm pregnant has no bearing on the subject line of this email. I mean, I've thought about all this and I realize a baby will complicate some things, but I'm ready. I can do this. I feel like things are starting to make sense in my life, actually.

Now to the crazy idea: okay, so I've spent the last few days rereading some of mine and Adin's correspondence over this last year. I've just been in a sentimental mood, you could say. The material consists of letters, emails, text messages, etc etera. Think of a puzzle—what I have are lots of pieces, but when put all together, a story starts to take shape. A good story. A great story, maybe.

Here's my idea—let me pitch this idea to Adin. He's the one person who could help me write it.

Maybe this sounds crazy, but please trust me. I think there's something good here.

Anyway, just get back to me when you can.

Lilly

•••

from: Nate Samuels
to: Lilly Jameson
sent: May 18, 10:01 p.m. EDT
subject: Re: A Crazy Idea?

Lilly!
Big congratulations!

I know Adin must be thrilled. I'm happy for you both. You two seem happy together and it's pretty rare to see that in adults. I hope that didn't come out wrong – all I mean is that you both are clearly very in love and that's very special.

I hope there are no hard feelings about Tampa, by the way. I think the world of you and Adin is a good guy.

Now, about the book idea: I like where you're
headed. I like the idea of a love story across time (who
doesn't?) and I kind of like the idea of putting notes,
correspondence, journals, emails, all into one book (sounds...
comprehensive)!

Maybe think about a title that could work for the
project. Sometimes getting the title right can spur
everything else. At any rate, I'm looking forward to
seeing what you come up with. Feel free to email me
with any questions or when you get the outline done.
Take your time. No rush.

Wishing you and Adin all the best.

Nate

• • •

from: Lilly Jameson
to: Brenda Jameson
sent: May May 20, 10:05 p.m. EDT
subject: Busy Wednesday

Mom:
I just got your voice mail. I can't go shopping tomorrow. I'm
doing this charity 5K run. Maybe later in the week? I've already
got the nursery picked out. I've decided I want to do the room
in beige, but decorated with all things puppy-related. Dog
stuffed animals, bedding with dogs and well, I mostly want
to keep it simple.

Gotta go—phone is buzzing.

Lilly

• • •

from: Adin Driscoll
to: Lilly Jameson
sent: May 20, 11:03 p.m. EDT
subject: Yellow Sheet of Paper

Lilly,
I wish you had answered your phone. I'm not crazy about doing this over email, but I guess I have to.

So you'll never guess what I found. Or maybe, since you read the title of this email, you will immediately guess. In case it's still a mystery: I found some crazy shit on a little yellow piece of paper you tried unsuccessfully to dispose of. Your little list, your summation of my merits and drawbacks. You were tallying up, apparently, whether or not I would make a good father.

I don't know what to say about this. I mean, I was reading the thing and one second I was flattered, the next I was practically screaming at it. I folded it up and put it in my wallet. I keep taking it out and rereading it.

My God, Lilly. I feel like you've been lying to me. You *have* been lying to me.

You're pregnant, right? Right. And the fact that you've not told me, that you outright told me otherwise, is making me think things. Here are some of the things I've thought:

- *You're pregnant and you don't want me to be a part of your life.*
- *You think I won't love you if you're pregnant.*
- *You think I'll bolt because I'm not ready to be a father.*
- *You're waiting for the 'right time' to tell me, which, if it wasn't this weekend, probably won't be ever.*
- *You don't want to push me into a relationship with you for the sake of raising a child together.*
- *You've decided I just wouldn't be a good father.*
- Damn. That last one was really hard to write.

Look, I will be on Amelia Island tomorrow. Please, please answer your phone. I'm Adin; I'm not a stranger and I'm not someone you should be keeping secrets from. This is something we really need to talk about.

And in case you somehow forgot in all this mess: I love you.

Adin

⊠ ⊠ ⊠

May 20th
Las Vegas, Nevada

Adin

LILLY HAD LEFT VEGAS ON SATURDAY MORNING, WHILE I stayed an extra day for some post-nuptial partying with my old college friends. Things progressed very much like they had in our old days—we hit four different bars and then taxied back to my big hotel room, now extra empty without her, for a sort of after party, although what the after party fell *after* we couldn't have told you. I was teenage-drunk in an old man's body, and while the rest of the guys (who hadn't ever really slowed down in the years we were apart) raged on around me, I just lay on my bed and clumsily riffled through my memories of the past several days.

It was only distantly, then, that I overheard one of the guys say, "Hey, Adin! Your woman's been makin' a mess!" There was a loud crinkle of paper, and: "Heeey, she's takin' notes! Story time!" This was followed by a chorus of *Story time!* from five different male voices.

Yes, this is actually how grown men behave around each other.

I wasn't especially interested in the story notes. I was busy putting a muzzle on my growing nausea. I had had way too much to drink, even by a young man's standards. It was only when the room started to get really quiet that I resurfaced in the external world. I struggled up onto my elbows to check. The guys were all standing in a huddle, reading an uncrumpled yellow piece of paper. When they heard me moving, they all kind of slowly raised their heads and gave me the same worried look.

I felt my heart stumble over itself. "What?"

George, Tristan's brother, carried the note over to the bed and handed it to me. I read it, the whole thing, all the way through. Then I read it again. Then I got so dizzy I thought I was going to die, and I threw up right there on the hotel room carpet.

BY TUESDAY NIGHT I HAD LEFT FOURTEEN MISSED calls, seven voice mails, and a dozen texts on Lilly's phone. At first I was worried that something had happened to her on the way home, but when I called her house in Beaufort her mother said no, in fact, Lilly had called to let her know she was home Sunday afternoon. They had spoken again on Monday night, making plans to go shopping sometime that week. Was I coming to the 5k on Wednesday? she asked. Lilly would need supporters. It was the first I'd heard of it.

It was strange—on so many occasions I had worried incessantly that Lilly was ignoring me, when she was simply busy or away from her phone. Now that she *was* ignoring me, I felt numb. Worse—I felt amputated.

I drove to Dad's house after I sent her the email. Dad was in his green bathrobe, which he was hurriedly tying as he opened the door for me. "What the hell are you doing here?" he asked, not angry, just bewildered.

I walked in and past him without a word. He followed me into the kitchen, where he watched me pour myself an unholy amount of gin and swig back a good half of it. I gagged; it tasted like Sunday night. And I had worked so hard to be such a teetotaler.

"Boy," he muttered, leaning against the doorway, "I am not an open bar. Or a hotel. That's my best gin. You just drank about four bucks."

"I'll write you a check. I make money now."

He returned, slowly, to his pulled-out chair at the table. I would have felt worse about this, except Dad was a night owl like me. I knew he'd be up for another two hours. "What is it this time?" he asked, taking up his pencil. I saw he had a pad out, yellow, like Lilly's. He was taking notes for his column.

Now I felt bad about coming.

"What happened? She smile at another man? Did she, I don't know, offer too little comment on your wardrobe?"

"This isn't funny, Dad."

"You're damn right it's not funny. It's after midnight. My deadline is tomorrow. Now what in God's name do you want?"

I held the glass up to my lips again, like I was hiding behind it. "Lilly's pregnant."

His face didn't change in the slightest. He did, however, put down the pencil. Then removed his glasses. "Is that...good?" he asked, and all the bitterness had drained from his voice.

I shrugged. "I don't know. I mean, I'd love to raise a kid with Lilly. That was part of my plan anyway. But she left this god-awful note back in the hotel room in Vegas, like a private list of my pros and cons. For her eyes only, from what it had on it. And it was pretty...vicious."

"You're not perfect, Adin. I coulda told you that. It's a big decision for her—no sense lying to herself about it."

"Yeah, but she also flat-out lied to me. I all but demanded to know, and she all but promised she wasn't. And I've been calling her for the last two days, and she hasn't answered."

"Maybe she's not ready to have you in her life that way."

"I know." I swigged the other half. "That's why I'm here."

Dad shook his head. Then he got up, took a glass from the cabinet, and poured his own gin. Then he shoved me aside and got himself some tonic. Then he shoved me aside again to get to the fridge. "You want some lime, or are you content to guzzle my liquor like a nervous freshman?" he inquired.

"Freshman."

"Suit yourself." He emerged from behind the door with his completed drink. "Sit down."

I sat. He shut the fridge door.

"Son," he began, and I knew that I was now probably going to keep him up past his bedtime, "you have been stewing about this woman, for one reason or another, for more than six months. Now I'm your father, and I support whatever makes you happy. But at this point, I really have to ask, *Does she make you happy*?"

I stared into my empty glass. Dad took a few dainty sips. The ceiling fan clicked an off-beat rhythm. "Yeah," I said at last. "I'm pretty sure she does. I mean, it's a complicated happiness. It's a happiness that requires a lot of work. And I always thought real love wouldn't require work, but maybe I was wrong."

"Of course you were wrong. But that's a whole different lecture." He resumed his seat again. "You're a twenty-nine-year-old man. If Lilly makes you so happy, why have you spent the better part of a year acting like you're seventeen?"

"I don't know," I admitted, sighing. "I *was* almost seventeen, when I met her. Lately I feel like she's turning me back into that kid. She's like a wrecking ball to my life, but she's also like a Habitat for Humanity crew at the same time."

"Thank God only one of us is a writer," Dad muttered into his drink. I thumbed my glass and pretended I hadn't heard. Then he said, "Well, I'm tired of being your sounding board. I'm sure Tristan is, too, and don't *even* pretend like you haven't been bothering him about everything. You've spent all this time either expecting too much of Lilly or worrying that she expects too much of you. If you're going to lose her, you're *going* to lose her, and there is *nothing* you can do to change it, short of becoming an entirely different person, which you know damn well it's impossible to do. So why the hell aren't you just—" he struggled with his words, a rarity for him, "just doing what comes naturally to you? I hate to fall back on something as trite as *be yourself*, but that's what it amounts to. Decide what you want from her, and tell her you want it. And if it's not good enough, mourn her for the appropriate amount of time and then find someone else to bother yourself about. But you won't save anything, the way you're going. You'll wreck it, sure as shit."

He took a long drink, perhaps to make up for the time lost making speeches.

I thought about it for a few minutes and then pulled out a chair beside him and sat down. "I have been at this for six months, haven't I?" I asked. He nodded. "It's just...I forget, sometimes, that it's been going on that long. I've spent six months in love with someone who has made my life a living hell. Well, someone over whom I've made my own life a living hell. I haven't really been happy, not for more than a few days at a time."

I put my glass on the table. Dad took a coaster from the pile ten inches from my hand and placed it underneath, pointedly. "Your mother and I fought once a week," he said. "It was practically penciled into our schedule. *Sunday: laundry, budget, fight.* We had to break each other down and build each other back up, every time. It was like the end of the world, every time."

"How come I never saw it?"

"You were out lighting firecrackers under neighbors' porches like a good little bastard. We waited for you to go to do it."

I leaned back, buried my fingers in my hair. "Oh."

"But Grace wouldn't have been my whole world if we hadn't fought so hard. If we were easy-breezy, we would have been another one of those bored, passionless married couples, the ones who sleep in separate beds and have separate bank accounts and don't ever have sex."

I scrunched my face. "Dad."

"Oh, grow up." He took another drink. "I was happy because I was miserable. *That's* love. We didn't half-ass it—we went all the way, good times and bad times. We yelled and screamed, and then we held each other and wept and then I took both of you out for Italian and ice cream."

"That part I do remember."

He smiled, in that way that always made me feel a little awkward, the way that was a little bit love, a little bit sadness. "You're not a whole lot worse off than we were. You just think you are, and that's your problem. You both want to keep your own lives, and you both want to sacrifice them. You *should* just be sharing them, like normal people."

I imagined us on the balcony in Vegas, her telling me she was pregnant, me saying, *That's great, Honey, let's shop for bassinets when we get home.* I imagined posing our baby on the steps of an old schoolhouse; I imagined buying a house in Columbus for those late summers when the Georgia humidity was like puddles in the air. I imagined standing at the back of every reading, clapping next to Nate, and Christmas with her parents, an early winter morning in that old bookstore that began with a kiss instead of ending with it. I had spent so much time lately figuring out my direction and comparing it to hers that I forgot you could have more than one.

"Can I write my column now?" Dad asked politely. "It's about sushi, and I hate sushi, so I need all the time I can get."

I rose and clapped him hard on the back. "Dip it in soy sauce. Everything's good in soy sauce."

⊠ ⊠ ⊠

October 2, 2004
Ohio University, Athens, Ohio

Lilly

I HUGGED MY BACKPACK TO MY CHEST, STARING out the cab window. I felt tiny, there in the enormous back seat, swimming in an oversized, rust-colored wool sweater that I'd nabbed from Mom's closet. Funny, over the last five months I'd lost twenty pounds, but I kept reaching for bigger clothes. Bigger clothes were comfortable. And *comforting.* I was sure they helped me maintain my grand illusion of being a happy, well-adjusted, high-achieving twenty-year-old. Most importantly, they kept my mother off my back about all the weight I was losing.

I couldn't get over it—Athens really hadn't changed all that much. It felt like I'd been gone for years, but seeing how the roads all led to the same places and how the students followed the same paths to classes in buildings I knew the name of, it was clear I hadn't been gone as long as it felt like I had. Mine and Adin's bench in front of the cafeteria was still there. The maples were losing their leaves in front of the freshman women's dorm. If you looked close enough, you could see that the Sigma Chi house still had a lone Solo cup drifting near the shrubbery. I stared out the window, one hand on the glass, marveling, not just at the campus but also at how close I felt to the place. I felt like I was *back*. I was home.

I'd been gone for about five months. Five long months filled with me working a summer job in a marina in Beaufort where I waited tables and eavesdropped on all those dreamy-eyed sailors who were doing what Adin and I used to talk about doing—sailing the coast. I enrolled at USC, where I knew virtually no one, befriending the one person I was matched up with in the Honors Program—my mentor, the Director. Every student got a mentor, and all were paired with faculty. I was the newcomer, the new transfer student. The Director, a white-haired man who looked to be approaching seventy, took me under his wing, since no one else was available. I met with him and talked books on Friday afternoons for an hour or so. He showed me where a cafe was in the building, and sometimes we got coffee together. That was the nice part of my week, and my weeks usually went unnoticed and were quickly forgotten. When I wasn't in class, I tended to burrow in the tiny bedroom of the apartment I shared with three other girls. I worked on taping up posters to cover every square inch of the walls, I read submissions for my Fiction class, highlighted my textbooks, and occasionally went on long walks around the edge of campus, a caged animal, looking to escape. I still had my journal. I taped in little menus, receipts, and greeting cards sent by my mom. I penciled in quotes from books I liked. I didn't have much at that point in my life, but I held on to the belief that what I was living through was some kind of teacher. I sensed, even then, I would need to remember all of this.

I went home every weekend, lugging my backpack to my room (containing no fewer than eight books at a time) and barely emerged until 10 a.m. on Sunday—just enough time to sleep in, eat Mom's pancakes, and skip church.

It was on a weekend like that, a Sunday morning in late September, that Mom and Dad surprised me with a plane ticket to Athens. Mom slid the envelope under my bedroom door around 9 a.m. while I was perched in the middle of my bed, three French dictionaries spread in front of me and a printed-out Victor Hugo poem I was working to translate. I had my headphones on when I saw an envelope slide under the door. The big block letters said *LIL*. I scrambled down from the bed and went to the door and opened the envelope. It was a plane ticket. To Ohio. Tears streamed down my face, smudging the print.

An hour later, she was telling me how she and Dad sensed I missed my friends, that USC just didn't make me happy the way OU had. They wanted to do something special for me.

So instead of heading back home to Beaufort for my fall break, I got on a plane to Ohio. I had one day there. That was it. But I was massively grateful. And they knew it, too. When I looked downstairs, over the banister, Mom was watching me, biting her bottom lip, willing herself not to cry, too. She understood. Despite everything going on inside me and all the things I just could not tell her, she understood.

That morning I hurried downstairs, feeling alive in a way I hadn't for a long time. The plane ticket had opened the door to a longer conversation about whether I should or shouldn't go back to USC. Mom, Dad, and I poured more coffee, spent an hour around the dining room table having the most civil conversation we'd ever had. I was shocked when Dad said he would fully support me going back to OU, if that's what I wanted to do and Mom said she would, too. "We'd make it happen, Lil," she'd said. It was the first time I felt included in one of their decisions that dealt with my life. I told them I would think about it.

I went to my room, my stomach in knots, plane ticket in hand, and just stared at it, thinking it through. I hadn't planned to return. But what if I did? I got on my computer, just to see if there was any way I could be readmitted for the spring semester. Turns out, I could. All I had to do was turn in a form by October 11. I printed off a re-enrollment form, filled it out, and slid it into my backpack, noticing a brochure for a study abroad trip next summer that my USC French professor had handed me on Friday. I'd accepted it the way I greeted most everyone and everything at USC—passively, barely, begrudgingly.

Sure, Paris, France was a good idea. But OU was a better idea.

I fired off an email to OU Admissions, stating that I would personally drop the re-enrollment form in their drop box on Saturday afternoon, before I went back to the airport. The next month passed in a blur. All I could think about was how it'd feel to be back with Jane, Jason, Adin, and all the other people I spent so much time thinking about and wondering about.

I rested my head against the cab seat, taking a deep breath as it passed the large, red stone OU *Welcome* sign, making my heart beat faster. I hadn't told anyone I may be coming back in the spring, just as I told no one I was leaving. Saying it out loud would make it real, and I couldn't yet grasp that this may all be real again. All Jane and Jason knew was that I was staying overnight. They didn't know I had a signed re-enrollment form in my backpack. I'd scrolled over Adin's number in my contacts, but I didn't dare call. By that point, I was embarrassed that it'd been as long as it'd been; I couldn't imagine he'd want to talk to me. I spent a lot of time beating myself up about not being able to reach out.

I was staying with Jane for the night. Initially, she'd been pissed off at me for not returning to OU, but it helped that she'd found herself a boyfriend and that she'd have a single, since I wasn't coming back. When she told me he was a Phi Tau, I thought she must have lost her mind, but she'd prefaced it by assuring me he was not some dirtbag fraternity idiot. His name was Philip, and apparently he was a senior and the vice president and I would like him if I met him.

So I told her I would meet him. I would go meet the amazing Philip. When I laughed and told her we needed to keep the fact she was dating a Phi Tau from Jason, she'd gone quiet on the phone and said she had to study for a Spanish midterm.

Mostly I wanted to see this new Jane that seemed to be replacing my best friend. She talked about Philip nonstop. She talked about where Philip wanted to go to grad school. I noticed she didn't mention parties, bar-hopping, or Adin. It felt like a lot of things were changing, most of which I couldn't see. She talked about her room. She was always moving things around, telling me about where she was putting her bed and how she had moved the desk around and how it made things *so much more spacious!* I wanted to catch up with her, maybe go to one of Jason's Sigma Chi parties...

I rolled down the window, letting the cool autumn air in. I remembered how Jason used to love going running on afternoons like this—when it was sunny but not hot, cool but not cold. He was another reason I had to come back. We hardly talked anymore. I knew he was the newly crowned Sigma Chi Recruitment Manager, but it felt like when we did talk, we had fewer and fewer things in common. He'd call me at eleven o'clock at night, when I was in bed, and he'd want to tell me about the new recruits, parties, and social events, which sounded more and more meaningless to me. Lately, he kept talking about this recruiter from an oil company who wanted to hire him to work in Texas once he had his Biochemistry degree. He kept talking about salaries, projecting how much money he could save up the first year and what he'd buy, the car he'd trade in for and then what he'd save up for. He kept talking about moving to Texas. And then one night, right after we hung up after being on the phone for two hours, I realized he hadn't asked me anything about my own life or what I'd been doing.

He and I had always been different. That wasn't the problem. In the past, I'd liked those differences. I liked that he could tell me scientific things that I could barely follow. I liked that he knew Latin. And that he was a great dancer. And held the door for me. Hell, I even liked the way he could be jealous and territorial, hotheaded and temperamental, but I knew I was starting to become a minor figure in his life and I knew that what he was seeing in his future (Texas, big money, biochemistry) was completely different from what I was seeing in mine, which, admittedly, I wasn't sure about, but I knew I wasn't interested in his top three at all.

The cab slowed down and I rested my head on the seat, idly gazing out the window. I zeroed in on a runner twenty feet away, some guy running with his shirt off. I recognized something about him, but I wasn't sure what. I leaned in close to the window, squinting. Then, as he got closer, I knew exactly who it was. *It had to be...*

I jerked upright, gripping the driver's seat. "I'm sorry can you please let me out here?"

The cab driver jumped a little and looked around. There were cars in the two lanes beside ours. "You want to get out *here*?" he asked, gripping the wheel.

"Yes!" I nodded, fumbling for my wallet. "Right. Here is fine!" I handed him cash. He thanked me as I scrambled to get out of the car. I ran across the lane beside ours, my backpack swinging wildly from my shoulder, dodging cars.

"Jason!" I called out.

His body stiffened and he turned toward me, coming to a stop about ten feet away. "*Lilly?*"

It was him.

I choked back a sob, some deep well of pain and sadness that I hadn't realized was there and smiled while running as fast as I could, throwing my arms around him, his skin wet and glistening in the afternoon light. It was only mid-embrace that I realized I was holding on for dear life, and he was barely holding on at all.

He had a quiet, curious look on his face. "I barely recognized you with short hair."

I smiled, fingering my shoulder-length hair. I took a step back and glanced at my watch. "I thought you were supposed to be meeting me over at Jane's, like, right now? We were going to head into town?" I said, catching my breath. It felt like my entire body was vibrating, pulsing with energy.

He forced a smile and looked away, steadying his breathing, his stomach rising and falling. He wiped his brow with the back of his hand. "I thought...," he took a deep breath and looked up at the sky. "I'm not actually going tonight, Lilly," he said, the words coming all at once as his eyes met mine.

"You...you're *not going*? To dinner with me and Jane and Philip? Do you have a chapter meeting? Or something?" I could feel the old familiar agitation rising up in me.

He took a deep breath and looked away. "No, Lilly. I mean, and this *is not* how I wanted to say this, *at all*, but I've been kind of seeing someone. I was going to tell you when you got to campus."

I took a step back, feeling a cool wind blow through. "You're seeing someone?"

He nodded, quietly. "Yeah, I'm seeing Julianna," he said, looking around. He looked uncomfortable, like he was worried to be seen with me.

I was confused. "But, you're seeing me. I don't understand."

"That's the thing, Lilly. We *aren't* seeing each other. At all. Not anymore."

I stood there, speechless. My mouth opened and closed.

"Look, Lilly. You know, a lot has changed. Jane is with Philip. You've moved on. Even Adin has a girlfriend now. Everything's just... *different*. You know, we're all completely different people now."

"What?" I shook my head, trying to catch up. "Did you say Adin has a girlfriend now?"

This made him smile and relax a little. "Jane didn't tell you?"

I quickly shook my head, trying to absorb everything.

"Yeah, he's dating some freshman—"

"Okay..." I said, the word locked in my throat. "Huh." I looked up at him, trying to take all this in. "I just..." I said, my voice breaking.

"Hey, are you okay?" he asked. "You look...*different...*," he said, lowering his voice, choosing his words carefully.

I sputtered something unintelligible and choked back tears, quickly nodding since I was unable to speak. I wiped my face with the heels of my hands. I knew if I started to say something, it would come out in thick heavy sobs and the emotions would spill forth, undecipherable. It would get embarrassing. Instead, I said nothing and tried to choke it all back. I knew he was too nice to leave me there in that state. He would at least give me another minute, but I knew I had to calm down.

"Look, I was going to tell you about Julianna. I just wanted to wait to tell you in person. I didn't want to be a dick and say this over the phone."

You didn't want to be a dick...

I was shaking by that point, the tears coming fast. I couldn't hold it back. Just then someone's backpack knocked my shoulder, reminding me we were on a main path, people streaming around us as they headed to classes, cafes, and the library. Some of them did double takes, after seeing the shape I was in. A maple leaf fell between us, and I watched its sweeping fall, wiping my right eye with my sweater sleeve. Jason stood out, wearing only his black jersey running shorts and no shirt. It looked like we weren't experiencing the same seasons. He looked like he was ready for summer and I was bound for winter. I knew I stood out, too, a castaway among friends. If Jason of all people had barely recognized me, it was likely no one else who knew me would, either. My eyes drifted to his shoulders, his pale stomach, flecked with a few brown wisps of hair. How well I knew all those curves. He had been my first. And now we were running a million miles away from each other. There was a time he made me feel safe and understood. I'd been feeling all that slip away for months. And I knew he probably had, too.

He reached for my hand, and I snatched it away.

"Lilly—"

"Don't. I just...," I said, my voice catching in my throat. There were so many people around. I felt stupid. I felt like an idiot for even showing up. I knew I wouldn't stay the night.

"Come on. Talk to me. How are things going at USC? You're always so quiet on the phone."

I looked up at him, not at all sure who I was seeing anymore. Of course I wasn't okay. I hadn't been okay for some time. Was he trying to be a friend to me now? He was seeing Julianna? He was *going to tell me*?

"It's great!" I said, dabbing my eyes, forcing the words out of my mouth. "I think I'm going to France next year." I said, the word *year* catching in my throat, the announcement coming in a rush. I could barely keep track of what I was saying, but the words came from some place that was beyond that moment, from some far-off horizon where a part of me still knew how to protect myself and find a way to be okay when nothing was okay. Call it self-protection. Call it self-preservation. But as soon as I said the words, I knew it was all true. I'd never return to OU, and that, too, was almost too much to bear.

He smiled weakly as if seeing through me, and I smiled and felt the tears release themselves down my cheeks. Nearly two years we'd been together. I told him I needed to go, trying my best to steady my breathing and talk normally. I turned a little, giving him the impression we were done. Done with talking. Done with us. And I watched as he turned from me and began jogging away, just as he'd been doing five minutes earlier. I watched him leave me, the tears spilling down my face. He was out of my life now, I thought. He would go places I would never know, never see. He would go be someone else's. Who was I kidding? He already was someone else's. I turned and continued up the hill in the opposite direction of him on the sidewalk, crying openly now, unsure of where to go. I was trying to think of the quickest way home.

⌗ ⌗ ⌗

May 21, 2014
Amelia Island, Florida

Lilly

I KNOW, I KNOW. I SHOULD HAVE ANSWERED Adin's calls. And I should have responded to that email, but I couldn't muster up the courage to say the word *pregnant* to him via electronic device. I needed to actually see him if I was really going to let him know what was going on. I couldn't lie anymore about it. But I was scared of what his reaction would be. I imagined breaking the news to him only to get a blank stare or an audible swallowing of air. I wanted none of that. I didn't have the heart to tell him that if he wanted to do this with me, I'd need him to man up and get on board with this. I didn't like asking people for things anyway, and this felt like I would be asking the biggest favor, ever.

Of course, I wanted us to raise a child together, but I couldn't have Adin give me 60 percent or 80 percent. I needed him to be 100 percent in this with me. And our track record, let's face it, was spotty.

So that morning I listened to his voice mails on speakerphone once more, while double-knotting my tennis shoes and pocketing that one picture of us from college. It would be my new lucky charm, I'd decided. I'd been a runner pretty much since middle school, when I was drafted to run on the high-school cross-country team. When one of the local city council members asked me if I'd consider running in a 5K for literacy, I signed up immediately. Mom wasn't crazy about the idea because of the pregnancy, but I did some research and found that it was okay and wouldn't harm the baby.

I put my cell phone, keys, and ID in a small, black, fanny pack I always wore when I ran. I had decided that I would answer Adin's call if he called today, or I'd call him tonight, whichever came first. Today he was going to learn that in about six months he would be a father. I drove over to the lot where the race began and milled around. I did some stretching and talked to some of the locals I'd gotten to know since living on the island. I saw mothers getting strollers out of cars and fathers pushing strollers to the starting line. There were little groups of friends clustered here and there, some teenagers, and lots of dogs on leashes.

I wondered what my life would look like a year from now.

It was almost 9 a.m. Everyone began making their way to the starting line. I checked my phone one more time and touched my stomach. It had become a nervous habit, checking in on our baby, making sure all was right in his or her world.

"Today your daddy's going to find out about you," I whispered.

I'd been trying to detect movement since feeling what I thought was a kick last week. It always steadied me. Adin hadn't called. I wondered if he was actually serious about showing up on Amelia Island, and then I remembered his Valentine's Day stunt in Tampa, how he'd shown up late without calling. I put my phone on vibrate, zipped my fanny pack, lowered my baseball cap, and tightened my ponytail one last time before the race started.

The gun was fired. Everyone slowly began to shuffle into a steady jog, carving out a regular pace in the crowd. I moved past some people, picked up my pace, and found a clear path. I'd left my iPod at home in order to have some quiet time during the race and to be more aware of the baby. I jogged past a group of four girls who looked to be about fourteen years old and then I passed by a guy running with a stroller made for twins, the babies wearing caps to shield their faces from the sun. I fell into a steady pace and thought about our baby. I was pretty sure Adin was somewhere hating me right then, and I couldn't blame him. I hadn't meant to exclude him, but I didn't want him to feel compelled to raise a child with me either. Not when he had a good life in Savannah. He had seemed so happy in Vegas.

Just then I noticed my neighbor, Tammy Mills, running a few steps ahead. Tammy worked in Jacksonville at a law firm and had organized the race. She was a born multitasker. I sped up a little so that we were running side by side. She was pushing a stroller that held her Pekingese puppy, Melon, and her one-year-old son Baron.

"Hey, Tammy!"

Tammy glanced toward me. "Lilly! I see the two-mile mark!"

"Good! Good!" I tried to steady my breathing. I glanced into the stroller. Melon's soft pink tongue was flapping in the wind. It looked like she was smiling, enjoying not having to work at all for a ride through Amelia Island.

"Oh, Lilly, did you ever talk to that guy who was looking for you?"

I kept my pace steady. "Someone wanting me to sign books?"

"Don't know." Not slackening her pace a bit she reached into the stroller and handed her son a small teething ring that had slipped under a cushion.

As far as I was concerned, Tammy was superwoman.

"It was before the race started. I couldn't find you. I gave him a goody bag."

A wave of nervousness ran through me.

"Lilly, there he is! That guy."

Tammy was pointing to some distant figure near the next water station at the two-mile mark. The sun was very bright that morning and there were at least ten volunteers and workers huddled at the water station, some with cameras, some recording their relatives, and there were a few people with posters. It was like a miniature version of *Today*.

"What?" I shouted over the shouting, scanning the group of people.

"The blondie!"

That's when I saw Adin. He was breaking through the crowd, maneuvering past people.

He's really here, I thought. I felt a rush of excitement and adrenaline. I'd have to tell him.

"Be right back," I said to Tammy.

I jogged over to the water station and inhaled a cup of Gatorade, wishing it were something stronger. I had not wanted to tell him like this. I had envisioned sitting someplace quiet, holding his hand, looking him in the eye, maybe over tea or coffee.

"Lilly!"

I smiled and walked over to where he stood.

"Hey! I'm glad you're here. *Really* glad."

I reached out and took his hand, hoping that by this he understood that my distance was not for lack of feeling but because I really did want the best for him. I didn't want to feel like an obligation to him. I watched Tammy stop just ahead and get a cup. I tossed mine into a trash bin and held on to his hand while trying to get a handle on my breathing.

He led me to a small patch of grass alongside the track.

"Okay. I have something to tell you..."

"Lilly, I've emailed. I've called. I left Savannah at 6 a.m. to get here to see you. Please tell me what's going on."

I nodded and wiped my eyes. "I know. And I didn't know how to tell you. But I'm pregnant."

"You're pregnant?"

"*I'm pregnant.*" I reached behind me to tighten my fanny pack. "I didn't want you to feel like I was an...obligation, or like *this* was an obligation," I said motioning toward my stomach. "You have a good thing going in Savannah, and I'm sorry that I've been distant. I'm *really* sorry for how that must have made you feel."

He reached for both of my hands. "Lilly, you're pregnant? You're worried about how that makes me feel? That makes me feel great. You're pregnant with our child, Lilly."

I laughed and choked up a little. "Oh, really? That makes you feel great?"

He nodded, taking both my hands. "That is maybe the best news ever."

I squeezed his hands. I felt like a huge weight had been lifted. "You really mean that? You want to do this?"

"Definitely," he said, wrapping his arms around me.

"You kind of knocked me up," I said, choking up a little.

"I guess I kind of did, but to be fair, I didn't mean to. Still...College Adin would be thrilled about this development."

"I'm sure my dad will be," I said, glancing at all the runners.

"He'll really hate me now, won't he?"

I shrugged. "He kind of hates most things, so that's no big deal."

I felt like I could breathe again. I'd been so anxious about telling him and how he'd react.

People were tossing the small plastic cups near our feet and I noticed we were standing right beside a trash can.

"Hey, would you want to finish this with me?" I asked. "There's only a mile left. Well, 1.1 miles," I said, squinting in the distance.

"I want to talk to my child first," he said.

I shot him a look. "What do you mean? Your child is in my stomach at the moment. Incubating."

"I know. I want to tell him or her about his mother. And how she likes to keep secrets and be evasive and how she should really stop doing that."

"No, absolutely not," I said, darting away from him, but he pulled me back into his arms. I leaned into the crook of his neck and he gave me a kiss.

I pulled the picture of us out of my pocket and held it out in front of us. "Besides, I've been telling our child about their father a lot lately."

"Good things I hope," he said, wrapping his arms around me, staring at the picture.

"There are only good things to tell." I turned to face him. "Come finish this race with me."

Adin looked at me like I just suggested we relocate to Uranus. "You're pregnant! With my child!" He laughed and looked away. "I can't believe those words just came out of my mouth."

I put my arms around his neck and pulled him close. I couldn't believe those words came out of his mouth, either.

"You're sure?" he asked.

I nodded. "Absolutely." Another tiny, dented cup popped onto the ground on my left. Runners sped past. "Really, it'll be fine."

I took a step back, still holding on to his hand, and started jogging, and he joined me. We ran steadily beside each other and it felt good to be there and to be connected to what I realized was my whole life. Something very real had been put in motion and it felt rooted to the earth, no longer a fantasy or solely in my imagination. We passed a lot of people. He mentioned the yellow list, and I winced and apologized. Then he started trying to convince me how he could change some of the cons. For instance, his handwriting could be improved, rather easily, in fact. He'd been reading something on the internet about it, so he had that going for him.

And he said he just wanted to be with *me*. It didn't matter where.

I listened to him talk about what we could do, how we could live on Amelia Island or Tybee Island. We would be okay. We would be *more* than okay, he said. And I believed him. I listened to his ideas, keeping a steady pace as he jogged along beside me. It occurred to me that we were a family running together.

As he was talking about life on the island and areas he'd like to photograph, I felt comforted, almost dissolved by my own happiness and the unexpected pleasure of being right where I should be, though I couldn't tell you how I got there. I felt a wave of feeling that I recognized as being culled from some far-off dream or far-flung memory. They say you only dream about what you care about. Maybe it's like rehearsing for a life that's not yours but could be. Someday.

"Hey, there's Tammy!" I said.

"Holy shit. Is she pushing a stroller?"

"She is. She's superwoman." By this time, Tammy had managed to get Melon running alongside her. The dog seemed happier than she'd been in the stroller, her mouth spread wide, grinning.

"See that? I would do that for you," Adin said, pointing to a man running with a stroller up ahead.

"What do you mean?"

"I mean that I would be the guy pushing the stroller!"

I burst out laughing. "But your manhood!" I said, trying to push through a cramp in my side. "Maybe that'll be you. This time next year."

"Hey, I'm *very* secure in my masculinity," he said.

"Deal," I said, catching sight of a sign up ahead that told us we had a half mile to go. "Hey, we've almost caught up with her."

Adin followed my lead and sped up a little to reach Tammy. We all ran together for a moment.

"Want me to push him for a minute?" Adin asked.

"Oh my God! Would you mind?" she said, clearly grateful for the offer.

"Not at all," he said, taking the handles from her, never once stopping, allowing Tammy to sprint ahead.

I watched him take over, amazed by how good he was. I marveled at the fact he was running with me—with us—actually. Baron had fallen asleep. The air was heating up. We kept the same pace, and the finish came into view. It was so close now.

I wanted to hold on to the moment and I knew the minute I commented on it, it would be gone forever.

A dense crowd was waiting for us at the end, so dense that if a white finish line was spray painted on the dirt, we couldn't see it. Too many banners and too many balloons clogged the air, competing for our exhausted senses with the cheers from the crowd and the songs from the brass band. Slowly we stopped running and let ourselves be carried by the waves, music, and laughter. By the time we cleared the noise and stumbled away from everyone, we felt like an invisible tide of goodwill had brought us to this moment. We fell into the grass, still catching our breath.

We stumbled away from everyone and everything and lay there for a long time, taking in the day, his hand on my stomach, whispering things about me. I don't know how long we were there, talking about what to name our child. Would it be a boy or a girl? How would we decorate the nursery? The beginning of my life had kicked into gear, and everything was happening so fast and was so exhilarating I couldn't tell what would happen next.

THIS IS WHAT LIFE HAD BEEN PREPARING ME for, giving me a little nudge that it wasn't through with me yet. That one day all the pieces would come together, revealing one picture of us.

꘎ ꘎ ꘎

December 14th
Amelia Island, Florida

Adin and Lilly

Dear Grace Lillian Driscoll,

It's almost Christmas in Florida. That means something a little different from most places, because it's about sixty degrees right now, but there's a tree up in the living room and some Harry Belafonte on the stereo, which is close enough. Your father insisted on a real tree, to which your mother finally relented on the condition that he procure and install it on his own, which he did. So now the whole house smells like pine, and all is right with the world. (Your dad would like you to know he's a manly man, Honey. Don't forget it.)

Next to us, by the way, is you. You, one month old today, in your little sky-blue cap and booties. You, with your pinchable fingers, your little pensive frown. It's funny, having present you right here in the room and future you with us in the words on this page. It's like having two kids. Do we have two actual kids yet? (Mom says, "Slow down, Cowboy.")

We're sitting here writing you a letter to celebrate your first mini-birthday. We felt it was appropriate, seeing as it was letters, really, that brought us together in the first place. Mom thinks we should put it into a book, along with all the others, but Dad thinks maybe there's some stuff in there that he's not wild about all his friends and relatives reading. Don't worry—he'll come around.

Mostly we're doing it because there are things we feel are important for you to know, things we wish we had known a long time ago. We've talked about it a lot, and God knows there's a lot that we don't agree on, things which we will someday yell and scream and tear our hair out over. But that's okay. Sometimes we need to be reminded that what we have is worth yelling and screaming about. You helped us realize that. So now we're going to help you figure out some stuff:

Don't lose track of good friends or anybody important to you. Even us. The longer you know somebody, the better they are for you, the more well equipped to help you be the person you want to be. And don't be mad at them for telling you the things you least want to hear. If you're mad at something your friend has said about you, that's probably what it feels like when they're right.

We hope, though, that someday you meet someone who seems unlike everybody else, someone who becomes your best friend. We hope that person helps you figure out who you are and what's important.

People will tell you that real love doesn't happen. They'll say that nothing lasts. They'll insist to you that you could not really love that man or that woman like you think you do, and they'll make you feel bad for believing otherwise. Those people are wrong. We spent nine years apart from each other. Your father stumbled through a series of bad breakups. Your mother got married and divorced. And not once in all that time did we stop loving each other.

Don't rush anything when it comes to love, either. Shakespeare once said, "The course of true love never did run smooth." That's true.

We hope that you take a lot of pictures and keep track of your life. Don't let good moments pass you by. Pay attention to the world around you—it's a pretty interesting place. There are mountains and shorelines, palm trees, and white sailboats on the water just outside your window.

Please know that your grandmother will keep you in constant supply of clothes you'd probably rather not wear. She likes neon. She likes electric orange and hot pink. She will want you to like these colors, too. Maybe you will. Don't feel like you have to wear the clothes. But always make her feel like you appreciate everything she brings you. (That's good manners.)

And finally, know that at some point, a really long time ago, your parents were real people, the same as the sort of real person you are right now, reading this. Back before they were old people with gray hair and bad taste in clothes, before they had to have the plots of movies explained to them halfway through, before they showered you with advice you were probably well on your way to figuring out on your own anyway, they were young, and confused, and furious, and terrified, and in love. Really, really in love. And they hope—they promise—that in whatever world you're living, no matter how different, no matter how overwhelming, they still are. With each other, and with you.

Happy Birthday, Gracie,

Dad and Mom

ACKNOWLEDGMENTS

Tasha Cotter

Thank you to my wonderful teachers and mentors over the years: Nikky Finney, Lisa Williams, Young Smith, Mary Mollinary, and Julie Hensley, to name a few. Thank you to the University of Kentucky Honors Program for providing a perfect home for me to explore ideas, learn from the best and the brightest (Cheryl Cardiff and David Durant, especially), and follow my own creative inclinations wherever they led me. Thanks for letting me spend a lot of time with Tolstoy. Thank you for letting me spend some extra time with poetry. And for the scholarship that let me go to Paris for a summer. (It changed my life.) To the UK College of Arts and Sciences: Thank you.

Deep, unending gratitude to all the folks at The Kentucky Center. It was at the Governor's School for the Arts that I first met other people who loved the arts as much as I did. Thank you for creating a home for young Kentucky writers and artists. What you do is so important. You make Kentucky a wonderful home to be a writer.

Huge thanks to my amazing husband Daniel: my counselor, my best-friend, main adventurer, constant companion, my big love. Thank you for sticking around all these years and for encouraging me to keep going. You are the funniest and wisest person a girl could choose to spend her life with. Most of all, thank you for giving me the time (and space) for my writing.

Thank you, Alice Speilburg, for loving this book right from the start. Your enthusiasm provided a much-needed jolt of confidence when I needed it most. I'm certain that your feedback and editorial eye made this book as strong as it is. Thank you for believing in this story and for being such an advocate for the story we wanted to tell.

Virginia, I'm so glad we met all those years ago! You and Stephanie have worked so hard to make this book shine. Thank you for your editorial feedback and for taking a chance on this big love story.

Christopher Green, you're the Laurie to my Jo March, Adin to my Lilly. Thank you for collaborating with me on this epic romance; it's a story I never get tired of reading. How we managed to tell this story, I still don't know, but I couldn't have pulled it off without you. Thank you for loving Lilly as much as you loved Adin and for caring for her when she was occasionally in your hands. Thank you for getting her through the thicket of her past, mostly unscathed, and for keeping the flame between them alive. Writing this book with you changed the way I saw the world. Thank you for occasionally breaking my heart along the way. Most importantly, thank you for mending it.

Christopher Green

Thank you first to my mother and grandmother, who raised me with a love of books and writing and insisted that I was substantially less awful at the latter than I believed I was. I have always struggled to believe that the things I make are truly worthwhile, but something that you both said must have stuck or I wouldn't be here, talking to you in the back of a book with its own Library of Congress number.

Thank you, Centre College, the place where I got to be more me than I have ever been anywhere else—even Brooklyn. Thank you especially to the people there who changed me forever: Dan Manheim, who taught me to love the discipline of English; Mark Rasmussen, who taught me to love my own service to that discipline; and Lisa Williams, who probably doesn't think she made much of an impression on me at all, and may in fact not remember who I am. I still sometimes write poetry too, Professor Williams, because of you.

Thank you to Virginia and Stephanie for believing in this book, and in me, even when I was late on all my deadlines because I was grading papers or laminating something. I learned how to love this thing we made even more by seeing you love it.

Thank you, Jane Bradley, for telling me that something I wrote could be published. Honest to God, I didn't know.

Thank you, Mary Gaitskill, for telling me that you would not *dis*courage me from continuing to write. This is the highest praise I have ever received for literally anything.

Thank you to the many, many people who have supported me or kept me going all these years: Cassie, Allie, Lauren, Karl, Mike, John, Allie, Edy, Kelly, Lindsey, Alicia, Johanna, Tiffany, Andrew—and all the people I will shoot up in bed thinking of at two in the morning in about six months. I promise I will call you (at a decent hour) and tell you you're on this list. I love all of you so much.

And of course, thank you, Tasha. You know, people ask me how we managed to create this thing whenever I describe it to them, and I'm not entirely sure how we did, to be honest, but trying to explain it is almost as much fun as actually doing it has been. In so many ways I think the title of this book refers to you and me as much as it does to Adin and Lilly. There is so much of us that's been left in these pages for everyone to see, mothers and strangers alike. Everything we've been and hope to be. I will almost certainly never get to share that mostly inexplicable experience with anyone else ever again, and I'm grateful that if it was going to be with anyone, it was you. You taught me that writing is work, but the best kind of work. So much of what I am I owe to you and to this, the first project I ever got to the end of. I can't wait for us to read it to people together.

ABOUT THE AUTHORS

Tasha Cotter is the author of three books of poetry. A graduate of the University of Kentucky and the Bluegrass Writers Studio, she makes her home in Lexington, Kentucky, where she works in higher education and serves as the president of the Kentucky State Poetry Society. You can find her online at www.tashacotter.com or on twitter at @tashcotter.

Christopher Green is an English teacher in the Bronx, where he tries very hard to convince his kids to care more about high school than he did. He has published pieces in many print and online journals including *The Baltimore Review, The Ampersand Review, The MacGuffin*, and *The Rumpus,* as well as in New York series such as Liars' League NYC. He currently lives in Manhattan with a cat named T.S. Eliot. He is a graduate of Centre College in Danville, Kentucky, where the roots of this book are laid.